The Pub Across the Pond

Books by Mary Carter

SHE'LL TAKE IT

ACCIDENTALLY ENGAGED

SUNNYSIDE BLUES

MY SISTER'S VOICE

THE PUB ACROSS THE POND

Published by Kensington Publishing Corporation

The Pub Across the Pond

MARY CARTER

KENSINGTON BOOKS
www.kensingtonbooks.com

KENSINGTON BOOKS are published by

Kensington Publishing Corp.
119 West 40th Street
New York, NY 10018

ISBN-13: 978-0-7582-5336-1
ISBN-10: 0-7582-5336-2

First Kensington Trade Paperback Printing: October 2011
10 9 8 7 6 5 4 3 2 1

Printed in the United States of America

To the Irish

In memory of Tony Bracken (Uncle Tony)

ACKNOWLEDGMENTS

There are so many people to thank for this book, I don't know where to start. So I will start with my agent, Evan Marshall, and my editor, John Scognamiglio, who both surprised and terrified me when he said he loved the idea for the book. Thank you, John, for your never-ending support.

From the bottom of my heart I want to thank Kevin Collins and the entire town of Kilmallock, Ireland. Thank you, Kevin, for showing me your home. Thank you for the all the crazy text messages you answered whenever I had an obscure question about Irish culture, the books you suggested (or bought for me), and your stories. I treasure the memories.

Thank you to Eileen Collins for reading all my books and for your gracious hospitality, your fabulous cooking, and a beautiful place to stay.

Thanks to Bridget, Seamus, and little James Collins, Mary Sheedy, Owen Sheedy, and my new best friends for life—James Sheedy and Ann-Marie Murphy—(if there are two nicer people on the planet, I've yet to meet them—Cows, Ann-Marie, Cows!), as well as Jamie Sheedy, Andy and Sarah, Mandy, and you too, Helen!

Thank you to Dermot O'Rourke: I wish I could go back in time to when you were a publican at O'Rourke's—it sounds like those were some days—but thank you for your stories, jokes, and hospitality; Mike and Joanne Collins; Sheila and Greg Flannigan at the fabulous Flannigan's Pub; and Mike Fitzgerald at Fitzgerald's Pub; Natalie O'Brien from Natalie's Café (you really do have the best cappuccinos). Thanks to the folks who played poker with me and forgave me a few mistakes. And thank you to Deirdre and Thomas—if any of my readers find themselves in Limerick, do make a reservation at the French Table.

viii ACKNOWLEDGMENTS

In a broad sense, I'd like to thank the regulars at both
Maguire's Pub and Murphy's Pub in Queens—Angus, Alan Cot-
ter, Jimmy Kehoe, Kevin Mcinerney, Eoin Wogan, and Martin
Tierney. If you said, "Don't put that in the fecking book," I listened. Likewise, if you said, "Put that in the fecking book,"
sometimes I listened too. Angus, thanks for giving me inspira-
tion for bits of one of the characters, and an idea for one of the
scenes. Thank you to all the musicians who play terrific traditional Irish music. Thanks to Peter Maguire.

Thank you, Val. I'm mentioning you mostly because you kept
asking me if I was going to mention you.

I'd like to thank the bartenders: Tony Bracken (quintessential
Irish bartender, perpetual good mood, never failed to call me
petal, give me a hug, or ask if I was all right. You are missed,
Tony), Sara Murray, Elaine McKenna, Anne O'Shea, Tony
Healy, Maria Molloy, and Colm Cahill. The talent, patience,
and humor it takes to entertain, serve, police, babysit, and coun-
sel is underrated. They are superstars.

Thank you to Siobhan and Thomas Hahn for reading my
books in English and German and inspiring one of the bits in
the book.

I'd like to thank Pat Ward and Martin Devaney for a few
good one-liners.

Locally, thank you to Susan Collins and Mary and Jimmy
Egan for their generosity and hospitality.

From my travels to Galway, I need to thank Declan O'Don-
nell and Alexander Riabykh for their company and some suggestions on the fictional name of the town, as well as some
amusing stories.

Thank you to cab drivers, musicians, tour guides, publicans,
and unsuspecting citizens on buses in Dublin.

I know I'm forgetting someone or many someones, so please
forgive me. If you'd like, call me on it and I'll buy you a pint.

Lastly, I just couldn't finish these acknowledgments without
thanking the Irish in my family (be it several generations removed, the spirit remains): my mother, Pat Carter, and in mem-

ory of my grandmother, Mary Cunningham-George; my aunts: Bessie, Jane, Margaret, and Florence; my second cousin Mary Christine and her husband, Dave; and my Irish ancestors from Ballymena, County Antrim. I've yet to make it there, but I'm sure when I do, it will feel a little bit like home.

May good luck be your friend in whatever you do,
and may trouble be always a stranger to you.
—*Irish Blessings quote*

The only sure thing about luck is that it will change.
—*Bret Harte*

Just tell yourself, Duckie, you're really quite lucky!
—*Dr. Seuss*

If one is lucky, a solitary fantasy can totally
transform one million realities.
—*Maya Angelou*

Luck is believing you're lucky.
—*Tennessee Williams*

Luck never gives; it only lends.
—*Swedish proverb*

My luck is getting worse and worse. Last night,
for instance, I was mugged by a Quaker.
—*Woody Allen*

I'm an American girl looking for a REAL Irish guy. Must come with an accent. I'm a fun girl! Facebook me!

■■■■■■■■■■■■■■■■■■■■■■■■■■■■■■■■■■■■■■

American woman looking for a well-off STABLE Irish guy who just wants to go out for a laugh. No crazies, married, or "separated."

■■■■■■■■■■■■■■■■■■■■■■■■■■■■■■■■■■■■■■

PLEASE COME FROM IRELAND AND NOTHING TOO PERVERTED. Thanks!

■■■■■■■■■■■■■■■■■■■■■■■■■■■■■■■■■■■■■■

I'm an American lassie looking for the stereotypical movie romance. Please have an Irish accent, be under 40 years old, and don't send me any pictures of your cock-a-doodle-doo. Here's your chance to sweep me off my feet.

■■■■■■■■■■■■■■■■■■■■■■■■■■■■■■■■■■■■■■

Looking for my Irish Prince Charming but tired of kissing drunk frogs. . . .

■■■■■■■■■■■■■■■■■■■■■■■■■■■■■■■■■■■■■■

I've always had a fascination with Irish men. I don't know if it's the accent or what, but I've always had a soft spot. HOWEVER, no drinkers, gamblers, cheaters, or redheads. May overlook ONE of the above if you can Riverdance.

■■■■■■■■■■■■■■■■■■■■■■■■■■■■■■■■■■■■■■

That's right, I am American and I love Irish men! I came on here hoping to find an Irish dude for love, friendship, pen pals? Whatever works for you! I plan on visiting Ireland, you can count on that. So, c'mon guys, hit me up! Bonus points if you play the banjo.

■■■■■■■■■■■■■■■■■■■■■■■■■■■■■■■■■■■■■■

I'm American and would love to explore the Emerald Isle with a charming Irishman.

■■■■■■■■■■■■■■■■■■■■■■■■■■■■■■■■■■■■■■

I am a hopeless romantic and the boys here are not exactly cutting it.

■■■■■■■■■■■■■■■■■■■■■■■■■■■■■■■■■■■■■■

I would love to meet a true man, one that I can trust and give my undivided love to. One that I would cross oceans to be with. . . .
Also I love the accents. . . .

■■■■■■■■■■■■■■■■■■■■■■■■■■■■■■■■■■■■■■

I am sick of the States, sick of the people here. They have no culture, no passion, no sense of being. I am three-quarters Irish and love it there in Ireland, love the Irish men, and would love to meet a few. I am looking to move to Ireland in the next couple of years after I get my divorce.

■■■■■■■■■■■■■■■■■■■■■■■■■■■■■■■■■■■■■■

Looking for my "Sunrise and Sunset"???

■■■■■■■■■■■■■■■■■■■■■■■■■■■■■■■■■■■■■■

I would like to find my sunset and sunrise. Partly cloudy okay too. R u out there somewhere?

■■■■■■■■■■■■■■■■■■■■■■■■■■■■■■■■■■■■■■

PROLOGUE

Declan
The Greatest Love Story Ever
Told in Ballybeog

It was the greatest love story ever told in Ballybeog when everyone was drunk but nobody wanted to go home and all other
great love stories had been told.

Name's Declan, but I'll answer to most anything as long as
yer thirsty and polite, and in that order. Ah, say nothin' until
you hear more. I've been a publican at Uncle Jimmy's going on
twenty years now. Most days it's good ole craic, but sometimes
when you're a publican, you've gotta be a bags. I wasn't sure
Carlene Rivers, the Yankee Doodle Dandy who won the pub,
had that in her. She had sweet written all over her, and I hate to
say it, but girls like that always seem to attract the wrong kind
of lads. I've seen many a sweet lass get the guy of her dreams,
only to watch him turn into her worst nightmare. Over time
their men belly up to the bar more than they do the bedroom.
Because the Irish men who "do" usually don't hang around
here. And Ronan McBride was no exception.

Nobody thought the lad would ever settle down. There are
three kinds of Irish men: those who do, those who don't, and
those who say they might but probably won't. Ronan McBride
was the latter. He was thirty-three years of age but still hadn't

worked out his boyish ways. I don't know why nature makes those marriage-phobic men so alluring to the women—a course, no one would disagree that he was the best-looking man in the family, and I'm not just saying that because he was the only man in the family. His father, James McBride (or Uncle Jimmy, as he was known around here), had passed, God rest his soul, leaving Ronan, his mother, and six sisters to run the McBride family pub. In heavenly retrospect, I bet James wishes he would've just left the pub to the girls; it would have been an insult to his only and eldest son, all right, but as I said, sometimes when you're a publican, you've gotta be a bags.

As the song goes, Ronan was a rambler and a gambler, although he was never a long way from home. I can't tell you what it was that made the birds go absolutely mental over him, except he was over six feet and had all his hair. Let's just say he had his pick of chickens in our little town, not to mention a hen or two who would've liked to sink their beaks into him.

But it was Carlene who got folks to whispering that maybe, just maybe, our terminal bachelor might mend his wayward ways. There was something in the air whenever those two were in the same room. A bit of a spark you might say, especially when they were arguing. Yep, things certainly hummed when they lit into each other, and for anyone watching it was great craic. Although we worried about Sally Collins, of course— she'd been absolutely lovesick over that boy her entire life. Still, it did me good to see that beautiful Yankee bird come into town and shake up his world, and my money was on her from the beginning.

But despite cheering the lass on, I understood Ronan's terror. For some, there's nothing more frightening than love, except maybe running out of ale. I was like him meself, one of the Irish men who don't. And let me tell you, many are the nights when I've regretted it. Cold, long, rainy nights when I'm lying in bed and I close my eyes and some skirt that I chased when I was a younger lad comes skipping into my dream, all pretty, bouncy, and smelling nice, only to start giving me shit for letting her go.

Worse than the terrors, those dreams. I've known Ronan since he was a squaller, and I didn't want him to make the same mistakes I did. I used to say, "What's for you, won't pass you," but I know it's a lie. I let them pass me. I always thought there'd be more time.

I'm in me seventies now, and it's probably too late for me. I'm a scrawny-looking thing with black wire glasses and I've a tuft of silver bird nest sitting on me head, but I've been told I still have a right nice smile (even if they're not all me original teeth), and believe it when I tell ye I got me share of tiddlywinks back in the day. I'm not much over 5'5"—which I read in some touristy-type book is average for an Irishman. The average Irishman, according to this book, is 5'5", drinks four cups of tea a day, has 1.85 kids, and spends three euros a day on alcohol. I don't know where the writer of these so-called facts was getting his information, but it sure wasn't here, 'cuz some of our lads spend five euros an *hour* on the black stuff. That's a pint of Guinness for you blow-ins.

To make a long story short, I'm just your average Joe Soap. I make up for it in other departments, if you know what I mean. Ah, but this story isn't about me or my regrets, so I hope you can put away all lurid thoughts of my national endowments. If you want to take that matter up on a one-to-one basis, and it goes without saying that you have to be a good-looking bird, then you can Facebook me. I didn't join the fecking thing until the pub went up for raffle in America, but now that I'm on it, I reckon I might as well make the most of it. On that note, if anyone has an extra goat to give away, I'm on that farming game and I can't seem to get a fecking goat no matter what I do, so send me one, so, if you please.

To make a long story short, we were a nice, quiet town until that fecking raffle went viral. That means a lot of people on the Internet saw it. The tickets were sold in Irish festivals all over America, and they went for twenty dollars apiece. Everyone and their mother wanted to win a pub in Ireland. And if Carlene's mother looks anything like her daughter, I would've gone for a mother-daughter combo, but the Young Yank came on her own. And in the wink of an eye, our quiet little town weren't so quiet n'more.

Situated on the West Coast of Ireland, we're nestled on the edge of Galway Bay. We might be small, but we're mighty. Close enough to Galway City we only need to follow the scent of heather and lager along the coast to lay our fingers on her thriving pulse, but tucked far enough away that until that fecking raffle, we didn't get too many blow-ins.

We'll call our little village Ballybeog, or, in Irish, Báile Béag, which means "Little Center." I picked it because it sounds pleasant and Irish-y and because nobody in their right minds wants me to use its real name. Not out of shame, mind you, but for fear of being overrun by Americans like what happened in Dingle when the dolphin showed up. Nothing can ruin a sweet little village faster than a gaggle of Americans tracking down their "Irish roots" with their iPhones and dodgy laminated diagrams of supposed family trees.

Regardless, everyone will be treated as if they're welcome at the McBride family pub. This is the place to be. Drink away your troubles, catch up with the locals, watch a horse race, listen to traditional Irish music, play a game of pool, or darts, or cards, and see how much better life treats ye after a nice pint. Or two. Or twelve. Nobody keeps count except the Americans. Right now the place is jammers. We're waiting on a bride. So let me tend to my other customers now, but doncha worry. I'll check back to see how you're doing or freshen your pint. And if you get half a mind to be neighborly, don't forget to send me a fecking goat.

Chapter 1

Declan
Going Gaga

"She was the most beautiful bride ever," Katie says. She clasps her hands and holds them over her heart. She's the youngest of the six McBride girls, or the half dozen, as they're known around Ballybeog. At six foot, she's also the tallest. Even her brother Ronan only has a few inches on her. She was born last, born tall, and born almost blond. Of all the names given to her hair color—cornflake, strawberry blond, dirty blond—it's actually honey that fits it best. Honey-colored hair that's more often than not in tangles. She was a devoted practicer of bedhead before it became a sexy trend.

Hopeless romantic, they call Katie. Katie agrees with all but the hopeless bit. She likes to think of herself as an optimist, even if it's only true about 10 percent of the time. She's twenty years of age, but nobody thinks of Katie McBride as grown-up, least of all herself. She looks around the pub, demanding an audience. Guests are still piling in, shedding their winter coats, revealing long satin dresses that will shimmer when the ladies dance and smartly pressed suits the men only wear for weddings and wakes. Women discreetly slip off their heels and massage their toes, men loosen their ties, their belts, and their wallets, and then finally their tongues. The band is lively and drunk. They've yet to start playing.

"A fairy tale," Katie adds, with a loud sigh.

"Only you would call that ordeal a fairy tale," Siobhan says, slapping her handbag on the counter and eyeing me. She thinks that one sultry look from her will be enough to send me running. And let me tell ye something. It works. Siobhan's the oldest, the only redhead of the sisters, and practical about most things, especially love. In trounces the other four McBride girls, and whether by habit or coincidence, they sit down in order of their birth. From youngest to oldest it goes: Katie, Sarah, Liz, Clare, Anne, and Siobhan.

At the end of the bar, and no relation to the girls, sits Riley, whose real age is a bit of a mystery all right, but he's at least a thousand years old in drinking age, and more of a fixture at Uncle Jimmy's than the stool he's perched on. He leans in conspiratorially and winks at the girls.

"So?" he says. "What was the result?" Even I move in to hear the answer.

"The result?" Katie says. "Why, what a way to put it."

"Did the groom flee the scene?" a voice calls from the doorway. Laughter rolls forth, I must admit, even from me. Ah, but there's no harm in it, we all love the bride.

"It 'twasn't him that flew out of the church, it 'twas her," another voice adds. The laughter doubles, and there are a few cheers, mostly from the women. Katie has her audience now. Her broad smile is lit from underneath by one of the dozen tea candles that float the length of the bar like lilies on a pond.

Into the mix slips a young German man. He looks like a student. He's wearing denim trousers and a striped sweater, and he has an oversized backpack strapped to him. In his right hand, he holds a long piece of rope. Just about enough to hang yourself with. We don't have too many high bridges around these parts, so students under stress get creative. He stands sideways at the edge of the bar like a puppy trying to squeeze himself into another's litter. He orders a pint of Guinness. The chin-wagging momentarily halts, partly so I can take care of him, partly because everyone wants to ask him about the fecking rope but we're all too fecking polite. In addition to his pint, he orders a shot of whiskey, then another shot of whiskey, then another shot of whiskey. He drinks them without ever letting go of the rope.

"Woman trouble?" I ask him. When you're holding rope, no use taking the long way to the point. The young man nods. I pour him another whiskey. Everyone is looking at him. He has a square jaw, high cheekbones, and black eyelashes so thick that even I notice. It looks like two daddy longlegs superglued themselves just below his bushy eyebrows. His hair is fair and cropped short, and in the dim light of the pub I can't really tell what color his eyes are. Dark, I would say they are dark, all right. Dark eyes for a dark horse. Now that I look at him, I would've pegged him as a wrist cutter or a jumper. Just goes to show, you never know, do ye?

"I love Lady Gaga," the German says as if it's just occurred to him. His voice fills our little pub. He puts his hand over his heart. "When I see Lady Gaga, everything is all right." I nod and smile, the two biggest tools of the trade. A tear comes into his eye—looks like we've got a squaller. Alcohol affects everyone differently. Some people get in fights, some take off their clothes and knock boots with strangers, others have a good cry. When it comes to the ladies, I prefer the ones who like to lose their knickers, but not as much as I hate seeing a grown man cry.

"Some days, Lady Gaga is the only reason I don't hang myself," yer man continues.

"Well, here's another reason for ye," I say, setting another pint in front of him. I turn to Katie and whisper, "Who's Lady Gaga?" Katie tells me she's a singer and turns back to the suicidal student. She starts introducing everyone in the entire pub. It takes a while, especially when she starts saying where they live and who their young ones are, and gives a quick update on the status of their occupations, hobbies, living situations, health, recent deaths, births, or graduations, and lastly an update on their romantic entanglements. When she's done the suicidal student looks all glassy-eyed, blinks his spider lashes slowly, and he tells us his name is The David. That's how he says it, all right.

"I am The David."

"Boy George thinks Lady Gaga is weird," Sarah says out of nowhere. Sarah's an avid reader, always has the latest tabloid clutched in her hand. The David looks stricken. "After one of his concerts she asked him to sign her vagina," Sarah continues. "He signed her hat instead."

"Are you on holiday, then?" Siobhan asks the man.

"University," The David said. I knew it, but I keep my gob shut. A humble man eats more pie.

"Galway?" I ask. The David nods.

"But now I'm thinking of killing myself," he says. None of us are surprised, but we do a good job of hiding it. Most of us anyway. Riley is too old to hide anything. He points at the rope.

"I think it's a bit too short to do the job," he says. "If ye like, I've got a bigger piece that'll do ye."

"D'mind him," Katie says. "We'll sort ye out."

"Cheer up, things will get worse," Siobhan says.

"Just keep thinking of Lady Gaga's vagina," I say. "Shite. I mean her hat." The David nods, but tightens the grip on his rope. I don't know what it is, but I'm starting to like this lad.

"Why do you want to kill yourself?" Liz asks.

"He already told us," Anne says. "Woman trouble."

"You think you have woman trouble," Sarah says. "Try growing up with these five."

"D'mind her," Katie says. "Never give up on love. Ever. Do you hear? We have a love story that might cheer you up."

"Ah, bollix," Riley says. He bangs his pint on the bar. Beer sloshes over the edge.

"Mind your pint," I say. "Yer wastin' resources." Riley lowers his head and hides his face behind his Guinness.

"Which love story are ye on about?" Liz pipes in.

"Is there more than one?" The David asks.

"Depends how you look at it," Liz says. "Right?" Like all good middle children, she and her fraternal twin, Clare, are dutiful, exact, and the self-appointed diplomats of the lot. Always mad to get the details right. In other words, right pains in the arse.

"I've been married forty-six years," Riley said. "Now that's love."

"Not when you've spent forty-five of them sitting right here," I say. Riley pretends he didn't hear me and turns to The David.

"Would you look after a woman for forty-six years?" Riley asks.

"I wouldn't look after you for forty-six minutes," Anchor says. I turn, startled. He's sitting in the mix, drinking his pint, happy as a clam. He's such a big man, it's hard to figure how half the time I forget he's there.

"Forty-six years," The David says politely. "What's your secret?"

"Even if you come home intoxicated, always come home with something for her," Riley says. The David nods.

"The clap doesn't count," Anchor says. I shush him with a look. You can't let the young lads get too fresh, even if they aren't so young anymore, and even though Riley's too hard of hearing to cop on to the slag. I too wonder when the last time was that Riley brought something home for the missus, but once again I keep my gob shut.

"Can we get back to our love story, like?" Clare says.

"Better get us another pint, then," Anchor says. He holds up his glass, which is half-full by my account, but of course when it comes to the pint, most lads around here say it's half-empty. By the time he takes his last sup, he'll be expecting a new one. I'm happy to oblige.

"Get us all one," Anne says.

"I'll just have a mineral," Liz says.

"Good girl," I say.

"Good girl?" Anne says. "She downed seven glasses of champagne before the bride walked down the aisle."

"Walked the plank is more like it," Sarah says. The girls all laugh at the same time. I've got to tell you, when they all go at once, they'd bounce the bubbles out of a glass of champagne. I can't imagine Ballybeog without the half dozen. Sometimes I feel lucky just to be in their presence, and I realize there are millions of people who will never meet these girls, never hear them laugh at the same time, and I can't help but think, those poor fucking bastards.

"I only drank six glasses," Liz says when their laughter ebbs. "The first one never counts."

"I'll drink hers," Sarah says.

"Why are ye all here?" Riley says. He looks bewildered, as if he's just awoken from a long nap.

"We're waiting for the bride," Clare reminds him. I set down a fresh round of pints. "From the beginning, pet," I say.

"I just want to drink in peace," Riley says. A collective "Shut yer gob" rises from behind him. The crowd moves in even closer. After all, besides the whiskey, and the beer, and the music, and the games, and the races, and the rain, this is why we gather. We gather after weddings. We gather after wakes. Saint Stephen's Day, Saint Patrick's Day, Saturday. Monday through Friday. Sunday after mass. We come to celebrate. Birthdays. Births. We come for gossip. We come on rainy days, we come on sunny days. Cloudy days too, plenty of those. And don't forget windy days, and calm days, and slightly breezy days. Terrific storms. The calms before. Squalls. Wives sometimes come to drag husbands home. A few come to sip tea and listen to the music. But most of all, we gather for this, the stories. There's nothing we love more than a good story. And so far, this is not one of them.

"What're you on about over there?" Mike Murphy, the local guard (that's police officer to you Yanks) and banjo player, asks. He's warming up his instrument in his left hand while holding his pint in his right.

"A love story," The David says.

"Right, right," Murphy says. "Time for our break." He motions to the rest of the band, and they join our little cluster.

Katie looks at her sisters. "I'm not sure where to start," she says.

"Start where all good love stories begin," Siobhan says.

"Paris?" The David asks.

"Rome?" someone else ventures. "Venice? Las Vegas?"

"No," Siobhan says. "With a good woman and a fucked-up man."

CHAPTER 2

The Fucked-up Man

Ronan McBride leaned forward and rested his elbows on his knees. His right foot continuously tapped the ground, funneling all the energy in his body through his bouncing leg. He gripped his cards underneath the table. Across from him, Uncle Joe reclined in his chair. His right leg was crossed over his left, a cigarette dangled from the corner of his mouth, and he held his cards loosely in front of him, like a fan. The friendly game of poker, five-card draw, was going on its thirteenth hour.

In the beginning there were two tables of ten players. Around one A.M. it dwindled to one table of ten. As men lost, they smoked their last cigarette, swallowed the dregs of their pints, and stayed to watch. Nobody dared go home. Not when Ronan McBride and his uncle Joe were still at the table. Not when they could recoup some of their losses by betting on who was going to take the pot, and certainly not when the pot was up to fifteen thousand. Ronan was a bigger gambler, but Joe, a businessman and a teetotaler, was well suited to take him on. It was hard to believe they were related. Joe ran the general shop next door and hardly ever set foot in the pub.

In the center of the table, crumpled bills lay on top of each other like a massive pileup in a rugby game. They were out of cash and had switched to using bingo chips. It was never supposed to get up this high—it was five thousand when it came down to the two of 'em, and Joe was willing to keep the pot as it was, but Ronan had to push it.

Ronan tossed his faded yellow chip into the pot. "Twenty thousand," he said. He could feel his mates behind him: a chorus of shuffles, and grunts, and murmurs. He wanted to yell at them to shut their pieholes, but he didn't want to give anything away. He had four aces. Two on the deal, and two more sweet babies on the draw. It was a sure winner. He almost felt sorry for his uncle. Not sorry enough to stop. Uncle Joe had never given him a break, had never given his father a break, argued with him over the property until the day their da died, and even after, even at his father's wake, Joe was still onto Ronan to sell him the pub. He never understood his father's love of the drink, or the craic, or even the money that could be made from a pub.

Joe gave Jimmy grief over every twig or stone that landed on his side of the property line. He reported infractions to the guards every chance he got. His mother thought Uncle Joe had driven his father straight to the grave. Besides the drinking, and the smoking, and the fact that he never turned down a good feed, she was probably right; Joe was the one left standing.

But Ronan would take his father's short, boisterous life over his uncle's nervous, plodding existence any day. And he had four aces. No, he wouldn't feel sorry for Joe, not after his crass comments at his father's wake. He could still feel Joe's arm around him, his breath stinking of tea. He wouldn't even drink a pint to the oul fella.

"What are you going to do now, lad?" Joe said at the wake. Ronan looked at his pint, held it up by way of an answer. "I mean about the pub," Joe said. "I can take it off your hands." And then, by God if he didn't start in on turning the pub into a spa with sunbeds. Sunbeds. At his own brother's wake. Sunbeds, in fecking Ireland.

That's the beauty of it, Joe said. Pale, sun-deprived, Irish women would go mental over it. They'd be millionaires. Ballybeog had enough pubs. Uncle Joe had been thinking about this for a while. He'd purchased one sunbed, and it had been sitting in the back of his truck for months. Ronan told him he should just drive it directly to these sun-deprived women, whoever they were, but Joe said he didn't have the time, and besides, he needed a place for the sunbeds; one wouldn't make a profit, but think what he could do with twenty!

Like Ronan was going to let his father's pub become a roasting pit for the sun-obsessed. If they wanted the sun, they should move out of fecking Ireland. Besides, sunbeds gave you cancer. Ronan lit another cigarette and waited for Uncle Joe to react to his raise. Uncle Joe would take his sweet old time, as always. Ronan glanced with disgust at the overflowing ashtray. He smoked too much, he always smoked too many fags when he played cards. Declan quietly moved in, cleared the empty pint glasses, and replaced the ashtrays. Thanks be to God, Ronan didn't want to look at the evidence, not stacked up against Joe's little cuppa tea.

Four aces. Four aces. Four aces.

Joe dug in his pockets. He was such a thin man, and he was starting to look old. Was he shrinking? He and his father had never looked alike, his father so tall, so large, so full of life. Like two balloons, only somebody popped Joe and sucked all the air out of him. How was it that he was the one still alive?

Joe took out a set of keys. He was going home. This would all be over. He could probably sense Ronan's unbelievable luck. Four aces. Maybe Ronan had signaled his hand, shaking his damn leg. Well, it was all he could do to contain himself. He was too wrecked to keep up his poker face. He smiled and reached for the pot. Joe's hand slapped over his with surprising force. "Settle," Joe said. It was the same tone he'd used with Ronan when he was a child. "Settle." Ronan snatched his hand back and tucked it under his armpit. Joe dangled the keys over the center of the table. They swirled clockwise over the pot like a dousing rod sensing water. The men watching moved in, mesmerized. Once, around, twice around, three times around before they dropped with a clink.

Ronan stared at the keys. He looked at Uncle Joe. Ronan could hear his best friend, Anchor, standing behind him, smacking his lips. Anchor always smacked his lips when he was excited, which is why he was out of the game after the first round.

"What's that now?" Ronan said, pointing to the keys. "Your truck?" Joe's truck was a rusty old thing, not worth piss, even with the sunbed thrown in.

"Keys to the shop," Joe said.

"Keys to the shop," Ronan repeated.

"Now you put in the keys to the pub," Joe said. The lads reacted behind him. They said, "oh man," and "oh fuck," and "no fucking way," and he couldn't tell who was saying what because the loudest voice was inside his head, and it belonged to his father.

Joe's crafty. Did I tell ye about the time he tricked me outta me own shoes? You did, Da. Many times. *They were new shoes too. I'd only worn 'em one hour. Was sent home from school for walking around in me socks.* Quiet, Da. I have to focus.

Four aces. He had four aces. He had to have him beat. Joe was bluffing, or Joe thought *he* was bluffing. Joe never took Ronan seriously, always thought he was a fuckup, probably couldn't imagine him with pocket aces and two more sweet babies on the draw. You did not fold with four aces. With four aces you owned the table.

Ronan studied his uncle's face. Round, drawn, and lined like a basket. With his stick-thin body and round head, he looked like an aging lollipop. His hair was surprisingly still hanging on, soft curls that had long since turned gray and were in desperate need of a snip. Bushy eyebrows, thin lips, watchful brown eyes underneath heavy spectacles. He always looked slightly drunk—ironic wasn't it, for a teetotaler? He looked relaxed. Too relaxed?

Ronan glanced behind the bar to see if Declan was watching. He was wiping down the bar, as if paying no attention whatsoever.

"Declan?" Ronan called.

"Yes, lad?" Declan didn't look up, but he visibly flushed.

"Toss me the keys, will ye?" Anchor, so named because he

had the strength to hold most anything down, clamped his hand down on Ronan's shoulder.

"Roe," he said. "Don't." Despite his heft, Anchor was a softy, always looking out for the lads. He worked hard, he played hard, and he'd be the first to arrive and last to leave if you ever needed anything from him. But in this case, Ronan knew he was looking out for his own self. Anchor would go mental if his local pub suddenly morphed into Tan Land. Even if the place was filled with half-naked women. As the old joke went, a gay Irishman was an Irishman who would pick pussy over a pint.

"Throw 'em," Ronan said. Declan lifted the set of keys from the hook on the back wall and tossed them into the air. Ronan caught them in his left hand without even looking up. Had it not been such a tense moment, that kind of catch would have been cause for a celebration, and a round of shots would've been bought and downed. As it stood they were suddenly sober, and deathly silent. Even their cigarettes seemed to hover in midair. As Ronan gripped the keys to the pub, he and his uncle Joe stared steadily at each other from across the table.

"Wait," Anchor said. "Just hold on." Sweat poured into Anchor's goatee. He adjusted his baseball cap, then held both hands out. He took his cap off, wiped his brow with his massive, freckled forearm, then put it back on. "Just hang on here," Anchor said. He paced a stretch of floor. "This is fecking nuts. We have to have some kind of sit-down."

"We are sitting down," Ronan said.

"It's not your game, lad," Joe said.

"How about a fallback?" Anchor said.

"How's that now?" Joe said.

I have four fucking aces, Ronan tried to convey with his eyes.

"How about—a hundred thousand euros—within a month—or you get the pub?" Anchor said. "Or shop," he added with an apologetic glance to Ronan.

"Bollix," Ronan said. "Leave it be." Anchor put his hand on Ronan's shoulder and leaned down until his breath wheezed in Ronan's ear.

"I'm giving you a fucking fallback," he said. "Take it." Like

Ronan would ever be able to raise a hundred thousand euros. He looked at his uncle. Joe smiled; he was thinking the same thing. *Everyone is always underestimating me,* he thought. *Not this time.*

"A hundred thousand euros within the month," Ronan said.

"Or?" Joe said.

"Or my pub is your tanning bed," Ronan said. The men laughed. This time, Ronan didn't. "You want to give me the same deal?"

"No," Joe said. "If I lose, you get the shop."

"Fair enough," Ronan said. This was crazy. His uncle was losing it. Maybe he was getting demented. Maybe Ronan was taking unfair advantage of an old fella. A straight flush was the only hand in the whole world that could beat four aces. Who wouldn't bet with these odds? If Joe wasn't bluffing, he probably had a high straight at best. Once again, Ronan almost felt sorry for him. But there was no pity in gambling, and they were all getting tired, and it was time to end this. Ronan laid down his cards in one swift smack to the table.

"Four aces," he said. "Sorry, Joe." The lads whooped. Anchor cried out, tried to fist-bump Ronan, but caught him in the jaw. Ronan was too psyched to feel the pain. He'd just won Uncle Joe's shop. He didn't even know what he'd do with it, maybe see if his mam or the half dozen wanted to run it. Joe would turn it over all right, just like Ronan would've turned over the pub if he lost. An Irishman always honored his bets, even the foolish ones. Anchor put both hands on Ronan's shoulders and squeezed. It hurt like hell, but Ronan was too happy to yell. But then, something shifted. Uncle Joe fixed Ronan with a look, and instantly Ronan felt as if he'd been hit with a blast of cold air. He even looked down at his shoes, half expecting to see only socks, with holes in the big toe, laughing up at him. Joe smiled. A crafty fecking smile if Ronan ever saw one. Then, one by one, as if serving tea to the queen, Uncle Joe laid his cards on the table. As Ronan said, only one hand in the great game of poker could beat Ronan's four aces. And when Uncle Joe laid his high straight down on the table, Ronan's face wasn't the only thing that was flush.

CHAPTER 3

O Sacred Heart of Jaysus

It dawned on Ronan, as he sat in his mother's house at the kitchen table where he was reared, that given the choice, he would have rather faced a firing squad. Anchor, who had refused to leave his side since the game went down, sat across from him. Apart from occasional lip smacks, and chairs creaking as the lads shifted in their seats, the house was silent. Mary McBride was still asleep. Ronan hoped it was a good sleep; thanks to him, it could be her last good sleep for the foreseeable future. Despite the renovated living room with fireplace, and the den with a flat-screen television that Ronan built into the wall, and the screened-in porch with soothing rocking chairs, the kitchen was where everyone gravitated, no matter where else they began. It had never struck Ronan until now how white everything was. White walls, white tiled floor, white fridge, white stove, white cabinets. Except for the faded rectangular wood table where he sat, everything else was white. He'd grown up in this kitchen and he'd never really registered the shocking amount of white. It was like a celestial haven, designed to soak in the smells of home cooking and the laughter and chatter of children, and their children, and the occasional friend or neighbor who stopped in for tea. It was the heart of the house, the place where they all ran for comfort. It was fitting, then, to choose this location to break his mother's heart.

If only he could take the night back. Guilt churned in his stomach. But who could blame him? With three aces he would have folded sure, but for the life of him he couldn't imagine anyone folding with four aces—even those who didn't have a bit of gambling in their blood. That was the worst bit. If he had to do it all over, he would have done the same thing. It was a nightmare, the kind you had after too much drink, the kind designed to warn him that he was gambling too much; the waking lesson: Slow down. Was he just dreaming? Unfortunately, the hangover felt real, and Anchor's brooding presence reminded him it was all too real. Maybe he should have done this with a phone call instead.

It was too late to run now. He'd already woken up all six of his sisters, and they were on their way to Ronan's "emergency family meeting." In his thirty-three years, Ronan had never called an emergency family meeting. That was usually the MO of his mam and his sisters, always wanting to convalesce over some emotional upheaval. Ronan dreaded the family meetings. Five out of six sisters said they'd be there and left it at that, but Siobhan grilled him incessantly. She kept repeating, "What have you done now?" He refused to get into it on the phone. Siobhan would have been the fifth dentist, as in "four out of five dentists recommend." Siobhan is the one fucking dentist who just can't agree. Emergency family meetings were supposed to be treated like births in the McBride family—it was simply mandatory to show up for them, regardless of what was about to come out.

Anchor looked as if he was going to cry. Ronan only felt numb, although as the minutes ticked by, dread slowly crept in. His head was pounding, his mouth was dry, his hands were shaking. He was too hungover for this shit. When would he ever learn? This was it, this was his lesson, and by God he was going to learn it.

A pot of tea, a pitcher of milk, and a bowl of sugar sat in the middle of the table, along with nine porcelain cups on saucers and a pile of little gold spoons. In the "Tea Party from Hell" he was definitely playing the role of the Mad Hatter.

He thought about making a fry, but he knew he'd get sick. They all would. He'd put them through a lot in his lifetime, what with gambling, drinking, women, and the time he almost set fire to the shed, and the time he landed in the slammer at eighteen for drag racing, a stunt that ended with John O'Grady in traction after he smashed head-on into the town wall. And although he got out of it with nothing more than a few broken bones, John O'Grady never drove again; to this day he rode his bicycle everywhere he went. And there were many such incidents over the years to add to the list of dumb things Ronan had done.

But this was by far the dumbest. And there was no time to waste, no avoiding this one; by the time breakfast was being cleared in Ballybeog, everyone would know that Ronan McBride had fucked up once again, and this time he'd lost the family pub.

Ronan curled his fists up and stuck the right one in his mouth. Otherwise he was going to scream. He didn't know who he dreaded facing the most, his mam or the estrogen gang, as he liked to call the half dozen. He'd disappointed them plenty over the years. Disappointed them, angered them, and at times tortured them as only a big brother could. It was still hard to believe they were all grown women now. He still saw them as little girls. Vicious, evil little girls.

He deserved whatever they were going to throw at him. He was a grown man. Grown men should not be risking the family's livelihood in a game of cards. His mother would weep; oh God, he hated it when she cried—especially if he was to blame. She would pray too, she would pray for him, which would make it even worse. Jaysus, he didn't think about kindness. What if they killed him with kindness? Ronan shot up from his seat. The chair squealed on the tile floor.

"I gotta get outta here," he said. "Will you tell them?" Anchor pointed to the chair like the grim reaper. Ronan knew Anchor would physically restrain him if he tried to leave, nail his ass to the chair if he had to—he was that kind of friend. Ronan fell back into the chair, legs splayed, arms clutching his head. Then slowly, visions of racehorses circled the tracks of his thoughts.

What if he could rake in enough wins on the ponies to pay Joe the hundred thousand? He mentally jotted down names of jockeys and trainers who owed him; he'd call in all his favors, he would get some good tips. His buddy Racehorse Robbie would help him, wouldn't he? The man was a genius, he'd made big money on the ponies. Ronan could do it, he could pool all his resources and with just a little luck—

He was going to do it. This was meant to be. He'd always been afraid to really go for it, flat to the mat, like. Racehorse Robbie knew how to abandon all fears and plunge headfirst into his bets. That was the lesson Ronan needed to learn. How not to be such a chickenshit. This would elevate him from small-time gambler to the big leagues. This was the lesson he was supposed to learn. Nothing in life was risk-free. Fear was only in the head. From now on, his head would be fearless. He'd get the pub back and then some. He unclenched his fists and took a deep breath. He was starting to feel better. Excited even. This was going to work.

Unfortunately, he wouldn't be able to share his plan with the estrogen gang. Somehow he didn't think they would go for gambling as a way to pay off a debt he lost gambling. Women could be weird that way.

Siobhan was the first to arrive even though she lived the farthest away. She was also single and had no young ones of her own to slow her down, nor did it look like she took any time to dress herself. She wore a sweat suit, and her red hair was piled on top of her head, held precariously in place with a pencil. Her freckled face was unmade. She stood in the doorway and glared at Ronan from behind oversized navy spectacles that flared out at the edges like an eyepiece from a masquerade.

"Did somebody die?" she said. "You'd better fucking tell me right now if somebody died."

"Nobody died," Ronan said. Siobhan let out a sigh and

slammed the door. Ronan winced and looked toward the ceiling. He wasn't ready to see his mother. He wanted to delay it as much as possible. Siobhan dropped her purse on the floor next to the door and shuffled over to the head of the table. Even as a kid, Siobhan was never one for picking up her feet. She looked as if she belonged at a construction site, barking orders, shuffling through sawdust, and looking for the pencil stuck in her hair. It was funny to see her in public; it was the only time Siobhan would actually lift her feet off the ground like a normal person. And it was how Ronan always knew when she had a crush on a boy.

"Tea?" Ronan said.

"What did you do now, Ronan?" Siobhan said. She looked at Anchor. He kept his eyes on the table. "Shit," Siobhan said. She nodded at Ronan and he poured her a cup of tea. It was strange, the silence. Ronan wasn't used to it. He hated it. The table was always a hub of conversation, mostly the girls chattering away with their mother at the stove, soothed by the smell of a fry while gossip flew around the table faster than Ronan could catch it. Siobhan tapped her foot on the floor. She glanced at the clock above the sink and shook her head.

Katie was the next to arrive. She was dressed as if going out for the evening: heels, a pencil-thin skirt, and a soft lavender sweater adorned with ribbons. Her long honey hair hung in waves around her pretty face. She was wearing lipstick and smiling.

"Howya," she called. She shut the door quietly, stepped over Siobhan's purse, and threw her arms around Ronan from behind. When she leaned over and kissed both his cheeks, her lilac-scented hair tickled his collarbone. Maybe his mother crying wouldn't be the worst bit; maybe it would be seeing a little bit of the goodness go out of Katie's eyes. Ronan's hands, which had been resting on his knees, curled into fists under the table. She smelled flowery and eternally optimistic.

"Hey, Katie," he said softly. He wasn't worried about going to hell, he was already in it.

"Hi, Anchor," she said. "What's the craic?"

"For God sakes, Katie," Siobhan said, gesturing to Katie's

outfit. "Did ye think you were coming to a party?" Katie stood with one hip jutting out and slid her eyes over to her older sister.

"Siobhan," she said. "Nice glasses." Ronan poured her a cup of tea. Katie sat next to Ronan and looked at the stove. "Where's Mammy?" she asked. Siobhan and Ronan glanced at the ceiling. Siobhan folded her arms and stared at Ronan.

"Is it good news?" Katie asked. "Or bad?"

"For fuck's sake," Siobhan said. "Use your eyes, would ye?"

"Maybe he's getting married," Katie said. "And it's rendered him speechless." She laughed and winked at Anchor. Anchor tried to smile back but only managed to twitch his lips.

"Good Lord," Katie said. "Did somebody die?"

"Nobody died," Ronan said.

"Yet," Siobhan said.

"Should we wake Mam?" Katie said.

"Let's wait for the rest," Ronan said. Katie drummed her fingers on the table. Liz, Clare, and Anne were the three with young ones at home, and Sarah was not a morning person. Katie took out her cell phone and set it next to her cup of tea.

"Should I call them?" she asked.

"No," Ronan said. "They'll be here."

Liz and Clare, the fraternal twins, lived next door to each other and arrived together. Ronan was relieved that their young ones weren't with them. Although fraternal, the twins still resembled each other. They were heavier than the rest of the girls, although you would hardly call them fat. Voluptuous, Katie called them. Meaty, Ronan called them, but only when he wanted to get slapped. Both had shiny chestnut hair—Clare's still hung to her shoulders, but Liz had recently cut hers in short layers. Clare immediately took her place at the table, but Liz had to go up to each of them and make them feel her hair. For a moment the heavy silence was lifted by compliments and questions about who, when, and where she'd had it done. Ronan simply poured the tea.

"Anne was right behind us," Liz said. "Hope she makes it before it starts lashing." Ronan glanced out the window. Indeed, the clouds had moved in, casting dark shadows across the kitchen wall. Maybe it was for the best; it would feel wrong to deliver the news if the sun was shining. It made him think of Joe and the sunbeds that would soon litter the pub like vampire coffins, sucking the lifeblood out of their father's pub.

"Nobody died," Katie said before the girls could ask. Anne soon emerged struggling under a bag full of groceries. Since no one got up to help, she had to shut the door with her foot. She was envied by the rest of the girls for having the straightest, inkiest hair. When she was little, Ronan used to make her cry by telling her she was adopted and that her real parents must be Orientals. God, he was such a wanker, and not much had changed.

"I swear the wind was going to whisk me away," she said. "Oh my God, Liz," she said. "Your hair." Liz ran up to Anne and made her feel it. Anne put her other hand on her own head, also cut short. "Now we're the twins," she said. All the girls laughed. *Remember this sound,* Ronan thought; *they aren't going to be laughing for long.* Upstairs, Ronan heard his mother's footsteps. Anne set the groceries on the counter and looked around the table.

"Fuck me pink," she said as she made her way to the seat where Ronan pointed. "Who died?"

"Nobody," the girls answered in unison.

"What did you do, Ronan?" Anne said. She stood by her chair but remained standing. *Is that why God gave women bigger hips? So they could put their hands on them and stare at you condescendingly?*

"Just sit," Ronan said. They heard their mother coming down the stairs.

"Ma," Ronan called out. "Anchor's here."

"Ah right," his mother called from the other room. "Hello, hello. I'll just get changed and I'll make you lads a fry." They listened to her hurry back up the stairs, where she would change out of her robe and into clothes worthy of a guest.

"Maybe I should let you at it," Anchor said. He rose halfway. Ronan motioned him back down.

"Stay," Ronan said. "Somebody's going to have to carry out my dead body."

Siobhan's hand shot up. "I'll do it," she said.

"Ronan," Katie said. "You're scaring me."

"Just call Sarah," Ronan said.

Siobhan gave up her seat so that Mary McBride could sit at the head of the table. They were all there, including Sarah, who looked as if she'd literally been dragged from bed. Her hair was tucked into a baseball cap and there were smudges of mascara under her eyes. Mary fussed with the bun on top of her head, her once-lush brunette hair streaked with gray. She was plump like the twins, but still had a youthful look about her, a softness cultivated by years of service to her family. She was not comfortable sitting; it was torture for her not to whip out the frying pans and start cooking, and she had not expected to find all seven of her children, and Anchor, waiting at the table.

She looked at each of them, then crossed herself. She grabbed the hands nearest to her, which happened to be Anchor's and Sarah's.

"Sacred heart of Jesus," she said with her head bowed. "Who died?"

"The pub, Ma," Ronan said. "I killed the pub." Mary looked at her son and tilted her head. She patted a few loose strands of hair. She glanced at the stove. Siobhan shot out of her chair, smacked her hands on the table, and leaned into Ronan.

"What are you on about?" she said. "Did ye set fire to it or what?"

"O sacred heart of Jaysus," Mary said, crossing herself again. "Is anyone hurt? Just tell me nobody is hurt."

"Nobody is hurt, Ma," Ronan said.

"All right. Let's just breathe. We're insured. I know your father made sure we were covered against everything, even acts of God—"

"Ronan is not an act of God," Siobhan said.

"I didn't set the pub on fire, Ma," Ronan said.

"Oh, thanks be to Jesus," Mary said. She stood up. "Should I start the fry?" Anne took her mother's hand and gently pulled her back down.

"What did you do, Ronan?" Siobhan said. She stood, crossed her arms, and glared at him.

"I played a game of cards," Ronan said. Mary sighed; she'd made her views on gambling very clear.

"And?" Siobhan said.

"Siobhan, would you sit down and let him speak, like?" Sarah said. Siobhan shook her head, but sat.

"I had four fucking aces," Ronan said. "Do you know how good that is?"

"Language," Mary said.

"It was down to me and Uncle Joe," Ronan said.

"Oh, this has got to be good," Anne said. "You lost, did ye? And now—what? We're going to have to put one of his fecking sunbeds in the pub?"

"Is that it?" Katie said. "I wouldn't mind trying it out myself."

"You're close," Ronan said. "But it's not that simple."

"He put the pub into the pot and he lost," Anchor said. All heads jerked to Anchor. He put his hand up.

"Sorry, lad," Anchor said. "But this is getting fucking painful." He glanced at Mary McBride. "Pardon my language," he said, tipping his baseball cap.

"He put the pub into the pot," Mary McBride said slowly. She looked to her daughters to interpret.

"You what?" Clare said. "What is he on about?"

"I had four aces," Ronan said.

"But Joe had a royal flush," Anchor said.

"I don't understand a single word you lads are saying," Mary McBride said.

"He's saying that at some point in the evening, your drunken son ran out of dough. So instead of calling it quits—like a normal human being—he bet the pub. Our pub, our da's pub, now belongs to Uncle Joe, who quick as you can say Tan Land is going to turn it into our worst nightmare. Is that about it, like?" Siobhan said. She was on her feet again, hands raised to the heavens. Anchor nodded, but nobody was looking at him.

"Siobhan, don't be ridiculous," Mary said.

"I didn't start it," Ronan said. "Joe threw in the keys to the shop—then said, 'Now you throw in the keys to the pub.' "

"I knew it," Siobhan said. She began to shuffle-pace across the kitchen floor. "I bloody well knew it."

"Uncle Joe tried to raise you and you took the bait?" Sarah said. "Don't you remember Da telling us about his shoes?"

"I had four aces," Ronan said.

"Oh my God," Liz and Clare said in unison.

"O sacred heart of Jesus," Mary McBride said while crossing herself.

"I don't fucking believe you," Siobhan said. "Come over here. Let me punch you."

"Siobhan," Mary said.

"Don't worry, Ma, each of us will get a turn, but I jest have to have the first crack."

"We are not going to punch him," Sarah said.

"Thank you, Sarah," Ronan said.

"Anchor has bigger hands. Give him a good old wallop for us, will you?" Sarah said. "And don't hold back, lad." Anchor looked around the table. He looked at his fist. He looked at Ronan's face.

"Everybody wait," Ronan said. He screeched out of his chair and threw his hands up, just in case Anchor snuck in with a sucker punch. "Don't get your knickers in a twist. There's a fall-back." Anchor's head bobbed up and down. He pointed at himself with his thumb and looked around the table with a big grin. Only Katie returned it.

"Well, let's have it," Liz and Clare said at the same time.

"We have a month," Ronan said. "To come up with a hundred thousand."

"A hundred thousand what, luv?" Mary said. One by one, her children looked at her and kept looking at her. Finally, Siobhan rubbed her fingers together in the international sign for money until the light dawned. Mary's delicate hands flew up to her mouth. "O sacred heart of Jesus," she said. This time, the McBrides crossed themselves en masse.

CHAPTER 4

One More Chance

After two weeks of keeping his promise, the third Sunday Ronan was barely on time for morning mass at Saint Bridget's. He didn't intend on breaking the promise, exactly, but the past two weeks he'd learned his lesson. Too early and his mother would launch herself on him and drag him to her pew, front and center. Too late and Father Duggan would actually stop the sermon, fold his Bible against his ample stomach, and wait for Ronan to settle in.

"Glad you could join us," Father Duggan would shout. "God loves all of us, even those for whom time is as arbitrary and flexible as a sinner's universe." (Ronan had worked out that Father Duggan's God must be extremely hard of hearing, for he always shouted rather than spoke, something that was totally unnecessary given the incredible acoustics of the church, the bounce and the echo that followed his voice.) Then Father Duggan would thrust his Bible-wielding hand heavenward, while the entire congregation watched Ronan, as if expecting lightning to strike at any moment. The first time this happened, Ronan grinned and waved. This elicited a sermon the likes of which he'd never seen. From his mammy. He wouldn't dare do it again.

Ronan darted in, stuck two fingers in the holy water, crossed himself, and knelt. He had no problem with praying. Lately, he'd been doing little else. Today, he needed it more than ever. He finally had a couple of good tips on a gigi, straight from the jockey's mouth. There was a chance, however small, that he could win big. Big enough to pay off his debt to Uncle Joe. If there was ever a time to pray, this was it.

Ronan made the mistake of looking up and catching his mother's eye. There she sat, in the front row, motioning frantically for him to join her, her arm turning like a windmill. When she failed to elicit his reaction, she patted her bun, eternally searching it for escaping brown and white strands. Even after five years, it was so strange to see her sitting there without his father. She looked smaller with him gone, shrunken. Or maybe Ronan had done that to her. Wherever his father was, Ronan hoped there was whiskey; if he was looking down on them, he would need it.

Liz, Clare, Katie, and Anne sat with their mother. Siobhan and Sarah were probably sleeping. No rest for the wicked. But wicked or not, they were his flesh and blood. Which is why Ronan had to fix this. If his horse came through—he was 25 to 1—Ronan would have enough to tide Joe over. He was a long shot all right, but Racehorse Robbie assured Ronan his beauty of a horse was going to send serious shock waves through the Killarney Races. And Racehorse Robbie didn't take these things lightly; he'd made millions on his horses over the years. Furthermore, Ronan still had the Galway Races coming up—there was time, and there was hope.

In the meantime, Uncle Joe was already measuring the floor space in the pub, plotting where he would put his tanning beds. Ronan wasn't going to let that happen. He'd chain himself to the front door first. Of course, Joe would just go in through the back, but the point was, he was not going to let it happen. Not now, not ever. Ronan headed to his usual pew, situated in the very back row.

He was known as one of the "Last in Lads" aka "the Back Pew Boys." He and his mates sat in a cluster, so close to the back they were practically out the door. As Ronan tried to squeeze himself in, Anchor elbowed him in the gut and Eoin gave him a soft kick with his dirty work boot. Seven lads in all with barely enough room for their elbows and knees.

Ronan crossed himself and looked heavenward. *Please, Big Guy. I know I fucked up big-time.* He tried to think of something else to say, something more convincing, but he was distracted by the pitched ceiling. It was in disrepair. Its imperfection stood out only because its surroundings were so gorgeous. Hundreds of years old, soaring steeple, grand stained glass, and polished wood. Father Duggan asked Ronan if he would organize some lads to repair the ceiling. Ronan said of course he would.

That was over a year ago. He still intended on fixing it, but his prayer would've gone down easier if only it was done already. It was cracked, and it leaked. Ronan intended on fixing the crack and replacing the damaged wood, but he'd leave a tiny bit of the leak, just the part above the stained glass window, since there were folks who only came to church after a hard rain, just to see the Virgin Mary cry. Eoin shifted and stepped on Ronan's toe. Eejit. Who wore work boots to mass?

Speaking of work, he couldn't just sit there, he had to nail down his bets on the races. Ronan stood as if to stretch, jumped over Eoin's extended leg, and bolted out the door before Father Duggan had uttered a single word of his Sunday sermon.

The fastest way to the pub was through Paul Keals's field. An escape route—that was Ronan's definition of religious freedom. Paul had warned Ronan not to cut through his property, plenty of times. But he wasn't doing any harm, aside from spooking a few barnyard animals. He jumped the teetering wood fence separating Saint Bridget's from the Kealses' property and skirted along the edge. His boots instantly sank into the ground, weighing them down with muck.

Sheep stood in an awkward clump in the middle of the field like teenagers at their first dance. "Baaa," Ronan yelled as he clomped past. "Baaa!" That felt good. Nonplussed, the sheep blinked and chewed. God, what an existence. See, things could be worse. He could be one of those poor bastards with nothing but wool between his ears. Farther up the field horses stood grazing and lifting their long muscular legs to adjust or scratch. If he had a choice, Ronan would much rather be a horse. Those beauties could at least race. His heartbeat picked up at the thought of the horse "guaranteed to send shock waves" through the Killarney Races.

If only he could be there in person, standing next to the fence as the horses flew by, screaming his brains out, touching the horse that won him his pub back. He'd withdrawn every penny from his bank account to put down on the pretty pony. He was on his way to pick up some cabbage from the till at the pub too, every euro of which he'd replace. He wasn't trying to hide it from his mother or the half dozen, but he couldn't take the chance that they would get all preachy or freaked out and try to stop him. He had to lay down some serious dough on the horse—it was the only way he'd make enough to appease Joe. As long as he got close to a hundred thousand euros, Joe would have to take it. Listen to reason. Why did Anchor say a hundred thousand? Why didn't he say fifty thousand? What if Joe would have taken fifty? It was too late now, too fucking late, and he knew he had no one to blame but himself. Although it did make him feel a little better to share a tad of the blame with Anchor.

He'd watch the races at the pub. It would be good luck. He'd pop into the pub, get the dough, go to the bookmakers, place his bet, then come back to the pub to watch his horse cross the finish line first. If he stopped thinking and started running, he should have just enough time.

Today was the day, it had to be the day, he could feel it. He neared the Kealses' cow, a beast so old, her teats so saggy and wrinkly, if she was still making milk, it probably came out curdled. For luck, Ronan gave the old biddy a light slap on the ass as he passed. It was impossible to take life too seriously when you were slapping a cow on the ass.

The cow bellowed and gave him a look that shamed him to the core. Come on, he'd barely touched her, what was this? It was like Paul had trained the cow to hate him. Sure enough, here came Paul Keals lumbering toward him in tight pants and oversized wellies, shaking his veined fist, large face crimson with rage. Ronan did not have time for melodramatic cows or angry farmers. Paul Keals was another teetotaler in town, so Ronan's usual backup—an offer of a free pint—wouldn't help him out in this case.

"Aw, now, it was just a little love smack," Ronan said. "More like a tap. Love tap. Kind of in between a tap and a very affectionate smack." He threw up his hands. "She's all right, lad." He gave the cow a look, urging her to back him up on this one, tell her master she liked a little smack on the ass now and then. Instead, the cow bellowed again and turned her chocolate swimming-pool eyes on Paul. Women. Drama queens, every last one of 'em.

"You bollix you," Paul screamed. "I told you never to set foot on me property again."

"On my way," Ronan said. He didn't run; he walked backward as fast as he could without looking like he was afraid of Paul or his damn cow.

"Off to the pub, are ye?" Paul said. "On a Sunday no less. While your dear sweet ma is praying to God, you'll be praying to the pint."

"I didn't see you in mass," Ronan said. "Unless your congregation is a bunch of sheep." Oh, why didn't he just shut his trap? He didn't have time to antagonize anyone today, nor could he afford the negative karma. Positive thoughts, positive thoughts, positive thoughts. Paul was just too easy to poke. And this was all because Ronan had never gotten around to fixing Paul's fence like he promised.

"I'll get to your fence next week, Mr. Keals," Ronan said. God, he felt like a right eejit. Like he was back in school sucking up to Sister Ellen.

"Like hell you will," Paul said. "Next time I catch you on me property, I'll tie you down and let the old cow have her way with you, I will."

"Aw now, Mr. Keals, I appreciate the offer, but I'm not attracted to your missus in that way." Oh, why, why, why did he do it? He just couldn't keep his mouth shut. He liked Mrs. Keals too. Who wouldn't like a gal who'd put up with the likes of yer one for all these years? *Ah, impulse control, not your strong point,* Ronan said to himself.

Ronan stared at the old fella's ears as if expecting smoke to pour out of them. He waved and tipped an imaginary hat to the cow. "Apologies, ma'am," he said. He bowed. Paul Keals lurched forward. At first, Ronan thought the old fella was having a heart attack. Then Paul started to run. After him. The old guy was actually going to chase him down. Ronan almost stood there, willing to take whatever the old man wanted to do to him, but then he remembered he had a bet to place. So he ran.

So much for looking casual. He sprinted full on down the field with Paul Keals clomping behind him in his wellies. Just ahead of him, plopped in the middle of the field for no foreseeable reason, was a large rock. The kind you could sit on and have a nice picnic if you didn't mind the smell of cow shit with your chips and ham-and-cheese sandwich. Ronan saw it a second too late. He jumped it, caught his foot on the tip of the rock, and landed face-first in wet cow dung. Even with his ears to the ground, he could hear Paul Keals having a right old belly laugh.

Ronan stood, brushed himself off as best he could, and, chin up, headed for the road, as if cow shit on his face didn't bother him at all. He wasn't going to give the old man the satisfaction. He stepped out onto the road. He heard the roar of an engine and turned toward it. A blur of yellow, churning, belching metal was hurtling straight for him. It was Anchor on his tractor. He'd engineered it himself, doctoring it with a racing engine. Nobody believed it until they saw it, but Anchor could get that beast up to seventy miles an hour. Right now it seemed as if it were aiming for ninety. A blast of wind whipped up as the tractor sped by, unleashing a mini-tornado of dirt, pebbles, and glass from the road, pelting Ronan as he dove for the ditch. The tractor slowed, then idled beside him. Ronan looked up; Anchor was all teeth.

"I'm flying it," he yelled. He flashed him the horns. Anchor, a heavy-metalhead, always flashed the horns. Back of the hand out, index and pinky fingers up. Then, without offering Ronan a ride, he zoomed off again. Ronan put his head back in the ditch and pounded it softly against the ground. Maybe, just maybe, he should have stayed in church a little longer.

By the time he saw Galway Bay shimmering in the distance, Ronan felt like a new man. The sight of the bay never failed to soothe him. It was like the perfect pint of Guinness: dark at the bottom, buoyant in the middle, topped off with a nice, frothy head. Ronan pulled his racing card out and whistled a tune. Looking at the names of the ponies made him feel alive. He loved the little flip in his stomach, the tingle in his spine; he even loved the sweat that broke out on the back of his neck when he placed a bet. If he thought about it, in some ways this pre-bet feeling was even better than winning. Winning was grand too, winning was riding the crest of a wave, but still, there was something about the glorious thought of winning that he experienced before every bet, no matter if he won or lost, that raised his betting life to a near-spiritual level.

The lingering promise of—this could be it. This could be the one that changed his life. If he won big on this, he would change. He would. He would stop gambling altogether. Just one big win to carry him home. He would save the pub, pay off Uncle Joe, fix the ceiling in the church, mend fences, literally, with yer one, and maybe, just maybe think about settling down. He couldn't live above the pub forever, could he?

He had a tip that was "guaranteed to send shock waves through the Killarney Races." Howards End. Heard it from Racehorse Robbie himself: This young horse was going to go nuclear on the track. *This is it, Ronan, you're a right eejit if you don't listen to me on this one, take everything you've got, I mean fecking everything because this horse is going to be talked about for the next two hundred and fifty fucking years.*

Ronan visualized Howards End flying past the finish line. Saw the sleek curve of his neck, the whip of his mane, heard the roar of the crowd as his horse tore first across the finish line. Ronan rehearsed it over and over again in his mind. He imagined shock and awe spreading through the crowd. The men who bet on him shouted, pumped their fists, and grabbed the birds next to them and kissed them like they were coming home from war. Men who lost tore at their chests, threw punches, fell to their knees in agony—*Our Bookmaker, Who Sure Aren't in Heaven, Howards End Be Thy Name—*

Ladies fanned themselves and jumped up and down, boobs bouncing as far as the eye could see, and a few in very short skirts fainted, spread-eagled in front of him. Ronan saw lightning bolts shooting from the hooves of Howards End. Howards End would do it; he would come in first. He would be the horse that saved Ronan's life. Ronan would name his first son Howards and his second son End. Ronan had to scrape up every quid he could and throw them on his horse. Guaranteed to send shock waves through the Killarney Races! Only a few lads knew about it. They would keep their bets low until the very last betting second to keep the odds in their favor. Howards End would win. He had to. Otherwise Ronan was sunk, and so was the pub.

"Hello there, how ya keeping?" a female voice rang out. Ronan was so fixated on his upcoming win, he'd forgotten that he was walking right past the Collinses' hardware shop. Sally Collins stood outside smiling and waving. Petite, raven-haired, and perky. She was wearing a green jacket with rhinestones, a white cap with rhinestones, and jeans with rhinestones. Ronan was on such a high he had half a mind to swoop her up and give her a good-luck kiss, but knowing Sally, she would take it as a sign that he was madly in love with her.

"Grand, grand," Ronan said without slowing down. "What's the craic?"

"Damn all," Sally said.

"You're awful sparkly today," he said with a wink. She smiled. Every time she looked at him like that he'd think: ovulating.

Nod and smile, just nod and smile. Sally Collins had been

chasing him since they were kids. She was seven years younger, but still, getting up there. He really thought she would have married someone else by now. Instead, she was waiting for him. And waiting, and waiting, and waiting. She held on to any sliver of attention he showed her, even innocent things that were never intended as a romantic gesture, like the "romantic love letter" he'd left in the abbey when they were fifteen. He'd told her plenty of times to forget about him. He'd been nice about it. He'd been an ass about it. He'd avoided her. Now, he had to admit, he was slightly worn down. He couldn't help but admire her pluck; he couldn't help hating her for being so damn sure she wanted him. It was starting to confuse him.

"How does a June wedding sound?" Sally said.

"Expensive," Ronan said.

"September?"

"I'll get back to ye," he said.

"Any month will do," Sally said. She twirled a strand of dark hair with her finger and smiled. That wasn't fair. A guy could take advantage of that. She didn't know how lucky she was that he never had. He gave her a quick salute and headed on. Her disappointment trailed after him like a wet, smelly dog.

The pub beckoned like the proverbial light at the end of the tunnel. A good walking distance from Main Street, the pub and Joe's shop were surrounded by land. Ronan thought it was the best of both worlds, even if some customers were too lazy to make it out here. As he bounded up to the door, he heard the lads coming up behind him. Anchor's tractor was parked underneath the enormous ash tree that stood guard in front of the pub. Eoin, Collin, Billy, Ciaran, and Danny were coming up the walk. They all had newspapers and betting cards out and they walked on autopilot, feet heading steadily for the front door. Ronan prayed none of them would bet on his shock wave; he couldn't afford for the odds to decrease. He had to get the dough from the bar and run to the bookmakers.

Anchor was the first to smack into the door. The rest rammed into him like a six-car pileup. They grunted and swore, then swore some more, then stepped back, stared at the door, and swore some more.

"Christ," Anchor said. "The door's closed?" Declan always left the door open. Said it made it easier for the lads to saunter in and stagger-wobble out.

"Well, open it, you eejit," Eoin said. He had a wife and kid waiting at home; he was always hurrying people along. He stepped forward and gave the knob a rattle. Then he pushed on the door. It didn't budge. They all looked at Ronan. A vague worry flickered through him. He still had three weeks to pay off Uncle Joe. He put his shoulder against the door and heaved. The others joined in, adding their strength to the effort. Maybe Declan was upstairs sleeping off a bender. Soon their throats were sore from shouting, which reminded them that they were thirsty.

"Who wants to give the old window a smash?" Anchor said. He rolled up his sleeve.

"Don't even think about it." Ronan whipped around. Siobhan stood in front of him, hands on hips. Behind her the rest of the estrogen gang stood in a defensive line. What were they doing here? He didn't have time for another row, he had to place his bet. Siobhan reached into her handbag and whipped out a wad of dough wrapped in a rubber band. "Looking for this?" she said. He'd recognize that bulge anywhere. Ronan reached for his money. Siobhan snapped it behind her back.

"That's mine," he said.

"Not on your roll-of-the-dice life," Siobhan said.

"Can ye unlock the door for us while yous have your discussion?" Eoin said.

"No," Siobhan said. "The pub is closed until the new publican takes over."

"Declan quit?" Ronan said. When did this happen? Why was he being left out of everything?

"Declan didn't quit," Siobhan said. "But it will be up to the new owner whether or not he stays."

"What new owner?" Ronan said.

"We're raffling off the pub," Katie said. "To Americans."

"You're what now?" Ronan said. He knew his tone wasn't

nice. But this went beyond fucking with him. Katie stepped forward.

"It's for the best," she said. "It was my idea."

"What in the world are you on about?" Ronan said.

"Remember how Guinness used to raffle off a pub every year?" Katie said.

"No," Ronan said.

"Oh. Well, they did. It's kind of like an auction, only you buy a ticket," Katie said.

"Property sales are such shite now, a lot of people are doing it," Liz said.

"It's win, win," Clare said. "They get a chance to win a pub for twenty dollars, we get thousands of rich, desperate Yanks throwing money at us."

"Somebody better start making some sense here or I'm going to fucking lose it," Ronan said.

"Starting tomorrow, Irish festivals all over America will start selling raffle tickets," Siobhan said. "Twenty American dollars apiece. We only have to sell five thousand tickets to make our hundred thousand."

"I'll bet we make even more," Katie said. She brought something out from behind her back and held it up. It was a poster. Stunned, Ronan moved in to look at it. It was a photo of all six girls standing in front of the pub. They were wearing tight, low-cut dresses and smiling like they had just jumped the cameraman.

"You're joking me," Ronan said. He grabbed the poster and started tearing it into tiny pieces that he let fall to the ground like an unattended ticker-tape parade. The girls didn't make a move to stop him. "How could you even think of showing yourselves looking like this?" he said. Siobhan stepped closer.

"Looking like what?" she said.

"Like, like ..." Ronan's hands moved vaguely around his chest, not knowing where to land or how much he could get away with saying.

"It's already done," Katie said. "The posters are on their way across the pond as we speak."

"You cannot be serious," Ronan said.

"We're dead serious," Sarah said. "We've even contacted RTÉ. They're coming out to interview us today." RTÉ, Ireland's national television and radio broadcaster. This could not be happening. Ronan looked at Anne, the only one so far who had remained silent. Divide and conquer. Anne returned his gaze.

"We all agree," she said.

"You're saying some Yank is going to win our pub?" Ronan said. Surely, when they heard it said, out loud, like, they would come to their senses.

"It's better than watching it turn into a shake and bake," Sarah said.

"You can thank me for that," Anchor said. "I came up with the fallback." He smiled and flashed the horns.

"Did it ever occur to you that Uncle Joe would've taken fifty thousand, you eejit?" Ronan said. Anchor stopped smiling and shrugged.

"Yes," Siobhan said. "Some Yank will win the pub."

"What if they don't even run it?" Ronan said. "What if they turn around and sell it?"

"We can't control that," Siobhan said. "But George said that probably wouldn't happen." George was their trusty solicitor. Ronan couldn't believe they'd been consulting George about raffling the pub behind his back. "Most Americans are naïve," Siobhan continued. "To them winning a pub in Ireland is a dream come true."

"Wait until winter hits," Ciaran said.

"You can't do this behind my back," Ronan said. "You can't raffle the pub without my signature."

"True," Siobhan said. She removed a set of documents and a pen from her purse. She thrust them at Ronan.

"No," he said. "I still have three weeks."

"Two weeks," Anchor said.

"And what's your bright idea?" Siobhan said. Siobhan waved the money in his face. "Going to win big again, are ye?"

Ronan stepped forward, lowered his voice. "I have a tip," he said. "From Racehorse Robbie." Siobhan stared at him. He curled his hands up near his head as if trying to grasp something. "Shock waves," he said. "They're going to be talking about this horse for the next two hundred and fifty years." He was trying to whisper but could already hear the lads behind him madly speculating about which horse he was on about. He stepped even closer to his sisters.

"I know what you're thinking," he said. "I fucked up and I'm sorry. Truly sorry. I'm a right eejit, and you have every right to hate me. But this time—it's the real deal. And not for me. For you. I've scraped up every quid I could, and the odds are in my favor. If he wins—when he wins—it's going to pay off big. We'll get to keep the pub. No Uncle Joe, no tanning beds, and no fucking Yanks. It's my last bet. I swear to you, it's my last bet. Once more chance. Just give me one more chance, will ye?"

Siobhan looked at the cash, then looked at the rest of the estrogen gang, then looked at her brother.

"Ronan Anthony McBride," she said. "If we give you this money, and you put it on your 'shock wave,' and you lose—do you promise, do you swear on all of our graves, that you'll sign these documents and let us hold the raffle?"

Ronan looked at his sisters. He looked at the money. He looked at the documents.

"I still have three weeks," he said.

"Two weeks," Anchor said.

"It's a yes or no," Siobhan said.

"Deal or no deal," Anne said.

"That's my money," Ronan said.

"And this is our pub too," Liz said. "Or did you forget that when you were throwing it out the window like it meant nothing to us, like . . . like we meant nothing?" Her words were a rusty, dull knife to the heart, twisting, twisting. She was right. He'd taken more from them than they had from him. And he could still win. He could win and this ridiculous raffle would never go through.

"All right, all right," he said. "I promise. If Howards End

doesn't win, then I'll sign the papers and you can hold your raffle." One by one the girls nodded their consent. Siobhan tossed the money. It hit Ronan square in the chest.

"I'm going to win," he said. "A fecking Yank running the pub. Over my dead body."

"That can be arranged," Siobhan said. Suddenly, a familiar blast of dread-cold air ran through Ronan. He looked behind him. Anchor was still there, but the rest of the men had vanished.

"Where are the lads?" Ronan said.

"They took off," Clare said.

"The minute you said Howards End," Anchor said.

CHAPTER 5

The Good Woman

If there was anything Dublin, Ohio, knew how to do well, it was throw its annual Irish festival. Like Ireland, except smaller, their website bragged. Carlene Rivers thought the festival was just an excuse to eat, and drink, and drink, and eat some more, but to disguise that fact, the hundred thousand or so visitors who came through each year were also treated to Irish music, Irish dancing, Irish dogs (canines with credentials), sand castle–building contests, dart-throwing contests, whiskey-tasting contests, jigs, sheep herding (spelled h-e-a-r-d-i-n-g), and more green crap for sale than Carlene had ever seen in her life.

To be fair, the festival was always a fun day out. The food was delicious, the music was both live and lively, the people watching couldn't be beat, and the dogs could do some pretty awesome tricks. Parents were placated by plastic mugs of green beer, and children were bombarded with activities just for them. On Wendy's Wee Folk Stage, Skelly the Leprechaun emceed contests for children with the reddest hair, greenest eyes, and most freckles. If Carlene wasn't blond with blue eyes, and her best friend, Becca, wasn't a brunette, Becca would have been screaming ageism and dragging them up onstage.

The festival was held in the summer because Ohio in March was too unpredictable, and nobody wanted his or her shamrock-riddled tents flapping in the wind. Carlene and Becca, friends since they were in kindergarten, had been coming to Dublin's Irish festival since the summer they turned thirteen. Rebecca Weinstein was the only Jewish person Carlene had ever met who regularly wore *Kiss Me I'm Irish* T-shirts. She was wearing it today, of course, along with her plaid skirt, which was actually more Scottish than Irish, Carlene thought, but she kept this to herself. Carlene wasn't a physician, but she believed in their creed. First, do no harm.

Becca was pregnant and due to pop in less than a month. She was here to have a good time and "distract herself from her alien stomach." Carlene thought if she wanted to distract herself, wearing what amounted to a kilt and a tight T-shirt over her bulbous stomach wasn't the way to go, but once again, she kept this to herself. No good would come of belittling either her outfit or the Irish festival to Becca—she would defend every bit of it, down to the grown men who wore giant leprechaun ears and painted Irish flags or four-leaf clovers on their hairy beer bellies. Becca was thirty going on thirteen. She was also deliriously happy, so in turn, Carlene pretended to be deliriously happy, although she drew the line at wearing anything with a leprechaun, pot of gold, or shamrock. Most of these festival-goers, Carlene thought, put the sham in shamrock.

They ate their way down the street. Bangers and mash, shepherd's pie, curry chips, and salt-and-vinegar chips, and chips with mayonnaise, and chips with cheese, or just plain old chips with tons of salt. Chips, of course, weren't American potato chips, which the Irish called "crisps," they were big, fat French fries. Becca was yammering on about getting Irish soda bread when a man at a nearby tent called out to them.

"CmereIwancha," he said. Carlene stopped. In the entire festival, it was the first real Irish accent she'd heard. Becca kept walking. Carlene, drawn in by the man's lyrical voice and generous smile, walked into his tent. It was empty except for a large folding table on which sat a small white box. Beside the box was a poster of a little white house with a thatched roof. Six women in flashy low-cut dresses stood in front of the house, smiling seductively at the camera. WIN A PUB IN IRELAND, it said. Carlene was still studying the poster when she felt a huge stomach poke her in the back. *Please don't let it be a beer belly,* she thought.

"I was totally talking to myself for, like, ten minutes," Becca said.

"Sorry," Carlene said.

"How would you lovely ladies like to win a pub in Ireland?" the man said.

"Oh my God, oh my God, oh my God," Becca said. "Win a pub in Ireland?" She bent down as far as her protruding stomach would allow and looked at the poster. "Is it a pub or a strip club?" she said.

"It's a wee pub," the man said. "In Ballybeog."

"Oh my God," Becca said. "I'm totally game."

"Twenty dollars," the man said. Becca immediately dove into her purse and pulled out a twenty. The man handed her a slip of paper. "Name, digits, address," he said. "The drawing will be held in a month's time. Good luck to ye."

"Oh my God," Becca said. She began to fill out the slip of paper.

"What about you, miss?" the man asked Carlene.

"Oh, she won't enter," Becca said without looking up. "She's the unluckiest girl in the world." Even though there wasn't a mean bone in Becca's body, and she was telling the truth—Carlene *was* severely lacking the luck gene—it still hurt to hear it announced with such gusto by her best friend. Carlene secretly wanted to tell Becca to shut up. But Becca had made it clear that she was not responsible for anything she said or did "in her condition." Carlene couldn't wait until the baby was born so she could stop biting her tongue. The man in the tent was staring at Carlene with watchful eyes.

"You look very lucky to me, miss, if you don't mind me saying," he said.

"Thank you," Carlene said. "I really can't complain."

"What are you talking about?" Becca said. "You complain all the time."

Carlene smiled, hoping to cancel out Becca's declarations and show him that she was a gentle soul filled with nothing but gratitude for the good things in her life.

"I have things pretty darn good," Carlene said. She hated the sound of herself. Like an actress on an infomercial.

"You look good to me, miss," the man said.

"Oh, she's looks and brains lucky," Becca said. "Just not lottery lucky."

"Well, this isn't exactly the lottery," the man said. "But you know what they say. You can't win if you don't play."

"You've got to be in it to win it," Carlene said. Becca threw her a look. Carlene wished she hadn't spent the morning preaching about how she was going to start saving her money—how she only had thirty dollars on her, and she wasn't even going to spend it all. Unfortunately, ten bucks had already been spent on a stomachache. "Are the proceeds going to a good cause?" Carlene said. She knew then, good cause or no, she was going to enter the raffle. Becca's attitude was really getting to her, and she wanted to prove to this smiling Irishman that no matter how unlucky she was, she was still willing to get in the game.

"Well, I'm sure if the family is raffling off the pub, there's a good reason for it all right," the man said. Carlene stepped closer and looked at the picture. Up close she could read the sign above the pub.

"Uncle Jimmy's," she said.

"I believe he passed away," the man said. "And times are tough, as you know yourself." He quickly crossed himself. Becca did the same. *Oh, if your rabbi could see you now,* Carlene thought.

"That's so sad," Carlene said.

"Ah, but you can help out today with just twenty dollars." The man leaned in until he was only an inch or so from Carlene's face. He smelled of cigarettes and tea. "And you never know, do ye? Luck is like the weather. It can change like that."

He snapped his fingers. Carlene jumped. Becca folded her entry, kissed it, and stuck it in the box.

"Is it in Dublin?" Becca said. "The *real* one?" she added as if the fake one were listening.

"No, no, I'm afraid not. She's on the West Coast of Ireland, near Galway."

"That's so cute." Becca turned to Carlene. "Did you hear that? The pub is a she. Like a truck or a boat." Carlene didn't answer, she was back to looking at the women on the poster.

"Uncle Jimmy's daughters," the man said.

"Oh," Carlene said quickly. She hoped he didn't remember Becca insinuating they were strippers. Becca linked arms with Carlene.

"Let's go get soda bread," she said.

"Wait," Carlene said. She dug in her purse and counted out her money. Eighteen dollars. She thought for sure she'd only spent ten. With her luck she'd probably dropped two. Maybe the wind had carried it away and it was stuck to some beer guzzler's sweaty gut. She looked at Becca. "I'm two dollars short," she said.

"You didn't buy the Celtic cross necklace because you said you were broke," Becca said. "And it was only fifteen dollars."

"I know. But I want to help out Uncle Jimmy," Carlene said. Becca leaned in and lowered her voice.

"He's dead," Becca said. "I don't think your twenty dollars is going to help."

"His daughters, then," Carlene said.

"Ah, good girl," the man said. "Twenty dollars, luv."

"Come on, Becca," Carlene said. "I'll pay you back."

Becca sighed as if Carlene were her teenage daughter, hitting her up for an extra week's allowance. She rolled her eyes at the man as she dug two dollars out of her Coach purse.

"Don't complain about this later," Becca said. She handed her the two dollars.

"I won't," Carlene said. "And thank you."

"You're welcome," Becca said. "But if your luck does change, you owe me."

* * *

Carlene and Becca sat at a small green plastic table set up on the sidewalk and daydreamed over generous pieces of Irish soda bread, butter, and homemade jam. "Can you imagine winning a pub in Ireland?" Becca said. She spoke with her mouth full.

"It rains a lot in Ireland," Carlene said.

"That's the beauty of it," Becca said. "Job security."

"I don't follow," Carlene said.

"Remember when I lived in Seattle for six months and I called you crying every day because all it did was rain?"

"Yes."

"Well, I didn't tell you this because I didn't want you to judge me, but all I did to get through it was drink."

"You still drink. I mean, when you're not expecting. You own a wine bar," Carlene said. Last year Becca had opened Wine on the Flats, a wine bar in Cleveland, where they lived.

"That's nothing compared to how much I drank in Seattle," Becca said. "Rain, rain, rain, rain. It was all I could do not to throw myself off the Aurora Bridge."

"It's a good thing you're not selling those raffle tickets," Carlene said.

"I'm just saying—you'd make a lot of money."

"I hope whoever wins it isn't just after money," Carlene said. "Did you see how cute the pub was? It was family owned. God, it must be hard for them to sell."

"Maybe sad enough for them to keep drowning their sorrows at the pub," Becca said. Carlene laughed. "Oh," Becca said. She grabbed Carlene's hand and put it on her stomach. Carlene pretended to feel the baby kick. "Shane wants to win a pub in Ireland, don't you, Shane?" Becca rubbed her stomach.

"Shane?" Carlene said.

"Or Shania," Becca said.

"Shane or Shania Weinstein," Carlene said. "What does Levi think?"

"Loves them," Becca said. She gave Carlene a look. Carlene laughed.

"I would just die. I would just die to win a pub in Ireland," Becca said. "Wouldn't you?"

Carlene wasn't going to answer. It was probably a rhetorical question. Becca often pretended to listen, when in reality she wasn't listening at all. And you couldn't tell by looking at her because she had perfected the I'm-listening look. A slight tilt of the head, index finger poised by her lip, eyes on the speaker, chin up. Often, when Carlene was done spinning a tale or spilling her guts, she would discover Becca had actually been formulating the menu for an upcoming dinner party in her head, or rearranging the seating chart, or mentally grocery shopping, and once she even admitted to listing, in chronological order, every song in *Xanadu*.

And Carlene really would die to win a pub in Ireland. Unlike Becca, whose entire family, both maternal and paternal, had come from Israel, Carlene actually had Irish heritage. Her maternal great-great-great-grandmother, Mary Margaret, came to America from County Mayo when she was only sixteen. The Troubles were in full swing when Mary Margaret's mother passed, and her father joined the IRA. Mary Margaret was sent to Philadelphia to live with a cousin. Carlene's maternal grandmother, Jane, who lived four years longer than Carlene's mother, used to sit with Carlene drinking tea and regaling her with stories of far, far-away relatives who were from a magical place the Good Lord had blessed with soaring cliffs that hovered over the edge of the Atlantic Ocean, and rolling hills with a thousand shades of green.

Sometimes, Carlene's grandmother would put an album on the record player and sing along with an Irish ballad—"Danny Boy," and "The Fields of Athenry," and "The Rose of Tralee"—and Carlene would be transported into another world. A world of fiddles, flutes, harps, guitars, pianos, and tin whistles. Haunted windswept voices sang of life, land, beauty, death, drink, regret, mothers who were still alive, and hills with a thousand shades of green. There were days when her grandmother would refuse to sing because she "didn't have the pipes" or the pipes were leaking, so Carlene would try to sing along instead. When songs spilled into her grandmother's tiny, dark sitting room, Carlene's chest would fill and expand as if it were about to burst. On rare occasions, Carlene's grandmother would get up and dance.

Carlene loved these moments with her grandmother, but above all, it was her stories she cherished the most. When it came to hearing about her long-lost relatives, Carlene was a bottomless pit, constantly begging for more. There weren't nearly enough stories for Carlene to hold on to, so she would often replay the same ones in her head, adding and deleting details, until she could no longer separate fact from fiction. Stories about her great-great-great-grandmother walking to Catholic school and passing Protestant children who would yell out, "cat lickers, cat lickers," to which they would respond, "prote-stinkers, prote-stinkers!"

Or stories about James and Charles, the twins. Those great-great-great-uncles were black sheep, her grandmother said, but they still had hearts of gold. They must be something, Carlene thought, for like Mary Margaret from County Mayo, her grandmother said James and Charles were "great" three times in a row. Carlene wondered if she would ever do something so remarkable that she would be great times three. The twins were drinkers, and gamblers, and wickedly handsome. They moved to Atlantic City, and died, one week apart, at age thirty-three. The exact cause of their mysterious deaths, if her grandmother knew, was never articulated, but Carlene always assumed it was due to their wickedly handsome ways.

"You're Irish too, you know," her grandmother often said. Oh, Carlene knew. She knew it the way her lungs almost burst just listening to her grandmother play those songs on the record player. She knew it the way she could close her eyes and feel herself standing on a windswept cliff, see the ocean pounding the rocks below, or feel her small body rolling down the rolling hills with a thousand shades of green.

Becca made a fist and knocked on Carlene's forehead. "Anybody in there?"

"Sorry," Carlene said. "I was just thinking about Ireland. My great-great-great-grandmother was—"

"Wouldn't you just die?" Becca said. There it was, she wasn't really listening.

"I couldn't even imagine," Carlene said.

"Imagine, running my wine bar in Ireland," Becca said.

"It's not a wine bar, Becca. It's a pub."

"It doesn't have to stay a pub. It would be my place. I could change it into a wine bar."

"I don't know if it's a big wine country. They do seem to like their pints."

"I was in Dublin, the real one, remember? And I'm telling you, it's a very sophisticated city. They're, like, so European now."

"They've always been European," Carlene said. Carlene had never been to Europe, or Asia, or Australia, or the Middle East. Becca had been everywhere.

"You know what I mean."

"This pub isn't in Dublin. Near Galway, didn't he say?" Carlene said. Becca shrugged.

"Did you know there's a large Jewish population in Cork City?" Becca said.

"I did not know that," Carlene said.

"Oh yes. I learned all about it when we toured Cork. Apparently, when the Jews were fleeing to America during the war, the boat stopped in Cork, and when the captain, or like whoever, yelled out, 'New Cork,' a lot of the Jews thought they said 'New York' and they disembarked."

"Wow," Carlene said.

"Do you have any gum?" Becca said. "God, I hate this baby. I need something in my mouth all the time." Carlene stuck her hand in her pocket. She pulled out a couple of crumpled bills.

"What do you know," Carlene said. "Two dollars." She held the money out to Becca. Becca grabbed both of Carlene's hands and squeezed them so tight, Carlene wondered if she was in labor.

"You know I didn't mean it. You know I do not hate this baby."

"Of course I know that," Carlene said. "I never believed you for a second." Again, she held out the two dollars.

"Forget it," Becca said. "I'd rather you owe me." She looked at her watch. "Do the Irish eat sauerkraut? I've got a yen for some sauerkraut."

Carlene laughed. "Sauerkraut is German," she said. "But I'll bet we could find some cabbage."

"That's what I meant," Becca said. "Corned beef and cabbage." Carlene stood. Becca remained sitting. Finally she stuck her hands out and allowed Carlene to pull her up off the chair. Becca bought corned beef and cabbage and Carlene bought a beer, and they watched children ride ponies with green saddles. Becca reached over and took Carlene's hand.

"I hope this isn't making you think of Brendan," she said.

"Not at all," Carlene said. "Not at all." But even as the words were coming out of her mouth, Carlene could feel herself tense up. Becca was crossing a line, using her condition to talk about Brendan, something that she had already agreed not to do. Brendan was a long time ago, Brendan was in the past, and she didn't need anyone reminding her.

"Good," Becca said. "You deserved so much better."

"I know."

"Can you imagine if you won the pub in Ireland, and you ran into him, like?"

"Wouldn't that be something." Seriously, condition or not, she was pushing it.

"Or you fall in love with some other Irish man," Becca said.

"Never again," Carlene said. "They are the best of men, they are the worst of men."

Becca held up her soggy sandwich. "I'll eat to that," she said.

Carlene clinked her beer bottle with Becca's corned beef. "Cheers," she said.

Carlene worked at Jabs, her father's training gym for professional boxers. Her father, Michael Rivers, was an ex-boxer himself. When he failed to rise to the ranks of a professional, he opened the gym—just a few months before he met Carlene's mother. Growing up, Carlene spent more time at the gym than she did in their two-bedroom apartment above it. Now she managed the day-to-day operations. Her father had OCD, obsessive-compulsive disorder, and instead of growing out of it, as he always promised he would, he was just getting worse. Compared to the over-orderly, sanitized world her father lived in, Carlene loved the smell, sounds, and sweat of the gym.

She loved the squeak of tennis shoes on the linoleum floor, the patter of boxers' feet, the grunts and groans accompanying their jabs. She loved the ropes that hung from the ceiling, thick twisted vines that she would swing on when no one was looking, she loved the punching bags she would pummel with her fists, she loved the practice ring she would crawl into when she was all alone, punching and jumping and ducking. She loved the sound of whistles being blown, and sweaty men with towels thrown over their muscular shoulders. She loved it all. Her motto in here was "let 'em see you sweat." When it first opened, the gym was all men. Carlene used to sit on a stool near the ring, hold their towels, and suffer through teasing, hair ruffles, and play jabs. Her small fists would bunch up in imitation of theirs, and she'd strike at phantom enemies in the air.

Carlene knew that had she grown up with her mother, she would have missed out on all of this. But Renee Rivers died from a weak heart when Carlene was only six. Carlene was raised in the gym, and she wouldn't have missed it for the world. She wondered if it made her a horrible person to think such thoughts, but she just couldn't imagine her mother allowing her to be around all those grown men, all the swearing, all the sweating, all the punching. She probably would have taken ballet or tap-dancing class with the other little girls her age, maybe only allowed an hour a week at the gym, such as Saturday afternoons when her mother needed some retail therapy, or her hair done, or a mani-pedi. At least that's how Carlene always imagined it.

Now there were plenty of women who trained at the gym. It

had been Carlene's idea. First, she suggested women's boxing for fitness. She convinced the cutest boxer at the time to teach the class. It was a huge success. She added self-defense, then private boxing lessons, and then, slowly, the professional female boxers came to train. She'd doubled their membership. But on this day, she just didn't feel like working.

It had been one month since the Irish festival, and weighing in at a whopping ten pounds, twelve ounces, Shane Weinstein had been born the night before. Carlene had just come from the hospital. She'd never seen Becca so happy. Watching her friend hold her son in her arms was joyous. It also brought unexpected feelings of jealousy to the surface. Carlene was thrilled for Becca, but something ached inside her when she saw that fat baby, when Levi reached over and stroked Becca's cheek, and when the three of them just sat, and smiled, and breathed in the silence of what they had just become. A family. Carlene was a long, long way from being a mother herself, if it ever happened. In order to do that, she'd have to find a relationship she could sustain for more than a couple of months.

Carlene approached the door to her father's office. She paused, hoping just once she'd open it and find his desk littered with papers and coffee cups and loose change. She'd give anything to see her father sitting in the middle of clutter. She knocked four times, then paused, counted to four, and once again knocked four times. It was the only way he'd ever answer.

"Come in." She opened the door. Her father was sitting behind his desk. It was clear and polished. He wore blue rubber gloves. The tiny, immaculate room reeked of Lysol.

"Hey, Dad," she said. "Guess what? I'm an honorary aunt!" She sat down in the one chair across from her father's desk. She kept her hands where he could see them. He pushed over a box. She took a pair of rubber gloves from the box and put them on. She was taking the picture of Shane out of her purse when her cell phone rang. She held her finger up to her father, then slipped outside to take the call. He didn't allow cell phones in his office—he thought they caused brain cancer. The squeak of tennis shoes on the gym floor and sounds of the punching bags being hit made it hard to hear the caller. He had an Irish accent. Her first thought was—Brendan.

Even two years later, her heart caught in her throat at the thought of him, and even after the caller introduced himself as someone else, it took a while for the hammering in her chest to stop. When it did, and she could make out what the caller was saying, she was full sure somebody was pulling a prank on her. This was "hidden camera," this was "you've been punked," this was Becca doubling over with laughter and screeching, "You should've seen the look on your face."

The man was still speaking. He said something about Bally-beog, and Dublin, Ohio, and the Irish festival—and it wasn't until he said "raffle" that it hit her. And then she felt as if her heart was suspended in her throat again, a sensation that remained for a very long time, long after he repeated the words— "I told ye, ye looked lucky to me all right. Congratulations, you just won a pub in Ballybeog."

CHAPTER 6

Leaving Home

When the news of her winning the pub reached Cleveland, reporters came out in droves. Her father paled under the spotlight. Cameras snapped like turtles, microphones were shoved in their faces, and they were both asked way too many personal questions. It literally made her father sweat, and only Carlene knew that the handkerchief he used to pat the perspiration off his brow had been ironed no less than a hundred times that very morning. Yet somehow, they got through it all; somehow, no matter how many times her father begged her to stay, Carlene remained steadfast. Becca threw a small going-away party for her that her father didn't attend. But the day of her flight he held out a small jewelry box. Inside was a pair of teardrop emerald earrings.

"These belonged to your grandma Jane," he said. "And then she passed them on to your mother." Carlene held her breath. Her father rarely mentioned her mother. "She planned on giving them to you on your sixteenth birthday," he said.

"But I'm thirty," Carlene said. Her father just looked at her. "I love them," she said. She turned away as she put them on; she didn't want him to see her cry. When she turned back, she sported a huge smile and air-hugged him. What she would give to be able to actually touch him again, skin to skin, like she could when her mother was alive. She touched the earrings instead. Earrings her mother had worn. "I'm going to make you proud," Carlene said. Her father didn't reply. She touched the earrings again. *You too, Grandma Jane,* she said silently. *And you, Mom, always you.*

A six-year-old remembers her mother. She remembers her smell. Renee Rivers always smelled like laundry fresh from the dryer; something you couldn't wait to wrap your arms around and inhale. She remembers how she would stand at the stove stirring her famous stew while talking on the phone. A chunky yellow rotary tucked into the crook of her neck, the spiral cord stretching tantalizingly from the wall. Carlene would sit on the floor underneath the bouncing cord, and when she could resist no longer, she would reach up and tug the cord down to the floor, then release it and watch it bounce. She would do it until her mother yelled at her to stop, which was usually after the third yank.

She remembers carefully cut peanut butter sandwiches with just the right amount of jelly, and glasses of milk in tall colored-plastic glasses, and being sat in front of the television to watch cartoons. She remembers good-night kisses, and bedtime stories, and soft hands on her forehead when she had a fever. She remembers happy birthdays and cakes with candles, and Christmas celebrations. She remembers drives in the car to see Grandma Jane, her mother's elbow resting on the ledge of the passenger seat window, her gaze outward and slightly sad, as if she were leaving something behind. She remembers how the hugs and kisses Renee Rivers gave her father were different from the hugs and kisses she gave Carlene. Her mother always kissed her father longer, but she squeezed Carlene harder.

She remembers her last day with her mother. They took a trip on the city bus. They went to see a doctor. Her mother needed some vitamins. Carlene sat in the waiting room, swinging her feet off a padded chair. There was a pretty lady sitting at a desk.

She kept smiling at Carlene and even gave her a piece of gum from her very own purse. After the doctor's they went to a pharmacy where her mother was given some pills in orange plastic bottles. She remembers the bus ride home, although it's the one thing she wishes she could forget, it's the memory she plays over and over again in her mind, and because of what happened on that bus, when they got home, Carlene was sent to Grandma Jane's. Her mother didn't tell her that was why, but Carlene knew it. Carlene didn't get to come home that night. Her mother needed her rest.

She remembers coming home from Grandma Jane's the next morning. She remembers her father sitting up straight on the couch, all dressed up in brown linen pants and a white button-down shirt instead of what her mother called his "house shorts." She remembers the look on her father's face.

"Your mother," he said. He choked. It was the first time she'd ever seen her father look as if he were about to cry. It was also the last time she would ever see her father's hands free of the blue rubber gloves that would soon encase them. "Had a weak heart," he whispered. He held out his hands to her. Carlene didn't budge. Grandma Jane knelt behind her, wrapped her arms around her.

"She's in heaven watching over you," Grandma Jane said. "She's our angel now."

They wouldn't open the lid and let her see her. She wanted to see her. They were tricking her. If she couldn't see her, maybe she wasn't really dead. Maybe she'd run away. Maybe she was mad at Carlene for what happened on the bus. But then they buried the box and threw dirt over it, and her father cried—loud, gulping sounds that came from his throat. That was when she knew for sure that her mother was really dead. Her mother was in a box. They put her in the ground and threw dirt over her. Wasn't she going to be lonely down there? Wasn't she going to be afraid? How could she rather be down there than up here with them?

Hot spikes of guilt pulsed through Carlene whenever she

thought about that day on the bus. And she thought about it a lot. She ached to tell someone what she'd done, but every time she thought of telling, a huge ball of sick would land in her stomach and turn, and turn, and turn until she changed her mind about telling. If she told them, they would know what she'd done. They would hate her. They would leave her just like her mother left her.

A six-year-old remembers. Shadowy memories of a mother's love. But what she remembers most was that it was all her fault. Carlene was the one who was responsible. Carlene was the one who made her mother's heart weak. And flawed or not, her father was the only family she had left. She'd already broken her mother's heart; she could only pray she wasn't about to do the same thing to him.

CHAPTER 7

Air We Ever Going to Land

Irish Accent Voted Sexiest in the World

A recent poll of thousands of women from all over the world has decided: The Irish accent is the sexiest in the world. Thanks in part to actors like Colin Farrell and Liam Neeson, women from all over the world, even French women, are in agreement. Irish men have the sexiest accent in the world. They even beat out the Italians, who used to make them swoon with a simple *"Ciao, bella."*

Carlene finished reading the article, shaking her head and smiling all the way through. So she wasn't the only one who swooned like schoolgirl at the sound of the Irish brogue. She used to say that she could get turned on listening to Brendan read the "fecking phonebook." Becca constantly pointed out how much Brendan cussed. Although Carlene couldn't deny it, it didn't bother her. He said the F-word like it was simply an adjective, or a part of speech like "a," "an," and "the." Sometimes, he even said the C-word; not to describe women, usually a fella he was annoyed at. This one completely jarred Carlene's sense of right and wrong, and despite his attempts to defend the way the Irish he knew used it, she begged him to stop. But the difference between how he said "fecking this" or "fecking that" and how Americans said it was huge. It was all in the attitude. He rarely used it in anger—it wasn't a tirade, it was simply an additive, like a food coloring—something to spice up the fecking phonebook.

Or maybe it was just the accent. It sounded fecking good, helped out the rhythm of the sentence—Hamburger Fecking Helper. Sometimes it was with the "eh" sound, and sometimes with the "uh" sound. She questioned him about it once, apparently the "eh" sound was an attempt to be a little more polite. And although not all Irish swore, just like not all Irish people drank, or could Riverdance, Carlene had always wanted to take a year off, travel Ireland, and study the numerous forms and uses of the F-word. Fuck, an in-depth exposé.

At the bottom of the article, Becca scrawled: *Go get 'em*. Unfortunately, she added: *Don't forget Brendan*. It was capitalized and underlined and followed by multiple exclamation marks. For the first time in what felt like hours, Carlene's smile faded slightly. *There she goes again, bringing up Brendan*. Brendan Hayes. As if forgetting him was an option. She could still see him standing in the doorway of the Irish pub in Boston, grinning at her.

"Ten-dollar cover, gorgeous," he said.

"Oh," she said. She was just off the plane and had arrived at the pub where Becca had arranged for them to meet. Becca had just met Levi, who was going to Boston University, and she had been visiting him as often as she could. This was Carlene's first time in Boston, and, as usual, she wasn't exactly flush with cash. The gym brought in decent money, but her father was so nervous they would spend it all that most went into savings and bonds and retirement accounts. Carlene was surprised Becca would pick a place with a cover. She knew Carlene's situation with money.

"For the band," the man said. His smile looked like an apology. He was cute, wearing a soft brown scarf that matched his eyes. She thought he looked familiar, but she couldn't think for the life of her why. And she wasn't going to come out with "don't I know you from somewhere," so she didn't say anything. When he spoke, it sounded like a thousand flutes.

"I love your accent," Carlene said.

"T'ank you," he said. "I've been practicing it a long time." He winked and she flushed. She dug in her purse and took out a tenner.

"Are they any good?" she said.

"Let's see," he said. He held the bill up to the light. She laughed.

"I meant the band."

"Ah right, the band," he said. "They're fucking brilliant." A line was starting to form behind her. She smiled again, and then before common sense could stop her, she snatched the money back and wrote her phone number on it before heading into the bar. Becca was already there, and soon they were so caught up in conversation, Carlene didn't even think about the guy at the door until someone asked the bartender when the band was going to start. She'd never forget the look on the bartender's face.

"What band?" he said. "There's no band tonight." As his comment echoed down the bar, a rush of people, mostly men, headed straight for the Irishman at the door. Carlene got to the window in time to see him bolting down the street with at least five men after him. When the men came back to the bar, still fuming, she knew they hadn't been able to catch him. To this day, it made her laugh. If only it had been the last time she'd ever laid eyes on Brendan Hayes. If only she hadn't given her phone number to a con man. If only she hadn't remembered why he looked familiar. If only, when he called her a few days later, she had hung up.

Carlene put the article back in her purse and looked out the window. She wouldn't think about the past. Although she was dying to tell Brendan Hayes that she'd just won a pub in Ireland. *Some craic, eh Brendan?* Just to see the look on his face. Just so he knew that something so wonderful had happened to her that even the worst memories of him couldn't wipe the grin off her face.

Her seatmate, a man in his fifties, leaned over. "Do you mind me asking what you're so fecking happy about?" The question startled her.

"What?" Carlene said.

"I'm sorry to intrude," he said. "But ye haven't stopped smiling since takeoff. At first I thought maybe there was something wrong with ye. You know, like off in the head. But I'm starting to think there's more to it, and for the life of me I've never seen someone smile for five hours straight, especially on Air Lick Us or Kill Us, and it's kind of annoying me, if you don't mind me saying." Carlene laughed. He shook his head. "Are ye on drugs?" he said. "I've never been a fan. But I might make an exception for whatever you're on." Carlene looked at him.

"I won something," she said. "I've never won anything in my life. I mean anything." She leaned into him. "Until recently, I was the unluckiest girl you could ever meet."

"So what'd you win? The lottery?" he asked. She didn't want to rush her story. It was too fun to tell. So she told him how whenever she reached for pennies dropped on the ground, someone else would get them first. She told him she never won the milk-line lottery in kindergarten, where you'd get to line up first on break and get the chocolate milk before they were all gone, and how in the third grade she entered a raffle to win a giant, ugly stuffed rabbit.

Yes, he was bright orange, and wore a blue suit, and he was absolutely twelve feet of hideous, but she was madly in love with him. She scraped up twenty dollars—a fortune in those days—and she bought as many tickets as she could. Bobby Meijers, a ninth grader, won the rabbit. He immediately placed Mr. Orangey (as she had already named him) on the wheel-a-round on the playground and set him on fire. Carlene would never forget the smell of stuffed flesh burning. It even prompted her to start KETSA, Kids for the Ethical Treatment of Stuffed Animals. Nobody joined except Becca. Good old Becca. Her seatmate's eyes were glazing over; apparently, he didn't care what an unlucky girl she used to be.

She could have told him the real bad luck she'd had in life. Her mother's death, her father's obsessive-compulsive disorder, Brendan Hayes, the things he'd done to her, the things she'd done for him—

"I won a pub in Ireland," she said.

"What now?" Her seatmate was interested again. So she told him about the Irish festival. She told him about "CmereIwancha" and the table with the little white box and how she almost kept walking. She told him how when the call came that she'd won, she didn't believe it. She made the man give her his number. She hung up. She called him. His story didn't change. They'd just held the drawing in Ballybeog, and hers was the name they picked.

"Didn't I tell ye luck could change like the weather?" the man said. She still didn't believe him. She called Becca. Becca didn't believe her. She told her father. He didn't believe her. She Googled Ballybeog, and sure enough she found newspaper coverage on the raffle, and the drawing, and there it was again, a teensy, tiny picture of her pub. It was adorable. White with blue trim, and an actual thatched roof. She saw her name. Carlene Rivers from Cleveland, Ohio.

Then the call came in from the pub itself. She could barely hear the girl—it was hard to understand her accent on the phone, and there was so much noise in the background. She started to believe it. The girl said she would receive paperwork in the mail from their solicitor. It would take some time, and there were forms she had to fill out, including the application for the work visa, but the solicitor had done as much of the legwork as he could on their end and they would talk her through every step, and would she mind doing a few interviews for RTÉ? And then, then she started to think it was real.

Now here she was, a month later, on a flight to Shannon, and she couldn't stop grinning. Her father said she was breaking his heart, and Becca teased that she was entitled to a percentage of the pub because of the two dollars Carlene had to borrow. And it was still in the back of her mind that this just couldn't be happening to her, because she wasn't that lucky, but even through her doubts, she couldn't stop smiling. Her jaw was starting to ache. The overhead speakers crackled and the pilot's voice filled the cabin.

"Ladies and gentlemen, we're beginning our descent into Shannon. If this is home, welcome back. If you're just visiting, allow us to fill up your hearts and empty your pockets."

If this is home. Carlene turned away from her seatmate and placed a hand on either side of the little oval window. Through a parting of the clouds, she caught sight of the ground below. Not as green as she'd imagined, but real Irish ground. Iconic images of Ireland flooded her mind. Majestic cliffs rising above the ocean, her grandmother leaning back to kiss the Blarney Stone, ancient castles (the only castles they had in Ohio were White Castles), soaring cathedrals, Barry's tea, Father Ted, and sheep.

She saw the Claddagh ring her grandmother bought her when she was seven, her first birthday without her mother. She saw lines of people Riverdancing, she saw pubs, she saw edgy young musicians in need of a dollar and a shave playing on the street, she saw drunken fisherman singing at the top of their lungs. Even bars of Irish Spring soap floated through the conveyor belt of her mind. She'd be seeing leprechauns on the wing of the plane next. Before she knew it, her eyes had filled with tears. She could feel her grandmother and great-great-great-grandmother, and those wickedly handsome twins, and her mother sitting beside her. *Welcome home,* something inside her said.

Life had finally done it, it had finally surprised her—in a good way.

They were landing. They were landing in Ireland. Where her pub awaited. It was astounding. And she would not ruin it with doubts, or worry, or fear. Becca would not show up at her doorstep demanding a share of the pub, her father would not die without her, and she would never, ever speak to Brendan Hayes again. She wondered if she would ever be able to think of Brendan without seeing him in her underwear. Shortly after he disappeared, a man named Trent sent her a picture of Brendan. He was standing in a hotel room with nothing but a pair of her Victoria's Secret panties. They were red with little white hearts. He looked deliriously happy and better in the panties than she ever did.

Were Brendan and this "Trent" lovers? There was no return address, but the postmark was from Tampa, Florida. Was it just a drunken joke? Did Brendan even know she had the picture? She'd never know. When it came to Brendan there would probably always be a million unanswered questions. Maybe meeting him was a way of the universe foreshadowing her upcoming adventures in Ireland. Toughening her up so she knew what she was dealing with when it came to Irish men. Not that she would suspect all of them of secretly wearing women's panties, but she knew always to expect the unexpected. She was armed.

The airline she was flying wasn't so bad despite what her seatmate called them. Air lick us or kill us. She'd heard it called other names while waiting in line to board: Air Fungus. Air, what's that noise? Air we going to crash? Air kiss my ass. Air we going to linger in limbo after we crash? Now, why did she have to go and think such negative things? She'd had a perfectly nice flight with a quirky seatmate, and a private television with strange British sitcoms, and some kind of thick, meaty stew with bread and butter, and more offers for cups of tea than she'd ever had in her life. The attendants all had the required intoxicating accents, and big smiles. Now they were landing, and soon they'd be on the ground, safe and sound.

Please, God, please don't let the plane crash before I ever get to set foot in my little pub. She instantly tried to wipe the thought away. The Law of Attraction said that whatever thought you held in your mind would be drawn to you, and here she was focusing her powerful energy on crashing. Even if she repeated to herself, "We are not going to crash," she was still projecting crash to the universe. She had to send out the opposite energy. She imagined the plane floating gently to the ground on a four-leaf clover. She hoped it would be enough. She turned to her seatmate.

"I am so happy," she said. "We are gently floating down on a four-leaf clover." He just looked at her and turned back to his Air Lick Us catalogue. The page was turned to a dog bowl that filled itself. She suspected he didn't even have a dog.

She wasn't going to let him get to her. From now on, she wasn't going to let anything get to her. This was more than a chance to start a new life, this was a chance to finally be free, to find out who she was without her father's compulsions and her mother's ghost. *You can't win if you don't play,* she heard the raffle man say. *You can't win, if you don't play.* Her unlucky streak had officially been broken.

They bounced rather than landed. A bit rocky, but all in one piece. She had arrived. She flew out of her seat, a wasted effort since she was in the very last row. The group of boys who drank and partied as if there was no tomorrow, the ones who constantly reminded her why it sucked to sit so close to the bathrooms, chose now to sleep. Maybe she should tell them about her pub; from the amount she'd seen them drink, one night of their presence and she could probably stay afloat for the entire year. But no, she only wanted classy people at her pub. These filthy boys would not be welcome. She watched them awaken and stagger out of their seats. Her seatmate managed to skip ahead, as if he wanted to flee from her happiness. Screw him. She was not going to apologize for being happy.

Finally she was moving up. Just ahead there was a little old lady ever so slowly getting out of her seat. Carlene stopped so that she could go first. Good deeds! The flight attendant came down the aisle with the elderly lady's walker. She set it in front of the woman and smiled.

"There you are, pet," the attendant said. Carlene was behind the elderly woman when they'd first boarded as well. Life coming full circle. The flight attendant tried to get her to sit at the front of the plane, but the old lady refused, ranting and raving about survival rates being higher at the back of the plane, ageism, and lack of decent biscuits, which, from her tone, was clearly the worst of the lot. The old lady was trying to peer into the overhead compartments.

"You're all set, luv," the flight attendant said. The old woman stretched on her tiptoes and continued peering into the bin. She reached her hand up, but she could barely touch inside the compartment. She was so tiny.

"Let me help," Carlene said. Although she could clearly see it was empty, she pawed around the bin anyway. "It's empty," she announced. The old woman smiled. She was missing several teeth. Carlene wondered how she could even eat a biscuit. Finally satisfied she was leaving nothing behind, she inched her way up the aisle. There was an excruciatingly exact method to her exit-madness. First, grunting like a weightlifter, she heaved the walker in front of her, then she stopped and waited for it to hit the ground. Next she craned her head to the side as if listening for the thunk. Only then did she drag her faded yellow slipper up to meet it. Walker, lift, grunt, thunk. Slipper, shuffle. Lift, grunt, thunk, slipper, shuffle. Shuffle, shuffle, shuffle, grunt, thunk, thunk.

Carlene held her passport and work visa out and waited for the female immigration officer to take it. The woman looked as if she'd been rolled in flour, deep-fried, and stuffed into a green uniform three times too small. She had a slight reddish mustache. Carlene tried not to stare at it and absentmindedly touched her own upper lip. Finally, the officer took Carlene's passport and visa.

"Reason for coming to Ireland," she asked without making eye contact. Her voice could hardly be described as a soft lilt. Carlene cleared her throat. *Just say you're on holiday.* The officer finally looked at Carlene, then leaned forward and shouted as if Carlene was hard of hearing. "Reason. For. Coming. To. Ireland?"

"My great-great-great-grandmother, Mary Margaret, was

from Ireland," Carlene said. "County Mayo." The officer did not appear as if she was impressed. She'd heard this before. Everyone thought they were Irish. Wannabes. "Her father, I guess that would make him my great-great-great-great-grandfather—is that right? Four greats? Anyway, he joined the IRA when Mary Margaret was only sixteen—"

Carlene stopped. Was she allowed to say IRA in the airport? Was that like joking you had a bomb? Because even though her great-to-the-fourth-power grandfather died trying to protect Ireland, a proud IRA member himself, she didn't want to come off as political—at heart she was more of a Gandhi follower—peaceful revolutions and the like. Although now the Troubles had calmed down quite a bit, Belfast was the new Barcelona, and everyone was trying to play nice—

Still, she had better change the subject before she got herself in trouble.

"The Philadelphia Irish," Carlene exclaimed. " 'Complaining with a ham under each arm,' my grandmother used to say." The officer was openly staring at her now. Apparently, that wasn't a good thing to say either. "Did you know there are a lot of Jews in Cork City?" Carlene said. The officer suddenly stood up. She grabbed the sides of her shirt, near her massive bosoms, and leaned forward like a gorilla showing her dominance. Carlene waited for her to flash teeth. People around them were starting to stare.

"Reason. For. Coming. To. Ireland!" the officer shouted. But before Carlene could respond again, the woman slammed her hands against the pane of glass. "And I don't want to hear about your great-great-great-can of beans, so."

There was a long moment of silence.

"I won," Carlene said. *Just say you're on holiday*. "A pub."

"You what a what?" the woman said. She sounded quite alarmed, on the verge of panic, actually.

"I won a pub in Ballybeog," Carlene said. There, she'd said it. The officer leaned forward and exhaled on the glass. A small cloud of breath obscured her mustached mouth for a moment.

"You won a pub in Ballybeog?" the officer said. She hit each word with equal force.

"Yes," Carlene said with slightly more conviction. "I won a pub in Ballybeog."

"You're the raffle winner?" the woman said. Carlene was by no means an expert on the Irish brogue, but the stress had definitely been on the word "you're."

"That's right," Carlene said. "I'm a winner."

"How in heaven's name did ye win it?" the officer asked. Again, there was no opportunity for Carlene to actually answer. The officer kept talking. "Me niece entered that raffle. She bought ten tickets. She lives in New York. I wouldn't a mind winning it meself but it was only open to the Yanks, can you believe that? I said, now, wouldn't it be great, thanks be to God, if I could sit back and have a do-nothing job like running somebody else's pub? And I wouldn't be wasting company resources either because I've never had a sip of an alcoholic beverage in me life. I wouldn't have to sit here all day with yokes who sashay through here like they own the place due to some great-great-great-can of beans, so." She leaned forward and punctuated the end of her outburst with another exhalation of breath. "I wouldn't have to wear this outfit. It pinches me in the middle, it does. And did ye know I only get until half past for lunch? That's only thirty minutes, lad. Ah, stop now. How many tickets did ye buy? Cleaned 'em out, did ye?"

"One ticket," Carlene said. "I only bought one."

"Hmmph," the officer said. "I wouldn't be tellin' many people that, I wouldn't be tellin' 'em that a't'all. And you shouldn't say—you know—around here."

"IRA?" Carlene whispered. The officer shook her head. *Jew,* she mouthed. Then, with a disgusted shake of her head, she stamped Carlene through.

CHAPTER 8

The Ambassador of Craic

At the airport, Carlene boarded a bus to Galway. From there she was to wait by the fountain in Eyre Square for a man named Anchor, who would drive her to Ballybeog. She wasn't sure who he was, but on the phone he'd introduced himself as the "ambassador of Craic." Thanks to Brendan, Carlene knew "craic" was the Irish word for "fun," and not the cheaper cut of cocaine used by those who couldn't afford it pure. The bus was mostly empty, and Carlene sat up front. The driver caught her eye in the mirror and smiled. He was in his fifties with a trim beard and a pea green cap. He had warm brown eyes.

"Where are you from?" he asked.

"America," she said. No use leading with Cleveland, Ohio, and sucking the life out of the conversation before it even began.

"Ah, right. You'll love it here," he said. "You've got the Cliffs of Moher, Aran Islands, Galway City. Do ye like live music, do ye?"

"I do," Carlene said.

"They've got loads of musicians and young ones such as yourself in Galway."

Carlene nodded and smiled and took in the cows grazing by

the side of the road. She was in Ireland. She was on her way to her new life. She was glad she was in a bus; riding this high up, she felt safe. Even so, it was strange driving on the other side of the road, and every time she looked out the window, she felt as if they were about to get smashed by an oncoming car. Large signs leaving Shannon shouted: STAY TO THE LEFT.

"Galway's nice all right," the driver said. "And as I was saying, you should try to get to the Aran Islands. There's a ferry that leaves from Galway."

"I'm actually not staying in Galway," Carlene said. "Although I'm sure I'll eventually visit. I'm going to Ballybeog." The bus swerved slightly to the right. *Stay to the left,* Carlene shouted in her head.

"Do you have family out there?" the driver asked. This time she decided not to mention her great-great-great-can of beans. Outside it began to rain. Carlene didn't mind. Even through the drizzle, everything looked quaint and beautiful, even the road signs.

"No," she said. He was watching her again through the mirror. She wondered if it would be impolite to ask him to watch the road.

"This wouldn't have anything to do with the raffle, now would it?" he said.

"Raffle?" she said.

"I've had more Americans ask me about Ballybeog this past month than in me whole twenty years of driving," he said. *I see,* she wanted to say. *And how many accidents have you had in these twenty years? Please, oh please, watch the road, and for the love of God, stay to the left.* Instead, she smiled. "Some American won a pub in Ballybeog," he said. "Did ye hear about dis?"

"No," she said. She was probably going to go to hell for lying to the nicest people on earth, but she couldn't take the chance that he would react like the woman in the airport, not with her life in his jittery hands.

"Ah, it's all over the news here, sure," he said. "They're expecting him any day now."

"Him?"

"Aye, I think it's some big shot on Wall Street that's won it, all right. But if he's thinking he can swoop in and flip it, he's got another thing coming. Not a little shack like that, out in the bogs."

Carlene sat up straight. Flip? Shack? Out in the bogs? Suddenly she wasn't so concerned about him watching the road.

"You've been there?" she said. "It's a shack?" *Out in the bogs?* It was close to Galway, didn't they say it was close to Galway? Yes, she'd seen it on the map, it was close to Galway. Why did she let strangers rattle her?

"Ach, I've only driven on through it meself. But Ballybeog isn't exactly Galway, or Dublin, or Cork, or Limerick. It's just a wee little town. Ah, but greed is a mighty driver," the driver said. "A mighty driver." *Unlike some people I know,* Carlene thought.

"I heard it was a woman who won the pub," Carlene said. "She's a small business owner—a gym or something—and not greedy at all—just—lucky." Carlene smiled when she said "lucky." She still couldn't believe it.

"I don't know if I would call winning that pub luck," the driver said. "Out in the middle of nowhere, like."

"So you said," Carlene said.

"Are you going to make it to Dublin?" the driver said.

"Eventually," Carlene said.

"Now, winning a pub in Dublin. That would be lucky, all right," he said. "Nothing to bog you down out there." He laughed heartily at his own joke and looked at her to see if she was laughing. She was not. He winked and began to sing. "In Dublin's fair city, the girls are so pretty." He smiled again. This was getting annoying. She was tired of him smiling, and winking, and saying the word "bog." She really, really just wanted him to watch the road.

"Are ye here for long?" he asked.

"Yes," she said. "I'm here for a good, long while."

"A good while?" he asked. "How long is that, now? A fortnight?"

"Indefinitely," Carlene said, racking her brain to remember how long a fortnight was. "I'm here indefinitely." The bus swerved again. Carlene gripped the seat in front of her. "Stay to the left!" she yelled out before she could stop herself. The driver frowned at her in the mirror, and Carlene glanced apologetically at the rest of the passengers. Then she plastered her face to the window and closed her eyes. To her relief, it worked. The bus stayed to the left, and he didn't ask her any more questions.

It was easy enough to find Eyre Square, a rectangular park in the center of the city. At the top of the square, an impressive pair of cast-iron cannons stood guard. In addition to the fountain, which was where she was to find Anchor, there were patches of grass and benches on which to sit, several large trees, and flags dotting the perimeter, a statue of an Irish writer (a seated man with a suit and a hat—Carlene was too far away to read the plaque), and a bust of John F. Kennedy.

Apparently, after his visit in 1963, Eyre Square was renamed the John F. Kennedy Park. This was a good sign. Kennedy claimed Irish ancestry, and it seemed *his* great-great-great-can of beans were not only welcomed in Ireland, they were lauded as well. If only her last name was Kennedy. Then again, tragically, they weren't the luckiest clan on the planet either.

Carlene wandered over to the fountain. It was a rectangular pool, in the center of which soared a copper-colored sailboat, a lone mast with a large center sail, accompanied by two baby sails in the back. This, Carlene learned, was the Galway hooker, the sailboat most commonly used on the West Coast of Ireland, designed to withstand heavy seas.

The fountain was the perfect size to toss in a shiny penny and make a wish. Unlucky Carlene loved fountains. Lucky Carlene was no exception. She loved their forceful spray, she loved watching a wall of water spread its fanlike tips into the afternoon air, she loved the initial burst from ground to sky, waking everyone up with a whoosh. But unlike the former, Unlucky Carlene, Lucky Carlene also liked wading into fountains. Taking her shoes and socks off and dancing with the spray, even if large crowds were gathered, even if nobody else was doing it, even though, or maybe especially because, it was forbidden. Anchor, who was supposed to be waiting for her holding a sign that would read BALLYBEOG RAFFLE WINNER, was nowhere in sight. She would have preferred the ambassador of punctuality instead of the ambassador of craic.

It had been a long plane ride, then bus ride, and she was itching to relieve her cramped and sweaty feet. She stared at the fountain and made a dare with herself. She would take off her shoes and socks, wade in, run to the center, feel the spray on her face, toss her penny high in the air, make a wish, and run back out. The thought of actually doing it made her giddy. It was something the old her would have wanted to do, but never dared. College kids were gathered around the fountain, looking like hippies from the sixties. They might think she was odd, but she doubted any of them would pay much attention. The sweet, musky scent of marijuana filtered through the air. Maybe she was getting a contact high. Whatever the reason, she was going to go for it. She was a new woman, a lucky woman. Luck, she figured, was like a muscle. She would have to use it, stretch it, strengthen it. No pain, no gain. You can't win if you don't play. She took her boots and socks off, hiked up her skirt, and stepped bravely into the fountain.

CHAPTER 9

Make a Wish

Ronan tossed Anchor's idiotic BALLYBEOG RAFFLE WINNER sign into the nearest rubbish bin. He didn't need a sign; if Carlene Rivers looked like her pictures, he would have no problem spotting her. He'd waited until the last minute to inform Anchor that he was picking her up instead. He didn't want his mam and sisters to get wind of it, especially if they put two and two together and suspected his real reason in coming was to sneak off to the Galway Races. Which was exactly what he planned on doing. His mam had made enough money off the raffle to pay off Uncle Joe and have a nest egg for herself, so Ronan could afford to throw what little bob he had left on the horses. And even though he had a tip, he wasn't going to pay any attention to it.

After all, his last tip, the one guaranteed to send shock waves, hadn't even finished in the top three. It dawned on him that this American girl, lucky enough to win a pub, might just be the human equivalent of a rabbit's foot. He'd charm her, take her to the races, and let her pick the winner. Besides, his ultimate goal was to buy the pub back, and so therefore he had to make sure she liked him. Otherwise, Joe would worm his way in. Even if this girl did plan on running the pub for a while, eventually, the novelty would wear off, and winter would hit, and before she could say Cleveland Coliseum, she'd be on the first plane back to America. And who would she sell the pub to? An old begrudger next door? Or the original, affable, and not-bad-to-look-at Ronan? That was the plan anyway. He was a little late, and scanning the park, when he saw her.

From her picture, he knew she was blond, and beautiful. The lads had been jabbering about nothing else the past month. They were lined up to meet her. He was expecting to find her physically attractive, but so what, he found a lot of women physically attractive—that wasn't going to stop him from getting what he really wanted.

But he didn't expect to find her standing in the middle of the Eyre Square fountain next to the Galway hooker, skirt hiked up with both hands, revealing shapely calves and just a hint of thigh, head thrown back so that his first glimpse was of her long, pale neck, wavy blond hair cascading down her back, and full breasts thrust out. She looked slightly obscene and utterly beautiful in the dredges of light snaking in through the clouds and glimmering off the copper sails. She looked like a figurehead on a flaming ship. Although "wooden" would soon be the word used to describe him if he kept staring at her exposed flesh.

Jaysus. It was impossible to look elsewhere. He should have. She tossed a penny into the air, and as it twirled back down toward the water, she lifted her head. And since Ronan was standing directly across from her and hadn't diverted his eyes, not even for a second, not even to gather his thoughts, or quite frankly attempt to disguise the surge of desire he felt for this girl he didn't even know, before he could do any of that, she lifted her head and her eyes landed directly on him. And then she smiled. Her hand lifted in a little wave. Slightly stunned, Ronan waved back. He was hit with two equal urges: One was to tear across the fountain, take her in his arms, and carry her out. The other was simply to run.

His awkwardness remained, even as she came out of the fountain, sat on the ground, and began putting on little socks and short leather boots. He just kept standing and staring. She'd knocked all thoughts out of his head. He couldn't make sense of anything, couldn't make sense of what he was feeling, couldn't make sense of her. It was as if he'd imagined her in a certain way—uptight, loud, American, cheerleader, greedy, vacuous. Somehow, he couldn't reconcile any of that with the girl standing in the fountain. Now he was thinking beautiful, free, vulnerable, neck, breasts, thighs.

He couldn't go scheming to take the pub off her if he saw her as vulnerable. He wanted to take it off a greedy, loud, vacuous American. Just the thought of how she was already ruining his plan made him irrationally angry with her. He stood, hands on hips, watching her zip up her little boots, and even though she knew he was there, she had yet to look up. He meant to say, *Hello, I'm Ronan, you must be Carlene,* or—*Hey, pub winner,* or *How was your flight?*

"What the fuck was that?" he said instead. She took her time looking up at him. In fact, it wasn't until she put on her other boot, zipped it up, and stood that she looked at him again. The effect up close was even more disconcerting. She had fair skin, high cheekbones, and plump lips. But her eyes were the most remarkable thing about her. They were the lightest shade of blue he'd ever seen. So blue he tried to think of other blue things just to compare them to, but he was having a devil of a time formulating anything other than dirty thoughts. Blue, blue, blue. Blue movies. No. The sky. Well, not the Irish sky. Perhaps the skies above the Riviera. He'd like to take her to the Riviera. He'd like to take her anywhere. He'd like to take her right now in the fountain under the hooker. He was breathing heavily, and he felt like a complete eejit.

"What the fuck was what?" she said. Ronan lifted his hands in utter frustration and pointed to the fountain. Why did he even care? Why was he getting all bent out of shape because she waded into a fountain? Who was this girl?

"Nothing," he said. "It's just not normally done, like." She laughed, and it wasn't an obnoxious greedy laugh, it was light and airy, and made him feel ridiculously happy, and forced him to smile back. Jaysus, he should have let Anchor fecking pick her up. Then she was startlingly close to him, leaning in, and he could smell her. She was wearing a light perfume—vanilla? Yes. She smelled like a bleeding birthday cake. That wasn't right. That shouldn't be allowed. Fair play to her. Although if she thought she could cajole him into licking her icing, she had another think coming. Speaking of licking ... Her lips were slightly sticky, as if she'd just rolled gloss on them, and he couldn't look away as she whispered to him.

"You should try it sometime."

He couldn't even remember what they'd been talking about, and he didn't care. "Maybe I fucking will."

"Maybe you fucking should." Now she sounded a little louder, a little tougher, and her shoulders were squared back. Ronan felt a little bit of self-assurance slip back into his frame. This time, he was able to flash his signature controlled smile. It made her frown. That made him smile even more. "Come on," he said. He picked up her suitcase. "Is this all you have?" She nodded. He was impressed. He'd imagined she'd come with piles and piles of baggage, can't-live-without American crap.

"You're Anchor?" she said. He held out his hand for a shake, mostly because he wanted to touch her. "Where's your sign?" she asked.

"It took a detour into the nearest rubbish bin," Ronan said.

"Good to know I look like my pictures," she said. Was she flirting with him? Ronan flirted all the time. It was as natural as breathing. So why was he so flustered, so annoyed?

"You don't," he said. "You look better."

After tossing her suitcase into the boot of his car, they walked along Quay Street. Littered with shops, pubs, and restaurants, Galway's main drag also teemed with street performers.

Carlene saw a young man riding a unicycle while juggling knives, an older gentleman sculpting a large dog out of a little pile of sand, a young boy playing an Irish tune on the accordion, and a bald Asian man in an orange jumpsuit levitating crystal balls. Ronan saw only her.

"I can take you straight to Ballybeog," he said. "Or . . ."

"Or?"

"Well, the Galway Races are on—"

"I would love to go."

"Really?"

"Are you kidding me? I love horse racing. My dad and I always watch the Kentucky Derby."

"Ah, deadly," he said. "Let's go."

He felt much more comfortable talking to her in the car. Knowing that she thought he was Anchor also made it easier to settle into conversation. Even though the racetrack was a short distance from the city, traffic getting in was heavy, leaving plenty of time for them to get to know each other. It was probably wrong to get such a kick out of deceiving her, but he'd never again have the chance to be someone other than the man whose pub she'd stole. He'd actually been about to confess when she started quizzing him about the McBrides. What were they like? Why did they raffle off the pub? Were they happy? She sounded genuinely concerned, adding yet another layer of complexity to his mounting ambivalence.

"You didn't hear the story?" Ronan asked. Gossip flew so fast around Ballybeog, he'd just assumed the dirty details had already floated across the pond. Like scum. Maybe they did, and she was just putting on a show. If that was the case, she was a damned good actress. Was it all an act, down to her pretty little eyebrows furrowed in concern?

And then Ronan did something that surprised himself. He told the truth.

"They raffled the pub because the only son, Ronan, is a total fuckup. He almost gambled away the pub in a game of cards. Can you believe that shite?"

"Wow," Carlene said. She sounded genuinely surprised. She studied Ronan quietly.

"What?" he said. *Don't look at her, look at the road.*

"It sounds like you don't like him," she said.

"Really?" he said.

"Actually, you sound full of hate," she said. Her voice was quiet, frank. Ronan waited to feel angry or defensive. Instead, he felt almost relief.

"Sometimes I do hate him. He's caused the mother and the half dozen a lot of pain. Not to mention if the oul fella is looking down—"

"The half dozen?"

"His six sisters."

"Wow," she said. "One boy and six girls. No wonder he's fucked up." Her comment took him by surprise. He laughed.

"Yes," he said. "No wonder, indeed."

"You think it never would have happened? If Uncle Jimmy had been alive?" she said. It startled him, hearing her call his father Uncle Jimmy. He took his eyes off the road. She must have read his mind. "I've seen pictures of the pub," she said. "They all say *Uncle Jimmy's.*"

"Ah, right, so," Ronan said. "Do I think it would've happened? Are you joking me? Uncle Joe wouldn't have dared if my—my friend Ronan's father had still been alive."

She nodded quietly, then looked out the window. "Families," she said. "One of God's greatest mysteries." She was trying to be funny, but there was an edge to her voice. Ah, there was a story there somewhere. He found himself wanting to know everything about her.

"Indeed," Ronan said. Families were a mystery all right, and so was she. Had he just said "indeed" twice? He was going to have to get a fucking grip. Indeed.

CHAPTER 10

Cabernet Sauvignon

Carlene couldn't get over it. There was a castle in the middle of the horse racing track. A castle! Not a very big one, but it was the real deal. A rising rectangular mass of limestone walls with a crowned top, smack in the middle of the field. Ronan, who was still pretending to be Anchor, told her the castle was called Ballybrit. They stood just outside the entrance where bouncy children played in bouncy huts and adults paced with race cards. Carlene marveled at the castle while Ronan checked his wallet. Nobody but her seemed to think it was remarkable. If she had her way, she would stop the races so they could all storm the castle. She laughed at herself, and Ronan gave her one of his sideways looks. Only a few hours in his presence and she'd already learned that he seemed to have quite a repertoire of silent communication. Or maybe it just felt that way to her because she found his green eyes with flecks of gold—fool's gold, she warned herself—quite beautiful to look at. Set in a face with a strong jaw and sloppy black hair that curled under at the ends, there was something almost reptilian about his eyes. Or maybe it was just because she felt the slightest bit of danger when looking into them. He looked exactly like his picture. She was teasing when she called him Anchor, and had been waiting ever since for him to correct her. She found it fascinating that he didn't, and she wondered what angle he was trying to play.

Then, watching his jaw set when he called himself a fuckup, she first felt pity for him, and then something akin to anger. Was he trying to play on her sympathies? Catch her saying something bad about him? Was he always this insecure? Whatever else he was, he was definitely a complicated man. In her twenties, she would have fallen head over heels in love with him. Just like Brendan. But she wasn't in her twenties, and neither was he. And obviously, he had a serious gambling problem.

He insisted on paying the entrance fee, which she had been secretly counting on, since she'd yet to exchange her U.S. dollars into euros. Once they got through the line and entered into the main fields surrounding the track, Carlene stopped worrying about Ronan McBride. There were so many people, the excitement was palpable. You could walk right up to the fence and watch the race, or cheer along with the boisterous crowd in the grandstand. Lines and lines of bookmakers, dressed in trousers, blazers, and caps, called out as people passed by, holding leather bags, like country doctors, huge snap purses filled with cash. Next to them electronic boards flashed the horses' names and odds in scrolling neon. Rich or poor, every better's (or punter's as Ronan called them) money was welcome, and everyone was free to try their luck.

There were multiple food stands from fine dining to low-budget burgers. There were exhibitors selling their wares: racing memorabilia, purses, shoes, and jewelry. The women in the crowd were dressed in heels, skirts, and hats. Ronan must have been watching her watch them.

"If you think this is something, you should see them on ladies' night," he said. "Thursday. They dress to kill." He handed her a race card.

"Pick two winners," he said. "From any of the six races." Carlene refused to take the card.

"I don't know anything about horse racing," she said. "I just like to watch."

"It's just for fun," he said, thrusting the card at her again.

"Really," she said. "I don't want to."

"I'll tell you what," Ronan said. "Pick a horse for the first race. Doncha worry, I won't bet on him. I'm just testing a theory."

"You're thinking because I won a pub, that I'm some kind of good-luck charm?"

"Mind reader too, I see," he said. "Come on."

"Fine." Carlene took the card and read down the names of the horses. "Billy's Beauty," she said, handing it back to him.

"Seven to one," he said. "Sounds like a winner to me."

The horses thundered out of the gate. Ronan lifted out of his seat and shouted encouragement to Billy's Beauty. They were standing in the middle of the stadium, and the sheer volume of shouts and stomps from the crowd blew Carlene away. She was mesmerized by the horses' sleek necks as they flew by, noses lifted to the sky. She was having the time of her life. As they rounded the bend, Billy's Beauty pulled up to fourth place.

"Go on, ye boy ye," Ronan yelled. "Get on, get on, get on." Billy's Beauty pulled into third. Suddenly, Ronan's hand was on her waist. He pulled her into him. "Look at him go, Carlena," he said. "I think you are a good-luck charm." Nobody had ever called her Carlena. She vowed never to let anyone but him. Billy's Beauty kicked into high gear, and now he was vying nose-to-nose for the finish.

"Go, go, go," Ronan yelled. The ground thundered.

"Billy's Beauty is the winner," the announcer shouted. It was truly by a nose. Carlene screamed along with Ronan. He faced her, put both hands on her hips, and pulled her into him. His belt buckle slammed against her navel. She wanted him to do it again.

"Hi," he said quietly, as if they'd just met. As if they weren't standing in a stadium surrounded by screaming men, and women, and bottles of beer, and little cardboard boats of half-eaten sausages.

"Hi," she said. His lips moved in on hers, as if they had a mind of their own. She didn't resist. It was a celebratory kiss, slow and soft.

"You placed a bet on Billy's Beauty, didn't you?" she asked when he pulled away.

"You're fecking right I did," he said.

"How much did you win?"

"Enough to buy you a beer," he said.

"I'd prefer a glass of wine," she said.

"Not a bother." He grabbed her hand and they started down the steps. "How are Irish men like fine wine?" he asked.

"You get better with age?" Carlene guessed.

"No," Ronan said. "We start out like grapes, and it's your job to stomp on us and keep us in the dark until we mature into something you'd like to have dinner with." He said it with such a silly grin on his face that she had to laugh. By the time she stopped laughing, she wondered how long they'd been holding hands.

"Right then," he said. "Let's get you sorted."

His mood plummeted with each race he didn't win, until he was jittery and quiet beside her.

"Just one more," he said, waving the betting card. "Pick a winner for race number five."

"Ronan," she said. She didn't realize what she'd said until she saw the look on his face. It was like watching someone turn to stone. At first she didn't know what she'd done to upset him.

"Well, aren't you full of surprises," he said. "You knew I wasn't Anchor?"

She nodded. "I'd seen a picture of you too," she said. She wasn't going to apologize. He was the one who'd lied to her—he should be apologizing. She snatched the race card out of his hand and scanned it again. "Cabernet Sauvignon," she said. "It's what I just drank." He nodded, looked at her intently, then shook his head a little.

"Twelve to one," he said.

"Is that good?"

"It is if he wins." He smiled. "Why don't you place a bet on this one too," he said.

"I don't have any euros yet," she said.

"Why didn't you say so?" He dug in his pocket and handed her a twenty.

"I couldn't," she said.

"Ah come on," he said. "You took me pub, you might as well take me money." He said it lightly, and, if she wasn't mistaken, he'd also just dialed up his Irish accent, but the comment still stung. He immediately softened, palmed the twenty in her hand. "I'm sorry," he said. "I didn't mean it like that."

"I'll pay you back," she said.

"Especially if you win," he said.

She scanned the line of bookmakers. Ronan pointed out the ones who would pay out the most if Cabernet Sauvignon won. From among them, she chose a man in his fifties because he had the biggest smile. "Twenty on Cabernet Sauvignon to win," she said. He tossed her money into his pack, printed off a ticket, and handed it to her.

"Good luck, pet," he said.

Ronan took her to the parade ring where they watched the horses being led around for all to see. Cabernet Sauvignon was a tall and gorgeous animal. Deep black muscles rippled through his strong legs as he pranced around the ring like he owned a little piece of the world. He was a lucky horse if there ever was one. Carlene couldn't stop grinning. "He's going to win," she said. "I can feel it."

"Come on," Ronan said. "Let's get a spot by the fence. I want to be up close and personal for this one."

It was race number five, the first jumping race. The starting gate was on the other side of the fence, so they watched the race unfold on the giant television screen suspended above the track. Soon the horses passed the castle. Ronan put his arm around Carlene. They were standing directly in front of the fourth hurdle. The only way they could have a better view was if they were the jockeys themselves. As the horses took the first hurdle, Carlene realized she was holding her breath. The horses were jammed so close together, it was hard to make out the wine-colored hat and jacket of Cabernet's jockey. She didn't really even care who won—it was just so exciting to watch. Before she knew it, the horses were nearing the fourth jump. Ronan squeezed her waist. "He's right there, on the outside, see?" Ronan pointed. "He's doing good," he whispered. Once she spotted him, Carlene didn't dare take her eyes off her gorgeous, lucky horse.

Such grace, such power, such strength, such beauty. Carlene could see how you could get addicted to this. She shouted when everyone else shouted and jumped when everyone else jumped, mixing her enthusiasm with the frenzied crowd. And when Cabernet Sauvignon leapt over the hurdle, she lifted right off the ground with him. She braced for landing as his magnificent body seemed to defy gravity and hovered midair. The image of him suspended like that would remain with Carlene for the rest of her life.

Even though it was all unfolding in front of her, it took Carlene a long time to realize what was happening. Cabernet's back leg twisted. His body tilted sideways. The jockey, who was airborne, instinctively tucked himself into a ball and landed with a soft, sickening thud near the fence. Horrified, the crowd watched as Cabernet crumpled to the ground. He lay on his side, twitching. Carlene screamed, and Ronan pulled her into him. People cried, moaned, and shouted all around her, and an ambulance screamed into high gear. All the while, the rest of the horses kept running, their hooves pounded on. Despite the sirens, the shouts, and the smell of fear permeating the field, through it all they thundered on toward the finish line.

Paramedics lifted the jockey onto a stretcher. He lifted his head and reached his hand out as if to touch Cabernet, but his view was obscured; vets were already erecting a white tent around the fallen horse. Ronan clasped Carlene's hand and they began to fight their way out as the crowd swarmed in to witness the tragedy up close. Ronan never let go of her hand, and somehow, they made it through the grounds, out into the field, to the safety of the car. Ronan opened the door for her, and even leaned in and put her seat belt on for her. When he got into the driver's seat, a single shot rang out across the field. Carlene winced and hid her face in her hands.

"Are you okay?" Ronan asked after a minute. She took her hands away and nodded. The lump in her throat precluded her from speaking. When they pulled out of the lot, she didn't turn around, not even for a last look at the castle in the middle of the field.

CHAPTER 11

The Family Tree

As traumatic as the Galway Races were, Carlene made an effort to put it out of her mind. This was such a rare opportunity, and she vowed to enjoy the moments as they unfolded. There were so many sights to see and so many bits of Irish trivia running through Carlene's head, she felt as if she were having an out-of-body experience. Twelfth-century Norman invasions, and walled towns, and ringforts, and ruined abbeys. Rivers and bays, and soaring thirteenth-century churches, and castles, and town gates, and stone mansions, and Celtic crosses, and sheep and cows, and energy windmills, and roundabouts designed to keep the traffic moving, unlike the four-way stops at home, but that only made Carlene dizzy, and colorful shops, and cobblestone streets, and pubs, and pubs, and pubs, and pubs, and more pubs.

Not that she was able to take it all in at the speed they were traveling. Had she known Ronan McBride "drove it like he stole it," she might have opted for a bus into Ballybeog. As they drew closer to town, Ronan told her there used to be thirty-three pubs in Ballybeog, but now there were only eleven. The Celtic Tiger had been declawed. Ten of the pubs were located on

Main Street, an easy stagger from one to the other. The eleventh, i.e., her pub, she surmised, was the odd man out. Out in the bogs, in the middle of nowhere? It was late afternoon, and traffic on Main Street was surprisingly heavy. Carlene began to feel as if they were in a parade. Ronan beeped and waved at everyone he saw and everyone beeped and waved back. Carlene absolutely loved all the stonework and brightly painted shops.

"Wait until it's lashing down rain," Ronan said. "You won't be so cheery then." Carlene ignored him and feasted on the shop signs. John O'Malley and Daughter (the sign said they sold: Groceries, Fruit and Veg, and Ice Cream). Helen's Foodstore. East Ocean Chinese. Bridget's Gifts. Dally's Lounge, Undertaker, and Pub, rolled into one.

"One leads to the other," Ronan said with a wink when she pointed it out.

JP Moran and Company. Drapery and Books. Bank of Ireland. Philips Electronics. Although their signs remained, some hanging askew, at least half the shops they passed were out of business. Darkened windows covered in dust announced their sad state. Carlene wished she could bring them all to life. Many of the shops had gorgeous arched doorways leading to little cobblestone alleys she was dying to explore, and stone plaques she couldn't wait to read.

And of course, she saw all the pubs. Mickey John's, and O'Sullivan's, and Finnegan's, and she couldn't keep up with them all. She wouldn't worry about it, she would focus on her pub. Which was—where, exactly? She told herself not to panic; surely her street would be just as nice. Maybe it was good to be a little ways out. Before she knew it, they were exiting through one of the town gates, leaving the main drag, and turning left onto a country road. The cobblestone streets and colorful shops faded farther and farther away, replaced by paved roads and long stretches of green.

Was Ronan just showing her the beauty of the land? Surely her pub wasn't going to be in the middle of a farmer's field. Who would come to it? Cows?

Speaking of cows, they were all over the place. And unlike

the ubiquitous black-and-white cows she was used to seeing in Ohio, these cows were diverse. It was as if, like all Europeans compared to Americans, these cows had better fashion sense. These cows had caramel coats, and lush dark brown coats, and sun-kissed yellow coats. These cows had style.

After passing several farmhouses, many of which looked surprisingly new and not like farmhouses at all, but more like mini–limestone mansions, they turned left again, and here the road twisted and turned, trees hugging their every curve. Ronan seemed to think a winding road was an invitation to speed up. Carlene gripped the side of the door, too frightened to even yell, "Stay to the left!", and prayed she'd be able to see her pub just once before he killed her in a fiery crash.

And then, just when she was wondering why her life hadn't flashed before her—only, strangely, a pint of Guinness—the road straightened out, and Ronan slowed the car down considerably. A white clapboard house set just a little off the road with a sign above it came into view: UNCLE JOE'S GROCERIES. And next door, there it was. It was similar in size, and also white, but her pub was made of stone. For some reason it made Carlene think of the Three Little Pigs. Apparently, the Big Bad Wolf had already blown down the one made of straw, and she was grateful that Joe's wooden shop, and not her stone pub, would be next.

Mine, she thought, as she took it in. *That adorable little pub is mine.* The windows were accented with bright blue paint, and there it was, just like in the pictures, a thick, thatched roof. Her sign read: UNCLE JIMMY'S. She also had a small front yard with an enormous tree in front. But the biggest surprise of all was the large crowd gathered in the yard to greet her.

"Surprise," Ronan said. He pulled directly onto the grass. Carlene made a mental note not to ever allow him to do this again, but she decided to let it go for now. Carlene smiled when she got out of the car, expecting a big welcome, maybe even a few cheers. It took her a moment to realize no one was looking at her at all. Instead, they were all looking up at the sky. Carlene followed suit. A thick cloud was chugging along, making its way toward the pub, as if it were going to rain directly on it and nothing else. Still, hardly worth such a gawk, was it?

"What's going on?" she asked Ronan. The sound of an industrial-strength chain saw revving up obscured his answer. It was coming from the enormous tree that stood less than twenty feet away, towering over the yard like a friendly, old guard keeping watch.

"What in the fuck?" Ronan said. Halfway up the tree, in full rappelling gear, a small man was shimmying up the trunk. In his hand was a cordless chain saw. He revved it up again, and it roared like a racecar taking off. The crowd moved in and gathered around the tree as he climbed higher. Carlene turned to Ronan, but he had disappeared. She turned to a man next to her.

"Is it a sick tree?" she asked.

"Nah," he replied. "But I'd say it's a sick fella, all right."

"I don't understand," Carlene said. "What is he doing?" The man in the tree had reached the first large branch. It reached out like a giant arm offering to shake his neighbor's hand. The man hugged the tree and adjusted the saw so that its teeth were poised on the base of the branch.

"What's going on?" Carlene yelled again. She looked for Ronan but she couldn't find him in the crowd.

"Some craic, isn't it?" another man said. "He says the branch crosses over his property line, so he's going to cut it off."

"That's Uncle Joe?" she said.

"Joe Monkey, eh?" the man said.

"But it's not his tree!" At least she didn't think it was his tree. It didn't look like his tree—it was in front of her pub, so it looked like her tree. Nobody else seemed panicked.

"He'll get away with it, all right," the man said. "The new owner was supposed to be here this morning, but she's a no-show. Probably already scared off from all this fecking rain." Carlene stared up at the tree. Uncle Joe was still wiggling around, trying to position himself and the saw just so.

"Hey!" she yelled. She turned back to the man next to her. "Somebody should stop him," she said.

THE PUB ACROSS THE POND   93

"Ah, right," he said. "Can ye imagine? He's seventy-three. He's going to kill himself. And all because of some fucking Yank." Carlene ran to the base of the tree.

"Hey!" she yelled. "Stop!" Uncle Joe didn't look down at her. The saw bit into the branch with a screech. The crowd dispersed, people flew out of the way, yet they somehow managed to balance the pints they were holding without spilling a single drop. Carlene stayed put. "Stop!" she yelled again. Suddenly, arms wrapped around her and pulled her back.

"It's too late," Ronan said as the branch started to tilt. "Clear out." Carlene watched helplessly as inch by inch the giant branch fell, a loud, continuous breaking away. It was headed straight for the pub's adorable thatched roof. Carlene watched in horror as it missed the roof, but crashed through the little stained glass window set into the front door of the pub, and continued to fall, splitting the old wooden door smack down the middle. Carlene wouldn't have believed it if she hadn't seen it with her own eyes. The branch lay prone on the ground, half-in and half-out of the pub.

Carlene turned away and stared at Uncle Joe. He scurried down the trunk and stood at the base of the tree, hands on hips, grinning. The chain saw lay quietly on the ground beside him. Carlene walked toward him. Slowly, he sensed her gaze. Their eyes met and he tipped his cap to her.

"If you're here for a wee pint," he said. "I think they're closed for renovations." Carlene continued to stand and stare at him as he began to remove his rappelling gear.

"You okay?" he asked her after a moment.

"No," she said. "I'm certainly not okay." His eyes narrowed, probably at her accent. He stuck out his hand.

"Joe McBride," he said. Carlene stuck out her hand, and when they shook she squeezed his hand as hard as she could. "And you are?" he said, glancing at the viselike grip she had on his hand.

"The fucking Yank," Carlene said.

CHAPTER 12

The Welcome Party

Joe McBride was saved by the rain. It came fast and heavy, slipping sideways across the sky. He ran back to his store, toting his chain saw, and Carlene followed the pubgoers who ran around the side of the building, toward the back. There they entered a small, enclosed porch cluttered with bits of rusted metal, boxes, and bottles. A small table missing a leg was jammed into a corner, and a chair with no middle was shoved up against the back wall. On the table sat an ashtray overflowing with cigarette butts. *This must be the smoking area,* Carlene thought. *How charming.*

They entered through a back door and into a narrow hallway. The air was heavy with the scent of stale beer and damp stone. But Carlene also caught a scent of bleach, as if someone had at least made an attempt to clean up. The hall led directly into the main room. The crowd made their way back to their stools and seats at tables while Carlene stood and took it all in. The pub was the size of a large studio apartment. The long bar was made of sturdy dark wood that shone as if recently polished. Shiny brass foot rails ran along the base. On the back wall, in the space behind the bar, was an enormous mirror with an ornate gold frame. Liquor bottles lined the shelves like soldiers awaiting orders. Built-in cabinets housed row after row of mini-bottles of soda. She counted six beers on tap. Guinness had two taps. There was so much to look at, she didn't know where to focus her attention first.

Knickknacks and sports paraphernalia hung in every available space. The floor was made of thick wood beams. The bar stools were sturdy with high backs and faded red leather cushions. Guinness signs hung from the ceiling, along with an old-fashioned road sign that said BALLYBEOG at the top, with the Irish spelling, BÁILE BÉAG, below it. She'd learned its meaning after she won the pub. Little Center. This pub was going to be her world now, her little center. She stood, just taking in the sounds of her new world. Voices, laughter, footsteps, chairs squeaking, rain falling on the roof, glasses clinking. And the smells: ale, bleach, the scent of something cooking, something fried. The odd whiff of cologne, and she dared say, body odor, and the smell of mold were in the mix as well.

There was a small stage set up in the left-hand corner of the room, and three large, oval windows overlooked the front yard. A faded dartboard hung askew on the left wall, and beyond it sat a tattered pool table. Along the same wall, tucked into the very back corner, a set of stairs led up to a second floor. Only a railing, a small hallway, and a shut door were visible from below. *I love it,* Carlene thought with a breath of relief. Except for the tree branch, crashed through the old front door—that she could do without. Rain was coming in through the split, along with leaves, dirt, and bark. The wet debris hit the floor and turned into muddy bits that weaved their way through the grooves in the wood. Several men were gathered around the tree branch, speaking to each other while looking down at it, so from a distance it appeared as if they were talking to the branch, scolding it for crashing their party. Seconds later, they hauled it inside and stood studying the broken door.

"There's some wood out on the porch," Carlene heard

Ronan say. "I'll get it." Suddenly, a tall, beautiful woman with long honey-colored hair stood in front of Carlene. She had a beautiful, soft face and was all smiles. She stuck her hand out.

"I'm Katie McBride," she said.

"I'm Carlene."

Katie squealed, grabbed Carlene's hand, and held it up like she'd just won a boxing match. "Ah lads, look," Katie yelled into the crowd. "This is Carlene." There was a polite round of applause. Carlene waved. Everyone waved back, and many held up their pint glasses in salute. Suddenly, a man appeared to her left. He was huge. Tall and broad, with a soft, boyish face, at least what could be seen of it underneath his blue wool cap and thick red goatee. He was holding two pints of Guinness. He handed one to Carlene.

"This is Anchor," Katie said. Ah, Carlene thought. The ambassador of craic himself.

"Hello, Anchor," Carlene said.

"How ya keeping?" he said.

"I'm fine," Carlene said. "How are you keeping?" Suddenly, the noise in the pub dropped, and voices hushed one another, as if the curtain had just opened on a play. Were they waiting for her to make a speech? She hadn't prepared one. "Hello, everyone," Carlene said. Hellos came back to her twice the volume, and a few people clapped again. A camera snapped. A man stepped forward with a tape recorder and a small microphone. Behind her, Ronan and a few others came down the hall hauling a large sheet of plywood.

"I'm from RTÉ," the man with the microphone said. "Welcome to Ballybeog."

"Thank you," Carlene said. She took a sip of her Guinness. It was smooth, but stronger than she expected, and she'd taken too big of a gulp. She sputtered and coughed. The crowd laughed.

"She doesn't like the black stuff, so," a man in the crowd said.

"I do," Carlene said. "It's good." To prove it she took another sip, a longer one. The crowd cheered.

"Were you surprised to find your front door knocked down by the branch of the ash tree when ye arrived?" the reporter asked.

Ass tree? Carlene thought. *Did he just say ass tree?*

"She was, yeah," Katie stepped in and said when Carlene didn't speak.

"Very," Carlene added. Great, now she sounded like an American idiot. The men by the door had positioned the piece of plywood over the crack and were hammering it in. *Shit,* Carlene thought, *it looks like shit.* From what she could see of it, the original door had been beautiful. Dark wood, arched at the top with that little stained glass window. She would have to make sure she got it fixed as soon as possible.

"Ah right," the reporter said. "I suppose you would be, sure." He glanced around the pub. "Well, what do you think?" Well, waddayetink? She loved all of their accents. So buoyant, and upbeat, and lyrical, and hopeful. Sounds you could float away on, drown in.

"I love it," Carlene said, this time out loud. It was quaint, it was cozy, it was perfect, it was hers. Several women gathered behind Katie and moved in closer.

"Let me introduce you to my sisters," Katie said.

"Or the half dozen, like everyone else calls us," a redhead said. She held her hand out first. "Siobhan." The rest of their names came in rapid succession. Liz, Clare, Anne, Sarah. They led Carlene up to the bar and stared at the men sitting in the stools until one by one, the men left their seats to the ladies. All except one, a little old man on the farthest stool to the right. He didn't budge, but he did raise his pint glass a smidge and give her a nod.

Carlene took a seat at the center of the bar, feeling like a queen. A thin, older man was behind the counter. He wore eyeglasses and had a patch of white hair sticking out of his head, but when he looked at her and smiled, he appeared ageless.

"That's Declan," Katie said. "He's an institution around here."

"Hi, Declan," Carlene said. He pointed at her pint. She'd barely drunk any of it. "It's great," she said. "I'm just slow."

"Well, horse it into ye," Declan said. "It's your party. Get your drinking shoes on."

"We're so sorry about Uncle Joe," Katie said.

"He'll pay for that, mark my words," Siobhan said.

"Why were you so late coming in?" one of the twins said. Even though they were fraternal, they looked similar enough that Carlene couldn't remember which was which. Carlene opened her mouth to tell them about the races. She glanced around the room. Ronan was standing with a couple of other men. He caught her eye and smiled. She smiled back and had to force herself to look away.

"My plane was delayed," Carlene said. She watched as Declan moved fluidly behind the bar, gliding from one side to the other, always in motion, always doing several things at once. She had an employee! This was great. She had been worried about how she was going to run a pub all by herself. How silly to think she was going to be dumped into it without any help. And so much for her worry that she wouldn't have any customers. The place was packed. To her delight, a band was making its way onstage. She saw a banjo, a guitar, a tin whistle, and a funny-looking drum that the musician held in front of him.

"That's a bodhrán," Katie said. "It's made of goat skin."

"It's an old Celtic war drum," Siobhan said.

"Cool," Carlene said. She wished she sounded more sophisticated, less American. Carlene finished her pint, and she'd barely slid it forward on the bar when Declan was sliding another one toward her.

"Cheers, pet," he said. Katie linked arms with her, pulled her off the stool, and began touring her around the bar. She shook hands and posed for pictures. She felt famous. Everyone was friendly. *I'm going to love it here,* she thought. There was a loud pounding on the new front door. Several men flocked to the window where they gestured and shouted at the new arrival to go around the back. Carlene couldn't help but laugh. A few minutes later, a short and somewhat plump woman with a brown bun walked up to Carlene. Ronan trailed behind her. The woman held out her hand to Carlene.

"I'm Mary McBride," she said. "It's lovely to meet you."

"So nice to meet you too," Carlene said. Mary glanced at the boarded-up door, then looked back at Carlene with a shy smile.

"I see you're redecorating our wee little pub already," she said.

Carlene laughed. "I've just decided to shut everyone in," Carlene said. "So I'll always have customers."

"Was Anchor on time to pick you up?" Mary said. Carlene glanced at Ronan. His eyes remained steady.

"He was."

"I hope he didn't drive like a manic."

"He did."

Ronan raised an eyebrow.

"This is my son, Ronan," Mary said stepping back to make the introduction. Carlene could hear the pride in Mary's voice and see the loving gaze with which she looked at her son. Ronan held out his hand, and Carlene shook it.

"Nice to meet you, Ronan," Carlene said.

"Nice to be met," Ronan said. All of the McBrides were gathered around her now. As they slowly looked around the pub, an awkward silence fell.

"I'm sorry," Carlene said. "This must be so strange for all of you."

"It's better than Tan Land," Siobhan said.

"I wouldn't have minded trying it," Katie said.

"You would have burned like a shrimp on the barbie," Ronan said. He failed to pull off the Australian accent. Carlene might have laughed a little too loud, and Ronan might have grinned back a little too long, for suddenly everyone was looking at the two of them look at each other.

The half dozen swept her up again and brought her back to the bar. Carlene immediately began asking questions. When would her training begin, what days were the pub open, when could she go up and see her apartment? The girls ignored all of her questions, and Declan set a heaping plate of food in front of her. The band began to play. She didn't know the song, but they were skilled musicians, and it was a happy tune, a jaunty tune. She tapped her foot on the stool and stared at the plate of food. There were huge French fries, and sausages, and chicken fingers, and mashed potatoes, and beef with gravy, and coleslaw, and a salad the size of a tablespoon. An image of her father's horrified face rose before her. He'd been eating a macrobiotic diet for years. This was heaven. She could dig into this plate of fat and fried food openly. It was encouraged. It was a plate of love. She burst into tears.

"Jaysus," Ronan said. Carlene looked up. He was standing behind the bar, leaning against the back counter. His arms were folded across his chest. His green-gold eyes bored into her. "Don't eat it if it's going to make you weep," he said. Declan stepped forward and hovered over her plate.

"Is it all right, chicken?" he said. "I can warm it up for you if ye fancy?" He reached for the plate, but Carlene held out her hand to stop him.

"It's perfect," she said. "These are happy tears." To prove it, she dug in. Declan stood watching her until half the food was gone and she'd wiped her tears away.

"Good girl," he said. He patted her hand and slipped away to help the other customers. Ronan was still watching her. She took a moment to enjoy herself. Good food, good people, good traditional Irish music, and a beautiful, brooding man, watching her as if she were the most interesting thing he had ever seen. She tried to put away all thoughts of dead horses, broken doors, and tree limbs lying in the middle of the floor. She was suddenly exhausted, weary to the bone, yet alert at the same time. She wished her father were here to see this, sitting next to her, drinking a pint, eating thick French fries with his bare hands, instead of where he was now, at home, alone, wearing a fresh pair of blue rubber gloves, pacing the floors, and counting to fourteen thousand and forty-four.

CHAPTER 13

The Hangover

Carlene awoke with a start. It was pitch black and there was a chill in the air she felt all the way down to the bones in her toes. She looked down at her feet. They were bare and sticking out of the tiny bed. So tiny no man would ever be able to join her. Her head was aching, her pillow was stiff, and the wool blanket covering her was scratchy. She had no idea what day, or time it was, or for a split second, even who she was. Then it all came hurtling back. The pub. The party. The drinks. Oh God, the drinks. How many pints did she have? And shots, did she really do shots? Oh yes, she did shots. She'd morphed into some foolish little dog, showing off her tricks, drinking every shot they called out. Do an Irish flag! Do a baby Guinness! Car bomb, keg bomb, so many bombs, and they were concurrently detonating in her skull.

That's what she got for being a people pleaser, a people-pleaser hangover. There were so many shots, so many toasts, oh God, what was she thinking? Cheers, good luck, sláinte!

She must be in the upstairs room. She felt like such a fool. She'd imagined a large apartment upstairs, with a nice round living room, fireplace, and a standing harp (that she vowed she would someday learn to play); a huge walk-in kitchen where plump and happy Irish women would teach her how to make Shepherd's pie and Irish soda bread; a bedroom big enough for a sleigh bed, with a second fireplace, a cozy chair by the window where she would sit and read James Joyce (and now that she was practically Irish, she would understand every word of it on a deep empathetic level); and a claw-foot bathtub with lion paws for feet, where she would soak in Irish bubbles after a long day of standing on her feet.

Instead, it was a very small bedroom with a very small bath-room, with room only for a toilet and a shower. When you sat down on the toilet and closed the door, the doorknob jammed into your knee. For thirty solid minutes after she flushed the toilet, it sounded like a waterfall was in her room. The sink was outside the bathroom, next to her bed. There was one small window overlooking the backyard. She'd been too drunk last night to take it all in. She remembered stumbling up the steps and standing in the doorway. The party was still going strong when she passed out, and she could hear grown men below singing off-key at the top of their lungs.

Now it was silent. Had they locked up? Cleaned up? When was Declan coming back? Was she going to be open for business soon? Not today, she could tell them, couldn't she? Of course she could; it was her pub. But it didn't feel like her pub, not in the wake of her morning hangover. It was somebody else's pub, somebody's family pub. She closed her eyes. Getting up wasn't an option. Sometimes there was a lot of relief in running out of options.

The second time she woke up, the pounding in her head had eased to a dull thudding. From now on, she swore, she would serve the drinks instead of consuming them. Suddenly, she heard voices. She sat up in bed—big mistake, too quick, her head was exploding again full force. She lay down again and listened. Her heart hammered from the exertion of sitting up. There were definitely people downstairs. Men's voices, at least three or four, talking over each other. Were they still here from last night? What was she doing here? Who did she think she was? She didn't know anything about running a pub. She couldn't work with all this drumming going on in her skull. She wanted to stay in her stiff, scratchy, cold bed and listen to the rain. It was hard to tell what time it was. It was definitely lighter outside than when she went to bed, but the sky was an overcast, gunmetal gray, leaving open for interpretation exactly what time of day it was.

Oh, why wouldn't they go away? From below, the sound of laughter and glasses clinking filtered through the air. She sat up again, slowly this time, as if her head were barely attached and in danger of snapping off and rolling away, like a broken china doll whose glue hadn't had sufficient time to set.

Ouch, ouch, ouch, ouch, ouch. Where was her suitcase? Was it still in the trunk of Ronan's car? She'd been too distracted by the "tree trimming" to think of it. Sure enough, she still had on her skirt and top from yesterday. Her mouth was dry and tasted like copper. She slowly put her feet on the floor and pushed herself upright. She splashed water on her face from the little sink next to the bed. The faucet squealed when she turned it on, and the water was ice cold. There were no mirrors in the room. She went to the bathroom and smacked her knee on the doorknob. The toilet made its loud gurgling noises, and the waterfall sounds started up. She washed her hands in the cold water again. She was going to have to buy some soap. There weren't any hand towels. Carlene wiped her cold, wet fingers on her skirt.

She walked into the hall and peered down the railing to the bar below. The lights were on full blaze, and from her perch she could see four men sitting at the bar. How did they get in? How could they start without her? What time was it?

She eased herself down the stairs. Here she could see there were actually five men at the bar drinking full pints. The large tree branch was still in the middle of the pub, and a man was walking across it while trying to hold his pint. When he got to the other side without spilling a drop, shouts erupted from the bar. Money was thrown down and snatched up.

On the farthest stool to the right was the same old man Carlene had seen there last night. For all she knew he was superglued to the stool. He could have been any age from seventy to ninety. His face was gaunt and wrinkled, his cheeks concave, his lips thin and brittle. He had a full set of brown hair, hanging straight on his head like an upside-down bowl. It took a moment for Carlene to realize it was a hairpiece. He was wearing a striped shirt with suspenders and a cardigan sweater. He was the first to notice Carlene, maybe because she was staring at him. He gave her a gruff nod and raised his pint glass as if requesting a refill. Immediately, all faces at the bar turned toward her. The distraction proved fatal to the log roller. He lost his footing and slipped off. His pint glass crashed to the floor. Dark ale ran out and snaked along the floor. As the men at the bar looked on and laughed, he let out a long string of cuss words, only half of which Carlene understood. Shouts and groans rose from the men, and once again money was thrown down and snatched up.

"How ya?" the man closest to the stairs called. "What's the craic?"

"Hello," another said. "Which one of us beasts woke up beauty?" Carlene laughed.

"I see you've started without me," she said.

"If you come over and pull a pint, ye can catch up right quick," the one closest to the stairs said. He was an average-sized man who appeared to be in his thirties. He had a buzz cut, brown eyes, and dimples. He stuck his hand out.

"Name's Eoin," he said. "In case you don't remember from last night." Carlene shook his hand.

"Of course I remember," she lied. With the exception of the log roller, who barely looked eighteen, and the old man at the end of the bar, the other four men looked like they were either going to or coming from work—heavy boots, long hours, and dirty nails. They ranged in age but united in smiles. A surge of hope rose in Carlene. They seemed like genuinely nice men, even if they were drinking at what couldn't be later than eight o'clock in the morning. Carlene slipped behind the bar and eyed the pint glasses lined up in front of them. Had they just served themselves? Had they paid? As if reading her mind, the one next to Eoin spoke up.

"Ronan fixed us up," he said. He held up his pint glass. It

took Carlene a minute to recognize him. He didn't have his hat on, so at first all she registered was the thick, red hair.

"Anchor," she said. "The ambassador of craic." He grinned.

"Spot on," he said. He elbowed Eoin. "See? She remembers me." Next to Anchor sat a beautiful-looking man—or boy, should she say—with blue eyes almost as light as hers. He was wearing a T-shirt that said: SUPPORT YOUR LOCAL BARTENDER. Below it was a picture of a bra and thong. He caught her reading it and grinned. Eoin pointed at him.

"That's Collin." Collin waved. Carlene wondered if she should ask him for ID, although judging from the state of his pint, it was a bit too late. "Next to him is Ciaran." Ciaran, forties, light blond hair slicked back, nodded. "And the oul fella on the end there is Riley." Riley raised his pint glass again.

"I'm the baddest motherfucker in this bog," Riley said. The men burst out laughing.

"Don't forget me," the boy on the log said.

"D'mind him," Eoin said. "He's a bollix."

"Billy the bollix," Anchor said.

"Shut yer piehole," Billy said. He waved. He had reddish brown hair and a face full of freckles. He lay down on the log and stared at the wood-beamed ceiling like a kid trying to spot shapes in the clouds.

"He's communing with nature," Eoin said when he caught Carlene watching Billy. The men laughed.

"Feck off," Billy said.

"Meditation won't crack that walnut," Eoin said.

"Did you say Ronan was here?" Carlene asked Anchor. He pointed to a spot in the upper corner of the bar. There hung a television. Carlene hadn't noticed it last night. "He said we could watch the races," Anchor said. "But it's not working."

"Bet they forgot to pay the cable bill," Ciaran said.

"I'll look into it," Carlene said. "Where's Ronan now?"

"Bookies," Anchor said.

"Same old ding-dong," Eoin said.

"So, how ye keeping?" Collin asked.

"I'm keeping . . . well," Carlene said. *For someone who just woke up, is wearing the same clothes she wore last night, and hasn't even had a cup of coffee yet.* "Although I have a lot to learn," she said. *Like how to keep men from sneaking in before dawn and starting without me.*

"We'll teach you," Riley said. "Let's see you pour a pint of Guinness." His gravel voice carried the weight of cigarettes and bricks. The men straightened up respectfully as Carlene took a pint glass and held it under the tap. She couldn't remember if Declan had pushed it or pulled it. She pushed it. A collective groan rose from the bar. Carlene stopped. She kept the pint glass under the spout and pulled the lever instead. The men erupted in disgust.

"Start fresh," Collin said.

"Rinse the glass out, for feck's sake," Riley said.

"Somebody play some tunes, this is going to take a while," Ciaran said.

"Tunes?" Carlene said. "I have tunes?" Collin pointed. There, behind the battered pool table, was a jukebox. The discovery filled her with unexpected joy. Her pub. Her customers. Her tunes. From now on her life would be filled with surprises, and music. And men who liked to drink at eight o'clock in the morning.

"You think we'd come to a pub that doesn't have tunes, Yank?" Anchor said. "We have motorcars, petrol, electricity, and Facebook too," he added.

"D'mind him," Ciaran said. "His Irish charm takes about twelve pints to kick in." Carlene glanced at Anchor. "That's twelve pints into you, lass, not him," Ciaran added. Anchor laughed. He threw his head back and kept laughing. It was a laugh fit for a man of his size. So infectious, she had to laugh too.

"Focus on the Guinness," Billy said from the tree. "Become one with the pint."

"Don't mind him," Eoin said, jerking his thumb over to Billy. "We'll throw him out with the branch." Collin held up the plug to the jukebox.

"Drumroll," he said. The men pounded their hands on the

bar. Collin plugged it in and stood back. It didn't light up. He shook it. He kicked it. "Dead," he said. "Add that to the list."

"Now you can't drown out our shite talk," Eoin said. Collin punched the jukebox again. Carlene wondered if she should tell him not to do that, but she wanted to keep the few customers she had. She leaned in and whispered to Eoin.

"How old is he?"

"Drinking age in Ireland is eighteen, luv," Collin called from across the bar.

"Sorry," Carlene said. Wow, the young ones had really good hearing.

"But he's only sixteen," Ciaran said. Carlene must have look stricken, for they all laughed.

"Fuck off," Collin said.

"I second that," Billy said.

"They're nineteen and twenty," Ciaran said. "But some pubs let 'em in even younger than that."

"Am I going to die here waiting for that pint?" Riley said. Carlene turned her attention back to the Guinness tap. The men shouted instructions, and she followed along like a game of Paddy Says.

Pull the lever. Tilt the glass. Easy does it. Now you have to stop pouring halfway, put the pint glass down, and let it settle. That's right, ease up now. Put the pint down. Walk away from the pint. Busy yourself with the customers, but keep one eye on it. Never let a man's glass get empty. Take yer top off if you'd like. You don't even need to ask, just throw down a second one when there's only half left in the first one. Now go back to yer pint. Fill it until there's about this much head at the top. Billy, would ye stop laughing every time somebody says "head"? No, that's a pope's head. No, that's a bishop's head. That's right, you want a priest's head. So do a lot of other people around the world right now, but we won't get into dat now, will we? Speaking of which, will you be wanting mass times?

That's pretty good, but you were a little slow, so throw her out there and do another one. No, no, throw her out to one of us, not down the sink. Try it a little faster now. Remember. A pat on the back is only six inches from a boot up the arse. Give it to Riley, he's the oldest and ugliest. Did you know there's a bog in the backyard?

On what felt like her twentieth pour, Carlene got a loud cheer.

"Not bad, not bad," Anchor said, checking his watch and measuring the head. She smiled and winked.

"You got something in your eye, darling?" Ciaran said. She must not have the winking thing down.

"You're from Ohio, right?" Collin said.

"That's right," Carlene said.

"Cleveland," Collin continued. "Home of the Rock and Roll Hall of Fame."

"Metallica!" Anchor said. "Inducted in 2009."

"Cleveland," Collin continued. "Home of America's first traffic light, nineteen-fourteen."

"Really?" Carlene said.

"I swear on me pint," Collin said. "Ohio. 'Hang on Sloopy,' official state rock song."

"If you lived there, it would be 'Hang on Sloppy,'" Anchor said.

"Ohio," Collin said. "Seventeenth state to join the union. Indian name meaning 'longest river.' Home of John Glenn, oldest man to venture into space." Collin leaned over and looked at Riley. Riley put his fist up.

"I'll send ye into outer space," Riley said. Collin laughed.

"Ohio. The Buckeye State. Ohio. Home to Drew Carey. Ohio—"

"Okay, okay," Ciaran said. "Now we all know you can fucking Google. Now shut the fuck up about Ohio." He glanced at Carlene. "No offense, darling."

"None taken," Carlene said. Ohio was a long way away. Ohio was another world. She had a new life now, a new, glamorous life. She looked at all the pints lining the bar. "How do I wash the dishes?" she said out loud. Eoin joined her behind the bar.

"CmereIwancha," he said. She moved next to him. He held up a pint glass, then pointed to two small sinks below the bar.

They were both already filled with water. He picked up a yellow box next to one of the sinks.

"Just a smidge," he said, shaking the detergent in the first sink. He flipped a switch and a little built-in brush began to twirl. Eoin tipped the glass over it, swirled it around, then dipped it into the second sink, which he loudly proclaimed was the "sanitizing sink," before he brought it to rest on a nearby drying rack. When Carlene thanked him, he beamed as if he'd shown her how to mine for gold.

"No bother," he said. "No bother a't'all." When he walked back to the stool it was with a definite swagger.

"Did I tell you I'm the reason you won the pub?" Anchor said.

"You drew the name of the winner?" Carlene said.

"No, no, 'twasn't me," Anchor said. "But it was my idea to have a fallback," he said. "Otherwise, this would have been Tan Land."

"So I heard," Carlene said.

"Pale is the new tan," Ciaran said. Everyone laughed. He acknowledged them by lifting his pint glass and giving a nod. Carlene looked at the tree branch. She was going to have to figure out what to do about Joe McBride.

"So you owe me," Anchor said. He had a huge grin.

"What did you have in mind?" Carlene said.

"Take yer top off," Ciaran said.

"Says the married man in the group," Eoin said.

"Says the other married man in the group," Ciaran said.

"Ah, I'm just joking you," Anchor said. "Free drinks for life ought to do it."

"So what did you do back home?" Collin asked. "In Ohio?"

"I managed a training gym," Carlene said.

"What the fuck is that?" Riley said. He sounded offended.

"A gym where boxers train," Carlene said. She held up her fists and moved her feet in place.

"Fuck me pink," Riley said.

"So you go from sweaty men lifting weights to sweaty men lifting pints," Ciaran said.

"So it seems," Carlene said. Just as Carlene was wondering if she should ask the men if they were going to pay for the drinks, and how to use the cash register, Ronan walked in. She was definitely going to have to get the front door fixed; she didn't like not being able to see who was sneaking up the hall. Ronan started talking to the men about horses, odds, and tips, and within seconds, they were up and leaving the bar. They laid money next to their pints, smiled, and waved, and those wearing hats tipped them to her, and soon they were gone. All except Ronan and Riley. Carlene was starting to wonder if Riley ever left his stool. Carlene picked up the money on the bar, looked at it, and then set it next to the cash register. She removed their pint glasses and set them next to the sink to wash. She looked up when she heard Ronan laugh.

"You don't know how to open the cash register, do you?" he said.

"Declan hasn't trained me yet," Carlene said.

"Declan's not going to train you," Ronan said. "He's retired." Not train her? Declan was the nicest man she'd ever met. He called her chicken, and pet, and petal, and luv. Of course he would train her. Maybe he didn't realize she wanted training. And why did she get the feeling Ronan was slightly annoyed with her this morning? What had she done?

"Head hurting this morning?" he asked her.

"A little," she admitted.

"You weren't easy to put to bed," he said. Startled, she looked at him. Then slowly, an image of Ronan walking her up the stairs, or actually near carrying her up the stairs, rose in her bomb shot–foggy brain.

"You put me to bed," Carlene said, more as a statement to herself than asking a question.

"Don't remember?" Ronan said. There it was again, a sarcastic bite to everything he said.

"It's a bit fuzzy," Carlene admitted.

"Wish I could say the same thing," Ronan said. There it was again—a catch in his voice. Annoyance. Anger even.

"Why?" Carlene said. "What did I do?"

"Just pray you're never captured behind enemy lines," Ronan

said. "You get a few pints in ye and you sing like a canary." Carlene winced. She didn't have a clue what he was talking about.
What did she say? What did she do? Obviously nothing funny
happened—she was wearing all of her clothes when she woke
up. Great. Her and her big, drunken mouth—whatever it said.

"You seem to be enjoying this," Carlene said. "Why don't
you just tell me what I said—or did?"

"Never mind," Ronan said. "It's for the best." What was for
the best? Why was he suddenly so cool toward her? She couldn't
have said anything mean to him, could she? She wasn't a mean
person. Ronan walked over and stared down at the tree branch.
"Joe is going to walk all over you," he said. "Among other people."

"No, he's not," Carlene said.

"What are you going to do about it?" Ronan said.

"I'm going to return it to him," Carlene said.

"He's crafty," Ronan said. "You've got to watch him."

"I'll certainly never play poker with him," Carlene said. The
second she saw the look on Ronan's face, she regretted the comment. It was as if she'd slapped him across the face. But they all
joked with each other around here! How was she to know what
was over the line and what wasn't? And why was he acting so
weird—and what did she say to him last night when he'd tucked
her into bed? She was so tired, and overwhelmed, and hungover,
and Ronan should never have let those men into her bar so early
in the morning.

"I was wrong about you," Ronan said. Carlene just looked at
him. She had no idea what he was talking about. He looked
confused, and disappointed in her.

"You don't know me," Carlene said. "You don't know me at
all."

"I know enough," Ronan said. He hoisted Riley out of his
seat. Riley tried to protest. "Let's leave the Yank in peace,"
Ronan said. Riley grabbed his pint glass and allowed Ronan to
escort him down the hall. He never looked back. Carlene stood,
hands on hips, staring after them. She listened to the back door
open and slam shut. Then silence. She couldn't believe it. He

was so cocky, so cold, so sure that he no longer liked her. What the hell could she have said? And why did she care so much?

It was probably for the best. He was probably only being nice to her so he could warm his way into her heart and then get his pub back. She didn't come here to fall in love—

I love you. Why did she remember saying "I love you"? Did she say "I love you" last night? Oh shit. No. She couldn't have. Stumbling up the stairs. Ronan holding on to her.

What a little bed.

It is, isn't it? Sorry it's not the Taj Mahal.

It's perfect. I love you.

You've had a lot to drink.

I do. I know I just met you, but I love you. You have gorgeous reptilian eyes, did you know that? Primal. Like an alligator. Or a snnnnnnnaaaaaaaaaaake. She put her arms around him, nibbled on his neck.

Carlene, stop it. Go to bed.

I don't care if you're a gambler and a fuckup. I'd bet on you. I love you.

No pajamas. Okay. Just lie down. The sooner the better.

Come here, I want to tell you something.

Go to sleep.

Come here.

He did. He walked over and leaned down so that his face was only inches from her face.

What?

You smell nice.

Tank you.

And you're much, much nicer than my Irish husband.

Carlene put her head down on the bar. She would have pounded it into the wood, but that would have been redundant. Oh God. Saying "I love you" was humiliating, and she didn't mean it, of course she wasn't in love with Ronan, she was just drunk, and overwhelmed, and he was way too good looking for his own good. But why, why, why did she have to mention Brendan?

CHAPTER 14

Extending a Branch

Carlene grabbed one end of the branch with both hands and hoisted it off the ground. It was heavier than she thought. She took a few steps down the narrow hallway and headed out the back. The branch was rough and sticky, and it sounded like a dead body dragging along the floor behind her. She liked the smell of bark, but not enough to keep it, hang it in the pub like an air freshener. Every few steps she had to stop and rest. *This is totally crazy,* she thought, as she inched it next door. *Joe is going to walk all over you. They all are.* Ronan had hit a nerve.

He seemed to hit a lot of nerves, too many of them, which was why she'd opened her big mouth and let all that garbage spill out. Now he thought she was married. Maybe it was for the best. What good would come of starting a relationship? Hadn't she learned her lessons with Brendan? Besides, she would attract way more customers as an aloof, single woman. Which was why she was going to have to find a way to make sure Ronan kept his mouth shut. Just thinking of how he'd pushed her away when she made drunken advances on him filled her with shame. Was he the kind who didn't kiss and tell?

They're going to walk all over you. He was right. Normally, she was a very nice person. Some might even say too nice. Too nice meant you knocked on your father's door four times, then waited four seconds, then knocked on his door another four times, then waited yet another four seconds before performing your last quad-knock.

Too nice meant you wiped your feet fifty times, washed your hands a hundred, ate only macrobiotic food while in his presence, wore fresh blue rubber gloves, and paced the yard with him until three A.M. when he needed to go for a walk. It meant you worked long hours at the gym because he could no longer handle more than a four-hour shift; it meant you met men who saw "too nice" coming a mile away, then just as you were falling for them, dumped you with the "you deserve better" line, something that always made her feel a deep sense of shame. After all, shouldn't *she* have been the one to declare she deserved better? Too nice meant even your best friend in the world thought you owed her over a two-dollar loan. Too nice was a thief, robbing bits of your life out from underneath you, one experience at a time.

Funny, Carlene didn't always feel nice on the inside. Sometimes she felt filled with rage, sometimes she criticized innocent bystanders in her head, and sometimes she performed random acts of rudeness, like the summer she waitressed at a popular truck-stop diner and filled all the sugar jars with salt and all the salt shakers with sugar. It was time she yielded more to those feelings when appropriate, like when neighbors saw fit to shove trees through her front door.

There were at least twenty cars parked on Joe's front lawn. Carlene stood at the side of the shop, wondering if she should wait until the crowd died down. No. Let the locals see that she wasn't a pushover. There were plenty of people who'd witnessed Joe's timber tantrum, why shouldn't she have an audience as well?

A little bell sounded a welcoming jingle when she opened the door. The branch made a scraping sound on the floor tiles as she hauled it in. The shop was narrow but surprisingly long. It stretched back so far she couldn't see the end. Tall shelves in multiple rows were packed with canned food, cereals, sweets, chips, household products, gardening tools, patio furniture, decorative vases—and that was just the first few shelves. No space was bare. Carlene would have to be careful not to swipe any products off the shelves. Standing up for herself was one thing, knocking down a hundred cans of Murphy's Mushy Peas would raise the war to a whole new level.

Carlene picked up speed and tried to locate the counter. The shop was set up like a maze. She pulled ahead of the first row of shelves and stopped dead. A group of well-dressed people stood in a circle in the middle of the store. They were singing softly, and all of them held little glasses, raised in a toast. Suddenly, the singing stopped, and everyone turned and looked at her. She took a few steps forward. Here she could see they were all gathered around a young couple who were holding an infant wearing a little white dress. Next to them stood a stocky priest. He held his Bible over his stomach. A christening, they had just come from a christening. Why were they celebrating it in the store? Joe McBride stepped forward.

"Hello," Carlene said. "Sorry to interrupt."

"Ah," said the priest in a booming voice. "You must be Carlene Rivers from America."

"That's me," Carlene said. Was she supposed to wave? Shake his hand? Bow? None of them were possible while holding the tree.

"I'm Father Duggan," he said.

"Hello, Father," she said. She curtsied slightly, using the tree for support.

"What's this now?" Father Duggan asked, pointing to the tree branch. The baby started to cry. Carlene could relate. Everyone was staring at her, awaiting an explanation.

"Well," Carlene said. "I'm from Ohio. It's an Indian name meaning 'longest river.' And the Native Americans had a tradition that whenever a baby was born, they would extend a branch to the parents. You know—as a way of welcoming them into the family tree." There were murmurs all around. Joe crossed his arms, but said nothing.

"How lovely of you," Father Duggan said. "Ah, isn't that nice." He looked around the room for confirmation. Several people nodded and said, "Ah, yes, 'tis, 'tis."

"I shouldn't have brought one so big," Carlene said. "I'll take it back."

"I was going to suggest that m'self," Joe said.

"No, no," Father Duggan said. He tapped the baby's father on the elbow and nodded at the branch. The young father and two other men stepped up and took the tree from Carlene, holding it in the middle and on both ends. They stood awkwardly and glanced about the shop, like men with a canoe and no river. The tree shook slightly in their hands and dropped a few leaves.

"Thank you," the young father said. "Thank you very much."

"Ah, it's lovely," the young mother said. "But where are we going to put it?"

"Why, in the wee fella's room," the father said. Carlene looked at the baby again. It was a boy? He looked like he was wearing a dress. She decided to keep this to herself.

"Why don't you just set it in the back for now," Joe said. "Until you have it all sorted out."

"Ah, brilliant," the father said. He and the men moved out to the back with the branch. The guests all parted to allow them through.

"Well," Carlene said. "I'd better be on my way."

"Will you be wanting mass times?" Father Duggan asked.

"Of course she will," Joe said. "I'll give her all the details. Right after we sort out some neighborly business." He headed down the nearest aisle and motioned for her to follow.

Joe headed for the counter, situated against the back right wall. Behind him was a stool, a cash register, a newspaper, a plant, and a teakettle. Propped up on the counter was a cardboard cutout poster of a tanning bed. Across the poster in huge letters it read: I'LL BRING THE SUN TO YOU. Next to the tanning bed was a picture of a truck. Carlene stood awkwardly on the other side.

"Are you settled?" he asked her while tidying up behind the counter.

"I'm trying," Carlene said. "I've had a few setbacks. Branches and leaves to clean up, a front door that no longer works." Joe nodded as if that were all par for the course.

"You've got the Irish gift for blarney, I see," Joe said. "I'll give ye dat. A new branch for the newest member of the family tree." He laughed. "Would you like a cuppa?" he asked. Carlene glanced at the kettle, which Joe immediately began fussing with even before she accepted his offer of tea. What she really wanted, what she would kill for, was a nice cup of coffee. Not instant, but freshly brewed, real coffee. She made a mental note to search her pub for a coffee machine. If they didn't have one, surely one of the shops in town would sell coffeemakers? What was the Irish equivalent of Target? She had so much to learn.

"I'd love a cup of tea," Carlene said. She vowed, no matter what, that she would never refuse a cup of tea in Ireland. It was surely bad luck to do so. While he fussed with the tea, she took in more of the shop. Even back here, shelves were built from floor to ceiling, and once again not a drop of space was wasted. When the tea was ready, Joe poured it into a china cup with red roses painted on the side, topped off with a gold rim. He served it on a tray with all the accoutrements: a tiny silver spoon, a sugar pot, and creamer. It was as if he was having tea with the queen. He pulled a folding chair out for her and opened a package of chocolate biscuits as she doctored her tea with milk and sugar. He waited for her to take the first sip. His gaze was so direct and patient, for a split second she was terrified he'd poisoned it.

"So," he said. "Why do you want to own a pub in the middle of nowhere for?" The tea burned the top middle of her throat and she fought to swallow it.

"Oh," she said with forced enthusiasm. "Who wouldn't want to win a pub in Ireland?" She left out the "middle of nowhere" because she didn't like the pub being in the middle of nowhere, when just ten miles or so out was a very nice stretch of somewhere. "It's the opportunity of a lifetime," she said. What she didn't say was that sometimes she was so sick of Cleveland, Ohio, and the endless, mindless repetition that her life had become, she would have been thrilled even if the raffle had been for a Popsicle stand in Siberia. She kept this to herself; you never knew how the locals were going to take something. Joe nodded, sipped his tea. She nodded, sipped her tea. He nodded, sipped his tea.

"You like being around drunks?" Joe asked.

"I like being around people," Carlene said.

"Sloshers?" Joe said.

"That's not exactly—"

" 'Cause that's what you'll be dealing with. If you get any customers at all."

"Now why would you say that?"

"Ah, no worries," Joe said. " 'Tis miserable weather, 'tisn't it?" A light rain had been falling all morning. Carlene barely noticed it.

"I don't mind," she said.

"Ah," Joe said. " 'Tis gonna be lashin' out of the heavens all week." Carlene turned her attention to the wall behind the counter. It was the only space in the entire shop not filled with shelves. Instead, cuckoo clocks were hanging on the wall, all shapes and sizes. They appeared to be hand painted and made out of bronze. Carlene spotted motorcycles, cars, houses, and tractors.

"Those are great," Carlene said. "You must really like clocks."

"I like tinkering with time," Joe said.

"You made these?"

"Ah, I did indeed," Joe said. "With me own two hands and one heart."

"They're great," Carlene said. "I don't have many talents."

"Well, you'll soon be a publican. Or so you 'tink." The parting comment was tagged on in such a soft voice, Carlene decided to ignore it.

"I should get going," she said. "I just want to know what

you're planning on doing about my front door." Joe gestured to his wall of clocks.

"Pick one," he said.

"Thank you," Carlene said. "But I'd rather have my door fixed."

"Ronan will fix the door," Joe said. "That was our agreement." Carlene wasn't sure she heard him right.

"Ronan knew you were going to cut down the branch?" she said. Joe just looked at her. "Was it his idea?" Carlene couldn't think of why this would be, but something in her believed it, knew it to be true. His reptilian eyes flashed in front of her. He blamed her for losing the pub. Joe gestured to the clocks again.

"Ah, now, would ye go on and pick one?" When she didn't make a move, he plucked one off the wall and handed it to her. It was a yellow bulldozer with a clock face.

"Really," Carlene said. "I couldn't." Joe took her hands and set the clock in it. "It's very unique," she said.

"How much did that raffle ticket cost you?" Joe asked.

"I—"

"Twenty American dollars?"

"Yes." It seemed a lot of folks around here had a habit of asking her questions to which they already knew the answer.

"Well, that clock will be worth ten thousand euros to ye," he said. Carlene knew she was looking at the bulldozer a little too hard now—it was a nifty piece all right, but hardly worth ten thousand euros.

"You won't find gold in her," Joe said. "But by the time you give her back to me, I'll give you ten thousand euros."

"I don't understand," Carlene said.

"For the property," Joe said. "When you're ready. They raffled it off just to get my goat. This town doesn't need another pub." He pulled the advertisement for the tanning bed into his body. In the picture, the sun was shining. " 'Tis miserable here, 'tis. You'll see for yourself. You'll be wantin' a bit of the sun, ye will. This town doesn't need another pub. They need Tan Land. They were fully expectin' Tan Land. Nobody thinks you won that pub fair and square. They might not be saying it, but you can believe me, they're all thinking it."

"I see," Carlene said.

"You've got nothing but a bog in the backyard, did ye know that?"

"I haven't quite had time to check it out," Carlene said.

"It would cost you a lot of money to fix up that swamp land back there. You're not going to make that kind of money running a pub. Ah, but sure, try it. You'll see what I mean soon enough. When you're ready, give me the digger and I'll know you're wantin' to sell. I'll give you ten thousand euros, and we'll have a solicitor draw up the contract. It's not a fortune, mind you, but you won't get any better offers, I'm tellin' ye. Not with the old bog in the back. Ten thousand euros for twenty American dollars, now that's a beauty of a deal, if you know what I mean."

"I think it's a beautiful piece of land," Carlene said. Joe gave her a look that could only be translated as: *You would.*

"Americans. They like the promise of something for nothing, don't they?"

"Thank you for the tea," Carlene said. "And the clock. But I'm afraid you won't be getting it back."

"In time," Joe said as she headed out of the store. "In time." On her way out, Carlene stopped once again by the young parents, family, and friends, gathered for the christening. They were putting on coats, hugging each other, preparing to leave.

"Please come next door for another toast," Carlene said. "The first drink is on me."

"Ah, we couldn't," the young father said.

"You've been too kind already," the mother said.

"I insist," Carlene said.

CHAPTER 15

Three Black Swans

The next morning, Carlene's first act of business was to hang an Opening Soon sign on her pub. She made it out of a rectangular scrap of wood she found on the back porch, along with a can of red paint. She sat on her little back porch, painting the simple words on the sign, excitement building with each curve of the paintbrush. When was the last time she even worked with paint? Grade school? This felt good, this felt right, maybe they were onto something in elementary school, maybe they should have warned her there would come a day when she would stop painting, and coloring, and cutting out shapes, and she wouldn't even realize how much she needed the simple, creative pleasures in life. Maybe her third-grade teacher should have grabbed her by the shoulders and said, "Never stop doing this, do you understand? Do not stop." Then for good measure, given her a good shake. It might have scarred her in the short term, but perhaps she would have been a famous artist by now, or at the least, a little bit more in touch with that warm, calm, floating feeling she was experiencing right now, in her slightly damp, woodsy, yeasty, paint-smelling porch.

In addition to simply making her feel good, she hoped the

sign would build suspense, garner interest in the change of ownership. She thought about adding the phrase "Under New and Improved Management" just to piss off Ronan, but in the end she decided against it. She honestly didn't know whether Ronan was in cahoots with Joe. She'd seen Ronan's face when they spotted Joe up in the tree, and he'd looked just as surprised as she did. She was going to have to be careful as to whom and what she believed from now on.

The group from the christening the other day weren't big drinkers, but they brought loads of sandwiches in with them and showed Carlene where her teakettle and accoutrements were. It was strange to think that everyone in town knew her pub better than she did, but she found it endearing that they were more than willing to show her the ropes.

She learned the young father was a solicitor and the mother worked in the hair salon in town. James was their first baby. The couple had courted in Joe's shop, which was why they wanted to hold the last bit of the ceremony there. They stayed for several hours, and when they left Carlene was happy to have met new folks, but utterly exhausted. Despite it only being early afternoon, she'd fallen into bed and slept all the way through until this morning.

It was so nice to wake up without a hangover. She hummed as she came down the steps in her pajamas. Riley was sitting on his stool. She broke it to him as gently as he could that she wasn't going to be open for a few days, and when she did open, it would be at three P.M., and not a second earlier. Riley slunk away like a child who was just told that Christmas had been canceled that year. She was going to have to survey the entrances to the pub; obviously, it had been too easy for him to get in.

Carlene made herself a cup of tea. There was something cathartic about encountering a barrage of the new and simple. Filling up an electric kettle, plugging it in, setting up the teacup, spoon, and saucer. When would this no longer be novel and beautiful? When would she simply do it with her eyes closed and forget there was once immense pleasure in watching a tea bag steep in a cup of hot water?

She planned on going to a grocery store later and buying instant coffee. It would have to do until she bought a coffeemaker. She wandered around her pub with her tea, checking every nook and cranny. She felt a little guilty, especially when it came to looking at photographs of smiling strangers. She felt like a voyeur, a stranger who had swooped in on a foreclosed house and taken it over with the previous owner's possessions still sitting where they'd left them, where they'd lost them.

This was not my fault, she reminded herself. Someone had to win the pub, why not her? She would make the best of it. At least her intentions were good   she wanted to make her pub the best it could be, she wanted to fit in with the locals, she wanted to create a space where people felt welcome.

And she wanted Ronan right by her side, running the pub with her—

She didn't know where that thought came from, and she didn't like it. It was probably guilt, or sexual attraction, or fear of not being able to make it on her own, or loneliness. She did not need Ronan by her side. Although she wouldn't mind looking at him up close every day, learning the nuances of his expressions, unraveling exactly what kind of man he was—

That was enough daydreaming. She had work to do. After finishing the sign, Carlene headed for the stairs with a skip in her step. She stopped dead near the pool table. Lying across it, like a body she thought she'd buried, was the tree branch. Yesterday, Joe had insisted the young father take it with him. By the time they left the pub, they'd apparently forgotten all about it. Either that, or they really didn't want a tree in the wee fella's room. Go figure. She would just have to deal with it later. For now, she wanted to explore the town while there was a break in the rain.

It was a grand fresh day, as she'd heard some locals say. The air was indeed crisp, smelling as if it were on the verge of rain.

Carlene loved that smell. She loved the scent of fresh grass and damp earth. Birds chirped and twittered all around her, and she could have sworn that even they had an Irish lilt. She didn't quite have a plan worked out, other than to head down the road toward the main street and take in the sights. Major shopping might have to wait until she had a car, or maybe a wheelbarrow, but she could pick up a few bits and bobs in town. She wanted the folks of Ballybeog to see her face about town, to get used to her as someone who shopped, ate, and waved, like everyone else. She'd show them she wasn't a typical Yank, whatever that was.

Maybe she would buy a new outfit, since she'd brought so little with her. She could even get some new knickers.

Knickers, she'd said knickers. She'd barely been in Ireland and she was already picking up the lingo. Maybe she truly belonged here, although it might take more than saying "grand fresh day" and "knickers" to convince everyone else of that.

Rain boots, she would definitely buy some rain boots, her tennis shoes weren't going to cut it. What did they call those boots? Wellies! Wellies and grand fresh knickers.

She waved to the cows and sheep in the fields, she waved to the farmer hauling pails out of his barn, she waved at a car whizzing by. The cows and sheep simply stared, the farmer lifted his head in a nod, and the driver honked. She was happy. Even the stones at her feet were exotic and new. She'd grown up across from a gravel pit in Ohio, and she'd never once found the stones exotic. Here in Ireland, everything was nicer than she'd ever known. She wanted to touch everything, memorize everything, love everything. Like the sky with its slapped-up patches of blue and gray, the purple flowers spilling over the hedges on the side of the road, and the miles and miles of limestone walls that bordered the rolling fields.

It was a pleasant walk and soon she was nearing the arched entrance to Main Street. Bally Gate, as she remembered from her reading—the only one of the four original gates that remained of the walled town. Did the folks who lived here know how lucky they were? How cool this was? Would her countrymen have torn down the soaring stone gate and replaced it with McDonald's? Yellow arches for a stone arch? She hoped not, but it was a shameful possibility.

Passing through the gate, Carlene marveled at the history contained within its walls. They were the same stones that stood during the Norman invasion, and Cromwell, and the Black and Tans, and the potato famine, and yet here it was, still standing. She could touch it, feel its history beneath her fingertips, caress the wet, historic stone. She moved down the street, thrilled to be there, happy just to walk about and see the shops up close. Just ahead, she spotted Nancy's Café. She was starving, and maybe she could get a cup of coffee. Just like at Joe's, a little bell tinkled as she entered the café. She wondered if she should get a bell for the pub. If nothing else, she should put a bell on Riley.

It was a cozy, two-room restaurant with yellow and brick walls, a smooth stone floor, and a fireplace in the front room. The open kitchen ran the length of the back wall. In front of it, pastry cases beckoned with cakes, pies, and scones. She smelled bacon, eggs, and fresh bread, and by God—was that coffee?

There, on the back wall, sat a cappuccino machine. Carlene heard angels sing. Almost every table in the place was full. There were young couples, and families with children, and babies, and old people. They were chatting, reading newspapers, and eating from heaping plates of food. Many looked up and smiled when she walked in, others paid her no mind. Carlene squeezed into a small table by the fireplace. Within seconds, a young woman with a long, dark ponytail approached. She grinned ear to ear, handed Carlene a menu, and put her hand on her shoulder.

"How ya," she said. "I know who you are. I was hoping to meet you. I'm Nancy."

"Nancy?" Carlene said. "As in—this is your place?"

"This is my place, sure," Nancy said. "How are you settling in? The weather's been miserable for you, sure. I hope everything is treating you all right, and if you've any questions at all I'd be happy to answer them."

"Can I get a cappuccino?" Carlene asked, still suspecting it was some kind of trick.

"No bother a't'all," Nancy said.

"Make it two, please," Carlene said.

"No bother 'at'all," Nancy said. Carlene also ordered a scone with fresh cream and strawberries, to which Nancy said, "no bother a't'all." The cappuccinos were heaven. Carlene ordered a third to go, and invited Nancy to pop into the pub sometime, to which Nancy responded, "I will, yeah. No bother a't'all."

When she was finished, and caffeinated, and full, Nancy suggested Carlene take a walk to the ruined Franciscan abbey just outside of town. Carlene intended on doing just that.

"Mind yourself, now," Nancy said. Carlene smiled and thanked her, and felt an irrational stab of jealousy. Now, that girl was nice. Genuinely nice. She had nice coming out of her pores. She probably didn't have an inner critic judging everyone around her, and there was definitely sugar in the sugar jars. She was pretty too. Was Nancy single? Did Ronan fancy her? If not, why not? She was cute, bubbly, and friendly, ran her own business, and was full-blooded Irish. Not some wannabe, but the genuine article.

Maybe Nancy was madly in love with someone else. She hoped so. But even if Nancy wasn't in love with Ronan, surely some woman in town was? Why was she thinking like that, why did she even care? She had plenty to do—and fix, starting with her front door.

She'd stop into a hardware store and ask if there were any handymen about who could fix it. And she would send Joe the bill.

She would have to call her father soon too, let him know she was all right. She'd have to get the phone working in the pub first, along with the cable for the television. There was so much to do, but she looked forward to it all. This was how she felt when she'd rented her first studio apartment, when even going out to buy Windex felt like an adventure.

As Carlene made her way down the street, she made a point

of waving to everyone she saw. She rarely beat them to it; usually they waved and said hello first. Just ahead, a boy soared toward her on a bicycle. He had a round face and chubby red cheeks, and behind him loomed the town castle. She held the image in her head, wanting to capture it forever.

She passed a small stone house. In the windowsill sat a pair of porcelain dogs. They looked at her with cocked heads, floppy ears, pink tongues, and big painted brown eyes. She passed pubs that were open and pubs that had been long closed. She passed the butcher, the bookmakers, and the bank. The town was a blend of medieval and modern, and somehow it all just fit.

Carlene took a right on the street where Nancy told her to turn. Just look for Dally's Lounge, Undertaker, and Pub. It was easy to find the pub; Carlene remembered pointing it out to Ronan on her way into town. The sign for Dally's hung sideways at the top of the building, a circular wooden painting of an older gentleman with a handlebar mustache, holding a pint of ale. Dally's, Carlene thought. A good place to drink and die.

Across from Dally's was another string of small stone houses. Above the middle one hung a simple wooden sign that said: MUSEUM. She would have to check it out later. Here the street came to a dead end in front of an open field. In the distance, the old Franciscan abbey sprawled the length of a football field. She only had to walk over a small wooden bridge and down a short stone path to get to the abbey. First, she crossed over to the little museum. She tried the door, but it was locked. She peered into the little window but was unable to make out anything other than dark, lumpy shapes in the small room. She would have to come back later. Carlene was about to cross the field to the abbey when it started to rain. It was just a light mist, and Carlene figured she might as well take a quick look around, then she'd definitely be off to buy her wellies.

Carlene paused on the wooden bridge and looked down at the shallow river. Farther downstream, a white-and-brown horse drank from the muddy banks. He was tall, his legs taut and stretched, sinewy muscles reflexively contracting and relaxing, neck proud and long. A thing of beauty, but too thin; his ribs stuck out like a broken accordion. She would have guessed he was wild, but a thin rope connected him to a nearby stake. Carlene wanted to go to him. Free him, feed him, touch his soft nose, feel his fleshy lips tickle the palm of her hand. But this wasn't her country, and he wasn't her horse. She had a constant sensation of being watched, of invisible boundaries, which, if she crossed, she would be banned, she would remain forever not one of them.

The monastery, complete with a soaring round tower, beckoned. It amazed Carlene that she could just walk up to this abbey without having to buy a ticket or wait in line. It was just out here, in the open, an accessible, twelfth-century ruined abbey. Carlene walked through an arched doorway and stepped into the open courtyard. The stones that made up the surrounding wall were chunky and set on top of each other in varying directions, leaving small gaps between them. She walked around the courtyard, imagining what it must have looked like back in the day.

It just wasn't fair. Why couldn't she have grown up here? She could have played ball in the courtyard, climbed the rock walls up to the second story, made out with teenage boys in the bell tower. The excitement of the roller coasters at Cedar Point in Sandusky, Ohio, paled in comparison.

Who had Ronan made out with here in the ruins of the abbey?

Carlene gravitated to the outline of a five-light window on the eastern side of the abbey, its stained glass long gone. It was at least ten feet high, set twenty feet in the air. Diamond-shaped cutouts showed where the individual windowpanes used to be. On the opposite wall, stone faces were cut into a soaring pillar. Beneath her feet was gravel and dirt; the sky was the roof. She crossed through a doorway and entered an even larger courtyard. The rain was heavier now, shrouding the ancient monastery in a cloak of mystique. Across the courtyard and to the left, a set of stone steps led up to what remained of the round tower.

The stairs were long and steep, and by the time she reached the top, she was out of breath. Here, a massive iron door stood guard to the tower, chained and locked. It was disappointing, but the view from the top was well worth the climb. She could see all the way to town. From here she looked over to a steeple in the middle of the abbey. Unlike the tower, the steeple could not be accessed by stairs. But suddenly, Carlene saw two heads poking out from the window of the steeple. Teenage boys, most likely. They must have scaled the walls. It was nice to know that even in these modern times, these boys chose scaling walls over the Internet or video games. Of course, now she could see they were smoking cigarettes, so maybe video games without cigarettes would be better for them after all. She walked down the steps thinking about the monks who once built, prayed, and lived in the abbey. She was so engrossed in her thoughts, she didn't see the two figures at the bottom of the stairs until she was nearly on top of them. She let out a little shriek.

Two short, slightly pudgy women in identical black rain jackets with the hoods pulled up blocked her path. It wasn't until she had a good look at their faces that she recognized the twins.

"Liz, Clare," Carlene said. "You startled me."

"How do you like our little abbey?" one of them said. Carlene was going to have to ask someone who was who, she couldn't always go on wondering.

"I'm sorry, I—"

"I'm Liz," the one who had just spoken said. Carlene laughed, embarrassed to be caught.

"Don't worry," Clare said. "We get it all the time." They pulled off their hoods. Liz had short hair, cut in layers; Clare's hung just below her chin, making her face appear slightly longer.

"As long as you keep your hairstyles, I'll remember," Carlene said.

"Did you know this was built in twelve ninety-one?" Liz said.

"It's remarkable," Carlene said.

"Ireland's abbeys have a rich history," Clare said. "A hundred monks flocked here to build this abbey. They were French and Irish, they were, but after a while the Irish ran all the French back home, and from then on it was only Irish monks." The twins stepped farther into the courtyard. Carlene followed. They led her through the last doorway. Carlene stepped into the smallest room she'd seen yet. Against the back wall was a crypt. She followed the girls over. It was protected by a wall of iron bars. This section had both a roof and a floor. Inside were two tombs. On top of the closest tomb, a skeleton was carved on top of the stone crypt. "A White Knight lies here," Liz said. Clare pointed to the right.

"There are more graves over there, but the headstones were destroyed. The town paid to have this fenced in to prevent damage to the crypts."

"They're amazing," Carlene said.

"We're lucky this is still standing," Liz said. "Henry the Eighth ordered all the Franciscan monasteries destroyed."

"Wow," Carlene said. She wished she could think of something more sophisticated and intellectual to say, but nothing came to mind. She felt as if the girls were working their way up to telling her something, and it was making her nervous. "I'm glad it's still standing too," she said.

"Oh, we've withstood a couple of tragic turns in our history," Liz said. "But don't you worry, we're still here."

"Absolutely," Carlene said.

"No matter who blows in and tries to take us down, we eventually run them out," Clare said. She laughed, which started Liz laughing. Carlene couldn't muster up so much as a smile.

"I see," Carlene said. Liz and Clare moved on, back through the doorway, and took a left.

"This was where the monks took their meals," Liz said. She pointed out a recessed aisle in the wall. "That was the old fireplace."

"I'm so appreciative of this experience," Carlene said. "We don't have sights like this in Ohio." Thunder rumbled overhead, sounding as if the sky itself was cracking open, and it began to pour. The girls backed up until they were under a small roof that used to hang over the fireplace.

"In thirteen forty-nine the Black Death swept through Ireland," Clare said. "It was the worst plague they'd ever seen. The Archbishop of the Franciscan Order was beside himself. Himself and his priests had been tending to the sick and dying day and night. Priests were falling sick as well, even in the midst of performing their duties. One night the archbishop returned to the monastery after a particularly deadly night. Weary with exhaustion, he went to the chapel, got down on his knees, and prayed for an end to the plague."

"He prayed for a sign," Liz said.

"Do you want to see the chapel?" Clare said. "It's enclosed too, but we'll have to run for it."

"Sure," Carlene said. They tore across the courtyard, over to where Carlene had first entered the abbey. They were back at the huge window with diamond-shaped panes. The girls stepped through the column and into a little enclosed chapel that Carlene had completely overlooked. Inside was a large Celtic cross. Clare crossed over to it and placed her wet hands on either side of it. Carlene was wet and shivering, and she wanted to go home. But she also wanted to hear the rest of the story, and she didn't want to offend the girls.

"That night the bishop fell into a deep sleep," Clare said. "He was visited by an angel who told him if he wanted to end the plague, he must build a friary for all the poor friars of Ireland. He was told the location of the new monastery would be revealed to him when the time was right. The next day he gathered three of his most trusted priests, and they set out to find the sign promised to him by the angel in his dream. They began to have a walk about. Soon they found themselves by a river." The girls gazed out, as if looking upon the very river. Carlene followed their gaze, mesmerized. Liz picked up the story.

"There sat three black swans, with flaxseeds in their bills." The story stopped, and the twins looked at Carlene.

"It was the middle of winter," Clare said. Carlene nodded, still not understanding.

"Flaxseed doesn't grow in the middle of winter," Liz said.

"Oh," Carlene said. "Well, there's your sign."

"There it was all right," Clare said. "Lush, and full in their beaks."

"The swans rose into the air," Liz said. The girls looked up, as if watching them go.

"They circled the river three times," Clare said. "When they finally landed, the archbishop and the three priests ran to the spot. The swans were gone."

"It was as if they vanished into thin air," Liz said.

"But in their place, sprouting up from the frozen ground, was flax," Clare said. "In full bloom."

"A heavenly sign, just like the angel promised," Liz said.

"And that's where they built the new monastery for all the poor friars of Ireland," Clare said. "And true to the angel's word, the plague ended soon thereafter."

" 'Course the archbishop himself died from the plague before the monastery was ever built, so," Liz said. Clare nodded and shrugged, à la, "What are you going to do?"

"Wow," Carlene said. "And we're standing right here."

"I'd say we're not," Liz said.

"Nah, that might have been the Ross Abbey in Glengary I was on about," Clare said. "This abbey was built much later."

"Oh," Carlene said.

"You should go there sometime," Liz said. "There are so many places in our little country for you to visit."

"Indeed," Carlene said. Clare stepped up until she was only inches away from Carlene.

"We've seen plagues, we've seen famines. We've been invaded by the Vikings, and by Cromwell, and by the Black and Tans, and French monks," Clare said. She looked at Liz and spoke as if the two were alone. "I suppose we can tackle the odd American girl who thinks she can run one of our pubs, so," she said.

"Aye," Liz said. "But it would make it a little easier on us if she wouldn't overstay her welcome, now wouldn't it?"

"Ah, it would, so," Clare said. "Because she'll tire of it soon enough anyway."

"And we'll still be here," Liz said. "Just minding our own business." Standing so close, Carlene noticed a thin mustache above Clare's lip. She didn't point it out.

"If I were you, I'd be looking out for black swans," Clare said.

"Right, right," Liz said. "Maybe they'll show you where to go next." Then the girls straightened, smiled, and walked away.

"Have a grand day," Clare called over her shoulder.

"Mind yourself," Liz said. Carlene sat on the edge of the cross and waited until the girls disappeared into the mist.

CHAPTER 16

Mud and Secrets

After her encounter with the twins, Carlene went shopping. She wasn't going to let their little warning get her down, not after how happy she'd felt that morning. Why was this happiness thing so weak, so fleeting? Why weren't the twins going after the one person they should really be angry with? Carlene suspected they weren't comfortable expressing anger toward their brother, so she was the next best target. Black swans, flaxseed, and angels. Well, she was here to stay, even if swans did circle over the pub three times. She would simply take it as a sign that she was where she was meant to be. That was the thing about signs, they were open for interpretation. Meaning was in the eye of the beholder.

Carlene was excited to check out her yard and test out her new red rubber boots. She entered the property from the back and surveyed her land. She was blessed with a whole acre behind the pub. The first step she took onto the soft ground startled her. It made a slurping sound like it was a thick, frosty shake and her boot the straw. Carlene yanked her foot up, but the patch of ground had already started to give. Or rather, take, for she felt the earth pulling on her boot, claiming it as its own.

She lost her balance and lurched forward, driving her foot even deeper into the muck. What a shock, how quickly the Irish earth could swallow a red rubber boot.

Down, down, down she sank until she was buried up to her knee. She cried out, and for a second was embarrassed at the desperate bleat of her voice. She sounded like a sheep. *Please,* she silently pleaded, as if it would help, as if she could strike a bargain with the gods. *Not now.* Her pub was so close. She wanted a hot shower and a glass of wine. She wanted to mull over her encounter with the twins. She could see her back porch just over the hill. Maybe the woman at the shoe shop tricked her. Maybe there was some kind of concrete sensor in the bottom of this boot, designed to sink intruding Yanks. The shop woman seemed so friendly, so inquisitive. Carlene found herself telling her she was the pub winner, without hesitating, and the woman seemed happy for her, excited even, yet maybe it was all an act. Carlene glanced down at her free leg, and despite everything, admired her boot.

Carlene had purchased them in siren red, liking the idea that she would be easy to spot, even at a distance, even through the mist.

She looked at her boot again. Be honest. Who wore a red boot up to her knee unless she wanted to get noticed? The mysterious blond woman in tall red boots.

So much for getting anyone's attention now. Her only company was a giant cow twenty feet away, chewing its cud, openly studying Carlene with an almost human curiosity.

"What?" Carlene said. The cow blinked, lowered its head, ripped off another patch of grass, and resumed chewing. Panic, she thought as she took in her surroundings, would not do her any good, would not help rescue her leg from the deep, wet mud.

At least it was no longer raining. The countryside was certainly green. The morning air carried a floral-manure scent across the field. The cow, most likely the one responsible for the manure portion of the morning smell, stepped a few feet closer. He seemed mesmerized by the boot. She could see him wearing

four tall red boots—it would look smashing against his black-
and-white coat. "Help," Carlene said. She'd bought a cell phone
in town, but she didn't have any local numbers. Was 911 universal? Or did Ireland use other numbers? Was it fair to call 911
to ask for a hand out of the mud? Were cows ever dangerous?
Aggressive?

The cow, apparently bored of her, was strolling away. "Hey,"
Carlene yelled. "Help." The sight of the cow leaving filled her
with a profound sense of loneliness. *Cow ass. I'm stuck in the
mud staring at cow ass.* How long before a human stepped into
this field? Would Joe come out for an afternoon stroll? Did people stroll in Ireland? If she had all these green, misty fields, she
would certainly stroll.

Although look where it had gotten her.

Birds flitted through the patch of trees just ahead of her, bolstered her, offered her a tiny ray of hope. How bad could things
be if they were so chirpy? Carlene's good leg was starting to hurt
from supporting all her weight. She put her arms out to her side
and slowly lowered her butt to the ground. That was better.

No, it wasn't. Now her ass was wet, and muddy, and slightly
sinking. Maybe the ground would swallow her up, bury her.
*American woman dies in bog behind pub. Yank swallowed by
swamp.*

Carlene leaned back and pulled her leg as hard as she could.
It loosened slightly. "Thank you," she said to the universe, or
the cow, although she feared neither was listening. She scooted
back a smidge and prepared to pull again. But this time, her leg
sank deeper into the ground.

The first vestiges of panic grabbed hold of her. She would not
die here with her leg stuck in a mud pit, or a bog, or whatever
the hell it was. She would not die before making a go of her pub.
She would not die before making love to Ronan, just once.

A growl interrupted her thoughts. It came from behind her,
off to her right side. Goose bumps prickled her arms. She was
terrified to turn her head. Did cows growl? A dark patch invaded her peripheral vision. It was a dog, a killer dog, and not

only was he emitting a loud, long belly growl, he was baring teeth. Watch out for the bog, the woman at the wellies shop had called out to her as she left. But what if she'd misunderstood the accent? Perhaps she'd said "dog." Watch out for the dog. Either way, this couldn't be good. The cow was nowhere to be seen, Joe apparently did not take afternoon strolls, and even the chirpy birds had flown far, far away.

"Nice doggie" would be a ridiculous thing to say. He was certainly not nice. Obviously, the Irish charm did not apply to their canines. Don't show fear. Was she supposed to look at the dog, or not look at the dog? Don't look at the dog. She was in the submissive position, cowering on the ground. Wait a minute, wasn't she supposed to pretend to be the alpha dog? How could she be the alpha dog if she was cowering on the ground? "Fuck you," she said softly. No reaction. She said it a little bit louder. The growl increased.

"Morely. C'mere." The dog bolted toward the male voice in the distance. She heard his paws smacking happily in and out of the bog. Why wasn't the damn dog sinking? She'd probably stepped on the one and only spot on the property where you were guaranteed to get sucked under.

She heard his approach. Thick boots sloshing in her direction. Heavy boots; boots equipped for a bog. She saw his jeans. Tall, sturdy legs. His rain jacket, long. His baseball cap pulled over his thick, wavy hair, green-gold eyes looking down at her. He didn't speak. He stood over her, staring. "Fancy meeting you here," he said finally. There was definite sarcasm in his tone, and more than a flicker of amusement. It was astounding, like the number of stars in the universe, the nuances carried in his Irish accent.

"What are you doing here?" she said. He knelt down so that they were eye to eye. *There is so much beauty in this,* she thought, staring into his eyes. *Just looking, quietly, up close, into another person's eyes.*

"Is that really what you want to say to me?" Ronan said.

No. I want to say you're beautiful. You smell good. I'm not married. I'm mortified that I said I love you. Obviously I don't love you, I don't even know you. But there's something about you I think I could love.

"About the other night," she said. "I was drunk and I said some things—"

"Forget about it—"

"I'm not married." It felt good to blurt it out. Ronan stared at her for a moment as if she were a safe he was trying to crack.

"Divorced?"

"No."

"So you lied? Because most people tell the truth when they're pissed."

"I wasn't pissed. I was just drunk."

Ronan threw his head back and laughed. "Pissed means drunk," he said. "You'll catch on. We've got a million words for it. Pissed, langered, rat-arsed, gee-eyed, blotto, bollixed, ossified, paralytic, plastered, wasted—"

"I get it, I get it."

"So you're not married and you're not divorced. I believe I'm missing part of this story, Ms. Shakespeare."

"If you don't mind, I'd rather not talk about it while I'm stuck in the mud."

"Fair play."

"Can you pull me out, please?"

"That's what I thought you wanted to say." Ronan sat down on the ground in front of her.

"I stepped in the one and only spot where you can sink, didn't I?" Carlene said.

"Nah," Ronan said. "There's a few more."

"Great. Are you just going to sit there smirking at me, or are you going to help me up?"

"Do I really smirk?"

"Oh yes. You are a big smirker."

"I did not know that."

"Well, now you do."

"I'm learning all sorts of things from you."

"Please. I'm really stuck."

Ronan rubbed his hands together. "All right, all right. I'll sort ye out."

"Thank you."

"But it's going to cost you."

"I'm not giving you back the pub." Carlene hadn't meant for it to come out so harsh. Maybe her encounters with Joe and the twins had affected her more than she thought. But Ronan didn't seem offended; in fact, it elicited another laugh.

"Fair play to ye," he said. "How about a secret?"

"A secret?"

"Tell me something about you that nobody—I mean nobody—knows."

"Why?"

Ronan shrugged. "That's just the going price for helping a lady out of the muck, what can I tell you, Carlena?" She flushed at the nickname, and a rush of warmth spread through her body. He was smirking again, as if he could read her mind, as if he knew without touching her that that her body was reacting to him. She tried to concentrate on his question. A secret. She could tell him about her father's OCD. Or her awful wedding. She could tell him about the orange rabbit—but she'd already confessed that little gem to the dog bowl–obsessed man on the plane. She thought about telling him any number of things, yet instead, something flew out of her mouth that she had never expected to say.

"I can't pee in public."

"That's not a secret. You're a girl."

"No—not like that. If I'm in a public restroom—or even at a house party—and there's a line of people waiting—I can't go. It's called bashful bladder syndrome."

"What?"

"Bashful bladder syndrome."

"It's hard to hear out here." Carlene yelled it. Ronan was laughing so hard his shoulders were shaking. "Sorry," he said. "I actually heard you perfectly the first time."

"It's not funny. It's a serious affliction."

She thought it was the end of the subject, but he was fascinated, wanted to hear all about it. She told him how mortified she was when it first happened. She was ten, at a slumber party. The bathroom was right next to the living room where the six girls were laid out in their sleeping bags. They'd been drinking grape soda all night. They all made a mad dash for the restroom. Carlene reached it first. She remembered the girls giggling and pounding on the door, yelling at her to hurry up. She couldn't go. Not a drop. Her bladder was bursting one minute and just— frozen the next. She knew she still had to go, but her body just wouldn't cooperate. She had to wait until all the girls were fast asleep, until she verified that each one was breathing deep and not faking it, and even then, even running the water and visualizing each girl's sleeping face in her mind, it took her forever to go. And unfortunately, it continued to happen; it still happened.

What kind of person couldn't pee in public? There was a name for the condition, she'd Googled it. Not bladder-block, or tinkle-phobia, or the golden freeze, as Ronan happily suggested, but BBS, bashful bladder syndrome—a mild anxiety disorder, or according to the Internet, "The inability to initiate urine while in the company of others."

"It said that?" Ronan asked.

"It said that," Carlene said.

"Who talks like that?" he said. "Have you ever heard anyone say, 'Were you able to initiate urine?' Ah, the bollix. Did ye take a piss? That's what you'd hear."

Carlene laughed. "Nature calls. And even though I'm standing right in the phone booth, I can't answer." This time they laughed in unison. It was cathartic, somehow, shouting about her pissing problem while stuck in the mud.

"Is it only number one, or is it also—"

"I have never gone—would never *contemplate* going number two in a public place! Ever!"

"Never, not once? Not even after a burrito?"

"Never, not once, especially not after a burrito. Can you please help me up now?"

"What if you're midstream and someone walks in? You're full-on like Niagara Falls—"

"Midstream I keep going," Carlene said. There it was again, that deadly smile of his. He had a dimple, just one, on the left side of his face.

"Thank you," he said. He started to kneel behind her.

"Wait," she said. He stopped. "Now you tell me a secret." He loosened his grip on her, but didn't let go.

"Or what?" he said. "You won't let me pull you out of the mud?" All she knew was that she wanted to stall him, wanted him to keep holding her, wanted to keep feeling his laughter vibrate the base of her spine.

"Please," she said. "Between Joe, and the tree, and the twins, and this defective wellie, I've had a stressful morning."

Ronan's hands immediately dropped from her waist. "What about the twins?" he said. Oh no, why had she said that? The only thing worse than being the woman who swooped in and took over their family business, would be being the woman who tattled.

"That's just what I was calling my wellies," Carlene said. "The twins."

"You're a bit strange, Miss America. Did anyone ever tell you that?"

"I believe you've covered that already. Now will you please tell me a secret?" Ronan settled behind her again, and soon she felt his arms wrap back around her lower body. She wanted to lean back on him, but she didn't want him to think she was snuggling up to him.

"See that empty patch up there?" Ronan stuck his arm out and placed his cheek against hers, so that when he moved his head to the left, he gently pushed hers in that direction. She could feel herself getting turned on again, and mentally told herself to focus. Up ahead she saw what he was pointing at, a bare patch of dirt, abandoned by the grass.

"Yes." She hoped he didn't think she was shaking because of him.

"I used to have a pigeon loft there."

"Like homing pigeons?"

"Racing pigeons. I trained them myself. Had them for years."

"That's a secret?"

"No, Miss America, patience." He waited, and this time she let go and leaned back into him, allowing him to hold her weight. He adjusted his arms and pulled her in tighter. She would show him patience, all right. He could recite *War and Peace* if he liked, and she would just sit there, feeling him, listening to him.

"I reckon those pigeons are the reason I've never settled down with a woman."

Carlene sat up, forcing him to let her go. "What's that, now?" Was this just the famous Irish blarney, or was he going to turn out to have some kind of a fowl fetish? Oh why couldn't she just fall for the nice, normal guy for once in her life? She'd never heard of a fowl fetish, a penchant for pigeons, but you just couldn't count on anything these days.

"Pigeons are loyal," Ronan explained. "Once they're trained that this is home, they'll do anything to get back to it. A fella I knew once gave me one of his racing pigeons when he moved away. The loft wasn't even there anymore, just one stump where it used to be. Every day that pigeon would fly back to it and just keep sitting on that stump, waiting for his original owner to come home."

"That's so sad," Carlene said.

"Every day I'd ride my bike over there and scoop him off the stump, tuck him inside my jacket, and ride back here with him. And every day, he'd go back. Pigeons will fight anything to find their way home. They'll battle storms, hunger, sickness, predators, fear, and still keep flying toward home. I once had a pigeon who was shot at, and he still made it back."

"You are depressing the fuck out of me," Carlene said. Ronan laughed and wrapped his arms around her again.

"That's not depressing," he said. "It's loyalty. It's love."

"So you're saying you haven't settled down because you haven't met a woman who's proved her loyalty by getting shot at, starved, or battling predators to make her way back to you?"

"I'm saying when someone loves you—really loves you— there's this invisible line connecting them to you. You think of each other as home base. And nothing in this world could keep you apart. You're never afraid to let her go, because you know she'll do whatever it takes to come back."

Carlene was silent for a moment. "Who was she?"

"Who was who?" His voice was deeper now, edgier.

"The woman who left you," Carlene said softly. Ronan tensed behind her. He tightened his grip.

"On three," he said. It sounded like, "On tree." She wanted to make a joke about it, but she'd already ruined the mood. He started to count, and then he pulled. Finally, Carlene's leg came up out of the mud. Unfortunately, her new boot did not.

CHAPTER 17

Empty Kegs and Vampires

The next morning, Carlene awoke to a loud clanging noise. It sounded as if it was just outside the house. Was something happening in the shed where the beer kegs were kept? Carlene sat bolt upright in bed. Was it Wednesday? She'd barely slept two hours. Last night, after Ronan rescued her from the mud, she found Ciaran, Anchor, Danny, Eoin, Billy, and Riley circling her back door like stray cats. They just wanted a game of cards and a quiet drink. Couldn't she just let them in? She'd stayed open until four A.M.

It couldn't be much more than six A.M. now. Was the beer man just delivering the kegs, or was she supposed to do something, sign something? She pulled on her jeans, which were lying on the floor beside her bed. Her clothes were always neatly folded and pressed at home. Here, she was still living out of a suitcase, and she loved it. There was nothing like simplifying your life. She pulled on a sweatshirt, slipped on her flip-flops, and went out to the shed. On the ground, in front of the shed, she saw circular impressions, like mini-spaceships, indented in the grass. Keg footprints. No, no, no. She counted six of them. The deliveryman had been here all right, and someone had stolen her kegs. Maybe there was some explanation. Maybe someone had already set them up for her.

She opened the shed. The old kegs were still there. Crossing her fingers anyway, she went over and tipped one. Light as a feather. Even though she knew the outcome, she took a turn tipping each one. They were all empty. And since there was nothing else to do, she went back to the first keg and kicked it. A hollow sound rang out. Even empty, it hurt her foot. Still, pain was better than festering frustration, so she went ahead and kicked every single one of them. Oh, if her regulars could see her now.

She completely forgot that she was supposed to have carried the empty kegs out to the front of the road for the delivery guy to pick up. He was supposed to remove them and leave the full kegs in their place. She was supposed to find someone to help her roll the kegs to the shed. Why didn't someone remind her? And what exactly happened?

It was too early to play detective. However, a few things were apparent. The beer man had indeed arrived at some ungodly hour. Instead of leaving the full kegs by the side of the road, did he roll them down to the shed for her? Doubtful. Otherwise, wouldn't he have checked inside the shed and taken away the empty ones? Good Samaritans usually go all the way, don't they?

So she was dealing with three factors. Beer man arrives, and finding no empty kegs, dumps the full ones out by the side of the road.

Good Samaritan rolls all six kegs down to the front of her shed.

Bad Samaritan comes along and steals her kegs. Unbelievable. Who was involved? Ronan? Joe? The evil twins? Little boys playing pranks? Alcoholic cows?

It didn't matter, she had to fix this. Why couldn't she just have one morning where she woke up, drank coffee in her underwear, and read the newspaper? Was that really too much to ask?

She called the beer man to see if he would take sympathy on her, redeliver the next morning.

"Sympathy," he said, "comes between 'shit' and 'syphilis' in the dictionary." She would have to wait a full week before he could deliver again.

Carlene's regulars would have to survive a whole week without beer on tap. As a consolation prize, she offered the lads two-for-one bottles of beer. Riley, however, wouldn't switch. Instead, she had to lure him with whiskey, generous shots of Jameson that he drank in quick gulps.

"Big daddy," he said as he shuffled to the bathroom. "You're the baddest motherfucker in this bog."

Her regulars. Ciaran, Danny, Anchor, Eoin, Collin, Riley, and Billy. Billy was thrilled the tree was still there and was back to practicing his log roll. Anchor was by the jukebox, playing every heavy-metal song he could find. Carlene didn't understand how loud screaming could be considered music, but the lads loved it. They banged their heads and played air guitar, and even if she did have a splitting headache by the end of the day, the customers were always right. Today Collin's T-shirt read: I CAN ONLY PLEASE ONE PERSON A DAY. TODAY IS NOT YOUR DAY. TOMORROW DOESN'T LOOK GOOD EITHER.

Carlene tried to balance looking busy behind the bar with socializing with the customers. She was starting to get a feel for when they were talking to each other versus when they were including her in the conversation. At the moment, Eoin was treating her to a long list of platitudes, and she was happy to lean on the bar and listen. "There's only two things you really need in life," Eoin said. "A good pair of work boots, and a good mattress. Because if you're not in one, you're in the other." Carlene smiled and nodded, even though she owned neither a good pair of work boots nor a good mattress.

Gradually, she was learning something about each and every one of them. Collin was studying at the University of Galway. Danny was a farmer and aspiring songwriter who still lived with his mother. Eoin and Ciaran were married with kids. Anchor was Ronan's best friend. Billy was afraid of dogs. Carlene was also getting used to their drink orders and arrival times, and so she started to make a game out of having their drinks ready so that by the time their butts hit the stools, she was already sliding the first of many over to them.

Conversational patterns were also becoming predictable. It often started out slow. A simple, How ya, What's the craic, What's the story, Damn all, damn all. Then it would shift to a few comments about the weather. If it wasn't raining, it was a grand fresh day; if it was raining, Ah, 'tis miserable, sure.

When the conversation switched to sports, Carlene had to flee. She had no idea who the players or teams were, or what sport they were even on about. There were too many to keep track. Hurling, and rugby, and Gaelic football, and road bowling, and football—which was American soccer—and sometimes American football, and whatever it was, they analyzed it in great detail and with even greater passion. Once, when Carlene made the mistake of casually asking a question during one of their sports discussions, Eoin immediately whipped coasters, straws, glasses, and salt shakers from the bar and set up an elaborate demonstration, after which a wall of expectant faces stared at her until she gave a hearty reaction. She made the appropriate noises and exclamations, but all Carlene really learned was that the salt jumped over the coaster and headbutted the pepper before knocking down the red straws. She never asked for clarification again, although she knew if one of the lads was in a particularly sour mood, more often than not it had to do with one of his teams losing.

Carlene would listen carefully when they started in on local politics, trying to soak up as much as she could about the way things worked in Ballybeog. She was a little more lost when it came to Irish politics, and the scapegoat whenever they discussed the United States. They asked her so many questions about President Obama, it was as if they regarded her as his long-lost cousin.

Geography was another favorite topic, especially for Anchor. He would spit out trivia questions about this or that island, river, country, or capital, and Carlene would scurry away as fast as she could, busy herself in absolutely anything else so they couldn't accuse her of being one of those Americans who couldn't find the Middle East on a map. She made a mental note to start studying maps.

Danny loved to talk about music, and songs, and celebrities. They all liked to flirt with Carlene and fired numerous questions at her about her life, as if she was a puzzle they were trying to put together piece by piece. She often side-stepped these questions as well, it was best to keep any possible rumors at bay.

It wasn't until after the first few weeks of getting to know her regulars, that really personal information started to leak out of them. Ciaran was the first to start an all-out confession, and Carlene was thrilled to try out the psychologist role of bartender. He was in a mood, drinking twice as fast, and it had something to do with his wife, or "herself" as he referred to her. Carlene prodded him and plied him with drinks until he finally started to talk.

"For fuck's sake," Ciaran said. "It's herself. She's reading about some vampire. Everything is 'Edward this' and 'Edward that' and 'He's so passionate' and 'He's all over her like,' and whenever this chick in the book needs him he's like, 'there in a flash.'" Ciaran stopped and sipped from his bottle. The other lads were listening too, even though some of them were staring elsewhere, as if lost in their own thoughts. Carlene was dying to say something, but she held back, and sure enough, Ciaran kept talking.

"And he's beautiful, and his fecking eyes change color or some shite, and I'm some unromantic bollix who can't measure up to a fecking vampire." A few of the lads nodded in agreement. Riley scratched his chin and frowned. "I mean, what's so romantic about sucking on someone's neck?" Ciaran said. There were a few chortles, which Ciaran cut down with a look. "Feasting on their blood, for fuck's sakes."

"I once cut off a chicken's head in front of a bird and she didn't speak to me for an entire week," Danny said. Ciaran kept talking as if Danny hadn't spoken.

"And I donated last year when that fucking blood drive van came around, and do ye think she appreciated that? No. I didn't even get a fucking cookie. Just orange juice that tasted like shite. Throw me out a couple of bottles, will ye, Yankee Doodle?"

"Before he bites you on the neck," Anchor said.

"I read that book," Carlene said. She popped the top of a bottle of Budweiser and slid it to Ciaran. She took his empty bottle and threw it in the recycling bin.

"Oh, that's just fecking great," Ciaran said.

"It's not the bloodsucking that's romantic," Carlene said. "It's the thought of a man giving you undivided attention."

"You've got my undivided attention, luv," Eoin said. He held up his half-full beer.

"I can only imagine what would happen to that attention if I ran out of beer," Carlene said, serving him another, even though he wasn't finished with the one in front of him. Eoin threw his hands over his ears. Ciaran leaned over and put his hands over Eoin's eyes. Danny flew over an empty stool to slap his hands over Eoin's mouth. Eoin pushed them all off, and they laughed.

"Did ye cop on?" Eoin asked.

"Hear no evil, speak no evil, see no evil," Carlene said.

"She's not as dumb as she looks," Riley said.

"Not the dullest knife in the drawer," Ciaran said.

"Not the dimmest bulb in the bunch," Anchor said.

"Just a couple of fries short of a Happy Meal," Carlene said. They just stared at her. "Never mind."

"Any time I try to pay her undivided attention, she just rolls over," Ciaran said.

"That can be good too," Eoin said. "Back-door loving."

"Watch it," Ciaran said. "That's my wife you're talking about." Anchor shouted at her to turn the music up. His head was bobbing up and down so fast she was afraid it was going to fly off.

"I can do that?" she asked. "How do I do that?"

"While you're at it, would you dim the lights too? I don't really want to see what these wankers look like," Eoin said. They showed her how to turn up the music, a small dial set into the back of the bar, and another one to control the lights. Carlene didn't know she had so much control. Every discovery was delicious, like finding you had additional rooms in your house you didn't even know about. Although she still didn't like heavy-metal music, and every time she inched the volume up a notch, Anchor jerked his thumb in the air. Louder, louder.

So much for the live bands she pictured playing traditional Irish music. She was going to have to ask around and find local musicians to come and play. Anchor sang at the top of his lungs. She couldn't understand how he could understand the words. She turned back to Ciaran.

"I wasn't just talking about attention in the bedroom," she said. "I'm talking about showing a passion for her life, her dreams, her wishes. I'm talking about physically missing the scent of him when he's away."

Collin jerked his head up. "Him?" he said.

"Yeah," Eoin said. "Whose smell are you on about?" He leaned over and sniffed Collin on his right, then Ciaran on his left. They all laughed. Carlene hoped her face wasn't as flushed as it felt.

"Her," she said quickly. She'd been thinking about Ronan, the scent of him. Suddenly, she hated him, hated him for always smelling so good. Why else would you wear such nice cologne unless you were trying to torture someone?

"You have to love her fucking chairs," Danny said. Everyone just looked at him. *"Premonition?"* he said. "John Travolta? Gets struck by lightning and gets all psychic, like, and falls in love with this woman who makes chairs, you know what I mean?"

"No," Anchor said. "We haven't a fucking clue."

"Great fillum, you eejits. Great fillum," Danny said. He shook his head at Carlene, like, "Get a load of them."

"Gay, gay, gay," Ciaran said. "Yous all are gay. I'm not falling for fucking chairs and I'm not going to be sniffing after her either. So let's just change the fucking subject."

"I agree," Collin said. "You can't chase after a woman. She'll lose interest."

"See?" Ciaran said. "I'll be the bollix who gets kicked to the curb for being sensitive." He looked at Carlene. "Gay," he said. "Very fucking gay."

"You'll end up like Sally with Ronan," Danny said. The rest grunted in agreement.

"Sally?" Carlene said. "Who is Sally?"

"You could do worse than being stalked by Sally," Eoin said.

"Sally who?" Carlene said.

"Still, it's a turn-off," Collin said. "When someone is that in love with you."

"Got all those college chicks falling all over you, do you, stud?" Anchor said. He also looked conspiratorially at Carlene and rolled his eyes.

"There was this girl from photography class," Collin said. "We worked in the darkroom together every day like."

"That's what you want," Anchor said. "A woman surrounded by darkness. When she comes out, she's like blinded by you."

"Did you ride her or what?" Ciaran said.

"If he'd a known he was going to get a ride, he would've worn lipstick," Anchor said. Carlene started to wonder if she should cut them off.

"Nothing happened," Collin said. "You know why? Because I started paying too much attention to her. Totally screwed the pooch. You have to make a major effort to look like you don't give a shit," Collin said. "You have to be careful."

"I'm careful," Danny said. "I change me address every three months." Carlene lined six shot glasses up on the bar and poured whiskey into each one of them. She set them in front of her boys.

"What's this for?" Anchor said.

"Customer appreciation," Carlene said. "Now. Who's Sally?" Before they could answer, Riley let out a shout. Behind him stood a man in a police uniform. He was tall and thin, with a thick mustache. He kind of looked like the man on the painted sign at Dally's Lounge, Undertaker, and Pub. Riley pointed to him.

"Does anybody else see the guard?" Riley said. "Or is it just me?" Carlene hurried over and turned down the music. The policeman, or guard as the lads called him, rubbed his ears.

"Are you Carlene Rivers, the new publican?" the guard asked.

"Yes sir," Carlene said.

"I'm Michael Murphy," he said. "We've had a complaint about the noise."

"From who?" Anchor said. "A cow?"

"I'm so sorry," Carlene said. "I'll keep it down from now on."

"See that you do," he said. "I won't write you up this time, seeing as how you're new in town and all."

"Thank you," Carlene said. "Would you like a drink?" She was about to suggest tea or a soda when he took off his hat, rubbed his bald head, and nodded.

"Just a wee pint," he said. "I'm on duty."

CHAPTER 18

A Man Walks into the Kitchen

Some days, not an ounce of intelligent conversation floated around the bar, but Carlene could usually count on a couple of good jokes. Today, Eoin had one to tell.

"A man walks into his kitchen with a chicken under his arm. The wife is at the sink, doing the dishes. The man says, 'I want you to meet the pig I've been fucking.' The wife turns around and sees the chicken. 'That's not a pig,' the wife says. 'That's a chicken.' The man looks at the wife and says, 'I wasn't talking to you.' "

Everyone laughed except Billy, who was playing pool by himself and didn't quite catch it. He stopped and propped his chin up on top of the pool stick.

"Say it again," he said. "Man walks into the kitchen with a turkey under his arm, and what?"

"It wasn't a turkey, it was a duck," Danny said.

"It was a chicken," Ciaran said.

"Doesn't matter," Collin said. "Could have been a turkey, could have been a duck."

"What do you mean it doesn't matter?" Eoin said. "It was a fucking chicken." He pointed at Billy. "Not a fucking turkey."

He pointed at Danny. "Not a fucking duck." He leaned into Collin. "A chicken."

"Fuck a duck," Riley said. "I'm the baddest motherfucker in this bog."

"Yes, you are," Carlene said.

"I'm just saying that the punch line isn't contingent on what barnyard animal he had under his arm," Collin said.

"Listen to the college boy," Anchor said. "Contingent."

"I know you said chicken. But the joke still works if it's a turkey, or duck, or whatever," Collin said.

"Right," Ciaran said. "I see where you're coming from."

"What about a pig, smarty pants?" Eoin said. "It couldn't be a pig." He nodded at Carlene.

"You're right," Collin said. "It couldn't be a pig."

"Why not?" Danny asked.

"Because when he says, 'I want you to meet the pig I've been fucking,' the missus would just turn around and say, 'Oh hello,' " Collin said.

"Right, right," Danny said. "It couldn't be a pig, so."

"If I was screwing a pig, the missus would have a lot more to say about it than 'Oh hello,' " Riley said.

"I still don't get it," Billy said.

"That's because they've made a complete bollix out of me joke," Eoin said.

"You've got to build to the punch," Danny said.

"I'll give yous a punch," Eoin said.

"Whatever the yoke is under his arm, the point is, he's calling his wife a pig," Collin said.

"Look at Carlene's face, like," Ciaran said. "I think we're effing and blinding too much for her."

"You could clean it up," Danny said. "You could say—the turkey I've been screwing."

"It's a fucking chicken!" Eoin said.

"The bird I've been riding," Danny said.

"It's the pig I've been fucking," Eoin said. "The Yank can take it. Can't ye, Yank?"

"At least the wife is doing the dishes," Billy said. After that, Carlene gratefully lost track of the conversation.

Dear Becca,

Thank you so much for your letter, it meant so much to me. I'm so glad baby Shane is doing well. I showed his picture to all the lads at the bar, and even though they didn't come out and say it, I could tell they thought he was cute. They saw your picture too and had no problem saying how cute you were! It's hard to believe Shane can start Irish dancing lessons so young! How does that work, since I assume he's not even crawling yet? (Sorry, just curious.) And that's sweet that you've been playing him "Danny Boy," I'm sure he'll enjoy it that much more when he comes for a visit. Can you believe I've almost been here a month? I think I'm really starting to get the hang of being a bartender. I feel like I'm part waitress, part psychologist, part babysitter, and part eye candy. The boys do like to flirt, and of course I flirt right back—and it's not even for tips because they don't tip in Ireland! I didn't remember that until after the first week of no tips, and I thought, God, they must really hate me. But they don't, they love me, and even though they cuss a lot, it's not much different than working at the gym. Still surrounded by sweaty men, except the only exercise these ones are getting is lifting their pints. Actually, though, they're funny, and smart, and interesting. I'm starting to think of my regulars like turtles— they carry their stories on their backs!

The worst part of the job is cleaning the jacks— that's bathrooms for you Yanks—it's the one time I become a little bit like my father, with rubber gloves, and masks, and ritualistic cleaning. Yesterday Billy threw up behind the pool table. That was pretty

*disgusting—but it's all part of the job. He said it
must have been something he ate. Not the twelve
pints he drank, mind you.*

*I can't believe how much they can drink here, but
they really seem to hold it well. Riley isn't so good
on the whiskey, makes him talk to himself. He likes
to say, "Big Daddy, you're the baddest motherfucker
in this bog." It's kind of funny, but it also makes me
kind of sad. Could be the rain. It has a way of
dragging you down. That said, the sun was out all
day the other day and I felt like I was on heroin, it
was such a high. No, I've never done heroin—but I
can imagine how it feels now!*

*Both the men and women here have a habit of
calling me pet, or chicken, or bird—which kind of
put me in a fowl mood at first, ha-ha (remind me to
tell you a joke about a man who walks into his
kitchen with a chicken under his arm)—but now I
kind of like the endearments.*

*There are a few about town who aren't so crazy
about me, and the neighbor cut down a beautiful
tree in my front yard, and someone stole my beer
kegs, and I think I was slightly threatened by the
McBride twins—but it's really not as bad as it
sounds.*

*I'm going to try to get a computer and Internet
connection in here, and when I do I'll make sure to
send you some pictures. The food here is delicious,
but thank goodness I do a lot of walking, because
it's not exactly the macrobiotic diet Dad follows.
Speaking of which, I know he'd love to see the
baby—and I know it's a pain getting rubber gloves
to fit such a tiny infant, but if you do get around to
visiting him, I'd really appreciate knowing how he
is. I've talked to him a few times on the phone, but
it's just not the same. I'm trying to talk him into
coming for Christmas but he just keeps saying,*

"We'll see." You and little Shane and Levi are welcome during the holidays too! Although there's no room to sleep at the bar, but plenty of B&Bs.

You'll be happy to know I found a little café here, run by an adorable woman named Nancy—every other sentence out of her mouth is "Not a bother!" and she really means it. She makes the best cappuccino in town—I dare say it even rivals the Cleveland Cup. Although I do miss hanging out there with you.

Love you!

Carlene

P.S. To answer your questions: No, I'm not married to an Irishman yet. And no, I'm not getting any. And yes, I do have kind of a crush on someone, the one man around here I shouldn't have a crush on, and I haven't even seen him for a few weeks, and he's mad to gamble and probably has a string of girlfriends— oh, I know what you're thinking, another Brendan—you'll never believe it but I got totally wasted at my welcome party and ended up telling him about Brendan—among a few other things, but that confession will have to wait for a face-to-face!

Dear Dad,

Thank you for your postcard. I think it took longer to arrive because of all the plastic. Business is going well, and I really love it here in Ireland. It's so green. How is the gym? Please say hello to the boys for me! Hope you're still putting some thought into coming for Christmas.

Love,

Carlene

At first, Carlene loved having "her men" to herself, but now it was really starting to bother her that no women came into the pub. She knew women in Ireland went to pubs—they had hen nights, and ladies' darts and cards, and girls' nights. But they weren't coming here. Besides Nancy, whom she'd already invited, and the half dozen, who probably found it too painful to come, Carlene needed to meet more women. Maybe she should check out this Sally girl the regulars had mentioned. She loved her regular lads, but she needed a little estrogen to balance out the place. The conversation had grown stale lately as well.

He's getting it on with the Clancy girl, the missus doesn't know—

The missus doesn't want to know—

Me mam's in the hospital again—

Me father's tipping away—

She hadn't seen or heard from Ronan in weeks, and it was driving her mad. Where was he working now? Was he out gambling away his life? Was he seeing anyone? Thank goodness Becca couldn't read minds—she would have arrived in a flash, performing some kind of intervention. No more Irish men, she reminded herself every night as she fell asleep. No more Irish men.

CHAPTER 19

When One Door Closes

Something was underneath Carlene's dresser, scratching, clawing madly away at the wood. She ran out of the room, slammed the door, and flew down to the bar, where she picked up the phone and then slammed it down again because she didn't know whom to call. She ran next door where she found Joe and Declan standing in front of the shop.

"Are you okay, pet?" Declan asked the minute she ran up.

"There's something underneath my dresser," Carlene said. "Scratching."

"Scratching?" Joe said. Declan scratched his head. Carlene scratched her head. Joe scratched his chin.

"It sounds like a squirrel or a rat. I really hope it's not a rat. I cannot handle a rat."

"Let's go take a look," Declan said. To her surprise, Joe also followed them over. The three of them stood inside the bar and looked up at her bedroom door. "Do you have anything to catch it in?" Declan said.

"Like what?" Carlene said. Declan held up his hand and then disappeared down the hall. He came back with a broom and a box. Joe stood studying the wall where the bathrooms were located. Declan headed upstairs. The minute he opened her bedroom door, something furry darted between his legs and headed for the stairs. Carlene screamed as the thing flew down, a tiny, dark whirling ball. At the bottom, it skidded, tried to get its balance, and slid across the mopped floors until it came to a stop underneath the pool table.

"You know," Joe said. "I think this wall is actually on my property line." Declan ran down the steps. Carlene thought her chest was going to explode. She waited for the thing to come out. When after a moment it didn't, she kept her distance, dropped to her hands and knees, and looked underneath the pool table.

"I'll get it, chicken," Declan said. He waved the broom.

"Wait," Carlene said. "I think it's a cat." She crept closer. It was indeed a tiny black trembling kitten. Carlene cooed, and whispered, and coaxed until the poor thing stopped quivering. She reached in, plucked him out, and held him up to her chest. Declan tried to hand her the box.

"No thanks," she said.

"Black cat," Declan said. "Bad luck, isn't it?" Carlene kissed the kitten's tiny head.

"I only believe in good luck," she said.

"I'm going to have to get the property deed out and have a look at this wall," Joe said. "If I'm right, you're going to have to move the pub about three feet to the right."

Ballybeog's Department of Planning Commissioner, or whatever his title was, paced the wall with the property deed in his hand, measuring and muttering. Mike, the guard, was also present, along with Joe.

"I don't know," the commissioner said finally. "You could argue that a small portion of the wall is exactly on the property line, but if you took it all the way to court, the judge could go either way."

"Joe," Carlene said. "This is so silly. If you want tanning beds so bad, why don't you just expand your own store?"

"You can't expand into a bog," Joe said. "This is the perfect place for Tan Land."

"Well, take me to court, then, but I think we're done here," Carlene said.

"In the meantime," Joe said. "I reckon I should charge you rent for the walls."

"You've got to be kidding me," Carlene said.

"Mike? Can I do that?" Joe asked. The guard looked at the commissioner. The commissioner flicked his eyes between Joe and Carlene and then finally shook his head.

"You'd have to go through a judge," the commissioner repeated.

"Is she allowed to have animals in this establishment?" Joe said. The kitten was sitting on top of the bar, licking himself.

"Oh my God," Carlene said. "You just won't quit, will you?"

"That could indeed be a health violation," Mike said. The kitten had its leg straight up in the air, giving them a full-on on shot of its crotch. Carlene had no idea if it was male or female. Female, she hoped, since there were so few of them in the bar. Carlene lifted the kitten off the bar and set her down.

"I think members of the guard would be more respected with a tan," Joe said. "Feared even."

"You reckon?" Mike said. He lifted his pale face as if searching out the sun.

"People would think you've been someplace warm. Like the tropics, or Mexico, or 'Nam. Someplace violent and warm."

"I disagree," Carlene said. "A pale face says you can handle the cold. It says strength. Siberia."

"Siberia," Mike said. He pushed out his chest.

"What about the cat?" Joe said. "Is it a violation? I mean it was just up on the bar flashing everybody its hoo-ha."

"Unbelievable," Carlene said.

"It was obscene," Joe said.

"You know," Carlene said. "Cats need things. Toys, food, litter. Maybe a little kitty bed. You have all those things at the shop, don't you?" Joe didn't respond, but his lips were moving as if he was totaling up her purchases in his head. She turned to Mike. "I'll keep him out on the back porch," she said. Mike nodded.

"The porch would be all right, so," he said. He looked at Carlene's front door, which was still walled off with plywood. "This, however, is a clear violation. Blocking an exit." He took out a pad of paper and jotted something down.

"I'll have it fixed today," Carlene said. "I promise."

"It's too late," Joe said. "He already said 'violation.' I suppose you'll have to shut her down?"

"What do you think you're doing, Uncle Joe?" Startled, Carlene turned to find Ronan standing behind her.

"You heard the guard, it's a violation," Joe said.

"You're lucky she didn't press charges," Ronan said. "I'm pretty sure cutting down the tree branch was a violation—not to mention the damage it did to the door." He turned to Mike. "I'm going to fix it today," he said. "And we've plenty of witnesses to prove that yer man here is the reason this doorway is blocked." Mike took Joe aside, and he must have had words of wisdom, for shortly thereafter Joe took his leave. But not before looking at the kitten, who was once again curled up in Carlene's arms. Joe pointed at it.

"Is that thing old enough to be away from his mother?"

"Are you?" Carlene said. She couldn't believe it had just come out of her mouth. Joe shook his head and walked out the door. Ronan laughed and laughed. It was a deep, joyous sound, which lasted long after Joe was gone.

Ronan had instructions for her, along with a list. She was to go to the hardware shop in town and pick up supplies. Anchor and Eoin were coming over to help install the new door. It was from a pub in town that had closed down years ago, a beautiful, sturdy, arched wood door with a brass handle and little yellow window at the top. Carlene loved it. She stared at Ronan, who stood, hands on hips, intently studying the door. He caught her staring at him.

"What?" he said.

"Why are you always just showing up here right when I need you?"

"Why are you saying it like it's a bad thing?"

"I'm starting to feel like I owe you. What does rescuing a damsel in distress go for these days?"

"Free pints," Anchor said.

"Hear, hear," Riley said. He was sitting on his stool, watching the lads prepare to work. Ronan passed by Carlene as if reaching for something behind her.

"I'll get back to you on that," he whispered.

I'll get back to you on that. Carlene played the comment over and over again in her head, and each time it made her shiver. But she would not spend the rest of the day obsessing on it like some kind of schoolgirl. Where had he been for the past few weeks anyway? She didn't know where he was living or what he was doing with himself, or where he was working, or where he slept, or absolutely anything, really, about the man at all.

Brendan had been like that. He'd sweep in like a tornado, exciting, fast, and utterly devastating, always leaving his destruction behind for her to clean up. And she'd done it, like a fool, she'd come to give him special allowances, knowing if she wanted him in her life at all, she'd have to bend the rules for him, let him get away with things that she wouldn't have accepted from an American man. It shamed her now, how much she let him get away with. Little lies she believed, weeks without a call, then suddenly he was there lavishing her with round-the-clock attention, romantic gestures, little gifts, and talks of the future. Their sex life was lacking, but Carlene chalked it up to his drinking. He swore he didn't have a problem—"it's just the Irish way"—he'd say whenever she would urge him to get help.

So she made excuses for him. He drank too much because it was so accepted in his culture, he practically grew up in a pub, and Americans were too judgmental about drinking. So what if she found him passed out in front of her apartment door more than once? So what if sometimes he didn't remember their conversations the next day? So what if he married her during a blackout? Maybe her grandmother had cursed her when she regaled her with stories of James and Charles, the wickedly handsome black sheep.

Brendan Hayes, professional boxer from Northern Ireland. On their first date, she realized that's why he looked familiar, she'd heard his name mentioned and seen a few posters advertising his fights. It was uncanny, meeting him at a bar in Boston, and not at her father's gym. Coincidence? Curse? Luck of the draw? Brendan swore it was fate. She swallowed that notion too, along with all his other crazy ideas.

We should get married. . . .

Never again, wasn't that what she told herself? Wasn't there supposed to be some sort of lesson learned from the pain you went through? Otherwise, you were little more than a hamster on a wheel, endlessly spinning but never getting anywhere. The days she spent crying, and worrying, and pacing, and turning down decent men who asked her out, just because she had a tiny, tiny dredge of hope that he might come back. But life didn't have to be that way. No more Irish men, Carlene reminded herself. No more obsessing about Ronan McBride.

The hardware shop was in the middle of town, right next to Finnegan's, a little pub she'd been meaning to check out. The exterior of the pub was white, and trimmed in black. It had a little storefront window displaying Laurel and Hardy figurines. Finnegan's also had an off-license, which Carlene had come to learn was a liquor store. But she'd have to pay a visit to the pub another day; today she had a list, and a purpose.

Carlene entered the hardware store. Like Joe's shop, it was bigger than it looked on the outside. And like Joe's, the shelves were crammed, every available space in use. Carlene stood irresolute, more than a little overwhelmed. Suddenly, a petite girl with long black hair and breasts too large for her little frame popped in front of her. She was dressed in jeans, a long man's work shirt, and a brown apron. But the macho look stopped there. She was covered head to toe in sequins and crystals.

"Are you looking to get rid of a pest?" she said. Her voice was surprisingly strong for such a small girl.

"Pardon?" Carlene said.

"You got a rat, lad?" The girl pointed to the shelf behind Carlene. Carlene turned to find she was standing in front of mousetraps and rodent killing products.

"Actually," Carlene said. "I need an axe. Among other things." The girl's eyes widened.

"Kind of cruel, don't you think?" she said.

"It's not that kind of rat," Carlene said. "This one walks on two legs." The girl studied her as if she was contemplating calling for help. "I'm putting a new door in," Carlene said. "I don't actually have a rat. Just a kitten. Who I adore, by the way, and no harm is going to come to him, of course."

"Oh," the girl said.

"You looked at me like I was Lizzie Borden or something," Carlene said. The girl's unwavering stare continued. "You know. Lizzie Borden took an axe, gave her mother forty whacks? And when she had seen what she had done, she gave her father forty-one?" *Guess that one didn't make it across the pond,* Carlene thought, since no recognition, only deeper suspicion grew in the girl's eyes.

"Maybe you should speak with me father," the girl said. "He handles the tools."

"I like your sparkles," Carlene said. "Hi, I'm Carlene." Bingo. The girl smiled. "Sally," she said. "I'm a bedazzler."

"A bedazzler?"

"A year ago I ordered Bedazzle Me from an infomercial. Since then I've kind of been unstoppable, like. I bedazzle everything I can get me hands on. Rhinestones, crystals, studs. This is my father's shop. He thought I was absolutely useless until I started bedazzling the birds who come in. I bedazzle their purses, T-shirts, trousers, trainers, sunglasses. Even their knickers." This last bit was imparted with a smile and a barklike laugh. Carlene laughed too, although she was fighting to get the image out of her mind of this girl and Ronan, lying together on a blinding, bedazzled bed.

It was as if she read her mind. Sally leaned forward and lowered her voice slightly, which meant she was now speaking in a normal tone of voice instead of shouting. "There's only one thing in this town I haven't bedazzled yet," she said. "But I'm working on that one, if you know what I mean." Oh, Carlene was pretty sure she knew what she meant. And she certainly knew *whom* she meant. There was a synergy that existed between women who loved the same man, a connection you could feel, like dread, in the pit of your stomach. Carlene felt the urge to flee, and an equal urge to stay and glean everything she could about Sally.

"Are you sure you need an axe to get rid of this two-legged rat?" Sally said. "How about I give you a pair of heavy work boots and you just kick him up the arse? I could even bedazzle the boot for ye."

"As tempting as that sounds," Carlene said. "I'd better stick to the list." A burly man in overalls, carrying a large ladder, tried to pass unseen behind Sally. He would have had plenty of room had she just moved up a smidge. Instead, Sally turned on him.

"Can't you see I'm standing here, so?" she said. The man halted, blushed.

"Sorry," he said.

"Yes, you are," Sally said. "Didn't you know it's bad luck to pass behind a lady with a ladder?"

"I thought it was the other way around," the man said. "It's not bad luck if the ladder is passing you, it's bad luck if you're passing under the ladder. In the first case—"

"I know what you're on about, I just don't want to be taking any chances, so," Sally said. She put her hands on her hips and stared until the man finally began to back up with the ladder, taking the long way around instead.

"That's me father," Sally said when he was gone. "I swear I'm going mental in this place. Let's go get you an axe, so," she said.

Carlene bought an axe, paint, nails, screws, and hinges. She also bought kitty litter, cat food, and a cat bed. Despite her earlier proclamation, Joe didn't deserve her business.

Sally efficiently rang her up and insulted at least three more male customers while helping Carlene. They all apologized.

"You should come work for me," Carlene said.

"Where's that, lad?" Sally said. They stared at each other. Carlene figured Sally knew exactly who she was, but she played along anyway.

"Uncle Jimmy's Pub," she said.

"Ah, right, right," Sally said. She took off her apron and screamed for her father. He poked his head around the corner, as if afraid to show his entire body. "This is me two minutes' notice," Sally said. Her father looked at his watch, then raised his hand and nodded. Sally stood there for another minute, then threw her apron across the room. "Right, so, lad," Sally said. "Let's go."

CHAPTER 20

Bewitched, Bothered, and Bedazzled

You should come work for me. It was a joke, a flippant remark. It came with an implied *ha-ha!* Although Sally had a little silver car, so at least Carlene didn't have to pay for a taxi. Now here they were, standing in the pub, Ronan's mouth absolutely agape, Sally shooing Riley out of the pub with a broom. Ronan looked at Carlene, looked at Sally, looked at Carlene. She shrugged. What was she to say? *I didn't really hire her, but I'm deathly afraid of her so here's our new barmaid?*

Carlene didn't even know if she even had enough to pay her. Sally came back into the bar shaking out the broom. Carlene glanced at Riley's empty bar stool.

"I didn't mind him here early," Carlene said. "He must be so lonely."

"So's the missus," Sally said.

"Riley's married?" Carlene said.

"Forty-something years," Sally said.

"You've heard him go on about the wife, haven't you?" Anchor said.

"I always thought he was joking around," Carlene said. "My God. His poor wife."

"Don't you go feeling sorry for everyone," Sally said. "She's probably thrilled to bits to have him out of her hair. Pub widows spend a lot of time whining, but once their fellas are back in the house, they don't know what to do with them. It's not long before they're begging them to go back to the pub." Carlene didn't comment. Personally, she would hate being married to a man who was always off to the pub. But it was such an ingrained part of the culture here. And American men often stayed late at the office or the gym, or were glued to the television, or secretly watched hundreds of hours of porn on the Internet. At least at the pub there was human interaction.

There were jokes, laughter, music, and conversation. True, sometimes she could feel her brain cells being picked off one by one, but other days the conversations were just as brilliant as she imagined back in Paris in coffeehouses in the twenties where great minds solved the world's problems on a lazy Sunday afternoon over cups of tea, or coffee, or buckets of absinthe.

"I just wonder why the wives never come," Carlene said. "Or any women at all, for that matter."

"Oh, that's just because the women here don't like you," Sally said. It was said with such frankness, almost friendliness, that Carlene wasn't sure she heard her correctly at first.

"I'm sorry," Carlene said. "What?"

"Carlene?" Ronan said. "Would you like to come over and help me hold this door?"

"I'll do it," Sally said. She was there in a flash. And if Carlene wasn't mistaken, she'd unbuttoned the top few buttons of her work shirt. She stood as close to Ronan as she could get; the top of her head barely came to his chin.

"They don't even know me," Carlene said. "How can they hate me?"

"You're American," Sally said. "They wonder why you'd want to come over here and try to take what's ours when you live in the land of plenty." The candy, Good & Plenty, in its hideous pink, purple, white, and black rectangular box floated through Carlene's mind. She caught Ronan's eye, and he shook his head slightly.

"Somebody had to win the pub," Carlene said. "I'm so sick of being blamed for this." Was she going to cry? Were there actually tears coming to her eyes? And what was this girl doing here, standing underneath Ronan, all unbuttoned? Carlene didn't want to stare, but she was pretty sure Sally had crystals glued to her cleavage. "It wasn't my decision to raffle the pub off to Yanks," Carlene said. "And by the way—we're not all that bad."

"I'm just trying to answer your question, pet," Sally said. "Give you the overall picture."

"Thank you, Sally, you can move now," Ronan said.

"The half dozen like me," Carlene said. "Well, four of them, anyway."

"Which two don't like you?" Ronan said. Oh, why did she open her mouth again? She hadn't meant to start on any of this.

"The door looks beautiful," Carlene said.

"Which two?" Ronan said.

"I was just kidding."

"Which two?"

"The twins, okay?"

"Liz and Clare?"

"It's nothing," Carlene said. "Maybe I misunderstood."

"Misunderstood what?" Ronan said.

"It's just that—I ran into them at the abbey the other day."

"And?"

"Did you hear that?" Sally said. "The abbey." She gave Ronan a look. The kind of look you share with a lover over an inside joke. Ronan, Carlene noticed, didn't seem to engage in it. Despite her own feelings for Ronan, Carlene almost felt sorry for Sally. It was painful, watching her throw herself at him. She could definitely use a little American advice à la *He's Just Not That Into You,* but Carlene kept her mouth shut.

"Carlene, I'm not going to ask you again," Ronan said. "What did the twins do?"

"Seriously, Ronan," Carlene said. "Nothing, really. I just got the feeling they didn't want me around here."

"Told you," Sally said.

"I'll speak with them," Ronan said.

"No," Carlene said. "That will only make it worse. It will make me look like I can't stand up for myself."

"They're my sisters," Ronan said. "It's me they should be giving out to."

"I agree," Carlene said. "But please, just drop it. For me?" The minute Carlene said it, Sally's head snapped toward her. Carlene didn't dare glance in her direction. Ronan gave Carlene a nod and turned back to the door. Anchor and Eoin stood back from the door and gestured. Ronan opened and closed it. It squeaked.

"Bollix," Ronan said.

"I love it," Carlene said.

"It squeaks," Ronan said. "We'll fix it."

"No," Carlene said. "I love it. It's better than a bell."

After putting in her new door, the lads didn't hang around long. Carlene even offered them a pint, but they all had somewhere else to be. It startled Carlene; she'd almost stopped seeing them as people who had lives outside of her bar. And was Ronan really just going to disappear on her again? What about the little flirtation from earlier? The hurried, whispered, "I'll get back to you on that"? Get back to her when?

Sally, that's what happened to it. Did Ronan know that Carlene knew that Sally was in love with him? Did he think she'd personally hired his stalker?

Sally touched everything behind the bar, rubbed her hands against every surface, as if sizing up what could fall victim to her Bedazzle Me. None of them, was the answer, now Carlene just had to bring herself to say it out loud. Carlene went to the back counter and picked up the one photograph in the bar that belonged to her. It was taken the night of her welcoming party, with her and the half dozen. They were all smiling at Carlene, had their arms around her. She knew she was being slightly childish and should just let the subject drop, but she couldn't. She thrust the picture at Sally.

"See," she said. "They threw me a party. They wanted this picture with me. I really, really think the half dozen like me." At least four of them. "They were so friendly," Carlene added.

"Ah, pet," Sally said. "Irish women will always be friendly to you. It doesn't mean they like you. This was their pub. Their livelihood. Do you think they wanted to lose it overnight? In a poker game? I'll tell ye how much they like you. They like you slightly more than a tanning bed, that's how much they like you."

"Oh," Carlene said. She grabbed a rag and cleaning polish. She set upon the bar, wiping it down in a circular motion, counting as she did. Stranger yet, she had an urge to go in the backyard and pace. She suddenly missed her father. She wanted him there. Even if it meant putting on rubber gloves. She would happily spend the next eight hours silently scrubbing by his side. She would pace the bog without complaining. At home, sometimes she made a game out of their pacing. She'd listen to the sounds of the neighborhood, those you would only hear at two A.M. Crickets. The breeze through the trees. Cars going by, their shoes swishing in unison in the soft grass. They could have made an Olympic event out of it; synchronized pacing.

She missed the gym too. Shirtless, muscular, sweaty men with towels thrown over their shoulders, sweat dripping down their backs, squeaks and grunts, and punches, and big smiles for her. She missed Becca and their weekly glasses of wine, their daily coffees. She was missing out on little Shane. He was probably head of the swim team by now.

A punching bag. She needed her own punching bag, she needed to start doing her workout again. Rain, rain, rain, rain, rain. Maybe it wasn't healthy, all this rain. The next time the sun was out, no matter what she was doing, she was going to drop everything and go outside. Maybe she would fix up the little back porch. She would definitely fix up the little back porch. Why hadn't she thought of this before? She would get rid of all the junk, maybe put a few plants and some nice patio furniture out there. She would offer wine, just like Rebecca suggested, and she would put up a swear jar. Every time anyone cursed, they would have to put a euro in the jar. She'd use the proceeds at the end of the month to buy something nice for the pub. If it was true, if no one liked her anyway, she might as well start taking charge, really making the place uniquely hers.

"Are you okay?" Sally said. There was a lot of wood in the pub. Carlene was going to polish all of it. She was going to put on music, and she was going to enjoy the hell out of the regulars who came in tonight, because the women of Ballybeog might not like her, but the men certainly did. Maybe, for once, she would even dress sexy tonight. Maybe she would bedazzle her cleavage. The kitten jumped up and rubbed against Carlene as she polished.

"No, kitty," Carlene said. "This isn't good for you." Sally, who was flipping through a magazine and filing her nails, swooped over and picked up the kitten.

"Aren't you a luv," Sally said. She planted kisses all over it. Carlene hated to admit it, but she was jealous. It was her cat, her pub. "What's its name?" Sally said.

"I don't know yet," Carlene said.

"Midnight."

"No."

"Blackie."

"No."

"Smokey."

"No."

"Slinky."

"No."

"Guinness."

"Definitely not."

"Jaysus," Sally said. "I think it's a form of abuse to let this wee thing go around not knowing his own name."

"Her own name."

"It's a girl?" Sally turned the poor kitten upside down. "How can ye tell? No willy?"

"It's a girl," Carlene said. "And she likes me."

Sally pointed her finger at Carlene. "You've got some kind of naming phobia, don't you?" she said.

"What?" Carlene said.

"You haven't named the kitten, and you haven't named the pub either," Sally said.

"Named the pub?"

"You don't exactly look like an Uncle Jimmy to me," Sally said.

Named the pub. Carlene hadn't even thought of that. She could change the name. Could she? Well, why not? It was her pub. Why did she constantly have to remind herself that it was really her pub? Carlene looked at the kitten.

"Gypsy," Carlene said.

"Are you joking me?" Sally said. "Never."

"Why not?"

"Because it's bad luck to name your cat after a knacker," Sally said.

"A knacker?"

"Knackers, gypsies, tinkers, you know who I mean, like? The travelers? They live in the caravans on the road. Stay away from them."

"Why?"

"Because they're dirty, stinking whores."

"Oh." Carlene had heard this reaction to the "travelers" before. A definite bias existed, and it kind of made her cringe, just like whenever the lads jingled their change in their hands and asked her if she had a jar to donate to the black babies, even though it was said without a trace of prejudice. It was, Sally said, just what they'd always called them.

"They don't like us either," Sally said. "They keep to themselves, they steal, they stink."

"I heard you the first time," Carlene said. "I don't know anything about them."

"Well, you don't want to be naming your cat after them, that's for sure." Carlene didn't answer. At least she had goals now. Clean out the back porch and make a nice outdoor seating area, name the kitten, and name the pub. Her pub.

"The Yank's Pub," Sally said.

"No," Carlene said.

"The Bedazzled," Sally said, spreading her hands like a jazz dancer.

"Not on your crystallized little life," Carlene said.

CHAPTER 21

The Walled Pub

Carlene stepped back and looked at her sign. The Half Tree. Even though, technically, all but a giant branch of the ash tree was still standing, it still made for a perfect name. She liked the idea of taking something negative and turning it into a positive. This would show everyone, especially Uncle Joe, that she had a sense of humor and that they couldn't get to her. She'd painted the sign herself, the words in blue looping, cursive letters that matched the trim on the windows. Anchor and Eoin hung the sign for her. Between giving out free drinks for favors, and paying Sally, money was tight. But there was pride in naming the pub. Sally put a sandwich board outside and wrote: GRAND OPENING. COME SEE THE YANK!

Nobody but the regulars came, but Sally wouldn't let Carlene bring the sign back in. Despite her antics, Sally wasn't all trouble, and to Carlene's surprise, she was starting to like her. Sally helped Carlene clear out the back porch, which actually consisted of Sally barking orders to the lads to throw the bits that were rubbish into their cars to take away. Carlene fixed the wobbly table herself, then painted it, along with the two chairs, a lovely shade of blue. They swept and mopped the floor of the porch and cleaned the windows. The lads lingered around the porch, smoking in the backyard or standing in the hall and peeking in at them. The kitten was curled up on the cat bed in the corner of the porch.

"Are you doing all this for the cat?" Ciaran said.

"I've seen you do a lot more for pussy," Eoin said.

Carlene gave them both a look. "No," she said. "I'm doing it for my customers."

"I think it's lovely," Sally said. "And romantic. We should get candles and string lights out here."

"That's a great idea," Carlene said.

"That's a shite idea," Eoin said. "You've ruined the vibe."

"What vibe?"

"This was a great smoking room," Eoin said. "Now it looks like a ladies' tea parlor."

"There's no smoking in here now," Carlene said. "You'll have to smoke outside."

"Ah, bollix," they said.

"That reminds me," Carlene said. "Just so you're fore-warned—I'm going to put up a swear jar."

"A what now?" Eoin asked. Carlene explained the concept. "What a load of shite," Eoin said.

"Complete bollix," Ciaran said.

"Fucking useless," Anchor said.

"See?" Carlene said. "That would be three euros right there."

"Never mind that," Sally said. "A friend of mine is getting married. I'm going to talk her into having her hen party here."

"Ah, Jaysus," Eoin said.

"We'll be here with bells on," Anchor said.

"No, you won't," Sally said. "Women only."

"I love that idea," Carlene said. She did too. As much as she enjoyed being the only female surrounded by these funny, talka-tive men, she still missed the company of women. And she liked Irish women especially, even if, as Sally said, they didn't like her. They were funny, quirky, smart, confident, and fun. Most of all, they were fun. They didn't seem to overworry, or overthink things like she did. She wanted to be more like them.

"We could make special cocktails," Carlene said. "I'm also thinking of getting some nice bottles of wine for the pub." She whispered it, just because she didn't want to hear the men say "bollix" any more today.

"When can they come?" Carlene said.

"Leave it to me," Sally said. "I'll get it sorted."

The next night, a series of loud bangs woke Carlene from a deep sleep. It wasn't Wednesday. Since the keg incident, she'd never missed a drop-off. The driver, who at first said as little to her as possible, was now quite friendly, and had even taken to helping her roll the full kegs to the shed. There were a series of other deliveries as well: mini-bottles of soda, liquor, ice, napkins, you name it. But none of them came in the middle of the night, and none of them made this kind of racket.

It sounded as if someone was hammering right downstairs. Carlene crept out of bed and inched her way across the floor, afraid to make any noise. It was ironic, how quiet she was trying to be for the very loud person who had broken into her pub and was banging on something.

There was definitely someone down there. She was afraid to open the door. She grabbed her cell phone, opened the little window in her bedroom, and climbed out on the slanted roof. She slid about a foot before getting a grip. Her hands shook as she dialed. *Please answer,* she thought. *Please, please answer.*

"Hallo." He shouted into the phone. Carlene could hear loud noise in the background, voices, music, glasses clinking. He was at a pub. Somebody else's pub. For a second, she was irrationally furious, and almost hung up.

"Ronan," she said. "It's Carlene."

"Are you okay?"

"No," she said. "Somebody's downstairs with a hammer," she said.

"What?"

"I can hear someone downstairs—it sounds like they're hammering something."

"Somebody broke in just to hammer something?" Ronan said. "That's gas."

"Please," Carlene said. "I'm kind of scared to death."

"You in your room?"

"I'm on the roof."

"Jaysus," he said. "Don't jump. I'll be right there."

"Be careful," she said. "Take a taxi."

"Bye awhile," he said.

She stayed on the roof, hugging her knees, listening. It seemed quiet now, and she thought she heard the sound of a car door opening, then closing, then pulling away. She stayed on the roof anyway and wondered how things had come to this point. She had been joking the other day when she called herself a damsel in distress, but here she was on the roof, shivering, shaking, waiting for Ronan to once again come rescue her. How did someone get into her pub? Did the whole town have keys to the place, or what? She was going to have to think about getting an alarm system, which seemed like a very paranoid, very American thing to do. It was so hard to believe that her attack kitten just wasn't enough to keep people away.

"Jaysus," Ronan said. "You really are on the roof." He stood in the yard, just below her.

"Where were you?" she said. She sounded like a hurt wife, but she couldn't help herself. He was swaying slightly and grinning.

"Did you miss me, Miss America?" he said. "Is that what all this is about? Purposefully getting yourself stuck in bogs and up on roofs, making up some shite about hammering, just because you're dying for a piece of this?" Carlene laughed, then started to slip.

"Whoa," he said. "Steady." Carlene tried to inch herself back up, but she slid even farther down the short, slanted roof.

"Shit, shit, shit, shit," she said. Her feet pattered furiously as she slid, her palms scraped against the roof. And then there was the edge, and the grass, and Ronan, all staring up at her. It was a small house, and a short fall. She landed on her side. Instead of soft bog, she managed to slam into a patch of hard ground. Ronan didn't move an inch, didn't even make an attempt to catch her. He was laughing. He was laughing! Carlene was once again furious. A knight in drunken armor—some help he was. Was she hurt? Was anything broken?

"That was fucking brilliant," Ronan said. He bent over at the waist, laughing, trying to catch his breath. "I wish I had a video of that," he said. Carlene sat up and patted herself down. She moved her legs, wiggled her toes. She was alive. She stood, brushed herself off.

"Thanks a lot," she said. She headed for the porch. Ronan grabbed her, pulled her back. His arm slid around her waist, his mouth found her ear.

"Wait," he said. "There's a madman running around these parts fixing things up while beautiful women are asleep," he said. Carlene laughed.

"I heard a car pulling away," she said. "I think they're gone."

"Maybe they'll be back with a screwdriver," Ronan said.

"Funny."

They crept down the dark hallway toward the main room. Carlene wanted to show him how she fixed up the back porch, but Ronan wouldn't let her turn any lights on. Despite his earlier teasing, he was deadly serious now and made sure she stayed a good distance behind him. He stopped midway, and she bumped into him. He put his hand out protectively.

"I smell sawdust," he whispered.

"I do too." They crept forward again, stopped where the hallway ended, and listened. Their eyes were already adjusted to the dark, and it didn't take long to spot the new addition to the pub. There was now a gigantic plywood wall where the entrance to the bathrooms used to be.

"What the hell?" Carlene said. She ignored Ronan's arms, trying to keep her back. She marched in and turned on the lights.

"I told you to wait," Ronan said. "Fuck," he whispered

when the lights came on. The wall covered up the entrance to both bathrooms, and whoever had done it had used about a million nails to hammer it in. It would not be quick or easy to take down. Sawdust gathered on the floor below the handiwork. Splashed across it, in bright red paint, it read: GO HOME, YANK.

Ronan slipped behind the bar and fixed them both a drink. Carlene didn't argue. She watched him work, easily reaching for glasses and bottles, stumbling only when he reached for something she'd moved to a new spot. Suddenly she felt guilty for changing the sign, and the porch, even though she had every right. He looked so at ease behind the bar, and the familiarity with which he touched everything touched her. He made her a drink with Jameson and ginger ale. She loved it. He leaned across the bar, smiled at her.

"What's a nice girl like you doing in a place like this?"

"In my pajamas," Carlene added.

"In your fucking pajamas," Ronan said. Carlene looked at the wall. Ronan kept his eyes on her.

"Joe?" she said. Ronan shook his head.

"Not his style," he said.

"He climbed my tree and cut off a huge branch," Carlene said. "Ruined my front door."

"In broad daylight," Ronan said. "In front of everyone."

"True," she said.

"And I don't think he intended on the branch falling into your door," Ronan said. "I think his eyesight and aim were a little off."

"Okay, okay," Carlene said. "Then who?"

"Hey," Ronan said. He was still leaning on the counter, his face close to hers. "Hello," he said when she met his eyes.

"Hello," she said. He slid his hand across the counter and took her hand in his.

"You have the softest hands," he said. *I have a mushy heart too,* she thought. *Especially when I look at you.*

"I used to wear a lot of gloves," she said. He looked at her funny, and she laughed, and then before she could stop them, hot tears filled her eyes.

"It's okay," Ronan said. "I have that effect on women."

"I'm sorry," she said. "I just miss my dad."

"I miss mine too," Ronan said. How dumb of her to say such a thing; she hadn't been thinking.

"I'm so sorry," she said.

"Me too," he said.

"I feel like I know him," Carlene said. "From all the pictures, and all the stories, and I don't know, it's just like I can feel him here." They were still holding hands, and Carlene was holding her breath, hoping he wouldn't pull away.

"What's your oul wan like?" Ronan said. Carlene didn't know how to answer. She didn't want her father to be defined by blue rubber gloves, and pacing, and ritualistic knocking. But she didn't know how to talk about him without that. Did she tell him that in addition to a packed lunch he used to send her to school with industrial-sized bottles of antiseptic?

"He's a character," Carlene said. Ronan didn't pry any further, and she was grateful.

"What did you want to be when you grew up?" he asked.

"A National Geographic photographer and journalist extraordinaire," she said.

"What happened?"

"I dropped my Polaroid camera in the Cuyahoga River," she said.

"You what?"

"I was eating cheese fries, and my fingers got so greasy the camera slipped."

"You eejit," Ronan said. Listening to him call her an eejit with that melodic accent and huge grin filled Carlene with an inexplicable sense of joy.

"I was ten," Carlene said.

"And that was it?" he said. "No more lions in the Congo?"

"No more lions in the Congo," she said.

"Then what?" he said. "What was the next dream?"

"A vet."

"The nursing sick animals kind or the fighting bad guys kind?"

"Oh, the fighting bad guys kind," she said. "Definitely."

"Deadly," Ronan said. "I can picture you with a gun strapped to your chest. Of course, you're topless." She laughed, punched him on the shoulder. He grabbed that hand too, and now they were holding both hands. "So what happened?" he asked. "Did you drop your dog in the Cuyahoga River too?"

"I killed a hamster," Carlene said. "I cried for six months."

"What?" Ronan said. "You got a tiny scarf, like, and strangled the wee thing?"

"I fed him strawberry Slim Fast," Carlene said. "He was kind of chubby and I thought the vitamins would be good for him."

"How do you know that's what killed him?"

"Well, he didn't leave a note," Carlene said. "But he died in a puddle of pink vomit." She couldn't believe it, she still felt horrible about it. "What did you want to be?" she asked. Ronan looked away. She waited.

"A publican," he said. "Like my father." He pulled his hands away. *Great,* Carlene thought. *Nice question, Carlene. Perfect mood killer.*

"And now?" she said before she could stop herself. He took his time making eye contact again, and when he did he held it for a long time. "Besides knight in shining armor," she said.

"That's very American," he said.

"What?"

"All that 'what do you do' shite."

"Sorry," Carlene said. "You started it."

"No. I asked you what you wanted to be when you grow up."

"Well," Carlene said. "I was just trying to ask you the same thing." They slipped into silence. He pulled back slightly, but remained close. She liked looking at his face. He had a faint, thin scar above his left eyebrow. She wanted to touch it, lick it, sky-write with it. It was suddenly so quiet in the bar, she could hear them breathing. He was so beautiful. The muscles in his arms, the smell of his cologne, those gorgeous eyes. Should she tell him when she looked in his eyes, she thought primitive, and reptile?

"What?" he said.

"I have to go to the bathroom," she said. He looked at the wall and laughed. When she came back down, Ronan was standing on a stool in front of the wall, trying to pry it off with his bare hands.

"Ronan," she said. "Don't." He tore into it like a madman. He'd taken off his sweater. He stood in his white shirt undershirt, and the muscles in his back flexed as he pulled on the wall. With a loud, splintering crack, a tiny portion of the upper right-hand corner came apart in his hands. He turned to her with the piece of wood in his hands. Sweat ran down his face. When he opened his palm and let the piece of wood fall, she saw drops of blood on his fingers. "Stop," she said. "We'll get help."

"I want it down tonight," he said. Carlene pulled a stool over to him, stood on it, then reached for him. He stopped what he was doing. She put her hands on his face, ran them down his jawline. She moved in, and he let her. They stood on their stools and kissed, getting as close to each other as their balance would allow. After minutes of kissing, Carlene stepped down and held her hand out. Ronan took it, met her on the ground, and pulled her into him. He backed her up against the wall and kissed her with a gentler version of the passion he'd used to tear at the wall. She broke away, grabbed his hand, and started for the stairs. He stopped in the middle of the room.

"Come on," she said. "Let's go to bed."

"Are you sure?" he said. "Maybe we shouldn't."

"Why not?"

"Maybe I'm not good at this," Ronan said.

"Good at what?" she said. "Sex?" First, she doubted it, and second, she was surprised he would confess that kind of a fear.

"No, Miss America, not sex. Relationships."

"Oh," she said.

"Maybe it's all downhill from here," he said. "You know—after the mind-blowing sex."

"Maybe it is," she said. "But maybe it's not. Maybe it could even be something great." But he was already backing away. He went behind the bar, opened a cabinet she didn't even know was there, and took out a blanket and pillow.

"What are you doing?" she said.

"I'm sleeping down here," he said. "Until I can change the back locks and you get a security system in."

Then I'm never getting one, she thought.

"You can sleep upstairs. With me."

"No," he said. "I can't."

"We don't have to have sex," she said. "We can just sleep."

"There's not a chance of me getting in that bed with you and not having sex," Ronan said. "Now go on with ye, get upstairs."

What a fool she was. Throwing herself at him. Now here she was, alone, while he was right downstairs, underneath the pool table. Here she went again, falling in love with someone who knew how to pull her in with one hand while pushing her away with the other. She was so forward, he must think she slept around a lot. Oh God, was that what he thought? Did he have a small penis, or was he too drunk to get it up? Or was he just not that into her either? She wasn't going to turn into Sally, pining after a man who clearly didn't want her.

That settled it. She would never do this again. She was glad he said no. She would not go downstairs and slip in next to him, press up against him, kiss the back of his neck, slip her hands down his chest, kiss him all over, work her lips down his body. And even if he'd totally rejected her, it was still good to know he was nearby, keeping an eye out for her. Even so, it took forever to fall back asleep, as if a vital part of herself had been torn off and was sleeping downstairs underneath a pool table.

CHAPTER 22

They're Called Sheep

Word spread about the wall. Declan was the first to arrive. He stood back, photographed it, examined it, and then did his best to distract Carlene. He made her a cheese toastie. He poured her a pint. He called her pet, and darling, and chicken, and luv a hundred thousand times. Next, Mary McBride arrived. She hugged Carlene and made sympathetic noises, fussed with her hair, drank tea, and fussed over Carlene some more. Then the half dozen arrived. They brought cookies, steak pie, and bags and bags of crisps. Clare and Liz paid her the most attention of all, and Carlene wondered if Ronan had spoken to them despite his promise.

Father Duggan was next. He prayed over the wall. He assured Carlene that he would mention this atrocity at mass, insist that whoever was intimidating her would immediately cease and desist. She agreed to come to mass soon.

Then people from the town, armed with food and sympathy, spilled into the pub. Nancy came bearing cappuccinos. The schedule for tearing down the wall was delayed, and delayed, because everyone wanted to have a gawk at it. It was great for business, and suddenly women were in the pub too. Unfortunately, it meant they had to traipse upstairs to use her personal bathroom.

Over the next few weeks, business continued to be so good that Declan started to pitch in along with Sally. Ronan, she noticed, wasn't coming around as much, but Carlene was too busy with customers to obsess. Even Joe stopped in now and again to assure her he had nothing to do with putting up the wall. He did, however, inquire whether it was legal for customers to use her upstairs bathroom. He was quickly tossed out by a few eavesdropping drinkers.

Mike the guard arrived one day. He photographed the wall, stayed for a wee drink, and as he said, "documented everything." Sue Finnegan, owner of the little pub Carlene had been meaning to check out, came, along with a few other pub owners in town, making a speech that all publicans needed to band together. Carlene was shocked how quickly everyone rallied around her. Whoever had been vandalizing her had actually done her a huge favor. She hoped, whoever they were, they had learned their lesson.

Finally, a date was set to take down the wall. A band was hired, and Declan arranged catering from several women in town. The place was packed. The band played Irish music while her regular lads prepared to begin the destruction. At the last minute, Eoin suggested they cut doorways into the wall for the bathrooms, but leave the rest of the wall up. He wanted to turn it into a mural, and Carlene loved the idea. They painted "Mna" and "Fir," the Irish words for Male and Female, above the respective doorways. "Go Home" was painted over and replaced with "Stay," so that the wall now read: STAY, YANK.

Eoin, to Carlene's surprise, was a fantastic artist. Over the next few weeks, he painted a beautiful mural of the Irish countryside on the plywood wall, complete with rolling fields, a stream, and towering trees. Then the people of Ballybeog were encouraged to stop in and sign it. It was a living petition, a town apology, a public stand against the begrudger who wanted her gone. Carlene had never felt so happy, and so welcome.

* * *

After that, things quieted down until Sally came through with the hen night. The girls were already drunk when they arrived. All ten of them were decked in fancy dresses and outlandish headpieces. Everyone, courtesy of Sally, was bedazzled, including Carlene. She felt foolish, wearing a headband with a giant blue crystal in the middle of her forehead, but she was learning to go with the flow. Roisin, the bride-to-be, wore a wedding dress that had been cut off way above the knees, neckline plunged low. She also wore a bedazzled veil that was longer than the dress.

The women immediately swept Carlene up in the fun and demanded she keep up with their drinking, shot for shot. Luckily, Carlene had suspected this was coming and had already doctored up a bottle of whiskey for herself that actually contained ginger ale. Sally was in unusually good form, touching Carlene's arm or giving her a little hug around the waist whenever she was near. It could have been the presence of all that crystal, or it could have been the bottle of Jägermeister she sipped from the entire evening.

There wasn't a band, but the girls played the jukebox, and drank, and danced, and swore, and joked, and gossiped, and swayed their hips to the music. Carlene watched them, once again mesmerized by their ability to let go and have fun without giving life a second thought. They laughed loud and often. They shrieked. They touched each other all the time; a hand on the shoulder, a hand on a hand, a hand on a knee, an overflowing display of connection and affection. All done with ease, without a second thought. None of them, Carlene noted, wore gloves.

Carlene felt like a phony, an observer, a reporter. She didn't remember all of their names, didn't know what they did for a living, where they lived, who they loved, or what their secrets were. But she was thrilled to have women in the pub. It was a start.

"We need men," one of the hens shouted. She was a tall girl with dark hair piled on top of her head, held in place with a tiara that read: BITCH. She had beautiful light blue eyes lined in heavy green eyeliner. She grabbed Carlene and tried to stare into her eyes. She couldn't focus for long, and she shifted her weight from one gold stiletto to the other, as if trying to keep her balance. "Where are all the men?" she said. Between her accent and her slur, it took Carlene a few tries before she understood her.

"It's just us girls tonight," Carlene said. She looked to Sally for support. Sally was holding a shot glass in one hand, and a crystal and superglue in the other. She stuck the crystal on the shot glass, then watched as it slid down, leaving a smear of glue like the trail of a slug.

"Bollix," Sally said before trying it again.

"I know," Miss Tiara said. "We should call you-know-who over here for Sally." Sally looked up from her shot glass and smiled.

"Oh yes," Sally said. She came out from behind the bar holding the bottle of Jägermesiter. She leaned against the bar, slid the bottle down to her crotch. "Yes, yes, yes." The girls howled with laughter, but Carlene was slightly appalled. She'd never seen girls act like—well—guys.

"Oh, Ronan," another girl shouted. "I love your big cock."

"Have ye bedazzled it yet, Sally?" Roisin yelled. Sally threw her head back and laughed. Then she guzzled straight from the bottle. When she came up for air, her eyes landed on Carlene and stayed there. Carlene suddenly felt as if the room was closing in on her. She felt someone's hands wrap around her waist from behind.

"Have you met Ronan McBride yet?" the girl whispered in her ear.

"Of course she has," Sally said. "He's been spending a lot of time over here lately, hasn't he, Carlene?" Carlene didn't answer; she tried to move away, busy herself behind the bar. Miss Tiara stopped her.

"Maybe it's to see you," Miss Tiara said. She poked Carlene's chest a few times.

"He's gorgeous, isn't he?" a pretty blonde said to Carlene. They all looked at Carlene, as if demanding her answer.

"He's very good looking," Carlene said. She felt heat rise to her face and she tried not to look at the pool table where he'd slept just the other night, she tried not to think about his mouth on hers, his voice and breath in her ear, his arms around her.

"He's off-limits to you," Roisin said. She swept over to Sally, whipped her bridal veil off, and put it on Sally. "Sally and Ronan are soul mates," she said. "It was written on the abbey walls, right, Sal?"

"Not on the walls," Sally said. "He left me a note in the wall," she added.

"Really?" Carlene said. *Don't let them get to you,* she told herself. Thank God she was drinking ginger ale, and yet she still felt sick.

"They were fifteen years of age," the blonde said. "What did the note say again, Sally?"

"Be mine," Sally said. They all looked at Carlene.

"Oh," Carlene said. "That's very. To the point." She understood what this was now. An intervention. Stay away from Ronan. Maybe Sally was the one who'd put up the wall. After all, she had motive and access to the tools. "So," Carlene said. "Why aren't you two together now?"

"Irish men take forever to commit," Roisin said. "I've been after Martin to marry me for the past eight years."

"But when they do commit, it's for life," the blonde said. "We don't have 'drive-by divorce' like you Yanks."

Carlene thought about her marriage. A hit-and-run. Guess he was the exception to the life sentence.

"So you think he really wants to be with you, Sally?" Carlene said. "You think he's just, what? Playing hard to get?" Carlene told herself to shut up. After all, these women were tough and drunk and could definitely kick her ass. But she wasn't going to let them gang up on her either, not without defending herself a little.

"I wouldn't have such strong feelings for him if it wasn't mutual," Sally said. "That's just not possible."

Carlene could tell from Sally's intense expression that she believed what she was saying. She felt a rush of pity for her. Carlene had once thought the same thing about Brendan. How was it possible to have every cell in your body light up around a particular man if they didn't feel the same way?

"But he doesn't call you?" Carlene said. "Ask you out on dates?" *Does he hold your hands and stare into your eyes and ask you what you want to be when you grow up? Does he ask you to tell him secrets and rescue you from bogs and roofs? When was the last time he pushed you up against a wall and kissed you until you saw stars?*

Roisin staggered up to Carlene. She looked her up and down. Then she turned her back on her.

"All right, ladies," Roisin said. "Enough of this fucking talk about fellas. This is my hen party. Who wants to do shots off my stomach?"

"I've known him since I was five years old," Sally said. "We've done loads of things together. Our families do loads of things together. Jane's right." Carlene glanced at the blonde, whose name she now knew was Jane. "You don't know a thing about Irish men," Sally continued. "You will never get them like we do. Even if they get crushes on American girls—"

"Or Eastern European girls," Jane said.

"Or whoever the feck," Sally said. "The relationships never work out because at they end of the day, they know they can't do better than an Irish wife."

"Maybe so," Carlene said. "But in America, if he's not pursuing you, we'd say, 'he's just not that into you.' I know it hurts, but when you actually get the concept it can be quite liberating." The women just looked at her. "Become the man you want to marry," Carlene said, trying to muster up a peppy voice.

"What the fuck does that mean?" Sally said.

"Sounds like a load of shite," Roisin said. It looked like the swear jar would work equally for her female guests. Carlene was going to have to get started on that. She could have thousands in there already.

"They're all the same," Miss Tiara said. "All men are babies who want a mother in the kitchen, and a Madonna taking care of their babies, and a whore in the bedroom. And it's all because their Irish mammies treat them like they're gods. I am not going to raise my son that way. I am going to break the cycle. God, I fucking hate men. I wish I'd never gotten married. I wish I could be a selfish man who thinks of no one but myself and comes to the pub every night to tell the same stupid jokes to other sweaty, smelly men who are too cowardly to go home and be good to their wives and kids."

Carlene was starting to think the shots were a bad idea. . . .

Miss Tiara stumbled up to Roisin. "I just wish one person would have wrenched me aside before I said 'I do' and told me how much marriage can drain the fucking life out of you," she said. Her tiara slipped slightly. She pushed it back up, only managing to slide it to the other side. Roisin staggered back, as if struck by Miss Tiara's words, then suddenly dropped. She sat slumped over on the floor holding her bottle of whiskey. Mascara ran down her cheek. Her hair was filled with static and several strands were sticking straight up as if crying for her veil.

"Now look what you've done," Sally said. Carlene didn't know if she was talking to her or Miss Tiara. The women all gathered around the bride-to-be.

"Your marriage isn't going to be like that," Jane yelled down at Roisin. "Martin's a nice fella. He's quiet and likes to stay at home."

Roisin lifted her head. "I know," she said. "That's the fucking problem."

"What do you mean?" Jane said.

"He's boring," Roisin said. "I'm going to die of boredom." At once the women began assuring her that Gary was not boring.

"For fuck's sake," Roisin said. "He's having his bachelor party in the Aran Islands."

"The islands are lovely," Jane said.

"That is a bit odd," Sally said. "Do they have strippers on the Aran Islands?"

"Yes," Roisin said. "They're called sheep." At first there was stunned silence, then the girls all broke into howling laughter.

"Ciaran could stand to be a little more like Gary," Jane said.

"After his bachelor party he came home with a thong between his teeth. I didn't speak to him until the wedding day."

"Come on, Jane," Roisin said. "At least you can't say Ciaran's boring." Ciaran, Carlene thought. Jane was married to Ciaran? Her Ciaran? This was the woman who liked the vampire books? For some reason Carlene never pictured Ciaran having a wife that hot. It did make her wonder why he was in the bar all the time if he had someone like her at home. Jane stumbled up to Carlene, and for a second Carlene wondered if she had just blurted her thoughts out loud.

"What does Ciaran do here all night?" Jane said. "What does he say? Who does he talk to?" What she really wanted to know was, "Why isn't he with me?" and that was one question Carlene couldn't answer.

"Hey," Sally said. "Bartenders are like priests. No talking out of school."

"This hen night sucks," Roisin said. "It's been about as useful as a chocolate willy." She stumbled over to Sally, grabbed her veil back, and put it on. Then she grabbed the bottle of Jägermeister out of Sally's hand and stumbled down the hall. The rest of the girls followed. Carlene stayed in the bar to clean up. But even from the distance she could hear them singing, and laughing, and shouting, and eventually vomiting into the bog.

CHAPTER 23

Down the Hatch

Carlene wanted to fully explore the backyard before winter hit. It was nearing the end of October, and the mild fall weather was starting to develop a bitter bite. She had purchased a new pair of wellies, ones that fit tighter this time, and she began tentatively exploring the backyard foot by foot. On many of these sunrise expeditions, the kitten would join her. One morning, Carlene was picking a few wildflowers for a jar for the back porch. The kitten bounded up to her, rubbed against her leg, then shot off again. Carlene watched the kitten trip across the yard. One minute it was there, and the next it dropped out of sight, seemingly vanished into thin air. Carlene's heart dropped. She ran to the spot where the kitten disappeared, a clawing panic gripping her chest. She fully expected to dig the kitten out of the muck, lifeless and stiff.

She should have named her, Carlene thought as she ran. Why didn't she name her? And why was she letting a kitten run around a bog in the first place? She'd tried to leave the cat inside, but the little furball wouldn't have it. She'd morph into a devilish creature, yowling and scratching at the screen door, insisting she be let out. Sometimes the kitten squeezed her tiny body through cracks in the porch and slipped out on her own. Live and let live, Carlene finally decided. It seemed to be the Irish way. When Carlene reached the spot where she had last seen the kitten, she looked down and saw a small hole in the ground.

Carlene dropped to her hands and knees and examined the opening. She was terrified to stick her hand inside, but she could hear the kitten's pitiful meows coming from within. No matter what, she wasn't going to call Ronan. He hadn't come around lately, and calling him to rescue her kitten was taking things a bit too far. Besides, wasn't she the one who lectured Sally on not chasing men? Was it time she faced the fact that Ronan just wasn't that into her?

Carlene picked at the grass on either side of the hole, hoping to make it a little larger. She wanted to at least be able to peer into it before sticking her hand into the abyss. Thank goodness for Saint Patrick, she thought. At least this couldn't be a snake hole. To her surprise, pulling the grass around the hole revealed planks of wood, as if some kind of crate had been smashed on the ground and abandoned. Carlene tore at the grass. Suddenly, she was staring at what appeared to be a small door, or a hatch. The middle of the door had caved in, creating the opening the kitten fell through. Carlene grabbed the remains of the door with both hands and pulled.

It swung open quite easily, revealing a deep hole beneath it. It was big enough for Carlene to jump into. The kitten's meows grew louder.

"Hey, kitty," Carlene said. "I'm here." Carlene wished she had a flashlight. She didn't want to leave the kitten for a second, but it was too dark to see inside. She wasn't going to go in blind. "One second, kitty," Carlene said. She quickly closed the door. There was no one around, but she still had this feeling—this rush of adrenaline that came with discovering a secret trapdoor. She ran like a child to the shed where she'd stored all the tools she purchased from Sally's hardware shop. A flashlight was one of her purchases, and as she ran she mentally patted herself on the back for thinking of it.

She opened the shed, grabbed the flashlight, and turned it on. It worked! Luckily, she'd thought of batteries too. She ran back to the secret door, dropped to her knees, and opened it again. At first she shone the light over the hole so that she wouldn't blind the poor little kitty with direct light. The kitten hadn't moved. He was crouched at the bottom, which appeared to be about ten feet down.

Not a bad drop. Still, she needed something, maybe a chair or ladder to put down the hole. Even with such a short jump, she could sprain her ankle if she wasn't careful. Especially since, from the looks of it, the floor of this hole was covered with stones. In fact, it looked almost as if the stones had been deliberately built into the floor. Carlene shut the door again and ran back to the pub. If anyone was watching her run back and forth, they would have thought she was some kind of nutter doing morning sprinting exercises. Not that she would care. She couldn't remember the last time she'd felt so giddy. She felt like Christopher Columbus about to discover the New World. She grabbed one of the wooden chairs from the back porch, returned to the trapdoor, and opened it for the third time. She lowered the chair as far as she could and then let it drop. To her relief, the chair stayed upright and she didn't hit the kitten. In fact, the kitten remained curled up on the floor, watching Carlene's every move. Her cries had stopped; now she seemed merely curious.

Should she go back for her cell phone in case something went wrong? Before she could talk herself out it, Carlene lowered herself into the hole. She landed harder than she expected, but other than a shock to her ankles, she was okay. She scooped up the kitten and examined her. She gently touched her paws and the rest of her tiny body. She was completely fine, just shaking, and her little heart was pounding louder than Carlene's. She set the kitten on the chair and turned on the flashlight.

She only had about a foot of space in which to stand upright. The hole did seem to continue, but it wasn't until she got down on her hands and knees that she could see there was an actual tunnel burrowed into the ground. The floor of the tunnel was made of stone, the walls were simply dirt, and the roof consisted of crisscrossing wood beams. Whatever this was, it was man-made, unless beavers in Ireland had rapidly advanced their skill sets. Did Ireland even have beavers? Carlene hadn't a clue.

It was a very narrow passageway, and when she shone the light down it, she couldn't see to the end. The eternal question remained—was there a light at the end of the tunnel?

If she started to crawl into it, how long would it last? What was on the other side? If she panicked, was there enough room to turn around, or would she be forced to crawl backward? What if she started crawling through and the roof caved in? She could suffocate to death without anyone ever finding her body.

And what if someone was hiding in there somewhere? It would be all fine and grand to make it through the passage, unless waiting at the other end was a vagrant with a meat cleaver. She couldn't do this now. She was going to have to think this through. Who else knew about this? Should she tell someone? Ronan?

Maybe she should run next door and get Joe. He would probably laugh at her excitement, tell her it was an old—what? What was this thing? Ireland didn't have basements. And it couldn't be called a cave, this was definitely man-made. Was this the beginning of a trench someone had dug to drain the water from the bog? But it wasn't a trench; it was a tunnel, a passage. What if it was some kind of monument from the Stone Age, or some druid temple? The kitten mewed, a pitiful sound designed to pity her into getting her the heck out of this hole. "All right, Columbus," she said. "We're going." Columbus, the discoverer; Columbus, the capital of Ohio; Columbus, her kitten. It was set, she had a name. And she had a secret passage just waiting for her to grow brave enough to explore.

After her third full hour of obsessing, it dawned on Carlene that maybe she could learn something about her property at the Ballybeog Museum. She stood in front of the museum door and said a silent prayer before entering. Her positive thinking must have worked—the door swung wide open. She paused in the entry. "Hello?" She heard the ticking of a clock, the squeak of floorboards. It smelled musty and somewhat lemony. She stepped in. It was a one-room museum, two hundred square feet of memorabilia. Carlene felt as if she were standing in her grandmother's attic. She was alone in a space cramped with objects she could actually pick up and touch, if she so dared. This was what museums should be, not standing in line with a hundred seventh graders to look at something behind six-inch Plexiglas. Most museums left Carlene feeling overwhelmed, overstimulated, and totally useless because she knew all the facts, names, and dates she had just jammed into her brain would disappear the minute she stepped into sunlight. But here, she could breathe; here, she might even be able to remember.

Carlene stood irresolute, unsure what do first. Commandeering the center of the room, and the only thing under glass, was a model of the town. On the walls were photographs, mostly black and white, of Ballybeog throughout the years: IRA soldiers, businessmen, schoolchildren, and families. Shelves ran the circumference of the room, littered with artifacts: coins; bomb casings; keys to who-knew-what (keys to the castle?); old liquor bottles untouched, the alcohol coagulating inside the dusty bottles; medallions; small, defective toys, such as a china doll with long blond hair but only one blue eye.

The room also contained a small desk. Shoved in the farthest right corner, it was cluttered with books and papers, and a chair. On the chair sat a purse. Someone was around and would be back any second. They were the trusting sort, either that or they were convinced no one would come in while they were gone. It must be nice to live in a place where you felt free to leave your purse open on the chair. Carlene was disappointed. Being alone in here made her feel like she was trespassing, and she was hoping to find someone around to tell her if they knew anything about underground structures in Ireland. She had to be careful; she didn't want anyone to know she'd found one on her property. It was her delicious secret for now.

Unfortunately, the folks in Ballybeog seemed to have an insatiable curiosity for every move she made. She would have to proceed carefully with the chitchat, or "chin-wagging," as Riley called it. She stepped over to the model of the town and read the placard. BALLYBEOG, 1592. She loved the miniature replica of the walled town, showing all four original "gates" or entrances. A brochure next to the model provided the basic information she already knew: The town was invaded by the Normans, the Vikings, Cromwell, and the Black and Tans. And like the twins had informed her that day in the abbey, French priests. They truly had survived it all. Carlene was thrilled there was still so much of the medieval town intact.

The castle still stood in the center of the town, along with the remains of the abbey, and the still-standing Bally Gate. The model showed that in the original town square there was a church with a large Celtic cross. The original church must have been destroyed, for Saint Bridget's was now on the outskirts of town. Carlene had visited the church on several of her explorative walks. It was a gorgeous place of worship with a soaring steeple, exquisite stained glass, and a cemetery in the back with a mixture of new and old graves.

For some reason, Carlene assumed she would find only ancient graves, as if in her mind nobody in this sweet little town was still dying, still being buried. The new graves saddened her, the older ones fascinated her. Carlene turned her attention back to the church shown in the model. According to the brochure, the town square was where residents used to gather to buy butter, hay, and potatoes, as well as catch up with the news and gossip of the town. Carlene peered down at the model. Sure enough, down a small alley just off the center of town was a public house, Ballybeog's first pub. Carlene wished she could go back in time, walk into that pub.

Carlene moved away from the model and turned toward the door. A mannequin stood in the farthest corner of the room. It was terribly thin, even for a mannequin, and dressed in rags. It must represent a famine victim, Carlene thought. Ballybeog had a gorgeous public park dedicated to the victims of the famine. It was memorialized with a stone monument, underneath which was a mass grave. Carlene stared at the mannequin as she made her way out. It gave her the creeps, and little pinpricks of fear sprang up and down her arms. As she passed, the mannequin moved its eyes. Carlene screamed.

"I frightened ye, did I?" It was the palest, skinniest woman Carlene had ever seen. She had caved-in cheeks and dark hair peppered with gray, and a brown dress that hung on her body as if it were draped over a mop. Carlene couldn't answer—she was still trying to catch her breath, her heart was still in her chest. The woman had almost given her a heart attack.

"You certainly did," Carlene said. "I thought you were a mannequin." She shouldn't have said that. It just popped out of her mouth. Although it was better than what she'd been really thinking—*I thought you were a famine victim.* The woman looked almost pleased for having scared Carlene to death. "I just mean, you're so still, and thin—which isn't a bad thing—in America everyone wants to be thin, which is ironic, I know, since you think we're all so fat. We are. A lot of us are. But we have anorexics too and they're very popular. I'm not saying you're anorexic, I'm just saying you would be very popular in America. Do you know Calista Flockhart? Never mind. She's very, very skinny and she's married to Harrison Ford, so there you go. You know? *Raiders of the Lost Ark?* Sexy, absent-minded professor cum swashbuckling tomb raider? Speaking of tombs," Carlene stepped forward, "I'm doing a little research project on underground passages. Do you have any information on that sort of thing?"

Now that she was closer, Carlene noticed a bruise on the woman's face. It was faded, but there was a thin green line sunk into the skin below her right eye, casting a haunted shadow on that side of her face.

"There is an audio presentation that accompanies the model of the town," the woman said. "Would you like to hear it?" Carlene so did not want to hear it. She wanted out of this room. She wanted out in the fresh air, she wanted to breathe without this woman staring at her, she wanted to run to Nancy's and buy this woman a dozen doughnuts.

"Of course," Carlene said.

"Would ye like a cup of tea?" If there was ever a time she should refuse a cup of tea in Ireland, now would be the time, for if there was ever the sort of Irish person who needed every drop of sustenance for herself, it was this woman.

"I'd love a cup of tea," Carlene lied.

The tea was bland, a perfect accompaniment to the audio presentation. Carlene drank and listened to the monotone recorded voice for forty-five excruciating minutes. "Thank you," Carlene said the second it ended. "I'd better be going."

"It's souterrains you're interested in, is it?" the woman said.

"Souterrains?"

"Underground caves, passages, shelters," the woman said.

"Yes," Carlene said. "You've heard of such things?"

"Of course I have," the woman said. "Ireland has a wealth of mysterious places underground. Some of the caves date back to the Bronze Age. But most of the structures are man-made. Nobody knows exactly why, or even when some of them were built. Some say they're more recent—bomb shelters built by the IRA, but others say the IRA simply found these underground structures already built. Which could mean they were made by the Vikings, or the Normans. Others think they date much later in time and were simply constructed during the famine as cold storage to preserve food."

"Wow," Carlene said. "Are there a lot of them?"

"I had a book somewhere," the woman said. She moved over to the desk. Carlene couldn't help but notice that she almost floated instead of walked, as if she were so light she was carried by the air. She glanced around at the desk, then looked at the ceiling. Carlene looked at the ceiling. It was a very low ceiling. In fact, she was starting to feel claustrophobic, as if they were already in an underground structure. "It's probably up there," the woman said, continuing to stare at the ceiling.

"Oh," Carlene said. "I don't see anything." Nothing could have prepared Carlene for the shock of the woman's laugh. It wasn't exactly a warm sound, but Carlene didn't think her capable of it nonetheless. The woman walked over to the farthest wall and pointed out a small string hanging from the ceiling.

"There's a storage space up there," the woman said. "But it will take me a while to go through it."

"No problem," Carlene said. "Maybe if you come across it, you can drop it into the pub." *And I'll feed you a hundred cheese toasties.*

"I've never touched an alkie holic drink in me life," the woman said.

"I can give you a mug of tea," Carlene said. *And a hundred fucking cheese toasties.*

"I'll let ye know," the woman said.

"Please do," Carlene said. "I'm really anxious to read the book."

"And why would that be?" the woman asked. Carlene was surprised by her bluntness.

"I'm having a trivia night at the pub," Carlene said. "I'm hoping to stump them with unusual questions about the land-scape of Ireland." The minute it was out of her mouth, Carlene knew she had to do it. The lads would love a trivia night, and it was the perfect cover to ask a million questions.

"I see," the woman said. "I'll have a look for it, then."

"Thank you, thank you, thank you," Carlene said. The woman smiled, although it never reached her eyes.

"Mind yourself," the woman said as Carlene went out the door. *Eat something,* Carlene thought.

"You too," she said instead.

CHAPTER 24

Trivial Matters

Dear Becca,
   I'm sorry, I'm sorry, I'm sorry, I'm sorry. Of
course I haven't drowned in the Irish rain, nor am I
"sinking into a bottle." And no, I don't need any of
my buddies in the gym to come and kick some Irish
ass, but thanks for the offer. I've just been very busy.
Yes, still loving the bar business. Congratulations,
that's wonderful news about Shane, I had no idea
there was such a thing as Baby Menses.

Love,

Carlene

P.S. How's my dad? Have you seen him? Talked to
him? It's been so hard to get him on the phone!

Dear Carlene,
   It's Baby Mensa, not Menses. Obviously you were
never a candidate, ha-ha! Sorry to nitpick, but I just

can't have you going around saying that! I don't
know what to say about your dad, I think he's kind
of lost without you.

Love,

Becca

Riley was in a chatty mood. Apparently, he'd recently come
across a Scottish man in a kilt, although where or when, Carlene couldn't quite understand. Riley was slurring his words
more than usual lately, even before finishing his first drink.
"They have to have drawers under them kilts," he said. "What
if they're going over a hill and there's a big wind?" Carlene nodded in agreement. She did a lot of nodding and smiling these
days.

She still hadn't seen Ronan, but she wasn't obsessing over
him. She visited the underground passage almost daily. She'd yet
to make it more than a few feet into it. Every time she tried to
crawl farther, she was absolutely seized by a feeling of terror.
Was that how her father felt most of the time? Terrified? Was
that the demon he tried to chase by counting, and pacing, and
preparing? The next time she talked to him, she would bring it
up, see if they could talk through their fears. She would tell him
she loved him, try to get him to commit to a visit. She really
wanted him to come for Christmas, even though he'd mentioned her coming to Ohio to celebrate. She felt guilty, but there
was no way she was going to miss her first Christmas in Ballybeog. She still had a few months to work on him.

Even Sally seemed in good form lately. She had dropped all
veiled threats about Ronan. And, as usual, the regulars were—
well, regular, and always good company. Things were changing
too. Carlene had booked a trad band for Sundays as well as in-
stituted quiz night on Thursdays. Last Thursday had been the
first one, and although it was just a small group, as predicted,
the lads loved it.

They were good at trivia, and competed passionately for the

prize—Carlene would rip up the bar tab of the winning team. In addition to tidbits from local newspapers, Carlene collected the trivia questions from an Irish pub way down south in County Kerry. They posted their past quiz night questions on their website for free. Geography, sports, history, music, and Dumb Things Americans Do were their favorite topics. Carlene always asked the questions; it was a surefire way of getting out of answering them. Even so, some of the boys found ways to dig at her, especially Anchor, who was a whiz at geography.

"Carlene wouldn't want to answer that question," he'd say. "It involves Asia. We know Americans don't learn about the world in school."

"And you did?" Carlene said.

"Try me."

"What's the capital of Ohio?"

"*World* geography," Anchor said.

"Wrong," Carlene said. "It's Columbus." And then, because she couldn't think of any world geography questions to stump him with, she moved on to the next round of questions. "Which has the highest mountain: Earth or Mars?" Carlene blanched. She didn't even know Mars had a mountain. Although she would have guessed Mars anyway, because that's what you do when you're faced with such a question, you pick the most outlandish answer, and she was right, of course the answer was Mars. She had to come all the way to Ireland to learn there was a mountain on Mars. Damn her American education! The next question, thanks to the Rock and Roll Hall of Fame, she would have gotten right. Who was the Godfather of Soul?

"James Brown," all the lads shouted at once, disgusted at her for such an easy question. The third one was also a winner. Thanks to his sexcapades, Carlene knew Tiger Woods's real name was Eldrick. "Which country is bordered by both the Atlantic and Indian oceans?" Both teams wrote the answer easily. Carlene silently cursed her American upbringing. A slew of geography questions followed, and she felt smaller with each one. Which country had eight of the ten highest mountains, which area in the Pacific means "many islands," which country beginning with a "T" has a shoreline on the Andaman Sea?

Sometimes she knew the trivia questions when they didn't. "On which street did Bert and Ernie live?" Stares all around. "Sesame Street!" She said it with great snobbery, pride, and one of those little fist pumps she'd often see golfers do after a great shot. Danny knew Elvis died in 1977. Carlene learned it took the famine ships four or five weeks to reach America from Ireland. Snooker was invented in India by British soldiers. The two teams were tied. Anchor grabbed the list and turned the questions on her.

"Clean, jerk, and snatch are terms used in what activity?" he asked.

"Bartending," Carlene answered. She got several laughs, Anchor got claps on the back.

"We can guess who clean and jerk are," Ciaran said, jabbing his thumb first to Collin, and then to Anchor. "But I'm afraid, pet, you're the only one with a snatch in here."

"Are ye fecking saying I look like a bloke?" Sally said. She was perched on her usual spot behind the bar reading a magazine. She spread open her legs and rubbed her hand on her thighs. Carlene was grateful she was wearing jeans.

"Fine," Ciaran said. "My apologies. Two snatches in the room."

"Don't ye fucking call it a snatch," Sally said. "It's a fanny."

"What?" Carlene said. "Fanny means ass." Sally laughed.

"Ah right," she said. "I forgot you Yanks call it that. We call our—snatch—a fanny. You call your arse a fanny. I met these Yanks once and one turned around and showed me her arse and asked me if her fanny looked big. I was like—'Turn around and let me have a look at it.' " Sally covered her mouth and rocked back and laughed and laughed. Carlene and the lads had no choice but to laugh with her.

"How many terms are there for the female genitals?" Eoin asked. "Not as many as for men, do ye think?"

"Let's make a list," Danny said. They were off and running.

Pussy, vagina, cunt—which launched a discussion about how
Irish men often called each other cunt, which had nothing to do
with a woman, and how offended Americans were by this, but it
was the intention, and their intention was simply an affectionate
slag on each other—snatch, fanny, gee-bag (which Carlene had
never heard of and didn't interrupt for clarification), beaver,
love tunnel—

They got stuck and switched genders. "Go," Danny said.
Pecker, dick, cock, sword, rod, penis, pole, willy, staff, pencil—

Carlene took the time to wash the glasses, leaving them to
their male bonding, although Sally would often join in with a
new addition, said loudly and proudly at the top of her lungs.
Apparently, it was still a tie.

"One more question," Collin said. Collin wasn't holding the
list of questions. "For the tie-breaker," he added.

"Go on with ye," Anchor said.

"Who was Carlene with, hanging all over, like, at the opening
night of the Galway Races?"

Sally jumped off her perch and made a beeline for Collin. She
leaned over the bar so that his face was only a half an inch from
her cleavage.

"What's that now?" she said.

"Collin," Carlene said. "Very funny. You know what? Both
teams are winners. Drinks are on me," she said.

"I want to hear this," Anchor said. The rest of the lads me
too-ed. Collin was all smiles. He wasn't wearing one of his
usual T-shirts today. He had on a white pin-striped dress shirt.
His hair was stiff with gel.

"Who was she drooling all over?" Sally asked. "You've
opened yer gob, now ye have to tell us."

"Nobody," Carlene said. "Collin's just taking a piss."

Eoin laughed and pounded on the bar. "Taking *the* piss," he
corrected. "Not taking a piss."

"Whatever. Case closed. Do you guys want free drinks or
not?" In the end, free drinks won out over Sally's cleavage.

"One mighty wind," Riley said. "And they'd be showing
their sticks and pouches to the wind."

"Sticks and pouches!" Danny said. "We missed those ones."

"Collin?" Carlene said. "I've got that thing on the back porch you wanted. Do you want to come get it now?"

"What thing are ye on about?" Sally asked. "I'll get it for ye."

"Not necessary," Carlene said. As she led the way to the back porch, she could have sworn Collin had a definite bounce to his step as he followed. When they reached the enclosure, she immediately dropped all pretenses. Collin's grin seemed to be a permanent feature of his face today. He pulled out his iPhone, thumbed through it, and turned the screen toward her. There was a picture of Carlene and Ronan at the races, locked in a kiss. Carlene quickly put her hand over the phone.

"It was nothing," Carlene said. "Just the one time." Ronan was already avoiding her, just out of paranoia of anyone finding out. What would happen if he knew Collin had a picture of them together? He'd probably disappear from her life altogether.

"So you're not dating him?"

"No. Absolutely not." Collin kept smiling. "And I wouldn't want anyone to think we were," Carlene said. "You can understand that, right?"

"Absolutely," Collin said.

"Good," Carlene said.

"So you're not dating him."

"I told you, no."

"So you're free to go out to dinner with me Saturday night," Collin said. So there it was. It all clicked into place—how he was dressed, the grin, the gel, the bounce in his step. It was all part of his grand plan to seduce and blackmail.

"I have to work Saturday night," Carlene said.

"I'll fill in for ye," Sally said. She was in the doorway, listening. How long had she been there? How much had she heard?

"Brilliant," Collin said. "It's settled, then."

"But I like working Saturday nights," Carlene said. As soon as she said it, she realized it was true. She loved the weekends. The pub was attracting more and more visitors. Single girls were starting to come in from Galway, along with middle-aged couples out for date night. Weekends were when the pool table was in use, the jukebox never stopped, and the drinks flowed. Carlene didn't even mind cleaning up afterward; the routine helped her wind down before sinking into her little bed, her limbs weary from a hard day's work, the noise of the evening buzzing softly in her head.

"Ah, so, you are involved with a certain someone, aren't ye?" Collin said.

"Who?" Sally said. "Tell me."

"Collin," Carlene said. "I'm serious. I really, really like Saturday nights."

"All right," Collin said. "How does Tuesday night suit?" Sally was still staring. Collin was still grinning.

"Suits me just fine," Sally said.

"Okay then," Carlene said. "Tuesday it is."

"It's a date," Collin said.

"It's a date," Sally said.

Carlene had never ventured into the souterrain this late at night. She dropped to the usual spot and turned on the flashlight. The passage was becoming a familiar friend. So far she had been able to crawl along it to the count of ten. Then she crawled backward to the count of ten. It was damp and the stones were hard on her knees, but she had no idea where in Ireland to buy knee pads without starting some kind of bizarre rumor, or ladies' rugby team. Tonight, she would go to the count of twelve. The passage was so low her head grazed the roof as she crawled, sending dirt tumbling into her eyes. She made it to the count of twelve, then hesitated. She could go all the way.

No, she wasn't ready tonight. She still wanted to tell someone else, have some kind of a backup plan in case something went wrong. Besides, she was starting to enjoy the anticipation of what waited at the end of the tunnel. It was distracting and exciting. At least that's how she justified her inability to make it all the way.

Afterward, she stood in her shower and watched the dirt run down the drain. Did anyone else know about the secret space? The McBrides should be the first to know. If she wanted it, she had a good excuse to call Ronan.

And what was she going to do about her "date" with Collin? If only Sally hadn't inserted herself into the mix, and Collin didn't have that picture on his iPhone. Not that she wasn't allowed to go on dates. It wasn't like she and Ronan were an item. But it wasn't Collin she thought of day and night, thoughts of him taking up all room in her head, heart rising every time the pub door opened, secretly praying that he would stroll through the door and sit at her bar.

CHAPTER 25

Mending Fences

Ronan thought about Miss America constantly. He wondered how she was really doing with the bar business. Although she seemed to be doing just fine, he knew there were ugly sides to every business, especially life in the pub. Seeing people go from normal to drunk, their eyes drooping, their words slurring, sometimes their sadness pouring out. Fights, passing out, the shakes and tremors, drinkers coming in the next day for the "cure," which just meant starting the day drinking all over again. There would even be times when she would have to clean up vomit, or piss, or shit, and he hated the thought of her doing any of that. Although she seemed well equipped, the last time he saw her she was wearing these bright blue rubber gloves, and the place always had this just-scrubbed smell. Sally was opening her mouth about town too; apparently Carlene had gone to the hardware shop and stocked up on sanitizer, gloves, masks, and all sorts of industrial-strength cleaning products. If she was trying to scrub all the badness out of the bar, she was in for the long haul.

He'd been avoiding her ever since the night they almost made love. He wanted to, and he came so close, and he still wanted to—he thought of little else these days—but there was just too much to think about. He couldn't jump into anything right now, and what kind of catch was he anyway? He was out of a job, except for a couple of bar shifts he'd picked up from Mickey John, but really, where was his life going? He was living with his mother again, and although he was well fed, he was too old to be living at home. And besides, wouldn't there always be a doubt in her mind, maybe in everyone's mind, maybe even in his mind, that he was just trying to worm his way back into the pub?

And then he'd gone and made a ridiculous bet with Racehorse Robbie. He was winning so far, but it was absolute torture. He'd been about to confess to Carlene what he was doing when she up and hired Sally. He didn't need the drama. Sally was still gunning for the two of them, and even though he knew it was never going to happen, it seemed as if she was never going to give up. Carlene didn't need any more enemies, which brought him to his next rumination, the one that occupied his mind after he was done thinking about making love to her, and that was all the vandalism and "pranks" somebody was playing on Carlene. He didn't like it one bit, and he was furious that someone would even try something like that.

He had to see her, and he finally came up with a good excuse. Which was why he was standing in front of the pub, poised to knock. It was still surreal, having to knock on the door of the pub he grew up in, and worked in, and lived in, but there it was, it was her pub now. She even had a new sign to prove it. The Half Tree. He knocked, and within seconds she opened the door. He tried not to stare. She was wearing jean shorts, a red negligee top, and blue rubber gloves. She had a rag in one hand and a bottle of Lysol in the other. Her long hair was piled on top of her head and held in place with a pencil. He wanted to kiss her.

"Good morning, Miss America." Carlene stood aside to let him in. He stepped in and almost slipped. "Jaysus."

"Sorry. I just mopped the floors."

"I can see that." He looked at her body, openly this time, he couldn't help it. Gorgeous pink spots appeared on her cheeks and he forced himself to look away. "Do you always dress like a Victoria's Secret model to wash the floor?"

"It's laundry day. I've very little left."

"Me father almost put a washer and dryer in here," Ronan said. "He never got around to it. And then I was going to put one in, but I never got around to it either."

"Oh well," Carlene said. "Sometimes I wash things by hand and hang them on the line. Today would've been a good day." They both took a moment and looked out the window.

"Ah, it's a lovely day today," Ronan said.

"Gorgeous," Carlene said.

"Listen," Ronan said. "I have some outdoor things to do today, and I was just wondering if you'd like to come with me."

"Will I be back by five?" Carlene said.

"If you want. Otherwise I've talked to Declan and he'd be happy to fill in."

"Oh," Carlene said.

"I ran into him in town," Ronan said.

"I see." He tried not to look anxious as she mulled over his invitation. She put the Lysol on a nearby table and peeled off her gloves.

"I'll get dressed," she said.

"Wear something you can get dirty in," Ronan said. She nodded and headed up the stairs. *As opposed to what you're wearing now, which makes me want to get dirty with you,* he added silently as he watched her go.

Carlene had been there a few months and was still trying to get around without a car. Fair play to her, but it didn't strike him as an environmental choice, which meant she was afraid to drive on the other side of the road. When Carlene opened the car door and sat down, Ronan asked her if she wanted to drive. She shook her head shyly at the invitation. "You might want to get into the passenger seat, then," Ronan said. The look on her face was deadly. Then she saw the grin on his face and laughed.

She muttered something about never getting used to it as she got out of the driver's seat and headed for the passenger seat. Ronan reminded himself to drive slower; she'd seemed terrified the night he drove her from Galway, always gripping the side of the door and air-braking. He accidentally brushed his left elbow against her breast as he reached for his seat belt, and he racked his brain for an excuse to get out of the car just so he could do it again.

She didn't even ask where they were going, and he liked that about her. He liked a lot of things about her—too many things, if you asked him, and it was starting to annoy him. Did she think about him? Or was she just being friendly? Obviously, she was attracted to him, that much she'd proved with all the kissing and inviting him up to her bedroom like. But what did it mean? What did she really want from him?

"How's the kitten?" he said. Ronan got the wee thing from a buddy of his who was threatening to drown it. He figured Carlene could use the company. Why he didn't just offer it to her like a regular Joe Soap instead of sneaking it into the place, he wasn't quite sure. When it came to Carlene, a lot of things made Ronan unsure.

"I've named her Columbus," Carlene said.

"After the explorer or the great Buckeye State?" Ronan said.

"A bit of both," Carlene said. There was a catch to her voice, as if there was more to the story, as if she was holding something back, but he didn't ask any follow-up questions. He didn't want to seem nosy, and if he started asking her questions, it might lead to her asking him questions, like where do you work now and where do you live and he didn't want to say with my mammy and in someone else's stinky bar.

They fell into silence as they drove. She looked out the window, and he hoped she saw how beautiful everything was on a sunny day. The richness of the grass, the little bursts of color from hay at the side of the road, how inviting the farmhouses looked in the sun. They were coming up onto the church, where Ronan would take a left onto Keals's property.

"Are you taking me to confession?" Carlene asked.

"That depends," Ronan said. "Do you have anything to confess?" It was meant to be a joke, but when he caught her eye and they stared at each other, there was definite voltage going on between them. He pulled up Paul's driveway and forced himself to look away from her gorgeous blue eyes. As promised, Anchor was parked halfway up the drive, waiting for him. His red pickup was piled with the wood Ronan would need. Carlene and Anchor hugged while Ronan started removing the wood from the back of the truck. Obviously, the two were good friends now, he thought. Was he actually getting jealous? She was Anchor's bartender, of course he loved her.

"What's all this for?" Carlene asked.

"Ever build a fence?" Ronan said.

"No."

"There's a first time for everything." He winked at Carlene. Anchor grinned. "You sure he's not home?" Ronan asked Anchor.

"They'll be gone until half three," Anchor said.

"Ah, brilliant," Ronan said. After the wood was all lying neatly on the ground, Anchor saluted them both and screeched away, leaving behind a cloud of dust.

With Carlene around, it was easy to build the fence. Ronan was repairing a section about ten feet long. He simply asked Carlene to hold the wood in place while he did all the sawing and nailing. He pretended not to look at her, but secretly watched her out of his peripheral vision. He watched her take in the property, the church next door, and if he wasn't mistaken, she was doing an awful lot of looking at him.

"Whose property is this?" she asked.

"An old-timer name of Paul Keals," Ronan said.

"This is so nice of you," she said.

"No, it's not," Ronan said. "I'm the one who busted this fence years ago."

"Running away from church?" Carlene guessed.

"My idea of religious freedom," Ronan said. Carlene laughed long and hard. A guy could get used to that laugh. Suddenly, they heard a quivering moo directly behind them. Carlene turned and was nose-to-nose with the old drama queen of a cow.

"Whatever you do," Ronan said, "don't smack her on the arse."

They worked side by side for a little over an hour. By the time they were done, they had both worked up a sweat. Before they reached the car, Ronan grabbed her hand, pulled her into him, and kissed her. She wrapped her hands around his back. He hoped she didn't find him too sweaty, but she must not have minded, for they smooched for a long time.

"Thank you," Ronan said. "I knew it would be easier to do this with you," he said.

"What?" she said. "Kissing?"

"Funny. I was talking about the fence. But I reckon kissing is easier done with you too," he said. They got into the car and he gestured to a cooler on the backseat. "Lunch," Ronan said. "As soon as we get to my secret spot." He drove to the park beside the abbey, and they walked silently toward the river. He set the cooler down and looked at the grass. He should have brought a blanket. But Carlene had already sat down, without a single complaint. He took out the ham-and-cheese sandwiches, which he did not plan on telling her had actually been made by his mother.

"This is delicious," Carlene said. Ronan leaned over and licked a spot of mayonnaise off her bottom lip. She shivered. That was too much for him to take. The next thing he knew, he was all over her, which might have been romantic except for the ham-and-cheese sandwich in her hand. By the time he pulled off her, it was smashed to her chest. He thought she was going to have a fit; instead, she was laughing. She pulled the smooshed sandwich off her breasts. He offered to trade, but she had already taken another big bite out of it. So much for Sally saying she was some kind of neat freak. You couldn't call a girl who would eat a ham-and-cheese sandwich off her shirt anything but beautifully easygoing.

"I don't know what we're doing," she said out of nowhere just as he was about to tell her that she was the perfect woman.

"We're eating ham-and-cheese sandwiches," Ronan said.

"I really don't know anything about you." *Here it comes,* he thought.

"Ask me anything," he said, hoping she wouldn't.

"Where do you live?"

"I'm back at the house for now," he said. "Just until I figure out where to plant myself next."

"Do you miss the pub?" she asked.

"Like my right arm," he said. There it was again, that blush. Maybe that did sound kind of dirty—was she thinking that's what he meant?

"Do you have another job now?" What she really meant was, are you still gambling—he could see it in her eyes.

"I have a couple of things here and there," Ronan said.

"Like what?"

"Are there going to be a lot of these, because I'd rather answer them in the river."

"You want to swim?" she said. "Here?"

"Why not?"

"For one thing, I don't have a suit."

"Don't need one."

"For another thing, I'll bet it's freezing."

"Want to place a wager?" He waited for a lecture. Instead, she smiled.

"How much?"

"Fifty euros," he said. "But you have to strip down to your knickers." She was a betting woman after all. Before he could even get his shirt off, he was watching her run into the river in her little bra and black panties. Maybe he would forget all his doubts, just go for it. He jumped in and pulled her into him.

"You're shivering," he said.

"It's like the Antarctic," she said.

"It's refreshing," Ronan said. "Now, what are your other questions?"

"I can't think," Carlene said. "It's too freaking cold."

"My job here is done," he said. They couldn't go anywhere else in wet clothes. As much as he enjoyed seeing her in her skivvies, he'd realized his mistake. He had to take her back to the pub now. They rode back in a comfortable silence. He would ask her out, and soon. There was no use rushing it.

"Hey," she said when he dropped her off.

"Hey," he said.

"I've got a trad band booked for tonight. You should pop in. Johnny Spoons is playing."

"How do you know Johnny Spoons?" Ronan said. Johnny was the best spoon player in Galway. He'd never been able to book him.

"Sue Finnegan told me about him," Carlene said. "So I just called him up one day." Must have been the American accent, Ronan thought. Either that or Johnny Spoons had already heard that the new American bartender was hot.

"I might do," Ronan said. "I might do."

"Well, I hope you do," Carlene said. "Because actually, there's something I'd like to show you—but it'll have to wait until no one else is around." Ronan hoped the grin on his face didn't look as lecherous as he felt. Apparently, it did.

"Take it down a notch, cowboy," she said. "It's nothing like that." She held out her hand. He took it, turned it over, and kissed her palm. "Uh, thanks," she said. "But I was actually just looking for the fifty euros you owe me."

CHAPTER 26

The Curse of the Full Moon

Bartenders will tell you, people act funny when there is a full moon. They don't even need to look to the sky for proof, it's there in front of them, evidenced in the strange behaviors of their regulars at the bar. Carlene had never believed in that kind of stuff before. She wouldn't be saying that after tonight. To Carlene's dismay, Sally was dressed in a short, low-cut little black dress and her raven hair was swept up on her head with a few tendrils falling down. She was wearing stilettos. When Carlene asked her what the occasion was, Sally happily informed her that she had it on good authority that Ronan would be in tonight, and she was going to seduce him. Carlene looked down at her own jeans and leather flip-flops and soft turquoise shirt that looked more like an artist's smock than a seductive tool. Would it be suspicious if she ran up and changed?

The lads were more fidgety on this particular tonight, Anchor was tugging on his goatee, Riley could hardly set his pint glass down without demanding another one, and Ciaran was arguing with Collin about helium balloons, a conversation Carlene didn't even attempt to follow. When the trad band came, they were sans a spoon player. Johnny, the rest of the band assured her, was on his way. This gave Carlene the perfect excuse as to why she was constantly looking at the door. Everyone seemed to be drinking more, getting drunk faster.

"It's a full moon," Sally said when Carlene commented on this.

"Really?" The first chance she got, Carlene snuck out to the backyard and gazed at the sky. Sure enough, there it was, fat and happy on the horizon, a yellow-white, pulsing orb. It was nearing the end of October, a good time for a full moon. For Carlene it conjured up everything she loved about the season. Hayrides, and campfires, and the smell of leaves changing color, and back to school, and new sweaters, and new beginnings. New Year's never felt as fresh as fall. It was her favorite time of year, and once again she reminded herself how lucky she was. She would call her friends back home tomorrow and catch up.

She would insist that her father come for Christmas. Maybe she would start a blog about her time in Ireland, so everyone back home could read about how she was doing. What a great idea! Of course she'd yet to get a computer and Internet service, but she was making enough money now that it should be possible. She was humming to herself and even skipping a little when she came back into the pub.

And there was Ronan, seated at the bar. She couldn't see all of his face because Sally was leaning into him, and her cleavage was obscuring the view. Ronan, however, was looking around the bar, just as she had done when she was looking for him. When his eyes landed on her, he smiled. Carlene flushed with joy. Sally's head jerked in her direction. Carlene was too late in noticing this, her gaze and smile still on Ronan, so by the time she made eye contact with Sally, it was too late. In the split-second glance between them, Carlene knew that Sally knew. Sally immediately pulled away from Ronan and began lathering attention on the other boys, but from the stiff way she was now carrying herself, Carlene feared Sally wouldn't keep up the happy act for long.

The band was ready to play. "Drink up," the singer announced. "The more you drink, the better we sound. But if you start to think we're good looking, it's time to stop drinking."

Besides the regulars, there weren't very many people about, and Carlene could only hope they would come in later. Maybe people were night owls during a full moon.

It was Johnny Spoons who brought the crowd. He stumbled in the doorway with about ten people in tow. Carlene didn't know any of them, but they were all loud and drunk. They swarmed a table near the band. Johnny lurched forward to join the band. He knocked into the music stand positioned center stage and nearly took out one of the guitar players. The band jumped back as Johnny toppled over and fell. He lay facedown on the music stand, both man and sheet-holder splayed out onstage. Carlene expected the rest of the band to swear and drag him off the stage; instead, they cheered.

"Get him a pint," the leader of the band yelled. Sally moved to do just that.

"Absolutely not," Carlene said.

"What do you mean?" Sally said.

"We're not serving him any more," Carlene said. "He's had enough." The members of the band hauled Johnny to his feet and propped him in a chair. They began to play. Johnny did too, and damn if he couldn't still play. Those spoons traveled up and down his arms like they had a life of their own. He bounced his head and knee to the music while those spoons sprang to life. Carlene was astounded; he truly had a remarkable gift. She would never see cutlery in the same light again.

"Full moon," Anchor said.

"Where are the cheese toasties?" Riley said.

"Hungry, boss?" Sally said.

"I'd eat a nun through a convent door," Riley said. Carlene went to the small refrigerator. The cheese was gone. There had been a huge block in there last night.

"Do you have the cheese?" Carlene asked Sally.

"No," Sally said. Carlene looked around the bar to no avail.

"It's missing," Carlene said. "It was in here last night, I swear."

"There's bad news and there's worse news," Ciaran said. "The bad news is you've got a mouse. The worse news is, he's robbing bits off you when you're asleep." Ciaran laughed like it was the funniest thing he'd ever heard. Sally took money out of the register.

"I'll get snacks from the shop," she said. "You don't want to run out of food during a full moon." The boys watched her ass as she left the room. Carlene was starting to feel just a little bit apprehensive about this full-moon business. Seriously, what happened to the cheese?

The men Johnny brought with him could sing, and dance, and drink. They did all three with great gusto. They spread out, and soon every corner of the bar was filled—the pool table, the dartboard, the dance floor. At one point, one of the guys grabbed Sally's hand and brought her into the middle of their dance. The next thing Carlene knew, Sally was dancing on top of the table. She looked at Ronan. He was watching her too, but nobody seemed particularly alarmed. Carlene waited a minute and then walked over to the table. Sally was noticeably drunk. Carlene wondered when this happened—she hadn't seen her drinking behind the bar. Carlene reached her hand up toward Sally.

"Down you go," she said. Sally tried to pull Carlene up with her. She was surprisingly strong. One of the men grabbed Carlene by the waist and lifted her onto the table. Carlene was mortified. Sally started dancing with her, encouraging her to put on a show. Carlene tried to push Sally away, but Sally clung onto her.

"Somebody bring me a bottle of Jameson," Sally yelled, still hanging on to Carlene.

"Sally, let go," Carlene said. "Let's get down from here."

"We're going to have a wee shot first," Sally said. Someone handed her up the bottle. Sally managed to drink from it and hold on to Carlene at the same time. Carlene could have jumped off, but it would have meant taking Sally with her, possibly injuring her. Carlene was just about to yell for Ronan when there he was, standing by the table, ready to catch them. Sally slammed the bottle of Jameson into Carlene's chest.

"Drink," she said. Carlene looked to Ronan. Sally grabbed Carlene by the back of the hair and tugged until Carlene's head tilted back. She put the bottle up to Carlene's lips. Carlene's choices were drink or choke. Carlene drank, came up sputtering. Sally cheered.

"Jaysus," Ronan said. He reached out his arms and Carlene leaned into him, no longer caring if Sally fell on her ass. Carlene could feel Sally staring daggers into her as Ronan took her in his arms. Sally kicked off a stiletto. It hit Carlene square in the middle of her forehead.

"Whoops," Sally said. "Sorry."

"Somebody needs to get her out of here," Carlene said. A ripping sound erupted from behind her. The dartboard had come clean off, taking part of the wall with it. It crashed to the ground.

"You bollix," the dart player up next screamed. "I was winning. You owe me five hundred—"

"It came clean off the wall,'" the other protested. "That's a forfeit." Before Carlene knew what was happening, they were fighting. At first they simply butted into each other, then hopped around each other, then put their fists.

"Shit," Carlene said. "What do I do?" The regulars got off their stools and slowly gathered around, but nobody made a direct move to get in between them. "We need to stop this," Carlene said. The lads waited until the first two punches were thrown. It wasn't as elegant as a boxing match, Carlene thought. The band stopped playing, all except for Johnny Spoons, who continued banging out a solo. Finally, the regulars swooped in and each grabbed one of the fighters. They continued to swear, spit, and threaten. Anchor and Ciaran dragged one of them out to the front yard, Ronan and Collin wrestled the other out back. To Carlene's horror, Sally, who was finally off the table, was holding Columbus.

Carlene didn't know where she'd found him, Columbus always hid when there were people in the bar, but there he was squirming in her firm grasp. Carlene slowly approached and held out her hands.

"I'll take him upstairs," she said. "He doesn't like crowds." From the window overlooking the front yard, Carlene saw one of the fighters puking into her bushes. Sally ignored Carlene's request and took the cat behind the bar. Carlene followed her.

"Sally," she said. "I think you need the night off. Go somewhere else and have fun." Sally set Columbus on the back of the bar. The cat immediately tore off, knocking a Jägermeister bottle off as he went. It smashed to the floor and immediately permeated the room with the sticky scent of black licorice. Ronan and the lads came back inside. Collin gathered his jacket from the back of the chair and put it on. Carlene hadn't noticed his shirt until now. It read: I SLEPT WITH YOUR GIRLFRIEND. Underneath was a thumbs-up from Facebook along with: 324 people like this.

Sally stepped forward. "I bet you're excited for your date," she said.

"Sally," Carlene said.

"Where are you taking her?" Sally's voice was raised so that everyone in the pub could hear her.

"It's not a date," Carlene said. "It's friends going out for dinner."

"That sounds like a date to me," Sally said. "Doesn't that sound like a date to you, Ronan?" Ronan's face tightened and he shoved his hands in his pocket.

"I haven't a clue," he said. He wouldn't look at Carlene.

"I was here when it all went down," Sally said. "She can protest all she wants, but Collin here asked her on a date, and she said yes." Carlene shook her head, but knew she wasn't going to win any fights with Sally in this condition.

"Go home, Sally," she said.

"Will you take me home, Ronan?" Sally said. Carlene waited for him to refuse, and was just about to offer to call her a taxi when he spoke up.

"Sure," he said. "We'll grab something to eat first." He looked deliberately at Carlene. "You don't mind, do ye? It's not like going out to eat with a girl is a date or anything, is it?" Carlene, half-stunned, just stared at him.

"Be my guest," she said. They left, Sally draped around him, half dragging him out. Collin stood awkwardly by the chair. The lads resumed their places at the bar. Carlene looked at the clock. It was just after midnight; they would expect her to stay open for them for another three hours at least. Even though official closing times were half eleven during the week and half twelve on the weekends, it was well known that the pub would stay open for the regulars.

"Are we still on for Tuesday?" Collin asked. Carlene wanted to shout at him, throw something at him, tell him they were certainly not on for Tuesday. But he looked nervous and sweet, and this wasn't his fault at all. And no matter what anyone said, it wasn't a date.

"Sure," she said. "We're still on." He smiled and the lads wolf-whistled and Carlene went into her routine: pouring drinks, washing glasses, listening to the chatter around her. The lads started a game of cards, and things went back to normal for a little while. She even got everyone out by half two. She was just shooing the last of them out the door when she noticed two men standing by the road, just underneath the split tree, watching her. They were wearing frowns and tweed suits. Was it normal to be afraid of men in tweed? She wanted to call the lads back, but they were already stumbling down the road. The men stepped closer. Under the front light, Carlene could see they were considerably older than she first thought, in their fifties maybe.

"We're closed," Carlene said, hoping she didn't sound afraid.

"Is Ronan McBride here with ye?" one asked. He didn't sound friendly. They seemed sober, but it did little to ease the tickle of apprehension Carlene felt at the base of her neck.

"He no longer owns this pub," Carlene said.

"Aw, but he still comes here, doesn't he?"

"A bartender never tells," Carlene said. They looked at each other and laughed.

"You'll give him a message," one said.

"I told you—"

"Tell him Robbie says hi. Asked specifically how his lovely mother is doing," the man finished. They smiled, turned, and walked away. Carlene felt a sinking sensation in the pit of her stomach. She'd heard the friendly banter of the Irish before, asking after one another, lamenting the weather, catching up on news. This wasn't the same. They weren't really asking after Mary McBride, they were laying down a threat. Carlene picked up her phone and stared at it. If she called now, would he even answer? Would he just think she was jealous?

If everything had gone as planned, he'd be with her now, exploring the souterrain under a full moon. He'd be able to reassure her that the men were harmless and she'd misread the situation. He'd laugh when she told him she was worried they were fashion-challenged loan sharks. Where were Sally and Ronan right now? There weren't even any restaurants open this late. Carlene looked at the full moon and flipped it the bird. Then, knowing it had to be done, she picked up the phone and called Ronan, even though it meant he would probably think she was a jealous man-chaser.

CHAPTER 27

The Nice Guy

Carlene was delighted to hear that Collin was taking her to dinner in Salthill. Just a few miles from Galway's city center, Salthill was a beachside haven, with a promenade, restaurants, bars, and plenty of B&Bs. Carlene needed to get out of Ballybeog, put some distance between her and the pub. Declan agreed to bartend, Sally was MIA. Given that Carlene heard Sally had been discouraging everyone from coming to the Half Tree, Carlene took it that she'd quit. It bothered her that she didn't get a chance to personally fire Sally.

Unlike Ronan, Collin was a cautious driver, maybe because his little car didn't even look like it could go very fast without falling apart. After a while, Carlene realized it was just as scary, if not worse, to have cars beeping at them, then hurling past effing and blinding at them. Collin didn't react—in fact, nothing at all ever seemed to bother him, and Carlene reluctantly admitted that was one of the things that bothered her about sweet Collin. Was she doomed to fall in love with dark, brooding, complicated men? Could she admit to herself that Collin was just too clean-cut, too sweet, too nice? Just like Ronan basically accused her of being. *They're going to walk all over you.*

And were they? Someone was stealing kegs and cheese, and slapping up walls, and who knows what else they had in store? Could it have been the men in tweed? What she needed was an official investigation, some kind of Nancy Drew/MacGyver type effort. Would the folks of Ballybeog hate her even more if she morphed into some kind of Sherlock Holmes? *I mean, really, what kind of person steals a block of cheese?*

Collin took her to a little Mexican restaurant. It was cozy, painted bright orange, and had Mexican blankets hanging on the walls, along with an Irish flag. Little shamrocks were painted on the margarita glasses. The menu was typical Mexican, but also included chips. Carlene devoured her burrito and margarita, then noticed Collin had barely touched his enchilada.

"Do you not like it?" Carlene asked.

"I'm more of a meat-and-potatoes kind of guy," Collin admitted.

"Then why did you bring me here?" There were plenty of restaurants in the city, and Carlene would have been happy with any of them.

"I heard you say you liked Mexican," Collin said. A blush radiated from his cheeks, flooding his face with red.

"Shit," Carlene said. She ordered another margarita, Collin ordered a beer.

"What's wrong?" he said.

"You," Carlene said. "We've got to do something about you." *Don't say it, don't say it, don't say it.*

"I don't follow," Collin said.

You're too nice, you're too nice, you're too nice.

"You're in love with Sally, aren't you?" Carlene said instead. Collin's cheeks burned brighter. "I thought so," she said.

"Ah, but I reckon I could get to like you too, so. I really do." Carlene burst out laughing. After a minute he laughed with her.

"I do grow on people," Carlene said. "But why settle for that?"

"Sally is in love with Ronan," Collin said. "As is a slightly kooky American girl I know."

"So fight for her," Carlene said, ignoring the slightly kooky American bit.

"It won't work. I'm invisible to her. Unless she needs something."

"Told you. Too nice."

Collin's groan was that of a man who'd heard this before. "What the feck do women want? A man who beats them?"

"Of course not. But—we do want a man with confidence. With a touch of mystery and a dab of danger."

"Danger?" Collin sounded alarmed.

"You are a very good-looking guy. But you act like an ugly guy." There was something about being in another country that made Carlene feel free to say whatever came into her head.

"I act like an ugly guy?" He sounded angry. The red was gone. Carlene pointed at him.

"There," she said. "That's much better."

"Fuck," Collin said.

"It's very simple. Just play a little hard to get. Just don't try so hard to please them. Just . . . hold a little back." Collin looked totally confused. She wasn't explaining this right. What did she know about teaching a nice guy to be a bad boy? Besides, maybe there was some mousy girl out there who would love his sweet, shy, doormat routine. But he wasn't in love with a mousy girl, he was in love with Sally Collins. And she would not fall for a doormat. Carlene told herself that she was being altruistic, that this had absolutely nothing to do with jealousy, the gnawing images in her head of Sally and Ronan together. She'd left that message on his phone warning him about the mysterious men in tweed, and he hadn't even called her back! Was he lying in a ditch somewhere with broken legs, or was he just too heartless to call her back and thank her for potentially saving his life? Had anything happened between him and Sally when they left the pub? She couldn't think about it, she wouldn't, it was torture.

When the check came, Collin reached for it, then looked at Carlene. With a slow smile, he slid it over to her. She laughed.

"I should've started the lesson after the check," she said. She reached into her purse. He grabbed the check back.

"I can't feckin' do it," he said.

"Baby steps," she said.

They took a walk on the beach. Carlene tried to put everything out of her mind and enjoy the night sand between her
toes, even though it was absolutely freezing. Collin wanted to
know all about Ohio, and she told him all the good parts, without getting into anything too personal. Collin still lived with his
parents, something Carlene realized was very common in Ballybeog. He had a sister who was married and lived in the next
town, and two brothers in Australia.

"Have you been to visit them?" Carlene asked.

"Not yet," Collin said.

"Why not?" His eyes narrowed slightly and he looked away.

"Ah, the oul wan and the oul fella don't get around as good
as they used to. I think they need me."

"Ah," Carlene said. "I've been there."

"You have?"

"Yes." She didn't offer anything more, and he didn't ask.
"Eventually," she said, "you come to a point where you realize
that it's your life. And as much as you think they can't, they can
manage without you."

"You're filling me head with all sorts of things tonight,"
Collin said. "Whatdda ye say we go get a wee drink?"

She was home before midnight. Declan was alone at the bar,
playing with Columbus. Carlene hadn't expected Collin to try
to kiss her good night, so she was startled when he grabbed her
and crushed his lips over hers, even tried to pry her lips open
with his tongue. She pulled away. He gave her a sly smile.

"Just practicing my bad-boy routine," he said. And then he
walked away with a bit of a swagger, leaving Carlene to wonder
if she should have kept her mouth shut once again.

"Would ye like a drink?" Declan asked.

"Cup of tea?" Carlene said. She realized, she really wanted one
too. Maybe Ireland was growing on her. She'd be ordering chips
at the Chinese restaurant next. Declan fixed them both a mug.

"Did you have anyone in at all?" Carlene asked. Declan
shook his head. Carlene wondered what Sally had done to lure
Riley somewhere else. Free drinks, most likely.

"Don't worry, petal," he said. "It will all blow over."

"Or blow up," Carlene said. She sipped her tea. Declan sipped his tea. Without drink, the conversation stalled. "What's the name of the woman who works in the Ballybeog Museum?" Carlene asked.

Declan frowned. "Nobody works in the Ballybeog Museum."

"I was there. I saw her. Real skinny? Anorexic looking, to be honest. Short dark hair?"

Declan shook his head. "The Ballybeog Musuem's been closed for years."

"But I was just there. I stayed for a good half hour, then as I was leaving she nearly gave me a heart attack. She was standing in the corner. I thought she was a mannequin."

"Ah," Declan said as if that solved it. "Maybe she was."

"Nope. She walked and talked. At least—she talked."

"Sounds like someone was messing with ye. Maybe a tinker? That museum has been closed for years."

"I think they prefer to be called travelers," Carlene said. Declan sipped his tea, Carlene sipped her tea. "Who used to run the museum?" Carlene asked.

"Gerald Murphy. He's retired now. You'll find him at Dally's Pub most days."

"Oh. That definitely wasn't him." Declan sipped his tea, Carlene sipped her tea.

"I'm interested in secret underground spaces," Carlene said. "Do you know if there's anything like that around here?"

"Could be," Declan said. "Hit and miss with all the bog land." Carlene thought about it. The underground space was close to Joe's property line, and his side was drier than hers. Was the tunnel built simply to help drain the water from the property? Obviously, Declan, who'd worked here for the past twenty years, knew nothing about it. Or was he purposefully keeping it a secret?

"Would ye like more tea?" Declan asked.

"Of course," Carlene lied.

CHAPTER 28

Her One and Only

Sheep grazed just outside the backdoor of the McBrides' modest two-story farmhouse. Carlene was pleasantly surprised to see all six of the McBride women and their young ones at mass, and thrilled when Mary McBride invited her back to the house for a fry. Ronan was nowhere in sight, which was not a surprise, although Carlene kept hoping he would appear at any moment or that she'd at least get to hear some mention of him. As Mary cooked, the women all congregated in the kitchen while the children played happily underfoot. The smell of the fry was so tantalizing, Carlene had trouble focusing on the chatter around her. Siobhan and Clare were helping their mother with the breakfast, although Mary seemed quite capable of doing it herself, and once in a while she would shoo a daughter away with the flip of her hand, then use the same hand to pat stray hairs off her face. Liz and Sarah were at the table poring over a bridal magazine. Carlene wished she knew them well enough to ask them who was getting married. Anne was out on the front porch with a little girl, and Katie—well, Katie was glued to Carlene's side, practically holding her hand. For once in her life, Carlene felt like the popular girl in school.

"Does your mother like to cook, Carlene?" Mary McBride asked her.

"Or do you like to cook?" Siobhan added.

"My mother doesn't cook," Carlene said. *It's hard to cook when you're dead,* she wanted to add. Carlene didn't plan on withholding the truth, she just didn't want to ruin such a happy family moment, and she wanted them to like her. Family was important in Ireland, and Carlene was suddenly embarrassed of her dead mother. "I used to cook for my dad," Carlene said. *He kept to an unwavering schedule, the precursor to his macrobiotic diet. Monday was pot roast. Tuesday boiled chicken. Wednesday lasagna. Thursday boiled chicken because both days of the week started with a "T," and Friday was whitefish. The side dishes were always green beans boiled exactly twelve minutes and little boiled red potatoes.*

"Ah, lovely," Mary McBride said.

"Are you sure there isn't anything I can do to help?" Carlene asked.

"Not a thing, not a thing," Mary McBride said. "Would you like another cup of tea?" No, no, no, no.

"That would be lovely, thank you."

"Come with me," Katie said, linking arms and steering Carlene out of the kitchen.

"Don't disappear too far, hear?" Mary said. "Her fry is almost ready." Carlene smiled to herself, loving how she said "her fry" as if she were a guest of honor.

"No worries," Katie sang. She pulled Carlene into an adjacent hallway where a wall of pictures accosted her. Picture after picture showed a dark-haired boy with the eyes of a reptile and a lethal smile. In one—he couldn't have been more than five years old—he was sporting glasses with black frames. They swallowed his face, yet he was grinning ear to ear.

"He loved those glasses," Katie said. "He never took them off." Carlene felt a twinge of love for him and silently chastised herself to stop it. Another picture showed Ronan as a baby—a chubby infant wearing what looked to Carlene like a little white dress. He probably wouldn't want the lads at the pub to see that.

"His christening," Katie said. "That's what they dressed them all in," she added as if she could read Carlene's mind.

"Can I get a copy of that for the pub?" Carlene asked.

"And here he is on the hurling team. Just when he was changing from cute to heartbreaker."

"He's my one and only," Mary yelled from the kitchen. Carlene laughed. Katie rolled her eyes and shook her head, but all with a loving smile of her own. Whereas Carlene had grown up without any females, Ronan had grown up surrounded and loved by them. Then why was he such a mess? Had they just spoiled him too much? No, he was a grown man, and the responsibility for his behavior was his alone. Just like Carlene had always blamed her father. He was the reason she didn't pursue veterinarian school, he was the reason she never traveled, he was the reason she hadn't fallen in love and married. Now she knew it had been her responsibility to take charge of her life all along. It sounded so simple, as if she should have figured that out by now, but it had been difficult to figure out her own life through the webs of her father's rituals. She had finally left, and he was still alive. Her own guilt and beliefs had been holding her back, not her father.

"Aren't there any pictures of you girls?" Carlene asked.

"We're over here," Katie said. She pointed to the wall directly across from them in the hall. Carlene couldn't believe it. One lonely group picture of the girls. Katie laughed. "You should see your face," she said. "Brilliant. Yanks are such gas." She linked arms with Carlene again. "There's loads of pictures of us upstairs," she explained. "We've got an entire wall stuffed with our faces as well, like."

"Oh thank God," Carlene said.

"He's still my one and only," Mary yelled from the kitchen.

It was more food than Carlene normally ate in a week. One fried egg, with the promise of more. Toast with butter and jam.

Bacon, which was really ham. Sausages, as if the bacon needed a friend. Black and white pudding, which Carlene hated but ate out of respect. Baked beans. A fried tomato. Potatoes. Orange juice. A pot of tea. Carlene happily stuffed herself as the table buzzed with conversation. She would have joined in but she didn't want to speak with her mouth full, and her mouth was always full. She didn't even care to pry secrets out of them—secrets, say, about a certain golden boy—but in fact, after this meal, all she wanted was a place to lie down, where she and her whale of a stomach could die in peace. And perhaps that was their plan, for they waited until the meal was over, when she was too full to run. A silence fell over the table that Carlene mistook for happy satiation. Mary McBride fussed with her hair. The three of the half dozen who had children fussed with them. Only Katie looked directly at her, but her smile looked as if it had been played by a remote control and accidentally put on mute. For a second Carlene was convinced they knew about the soutterrain.

Were they furious with her for hiding it from them? Who told them? The famine victim? *That's awful, Carlene, you have to stop calling her that even inside your head.* Why did she have these constant horrible thoughts that she couldn't drive out?

"We thought you should hear this from us," Katie said.

"If you haven't already," Siobhan said.

"Girls, we should not do this, it isn't our place," Mary said. Clare reached over and took her hand.

"Ma," she said. "You won't be saying that when she tries to bedazzle yer Christmas tree next year."

Mary McBride put her hand on her heart. "O sacred heart of Jesus," she said. Clare patted her hand again.

"Sally?" Carlene said.

"So she knows, then," Liz said. "Right, that's sorted." Liz pushed back from the table and stood.

"Knows what?" Carlene said. "I don't know anything." Anne yanked Liz back down.

"Sally and Ronan are getting married," Clare said. Carlene felt as if she'd been punched in the stomach.

"No, they're not," she said. It wasn't possible. Yes, they went on a date, yes, she could even believe it if they fooled around, but married? Ronan?

"Do you want some more tea, luv?" Mary said.

"No," Carlene said. She stood up. "I have to go." Katie sprang to her feet and grabbed Carlene's hands.

"We know he doesn't love her," Katie said.

"Katie," Mary said.

"He's my brother and I'm allowed to speak. Something is still going on with him," Kate said.

"She's right," Siobhan said. "We thought losing the pub would be the end of his gambling—but he's been acting strange."

"What does that have to do with Sally?" Carlene added.

"Sally has money," Liz said. "Loads of it."

"You think Ronan is the type who would marry for money?" Carlene said. Maybe she didn't know him at all. Of course she didn't, wasn't that one of the things she said she loved about him? The excitement, the danger, the unpredictability? Suddenly what once seemed sexy just seemed like a waste. An impossible mess to clean up. If he wanted to marry Sally for her money, who was she to stop him? It meant he wasn't the type of man she wanted to spend her life with. She'd rather count and boil green beans exactly twelve minutes. "I have to go," Carlene said. "I can't do anything about this."

"He loves you," Katie said. "We know he's not perfect—"

"He's absolutely perfect," Mary said.

"But we know he loves you," Katie said. "You should have seen the change in him when you came into town. He's been in the dark for so long, and it was like a light suddenly came on. He loves you."

"It's true," Siobhan said. "We all know it." The girls nodded. "He wouldn't be doing this unless there was a serious problem. And before you start feeling sorry for Sally Collins, she's hardly a wallflower. If he's marrying her out of some warped need to pay off a debt or protect us—she's masterminding the whole thing, you can bet your last love. No pun intended."

"I wonder if it has something to do with those men who came to the pub the other night," Carlene said.

"Men?" Mary said. "What men?"

"A couple of scrappy-lookin' fellas in tweed," Carlene said.

"O sacred heart of Jesus," Mary said.

"Calm down, Mam," Siobhan said. "What did they say?" she asked Carlene.

"They just asked if Ronan was around," Carlene said. "Wanted me to tell him they were looking for him." Carlene couldn't very well say they'd mentioned Mary McBride, could she? Why didn't Ronan call her back so she didn't have to sit here with all the McBride women's ears perked up, and debate what to mention and what to leave out? "They didn't really say much," Carlene said. "But they seemed kind of—serious." She was going to say "sinister," but stopped herself at the last minute.

"Sacred heart of Jesus," Mary said. "They're murderers. They're going to murder my baby. My one and only." Carlene didn't say it, but she was thinking the same thing. Thugs, loan sharks.

"And what did you tell them?" Clare said.

"Nothing," Carlene said. "Just that he didn't work at the pub anymore. I swear." If Ronan was in deep debt and was being threatened by loan sharks, was that reason enough for him to go running to Sally?

"We have to call the guards," Mary said.

"And tell them what? We're scared of a couple of men in tweed?" Anne said.

"Maybe if he marries Sally and pays off his debt, they'll go away," Carlene said. "Maybe it's for the best."

"My arse it's for the best," Mary McBride said. There was a collective gasp at the table. Then the half dozen broke out into laughter. Carlene wanted to laugh with them but she felt greasy and sick. She told herself it had nothing to do with picturing Sally in a wedding dress.

"You have to talk to him," Katie said. She took Carlene's hand across the table.

"I don't know what I could say," Carlene said.

"Tell him how you feel," Katie said. "But only if he makes a light go on in you too."

CHAPTER 29

The Half Tree—Present Day
The David's Interlude

"Wait," The David said. "This is what you call a love story? He is going to marry the sparkly Sally woman for the money? She is going to know this and she is going to let him?"

"We never said it was a simple story," Katie said. "People are complicated. Love is complicated."

"Love is shit," The David said. He held up the rope and nodded. "This story is shit."

"We're not finished with it yet," Katie said.

"Just tell me now. What about this American girl? Did she ever crawl into the hole? Did she ever tell Ronan she loved him? Does she still own this pub? Why isn't she here tonight? Is she home counting those green of beans things?"

"They're coming," someone said. The door opened. Sally swayed in glittering like a walking chandelier. Guests greeted her with cheers and claps, and hugs and kisses, and complimented her radiance.

"Where's the old chain?" someone said.

"Are ya saying I'm the ball?" Sally said.

"I'm saying he's a right fool to let you out of his sight today," the man said with a wink and a raise of his pint. The David reached for his rope, but it was gone. Katie touched him on the arm.

"Look," she said. Sally was the center of attention. She literally and figuratively glowed in the center of the room.

"She is acting very happy," The David said.

"She is," Katie said.

"I am so confused," the German said. "Where is the groom?"

"I told you we didn't have time to tell this story," Liz said.

"We'd better get the cake," Siobhan said.

"We baked it ourselves," Anne said.

"Six tiers," Katie said.

"I know we are not on an island," The David said as they headed out the door. "But I was voting for the Yankee Doodle girl." It was true, The David was sad for the American girl, but he was happy to be part of the story. The Irish culture was new to him, but he liked it. He stared at the bride as he passed. She was dancing by herself, with her eyes closed to the world. He obediently followed the girls to the shop next door to get the cake. He didn't have anything better to do, and he wanted to hear the rest of the story, whatever it was. And, for the first time in the past twenty-four hours, he forgot all about his rope.

CHAPTER 30

A Few Stiffies

Carlene stood in front of Finnegan's like a married woman standing in front of a hotel, contemplating whether or not to meet a potential lover in his room upstairs. She'd heard so much about this pub, which had been in Sue's family for generations. It was on the main street in town, and Carlene liked the black-and-white façade with a gorgeous wooden door marking the entrance. It was raining outside, but like she'd heard several regulars in her pub say, "It never rains in a pub." She'd called Sally and insisted she work for her tonight, not once letting on that she knew about her engagement. To her surprise, Sally agreed. Apparently getting engaged had done wonders for her disposition.

Carlene would confront Sally later, maybe after a good dose of liquid courage. Speaking of which . . . She took a deep breath and walked into Finnegan's Pub.

It was three times as big as her pub. To the right was the main room consisting of an L-shaped bar and floor space with built-in booths and several freestanding tables and chairs. There was a corner with two video poker machines across from an area to play darts. To the left was another section of seating, at least six booths, past which was a hallway leading out to the restrooms and an outdoor patio and backyard. It was more like a house, and Carlene would soon learn why. Sue and her husband and five children lived there—their rooms were above the pub, and their kitchen and living room were through the door behind the bar. In fact, when customers sat at the bar, they could see into the Finnegans' kitchen; the door was always open, making way for the kids to easily come in and out, which they did with great frequency.

It was dinnertime now, and Sue was standing behind the bar peeling potatoes. The smell of lamb curry wafted out into the pub. Carlene felt instantly at ease as she headed for an empty stool at the bar. There were a few old men sitting nearby watching a horse race on a television hanging in the corner, above the spot where Sue was peeling potatoes. The walls, like most pubs in Ireland, were littered with memorabilia. There were a ton of horse-racing pictures, hurling posters, Gaelic football posters, family pictures, old Guinness signs, a hurling stick, a soccer jersey, and several trophies that upon closer inspection were won by playing ladies' darts. The back counter of the bar was well stocked. The same tiny soda bottles that Carlene had in her bar, only three times as many. She also had snacks Carlene didn't have, bags of Taytos, Bacon Fries, and salt-and-vinegar nuts. Carlene made a mental note that she should expand her offerings of snacks as well.

Sue looked up when Carlene took her seat, and smiled. They had only met briefly, the time the publicans came to show Carlene their support when the wall had been slapped up. Carlene had been too busy to chat with her and was happy to finally have the chance. Carlene had forgotten how nice it felt to be on the other side of the bar. All she had to do was sit, drink, and chat. Sue was a tall woman who looked as if she'd have no trouble tossing drunkards out on their ears single-handedly, but at the same time there was something very soft and feminine about her face, a glorious mix of tough and tender. Her hair was cut fashionably short, with spiky layers held in place with gel, and colored a dark shade of red.

"How ya," she called to Carlene.

"Grand, grand," Carlene responded. She was starting to not only pick up the local lingo, but like it as well. It was like learning a foreign language, she was always looking for the opportunity to speak like the locals.

"You okay?" Sue asked. Carlene knew this was simply the opening to ask her what she'd like to drink, but when Carlene opened her mouth to say she'd have a pint of Stella, she heard a wail come out of her mouth instead, and instantly she was crying. And not a pretty cry either, it was definitely more of the poor-me type, which Carlene loathed herself for, but once the floodgates opened she couldn't stop. She didn't belong here. She loved this place. It was so much nicer than her pub, and Sue knew the business, had grown up in the business, and was Irish, for fuck's sake. Who did Carlene think she was fooling? Who cared if some great-great-great-can of beans was Irish? Whoever her ancestors were, they certainly didn't leave her a pub. And what kind of idiot falls in love with a man who has trouble tattooed on his forehead? And what kind of father wouldn't answer his phone at any other time than 8:12 P.M.? And what kind of daughter hated her own father for his disabilities? And why was she so afraid to crawl through the passage?

The tears wouldn't stop. Sue wiped her hands on her apron and tilted her head back toward the open door to her kitchen.

"Kate?"

"Yeah, Ma?"

"Bring me a bowl of the lamb curry."

"No bother." Sue took a blue bottle of the wall, filled a shot glass, and slid it over to Carlene. Carlene wiped her eyes and tried to smile.

"What's that?" Carlene asked.

"It's a stiffie," Sue said. "I tell the fellas who come in they have to bring their own, but I always give 'em to the girls." Carlene laughed. Then she started to cry again. "Drink up, lad," Sue said. "The lamb is on its way." As if on cue, Kate, Sue's oldest daughter, appeared with an overflowing bowl of heaven. The girl was tall like her mother with the coltish body of a fourteen-year-old and fresh freckles all over her face. She set the bowl in front of Carlene with a shy smile. "Get some brown bread and butter, luv," Sue told Kate. Carlene drank the shot. It was so smooth, with a hint of blueberry. It was easy going down.

"No bother," Kate said and disappeared into the kitchen. Seconds later she popped back out with a plate of brown bread and butter. Carlene bit into the thickest, softest, sweetest bread she'd ever tasted. Sue refilled Carlene's stiffie. Two hours and countless stiffies later, the bar swelled with customers, and Carlene was having the time of her life. She threw darts, sang "The Fields of Athenry" at the top of her lungs with a group of old-timers, and pledged her love to Sue, her lamb stew, and her stiffies. She was the center of attention, and loved the way the Irish immediately swept you up in conversation, and not the typical "What do you do for a living" bullshit Americans were always so fond of. This was hanging out, this was shooting the breeze, this was living in the moment and having a good time. This was something that Carlene never even knew existed, but now that she did, she realized she'd been missing it, craving this kind of connection all of her life.

"Have you ever been to New York City?" an old man next to her asked.

"No," Carlene said. She'd never been anywhere.

"I used to live in the Bronx," the old man said.

"I hear they have a nice zoo," Carlene said.

"How many windows does the Empire State Building have?" the man continued.

"I have no idea," Carlene said.

"Six thousand five hundred," the man said. "Can ye imagine cleaning dat?"

"That's a lot of Windex," Carlene said. The man threw his head back and laughed. Not a fake or polite laugh. Not a shy laugh, even though when he opened his mouth it was obvious that several of his teeth had uprooted and left, but a genuine, in-the-moment belly laugh. Carlene felt so happy. She felt liked. She felt witty. She was going to break out in a rendition of "I Feel Pretty" if she didn't slow down on the stiffies.

"You're all right," the old man said. He signaled Sue to buy her a drink.

"No, thank you," Carlene said, but the drink was already in front of her.

"What do ye think of our little town so far?" the man asked.

"I love it," Carlene said.

"Yer man next door," the man said. "He's a bit of a bollix." Carlene figured he was talking about Joe, next door to her, but she didn't comment. Luckily, she was saved by the band, who somehow appeared and set up without her even knowing they were there. They played traditional Irish music. Carlene loved every song they played, and the crowd did too. The locals knew all the words. How many songs did Carlene know all the words to, songs she could belt out in a crowd? Not counting pop songs, not many. Whenever she was in a bar in Ohio, she couldn't remember a single time where the entire place raised their voices together in song.

And this wasn't *American Idol,* it didn't seem to matter here how off-key or off-color you sang, nobody made a move to stop anyone from singing; all voices were welcome. On fast songs, men got up to dance. They kept their bodies still, tucked their hands behind their back, moved their feet to the rhythm of the music. Sue's son and younger daughter wandered in and out and to watch the festivities or ask their mom about something. Every corner of the bar was filled and in use from the pool table to the back patio, where smokers chatted beneath the gray cloud of their exhalations. And just when Carlene thought she had seen it all, and was contemplating taking her leave, here came her favorite musician, with his swagger and pair of spoons.

God, she loved Johnny. He played as if he'd been born with not just one silver spoon, but two. He played them on his wrist, he played them up and down his arm, he played them on his knee. He jerked as he played, his head and shoulders accompanying the spoons. When the song was finished, the crowd rose to their feet and cheered. "Johnny Spoons, ladies and wankers," the lead singer and banjo player called out. Laughter spilled forth. Carlene stood on her stool.

"I love you, Johnny Spoons," she said. "I love you." More laughter and cheers, and maybe another stiffie would be good right about now. She felt a tug on her jeans.

"Down you go," Sue Finnegan said. "Or you're going to give them all stiffies." Carlene had forgotten she was wearing a short skirt. There were several boos when she came down from the stool.

"Love you, Johnny," Carlene said again. The music played on. The television stayed on. Darts were thrown. But suddenly, everything inside Carlene stopped. She felt the sensation of slowing down, cold water splashed in her face. She looked up. Ronan was standing in the doorway. Whether or not true love or love at first sight existed, energy between people did. Chemistry. She felt him before she saw him. And now, when their eyes met, a current ran between them, as sure as a live wire. A current that gambling, or threats, or even an engagement couldn't shake. Was that what made life and love tragic? Something so powerful being placed in careless hands? He remained in the doorway, watching her. Carlene's head was beginning to throb. She took a step back and stumbled.

"Easy now," someone said. Hands wrapped around her waist to steady her. Ronan was at her side in a flash, replacing the stranger's hands with his own. His grip was strong, his gaze was steady, and he was wearing that cologne that smelled so good she wanted to throw him down and bury herself in his neck. "What in the name of God," he said, bringing his mouth close to her ear, "are you doing?" She spun around. She felt good again.

"I don't know if I believe in God," she said. "I didn't go to church growing up, did you know that?" Ronan didn't answer. "Of course you didn't, because we don't really know anything about each other, do we?"

"How much have ye had to drink?"

"Are you taking a poll?"

"You're embarrassing yourself." Carlene looked around. Nobody was paying any attention to her.

"I might be embarrassing you," Carlene said. "But nobody else seems to mind."

"You don't know the Irish way," he said. "Believe me, they'll be talking about you over tea."

"I don't care," Carlene said. "I'm having a good time."

"You have a pub of your own," Ronan said. "Or have you forgotten?" Carlene removed his hands from her waist.

"You have a fiancée of your own," she said. "Or have you forgotten?" He stared at her for a moment as if he was searching for something in her. Then he looked away. Carlene felt the beginnings of a dull ache in her chest. She didn't want to cry in front of him. "When were you going to tell me?" she said. "At the wedding?"

"It's complicated," Ronan said.

"I think this is what the twins meant when they told me to watch out for the black swans. I think you're the black swan."

"What are you on about?"

"It doesn't matter." The band started playing a haunting song. When Ronan went to speak again she gently placed her finger on his lips. Then she moved past him and closer to the band. The most beautiful song she'd ever heard was being sung. It was called "Black Is the Color." One line struck Carlene like lightning: *And I love the ground on which she stands.*

That was how someone felt when they loved you, she thought. They loved the ground on which you stood. A later line proclaimed he'd suffer death a thousand times for her. Carlene wanted to cry again, for herself, for never having felt love like that. She was still pitying herself when Ronan touched her elbow and led her onto the dance floor. He pulled her into him and they danced. It didn't matter that the song was about a woman with black hair and she was a blonde, she imagined it was Ronan singing to her, and she rested her head on his chest, just below his neck, where she could feel his heart beat. When the song was over, Carlene pulled back and looked into his eyes. They were both breathing harder than usual. They were alone in a room full of people.

She wanted to memorize his face in case she never got this close to him again. She leaned up to kiss him, but his lips were already over hers. The kiss was strong, and it expressed all the yearning she'd felt since she first won the raffle. It said I never even knew you and I've missed you. It said I'm sorry you lost your pub. It said I'm sorry I accepted a date with Collin. It said don't marry Sally. It said I want to belong here. It said there's a secret passage under the earth below the pub. It said how could you do this to me? It said stay away. It said don't ever leave me. His said he still had a few thousand secrets of his own, and no matter what, she would never, ever unlock them all, maybe she would never even really get to know him. When they were done with the kiss, there was nothing left to stay. Silence thudded in Carlene's ears.

"Tell me you're not engaged," she said. Ronan was silent. "Tell me," Carlene said again, louder, loathing herself for pleading. He opened his mouth.

"I told ye—"

"It's complicated," Carlene finished for him. "So what are you doing here?" she said. "What are you trying to do to me?" Ronan turned around and Carlene watched him walk out the door. She didn't know how long she stood in the middle of the floor staring after him as if desire alone was enough to will him back. She must have stood there for a long time, for the next thing she knew Sue Finnegan put her hand on Carlene's shoulder.

"I've called you a Joe Maxi," she said. "It's time to go home, luv." Carlene nodded, started toward the door. Then she turned and hugged Sue Finnegan. Sue was stiff at first, then hugged her back, then lightly, shoved her out the door. Carlene heard Sue say, as the gorgeous wooden door shut behind her, "Those fuckin' stiffies get 'em langered every time."

CHAPTER 31

On the Edge

Dear Becca,

Can you believe it's already November? I've been here five months! To answer your question—no plans, although it's early yet. Thanksgiving isn't big over here, but Declan already said he'd make me a turkey sandwich. Still no luck getting Dad to agree to come for Christmas. He's already hinting that he'd rather spend it with the Elks. He's not even a member. Any suggestions? What are your Hanukkah plans?

Love you!

Carlene

Sally and Ronan were still engaged. Carlene was positive the whole thing would have blown over by now, it would be in the past, a hideous mistake never spoken of again. Had they set a date? Sally probably needed plenty of time to bedazzle all the bridesmaids' dresses. Luckily, Sally had been taking major time off from the pub, but now that she was back, it was excruciating listening to her yammering on about wedding plans. It was hard for Carlene to listen and simultaneously fight the urge to punch her in the face.

She couldn't take it much longer. Carlene was going to have to fire Sally, something she wasn't looking forward to. Firing someone. It would be so American of her, and once again she felt shame rather than pride. Today Sally was humming as she washed the glasses. Carlene had never heard her hum. Carlene wasn't going to ask her if they had set a date; she feared she wouldn't be able to get the words out of her mouth.

Collin looked at Carlene with a commiserating glance. Carlene gave him a sad smile back. Did Sally even realize how Collin felt about her? Even if she did, Carlene knew it wouldn't make a difference. Sally was under whatever spell or hormone or chemical it was that inflicted women with love. The kind that made them do crazy things, and when asked why, the answer was always *Because I love him.*

Sally probably bullied him into marrying her, and now here she was, humming. And Ronan was a grown man, so no matter what the situation, he was responsible for his half of it. Let them have each other. Carlene poured Collin a shot on the house.

"I'm taking the next few days off," Carlene told Sally.

"You can't," Sally said. "I have a ton of things to do to get ready for the wedding."

"When's the big day?" Eoin asked. Carlene braced herself. She didn't want to hear it, even if it was a year from now.

"Two weeks from today," Sally said. Collin choked on his shot. Carlene laughed. She couldn't be serious. "And no," Sally said. "I'm not pregnant. We're just in a hurry." Carlene walked out of the bar and headed upstairs. "Where are you going?" Sally said.

"I'm taking a few days off," Carlene repeated. "And I'm starting right now."

The tour bus to the Cliffs of Moher picked up passengers from in front of Nancy's. The Cliffs of Moher, otherwise known as the Cliffs of Ruin. What a perfect place to symbolically say good-bye to Ronan. Unforgiving cliffs jutting out six hundred feet above the Atlantic Ocean. Carlene would stand at the edge of the cliffs and let him go, let him be with Sally. She didn't come to Ireland to fall in love, she came to run a pub.

There were mostly older women on the bus, and Carlene sat back and enjoyed their chatter, and gossip, of which there was plenty. After an exhaustive back-and-forth about the weather, they talked about their children, their houses, and their spouses. They gossiped about who was getting what done to themselves and their homes, and tittered about neighbors and neighbors of neighbors. They spoke in hushed tones about who'd died, and harsh tones about who had yet to send a mass card. No one directly tried to draw Carlene into conversation; she sat in the back of the bus where the only other occupant was a man asleep in the very last seat. He was curled up in the corner with his hood pulled over his head. Most likely a drunk, Carlene thought; he'd probably sleep through the entire trip.

Carlene opened her book and put on earphones, although it wasn't music she was listening to, and she hadn't even started the book, which promised to be a thriller—instead it was the women in the front of the bus who captured her attention. She wanted to eavesdrop without having to be involved. She knew if she hadn't been on the bus, she would have been the topic of conversation. Or was she just being paranoid? Maybe a steady diet of rain, sheep, Guinness, and chips, and the superfluous use of the word "lad," had twisted her brain.

She waited for the conversation to light on Sally and Ronan's wedding, and it eventually did. She heard about how Sally had been chasing him forever, she heard how Ronan was a loose cannon, a mad gambler, nothing like his father, and never going to change. It seemed they felt sorry for Sally, but with a "careful what you wish for" attitude. They spoke of a woman named Ellen, some farmer's daughter who was depressed and never came out of her room. One of the ladies insisted the girl wasn't just depressed, she was "mentally disturbed." Carlene felt for her, whoever she was. Some days she didn't want to come out of her room; some days she felt mentally disturbed.

Carlene wondered if these women knew anything about the Ballybeog Museum or the men in tweed. They certainly seemed to know everything else that was going on in the little walled town. But Carlene refrained from inserting herself into the conversation. Asking too many questions would just swivel the spotlight back on her. That was the problem with walls, Carlene thought as she looked out the window. They kept people out, but they also trapped people in.

It was a long ride to the cliffs, then a long walk up them, but when Carlene finally arrived, she stood as close to the edge as she dared, opened her arms, á la standing on the bow of the *Titanic,* and lost herself in sweeping, endless view. The cliffs were staggering in height and depth, and Carlene felt dizzy as she gazed down the jagged rocks to the ocean cresting below. Gazing out, she felt so insignificant, so small, so temporary. The wind kept her hair blown back and stung her eyes with tears. Once she was over her vertigo, she felt invaded by a feeling of peace. All her petty worries, normally so insistent and large, seemed foolish and insignificant. Up here, she could breathe. Up here, nobody cared that she was crying. Of course, she would have preferred not to share the moment with a couple of hundred tourists. Not that anyone was paying any attention to her. They were endlessly posing for pictures, eating chips and sandwiches, kissing, and chattering.

Children were glued to their cell phones, paying no attention whatsoever, as if they stood at the edge of the world every day. Carlene had an urge to run up to them, one by one, grab their stupid phones that they huddled over protectively as if they were their newborn babies, and hurl them over the cliffs and into the dark depths below. How glorious that would feel! Why didn't she have the courage to do that? What was the worst that could happen? Would they gang up on her and throw her off the cliffs? Would she even care? Where were their mothers? They should be the ones yanking their phones out of their hands and feeding them to the ocean.

She decided, standing there, that she was going to insist her father come to Ireland. She would start an all-out campaign if she had to. And she was going to ask Nancy out for a girl's night, and she was going to find out more about the museum woman, and she was going to crawl all the way into the passage no matter what.

She should make a will first. Who would she leave the pub to? Joe? Let him turn it into Tan Land? Ronan—let him and Sally run it like some happily married couple united by a common goal? Or raffle it off again? Maybe this time to some lost little French girl who dreamed of running away to Ireland?

No, it was still hers, she wasn't leaving it to anyone, which meant she was going to have to make it through that passage without dying. Even though there was every chance that the ground could cave in on her and crush her, or God knows what was waiting at the end, perhaps some wild animal ready to tear into her flesh—what wild flesh-eating animals did they have in this part of Ireland? She didn't have a clue.

Yes, this was the perfect place to fall out of love, or a few steps further, to your death. Two weeks? Who planned a wedding in two weeks? Maybe, like Anchor pointed out, when you'd been engaged for fifteen years it didn't take long to get down to the actual planning.

Standing there, Carlene also thought of the mother she barely remembered. Would they have been good friends? Would her mother have been the comforting sort? The kind whose shoulders you could cry on when another hopeful romance was dashed? Would she have told Carlene to move on with her life and forget about Ronan, or would she have told her to fight for the man that she—

Liked, lusted after, was drawn to, couldn't get out of her mind—anything but loved, because love was a commitment, love was ten plus years of listening to them whine and washing their dirty shorts.

Her mother had been blond like Carlene, slightly thinner, a tad taller. Her mother's hair had been naturally curly too, but she always went to great lengths to straighten it. Did that mean she would have hated Carlene leaving hers in curls? Would she have chased after her daughter with a straightening iron? Carlene had too many questions, and the answers were gone for good.

Would her mother be shocked by the effect her death had on Carlene's father? If she were still alive, would he still be scrubbing, counting, and pacing? Did he blame himself, like Carlene blamed herself, and über-cleanliness was his punishment?

Maybe if Carlene brought her father out here, to the cliffs, he too could let it go, let her go. She would have to lead by example.

"Good-bye, Mom," she said to the wind.

"Good-bye?" Ronan answered. She was so startled, he had to grab her to keep from stumbling over the cliffs. He pulled her back a safe distance and pulled off his navy hood. He was the man who'd been sitting at the back of the bus. He looked so beautiful standing in front of her, eyes intent on her, hands shoved in his pocket, dark wavy hair blown back by the wind. Carlene didn't even think, she just launched herself into his arms. Two weeks from now she wouldn't be able to do that; two weeks from now he would have a wife. He held her tight, then pulled back. At first he looked as if he was going to say something, and then he simply pulled her in again and crushed his lips over hers. As they kissed, even the magnificent cliffs fell away.

"Hello," he said quietly when he pulled back.

"Hello," she said. She went to kiss him again. He pulled back.

"Tell me about your mom," he said.

Ronan led her to the visitor's center at the base of the cliffs. They sat at a small table at the café and had cups of tea. He waited for her to speak.

"She had a weak heart," Carlene said. She pulled her hands away from Ronan and wrapped them around her chest.

"I'm so sorry," Ronan said.

"Thank you."

"There's something you're not telling me."

"What do you mean?"

"I mean like—I can feel it, sure. I can feel you holding back on me."

Carlene opened her mouth to make a joke, but then stopped herself. When she spoke again, the words came tumbling out in one guilty breath. "It was all my fault. I'm responsible for her death."

"What do you mean?" Ronan said. She wanted to kiss him for not immediately jumping in to tell her it wasn't her fault. That's what everyone else had done the few times she'd dared to confess to anyone: Becca, a teacher at school, and once even her grandma Jane. Before she could even tell them what happened, they would cut her off with "Oh Carlene," or "Don't you worry your pretty little head," or "It certainly was not." She wanted to hear these things, but they meant nothing if they didn't know what really happened that day. So Carlene continued to carry the guilt of a six-year-old.

"Tell me," Ronan said.

They were on the bus, on their way home. Carlene jostled into her mother with each lurch, ding, and belch of the bus. Carlene was sitting by the window so she could reach up and pull the cord when they were close to their stop. It was the moment Carlene lived for, the only way her mother ever got her to go on the bus. The sun was beating in Carlene's eyes, so she covered them with her hands. It was only for a few seconds. Suddenly she heard a ding, and then before she knew what was happening, her mother had grabbed her hand and was lifting her out of the seat.

It was too late! They were at their stop and somebody else had pulled the cord. Her mother didn't even tell her; there was no warning, not even a slight squeeze of her hand. Carlene heard the ding, saw the red light come on above the bus driver's head. Carlene started crying. Her mother had that weary look on her face, the one that meant she was tired and getting a headache, and soon she would tell Carlene to please, please, just let her have a little quiet, just a little quiet. Instead, she told Carlene that six was too old to cry like such a baby and that if she continued to cry like a two-year-old, when she got home she was going to take a nap like a two-year-old.

Carlene dropped to the floor, in the middle of the bus with people in front of her and behind her, and refused to budge. People started murmuring, then talking about her, then yelling advice. The bus driver honked the horn.

"We have to move," he said. Her mother knelt on the floor of the bus, her pretty white linen pants now pressing on dirt and a squashed piece of gum, and she pleaded with Carlene to get up. Carlene didn't move. Her mother tried to pull her up, but Carlene screamed and grabbed onto a seat leg and clung to it for dear life. Sweat started to drip from her mother's upper lip.

"Please," her mother said. "Do not do this to me in public."

Carlene then demanded a peanut butter sandwich, and even though she didn't know how her mother was going to come up with a peanut butter sandwich on a city bus, she demanded it anyway, yelled for one over and over, all the while crying. She remembered as she started to perspire, her mother smelled like oranges, she remembered the palm of her mother's hand tight and slick in hers, she remembered the golden flare of her mother's hair from the sun beating in through the windows of the bus. Her mother put her hand on her heart. "Carlene," she said, her face pale and almost frightened, her voice cracking from the strain. "You are going to be the death of me."

CHAPTER 32

The Eavesdroppers

When she was done recounting her tale, Ronan got up from his seat across from her, came around, and sat next to her. He pulled her into him and held her. She felt his lips graze her ear.

"Do you know," he said, "how many times I've heard my mother say that to me? 'Ronan Anthony McBride, you're doing to be the death of me.' Carly, if I had a euro for every time she's ever said that to me, clutching her heart like she was going to drop on the spot, I'd be the wealthiest man on the planet. It's a very Irish thing to say, so I believe your mother had some Irish in her all right. And you've only an inkling of an idea of the things I've put me poor mam and the estrogen gang through in my thirty-odd years. It's on a colossal scale, like. Now, I can't say for sure that you didn't kill that wee poor hamster with yer pink Slim Fast, but you did not—I repeat, you did not play any part in your mother's death. It was not your fault."

"But she had a weak heart—and I put it under stress—she was sweating and she had to pull me off the floor of the bus, and—"

"Carly, Carly, Carly, stop." Ronan took Carlene's face in his hands and forced her to look at him. "It was her time to go. End of story. Full stop."

"But it was one of the last things she ever said to me," Carlene said. Ronan leaned in and kissed her.

"You were right to come out here and throw it over the cliffs. It was not your fault. I'll bet she's looking down—begging you—begging you to forgive her for that being one of the last things she ever said to you. While it's been eating you up down here, I bet it's been eating her up twice as much up there. Do you want that? Do you want her up there where it's supposed to be all heavenly, only she can't even enjoy a single cloud, or harp chord, or whatever shite they do up there, because you're down here blaming yourself?"

"Really?" Carlene said. "Cloud? Harp chord? Whatever the shite? That's all you got?"

"At least you're smiling now," Ronan said. They sat silently for a moment, looking at each other. Ronan took her hand again. "Mothers pull screaming children off buses every second of every day. You could have been peaches and cream on that bus and your mother's heart would have still been weak. But it's not me you need to talk to—it's your father."

"I don't want to burden him."

"Fuck that shite. It's not about him. It's about you. And you are going to tell him what you told me—and you are going to make him listen. And if he doesn't look you in the eye and tell you it's not your fault, I'm going to swim across the pond meself, dodging turtles, and sharks, and goldfish and tsunamis, and whatever the fuck, and make him look you in the eye like, and tell you as many times as it takes until the six-year-old in you gets, really and truly gets that it wasn't your fault."

Carlene squeezed his hands, leaned into Ronan, and tried to thank him with all her heart through her lips. When she pulled away, Ronan tapped on his lip again, and once more she leaned forward and kissed him.

When she pulled away this time, Ronan's grin covered most of his face. She absolutely loved looking at his face up close. It made her world brighter. She wanted to look at that face for the rest of her life. He winked at her. It was amazing how much better she felt.

"Tell me you'll at least think about talking to him," Ronan said.

"Okay," Carlene said. "I'll think about it."

Ronan glanced at his watch. "We've still got another bloody hour," he said. "More tea?"

"Love some."

When he returned with their tea, he once again sat across from her, and they switched to lighter conversation. Carlene soon found herself recounting her time in Ballybeog: learning the ropes at the pub, getting to know the regulars. She told him about the woman from the museum with a black eye, hoping to get just a little closer to telling him about the passageway, but if Ronan knew anything about the woman, he didn't offer it up. They laughed over Ciaran's wife falling in love with a fictional vampire, and how the first morning she found Riley at his stool at eight in the morning, and Billy walking the tree like it was a log on the river, and Carlene bursting in on the christening with the same tree branch, then pretending it was a gift for the new baby. They laughed over it all, and it was the best release Carlene could have ever asked for. She forgot all her problems.

Suddenly, a large woman seated at the next table yelled, "Yahoo!" She was American, fat, and loud. Shit. Carlene hated when stereotypes came true, and at the same time she felt guilty for judging the woman so harshly. A person on vacation was allowed to be obnoxious and yell "yahoo!" at the top of her lungs, wasn't she? The woman shouldered a clunky video camera and was following her husband with it, and shouting out instructions. Smile. Do something silly. Now look serious. Carlene didn't see how he'd be able to pull that one off given he was wearing a baseball cap with a shamrock, a T-shirt with a leprechaun, and enormous green sunglasses. When she grew bored of filming her husband, the woman panned the camera over to Carlene, then Ronan.

"She films everything," the husband said. "She even filmed

you two smooching out on the cliffs." The woman, camera still up to her eye, pumped her fist. "Woo hoo!" she said. "I think I got some tongue too." Carlene wanted to die. "Love your shirt," the woman said. Carlene was wearing a rain jacket. She looked over at Ronan. He had unzipped his navy jacket. Underneath he was wearing a sweatshirt that read: *Cleveland Rocks*.

"Would you take our picture?" the woman yelled as if calling to them from an adjacent cliff. Where did she get that twang? That wasn't an Ohio twang, was it? Carlene knew she didn't have a twang. She couldn't.

"I'd love to," Ronan said. The woman's face lit up.

"You're Irish," she said as if she'd just found him growing in her garden.

"You're American," he said with equal enthusiasm. He threw a glance to Carlene in case she missed his sarcasm.

"Maybe you can help us," the woman said. "My husband and the group we're with are looking for an authentic Irish pub." The woman leaned in and shielded her mouth with her hand, as if this would prevent her husband from hearing her shouts. "They're all accountants, but don't count that against them!" Ronan's smile grew exponentially. Carlene shook her head. She did not want a bunch of Americans in her pub. No way, no how. It was her pub. She could refuse service to whomever she wanted. Besides, her pub was a couple of hours away. Surely Ronan would point them to something more local, something fitting, something with shamrocks or leprechauns and rainbows in the name. Carlene shook her head even harder. Ronan pretended not to see her.

"Let me t'ink," Ronan said. Was it Carlene's imagination or had he just dialed up his Irish accent?

"We're Irish too," the lady said. "We're from Dublin. Dublin, Ohio." The couple screeched with laughter. Ronan wouldn't stop staring and grinning at Carlene. They introduced themselves as Lorraine and Michael.

"Ohio," Ronan said. "Lovely state. The Buckeye State. The seventeenth state to join the union. An Indian name meaning 'long river'. And of course, home to the great Rock and Roll Hall of Fame."

Lorraine's eyes were wide, almost as if she were slightly stunned. "Yes," she said. "And Ireland is. Very green."

"We've never seen so much green," Michael said.

"What about Seattle?" Lorraine said. "You agreed we saw the same amount of green in Seattle."

"We love your potatoes too," Michael said. He looked at his wife. "We didn't eat potatoes in Seattle, Lorraine." He punctured her name like a slap across the face.

"True," she said. "We had king crab, though. And it was very green."

"Not the crab," he said.

"It rains a lot there too," Lorraine said.

"Go to Galway!" Carlene said. "There are plenty of pubs in Galway!"

"Unless of course you're looking for something more authentic," Ronan said.

"Authentic," the woman said. "Absolutely we want authentic."

"We've got a group of fifteen or so," Michael said.

"But we don't drink alcohol," Lorraine said.

"Perfect," Ronan said.

"Galway is very authentic," Carlene said. She reached down and pinched Ronan's thigh as hard as she could. He didn't even flinch.

"Roll your camera," Ronan said. "I'll give ye directions."

CHAPTER 33

Tips to a Good Proposal

When the bus pulled up to Nancy's, Ronan hopped off with Carlene. Without discussing it, he walked alongside her as she headed back to the pub. When they passed underneath the town gate, Ronan flattened himself against the wall and pulled Carlene into him.

"You had it wrong," he said.

"What?" she said.

"It's not what am I doing to you. It's what are you doing to me." Ronan leaned in slowly. Carlene turned her head and his lips grazed her cheek instead of their intended target. Ronan stepped back, shoved his hands in his pockets. He gazed at the wall above her head as he spoke, and his voice dropped to a low whisper. "Before I met you, I had everything under control."

Carlene laughed, loudly and abruptly, and the sound of it echoed in the small passageway. Ronan's face first flashed anger, then he paused as if replaying her words in his head, and soon his laughter joined hers.

"Ah, right. Maybe 'under control' is a bit of a stretch all right."

"I'll say. You're life was a mess. Is a mess."

"But it was my mess—I was going to pay for it—"

"How? By marrying someone you don't love?"

"That's my business. I don't need you haunting me—"

"Haunting you?"

"Consuming my thoughts. Would you please get the fuck out of my head?"

"You're following me around all day just to tell me to get the fuck out of your head?"

"No. I'm following you around all day because I need to explain what's going on between me and Sally." They locked eyes. Carlene waited. "And," Ronan continued, "because I can't think of anyone else I'd rather follow around all day."

"Flirting isn't going to get you anywhere this time, bucko," Carlene said. "And you can save your breath. I know why you're marrying Sally."

"Bucko? Did ye just call me bucko?"

"You're avoiding again."

"All right, Miss America. You think you know so much. Enlighten me."

"Those men I told you about—the tweed brothers."

"Go on," Ronan said.

"I think they're loan sharks. I think you owe them money. I think you're marrying Sally so they don't break your legs or tie a cement block to your ankle and throw you in a river!" This time it was Ronan's laughter that echoed through the little space first. He laughed so hard he had to wipe tears from his eyes.

"Loan sharks," he said. "Deadly. T'row me in a river!" It was just impossible to remain indignant and angry when he was howling with laughter. Carlene hated that about him. She loved that about him. She hated that she loved that about him.

"It's a working theory," she said when he finally recovered.

"Fucking brilliant," he said.

"It wasn't even my theory—it was your sisters'."

"Jaysus," Ronan said. "That's gas."

Carlene started to walk away. Ronan grabbed her by the waist and swung her into him. "Hear me out."

"I'm listening." But she wasn't. How could she listen when

he was so close that she couldn't even think? When she knew he could feel her trembling? When he'd asked another woman to marry him, yet here they were, chest to chest, hearts beating against each other?

"What happened with Sally was a huge misunderstanding," he said.

"She misunderstood a marriage proposal?"

"Do you see a ring on her finger?" Carlene hadn't thought about it, but now that he mentioned it, she knew if Sally had a ring, she would have been shoving it in Carlene's face.

"So you haven't bought the ring yet," Carlene said.

"I didn't propose," Ronan said.

"She just imagined the words, 'Will you marry me?' coming out of your mouth?"

"She followed me to the abbey the other day. And so did George and Martin."

"Who are George and Martin?"

"You like to call them the men in tweed," Ronan said. "Which I'm dying to tell them." He stopped for a minute and laughed again. He looked so beautiful in the shadows, his dimple, his scar, his green-gold eyes. Why couldn't this be simple? Why couldn't he just be hers?

"So they're not loan sharks?" Carlene said. "They don't want to break your legs?"

"Well, they might want to break my legs all right, but they're more like babysitters than loan sharks."

"I don't follow."

"I bet someone that if I ever placed a bet again I'd owe them a hundred thousand euros."

"You made a bet that you would never bet again?"

"I did, yeah."

"And George and Martin?"

"Are allowed to follow me around twenty-four/seven until the person I made the bet with is satisfied."

"Who did you make the bet with?"

"Racehorse Robbie. He's a fella I know who gambles on the ponies."

"And what do you get out of the deal?"

"If I go one year without betting, I get the hundred thousand."

"And this person is good for it?"

"Are you kidding me? He's loaded. He's owned several racehorses who've made him millions."

"Why would he make a bet like that with you?"

"Because he lives to bet. Because he doesn't think I can do it. And I don't know—maybe part of him doesn't want to see me end up like him."

"A millionaire?" Carlene said. Ronan stopped and gave her a look. She smiled. He smiled back, but it was softer, more serious.

"A mad gambler. Even with all his money, he can't stop betting. He has to bet or he goes mental. He recognized a kindred spirit in me."

"So what does this have to do with asking Sally to marry you?"

"He set me up—that's what. The other day some fella gives me a bell and says he's got a tip on a horse."

"Gives you a bell?" Carlene said.

"Calls me on the cellular phone," Ronan said slowly in a mock American accent.

"What guy?"

"I have no idea—but I'm sure Racehorse Robbie was behind it."

"I thought you weren't betting anymore."

"I haven't placed one bet—not one. Even though it's been killing me. But then the fella on the mobile said he was going to leave the tip in the tower of the abbey."

"Isn't that where you used to get tips—when you were a kid?"

"Exactly. I knew it was a setup, sure. I was just going to confront Robbie—or whatever wanker he had lurking there to catch me. But when I got to the abbey, Sally was there. The same fella who called me called her and said I'd left her a note in the abbey. By the time I arrived, she already had the note in her hand. It wasn't my handwriting, but she didn't notice—or she didn't care. The horse's name? Ready for this? Marry Me."

"No," Carlene said. "You're making this up." Ronan pulled a folded-up newspaper out of his pocket and handed it to Carlene.

"Number eight," he said. Carlene glanced at the list, and sure enough, there he was, number eight—Marry Me.

"Next thing I knew, she was yelling, 'Yes, yes, yes,' and throwing her arms around me—then there come George and Martin out of the corner, like they hadn't been hiding there all along, asking her what the commotion was—so of course she tells them we're engaged, then they look at me and wait for me to tell her it's not true, ready to nab me if they thought I was picking up a tip on a horse—"

"But would you have lost the bet just picking up a tip? Don't you actually have to place the best to lose?" Carlene said.

"The bet was that I wouldn't so much as look at a racing card, go near the tracks, the whole nine yards."

"That sounds extreme."

"Racehorse Robbie likes extreme bets. I guess I do too or I wouldn't have accepted the bet in the first place. I was planning to go out with a bang—my last bet, never to bet again."

"I don't know what to say to you, Ronan." Carlene pulled away and started to walk. Ronan kept pace slightly behind her. The wind began to pick up, blowing Carlene's hair all around her face, long strands whipping across her cheeks and lips. She kept walking, not even bothering to clear her hair from her eyes. Let the wind do what it would.

"I panicked, Carly. She was so fucking happy, and I was so fucking miserable with myself like for even falling for it, like. I swear on me da's grave I was about to tell her the truth. But before I knew what happened she was telling her mam, her father—my mam, the half dozen, and the whole world that we were getting married."

Carlene smelled fireplace smoke, damp earth, and cow dung. She picked up the pace.

"If I tell her the truth—"

"You lose a bet," Carlene said.

"It's not just that. Yes, I'd lose the bet." Once again Carlene felt Ronan's hands on her waist as he stopped her. She remained with her back to him until he physically turned her around. She tried not to stare into his gold-green eyes as they searched hers, but it was futile. Ronan had to raise his voice to compete with the strengthening wind. "Do you think I'd take a hundred thousand euros off my mother just to pay off another bet? One I never really made in the first place?"

"The raffle money," Carlene said.

"There's no way," Ronan said. "I can't do it. I won't."

"Why didn't you just tell Racehorse Robbie you weren't going to look at the tip, you were just going to confront whatever wanker gave you a bell."

"It's not the way things are done."

"Well, obviously, I don't know the way things are done. But I do know this. You're not doing Sally any favors. She deserves to be with somebody who will love her the way she loves you."

"She doesn't love me—she's just infatuated."

"My point stands." This time, Carlene started to walk again, and didn't stop, even though he was still following her.

"I'm not allowed to make mistakes? What about you, Miss I'm married, oh wait, I'm *not* married. To another Irishman no less. Which number am I?" Carlene stopped suddenly, and Ronan had to veer off path to keep from slamming into her. For once she didn't mind the dark, damp Irish weather. It matched her mood.

"What do you want from me?" Carlene said.

"I want you . . . I want you . . ." Ronan folded his arms across his chest, dug at the ground with his toe. "I just want you. But I'm a fuckup. I've always been, and I still am. Sally knows that and she still wants to marry me."

"So marry her."

"Carlene."

A surge of anger rose up in Carlene. She couldn't handle this. Why wasn't anything ever simple? Why couldn't she, for once, just be the girl who got lucky? She didn't mean to yell, but next thing she knew, her voice was up to the heavens, and bitterness spilled from her throat.

"I didn't come here to get my heart broken. I didn't come here to pour out all my secrets and tell you about my phobias, and my mother. I didn't ask for this. I didn't ask for you. One minute you're all over me, and the next minute you're gone, and the next minute you're back, and the next minute you're kissing me until I can't see straight, and the next minute you're engaged. I don't know why you keep fucking things up—but you're right. You do. You don't think about anybody but yourself."

"So I'm a selfish bastard now, am I?"

"If the shamrock fits."

"Carlena."

"Don't call me that. Don't call me anything. Pretend I don't exist."

"You think I asked for this? You think I wanted to be absolutely mad about the woman who took over me pub?"

"And just whose fault is that?"

"I'm not blaming you. I'm just—"

"I shouldn't be running your father's pub and you shouldn't be marrying a woman you don't love. So don't talk to me about my mistakes—because they're all in the past. And you're right. This isn't my first rodeo. I've had my heart broken by an Irish man before, so you'd think I'd smarten up. And at first I thought there was no way in hell you were anything like Brandon—but I was wrong. You're worse. You're worse because with Brandon, what you saw was what you got. I had red flags slapping me in the face but I waved them around in my little love parade for one anyway. But you—underneath all that crap there's this amazing and beautiful man in there somewhere. And you let people see glimpses of him, but you just won't let him out, will you? You're your own worst enemy. So marry Sally, don't marry Sally—I don't care, Ronan Anthony McBride. And here's a news flash for you. There's no way in hell you're going to stop betting because you can't. Not as long as you remain such a coward."

"I'm a fucking coward now, am I so?"

"Yes."

"And just what am I so frightened of?"

"Yourself."

"Look who's talking? It's too late for me with my da, but yours is still around. Only you're too afraid to stand up for yourself, like. You've been carrying around all this guilt, and you wear those blue rubber gloves around the place like some kind of nutter."

"Go to hell."

"I'm already in it."

For the third time Carlene started to walk away, and this time, nobody followed.

CHAPTER 34

The Americans

Carlene was so jealous of the Irish people she met. Besides knowing how to let go and have a good time, they were really proud of being Irish. They sang about it, joked about it, wrote about it, and drank to it. She could only think of three songs about Ohio; one was thanks to the Pretenders, another was a very sad song about the shootings on the Kent State campus in 1970 ("Ohio" by Neil Young), and then there was some folk song about the "Banks of the Ohio" that she just couldn't remember. Still, none of them made her rejoice at the top of her lungs.

And if she were to walk into a dive bar in Cleveland, Ohio, she wouldn't have wanted to hear any of the stories from the drunks at the bar. But in her little pub in Ireland, she longed for their stories. Since her blowout with Ronan, she needed her pub and regulars more than ever. And they didn't disappoint. Even Riley had grown on her. Lately, he'd always hit the door talking, and now that she could fully understand his accent, she was starting to appreciate him all the more. Today he came in looking over his shoulder.

"If you see the wicked woman coming to drag me home..." he said with a wag of his finger.

"I'll invite her in and give her a drink on the house," Carlene said. Riley continued the finger wag until his body was on the stool and his hand rested on the bar. They were old hands, wrinkled hands, shaking hands.

"Even if you come home intoxicated, come home with something for her," he said. Carlene laughed as if she'd never heard him say this, and served him his pint and shot of whiskey that she had pre-poured. Riley was always on time for the pub. Carlene found comfort in being able to count on her regulars. He smiled, showing what teeth he had left, and winked at her. "She's looked after me for forty-six years," he said. "Would you look after a man for forty-six years?" A movie flickered through Carlene's mind. It involved kissing Ronan for the next forty-six years.

"I wouldn't look after you for forty-six minutes," Anchor said on cue. When he put down his pint, foam stuck to his goatee. He winked at Carlene too.

"You're so nice you remind me of myself," Riley said. He turned his attention to Carlene, although his words were directed at Anchor. "Show a little kindness, overlook the blindness of a mean-sighted people on a mean-sighted seat," he said. Anchor grinned and gave one of his head jerks to Carlene that she'd come to read as: Get a load of him. "I met my wife by the red mill on Jerome Street," Riley said.

"That sounds very romantic," Carlene said.

"I met my love by the gasworks wall," Anchor said.

"I wouldn't go there now without a machine gun," Riley said.

It had been six days since she'd met Ronan on the cliffs (then plunged off them), and even though she pretended otherwise, she'd been waiting for him. She was tortured by the things she said to him, and she wanted to make everything better. Every time the door opened, her heart skipped a beat, hoping she'd see him coming through the door. Worse, she knew his absence meant he hadn't told Sally the truth about their engagement. Carlene told herself to forget about him and move on. Now she was actually enjoying some peace with her regulars, and getting used to being around Sally again. Then, without warning, when she wasn't even looking at the door, he suddenly came through it.

"Hi, baby," she heard Sally say.

"Hey," Ronan said softly. Carlene turned around. Their eyes met and locked. Was it her imagination or did his smile fade upon seeing her? He adjusted quickly, rubbed his hands together, pulled up a stool next to Riley. He pounded Riley on the back.

"The Americans are coming tonight," he announced. This time when he looked at Carlene, his smile was back.

"Americans?" Riley said with great alarm.

"Her buddies," Ronan said. "From Dublin. Ohio, that is."

"Ohio," Riley said. "Now, that's a right nice place." Carlene was surprised. She couldn't imagine Riley outside of Ireland.

"When were you there?" Carlene asked.

"Oh, I was never there," Riley said. "But I heard it was a nice place, all right. A buddy of mine was on a train once that stopped in Ohio. He said they had nice ham sandwiches there, all right." Sally served Ronan a pint. Carlene wanted to dump it, but she was torn as to whom she should drench first.

"It's on me," Sally said. She leaned across the bar and kissed Ronan on the lips. Ronan didn't let it last long, and Sally wasn't thrilled when he pulled away. "You'd better not be this shy when we're married," Sally said.

Carlene moved as far away from Ronan as possible and busied herself with the customers at the opposite end of the bar. She had been anticipating the arrival of the Americans as well. It was a Thursday night. She'd invited all the locals and paid the trad band extra to play tonight instead of Sunday. She'd even invited Joe, although she highly doubted he would come. The half dozen said they'd try to make it, but Mary McBride didn't like coming to the pub, which made Carlene immeasurably sad, even if she understood it. But the others, it looked like were going to come through. The place was already buzzing, and it was early yet.

Billy arrived with a couple of girls on his arm. Collin arrived, took one look at Ronan and Sally, and started flirting with Carlene. His T-shirt read: MAKE AWKWARD SEXUAL ADVANCES, NOT WAR. Ronan watched him with a scowl on his face, and practically jumped out of his seat every time Collin touched Carlene on the arm. Let him be jealous. It had been too long since their meeting on the cliff and the little seductive interlude underneath the town gate, then his refusal to come, all under the guise that he had to set things straight with Sally first. She didn't need games or thoughts of how good things could be between them if only he weren't so afraid to commit. Maybe she should give Collin a chance. Maybe the kind of love that made your heart leap into your throat was the kind that could kill you. Maybe she'd be better off with a nice guy like Collin. Her thoughts were disrupted by Anchor, who lifted his head and started to sniff.

"You burning something?" he asked.

"Oh shit," Carlene said. "The cheese toasties." She ran to the little toaster oven and threw open the door. Her little sandwiches were black and hard. If Sally hadn't been so busy throwing herself at Ronan, she would have noticed.

"Is that how the Americans like them?" Ronan asked. He was cheerful again. Carlene pried what was left off the rack and dropped it on the counter in front of him. She leaned in so only he could hear her.

"Just like your heart," she said. Immediately, she was horrified that she would say such a thing, but it was too late to take it back, so she just smiled. "Only messing," she said loudly. The band arrived in time to save her from having to listen to heavy metal. Anchor groaned as she shut off the jukebox. The fiddler, tin whistler, and guitar player started to warm up, and Carlene got them pints. Her second batch of cheese toasties was perfect. Declan walked in the door.

"How ya," he called.

"What's the craic?" several of the lads answered.

"Damn all," Declan said, slipping behind the bar. He started on the third round of cheese toasties, refilled drinks, and began chin-wagging about football scores, babies being born, and gossip about who was doing what work these days, or buying what property. He did the job with the skill and finesse of an Olympic gold medalist. She was amateur, he was all pro. If he had been forty years younger, she would have married him on the spot.

"Ran into Katie in town," Declan said. "The girls should be here shortly—at least, the three single ones are beautifying themselves." Billy perked up at the mention of the girls.

"Katie's coming?" Billy said. The two women with him exchanged disappointed glances. Billy put an arm around each. "There's plenty of me to go around," he said. The band started to play, and second, third, fourth rounds were bought. So far no sign of the Americans. Maybe they wouldn't show. True to Declan's word, the three single McBride girls walked in the door. Katie, Siobhan, and Clare were wearing fancy dresses, high heels, and matching bags. Billy let out a wolf whistle and all eyes were on them, including the band. Carlene was just thinking how lucky she was, what a great evening this was going to be when suddenly, in the corner, she saw the woman from the museum.

She was wearing a navy skirt, black top, and black hat. She was tapping her foot to the music even though her hands remained clenched on her purse in front of her. Her black eye was either all healed or she'd covered it with makeup. Carlene hoped she would stay long enough to try to have a chat with her, but right now she was too busy to stop and talk.

The conversation rose and fell all around her. Carlene loved standing back and listening collectively to all the chatter. It was like a symphony of words. It had its own life, breath, and rhythms, just like music. It would grow loud and fall soft. Male and female voices blended together in harmony. She heard deep laughter and high trills. Banter back and forth was like a waltz. A long story was a ballad, a grumble about a bad day was heavy metal, jokes and gossip were pop music—but the really good ones, the phrases that stuck in your mind forever, were rock and roll. The girls finished their tour around the bar, then pulled up stools around their brother.

"Not here for a long time," Siobhan called.

"Just here for a good time," he answered. Siobhan grinned and smacked Ronan on the head with her clutch purse. Carlene wished she'd do it again.

"What did we have to see?" she asked Ronan. He threw her a warning look. Carlene was about to gloat that the Americans weren't coming in after all when the first of several video cameras came through the door. All the noise in the pub couldn't have possibly come to a screeching halt when they burst in, but that's how Carlene would always remember it. She couldn't hear anything but a buzzing in her head.

There were indeed fifteen of them, in khaki shorts and sandals with white socks, and T-shirts with shamrocks and pints of Guinness and leprechauns, and so many things hanging off their necks (maps, cameras, binoculars, sunglasses) it was a wonder they could stand up straight. If they had it, they hung it. Or, in the case of their video cameras, they swung it.

"Top of the morning to ya!" one of the American women yelled out.

"Play 'Danny Boy'!" one of the American men shouted to the band. Then they stood at the edge of the crowd, grinning, as if waiting to be greeted, or perhaps announced, like the honored guests at a surprise party they'd secretly thrown themselves. When no such announcement came, they commandeered a table in the center of the room to which the band had already laid claim. Carlene watched in horror as they removed the empty instrument cases and put them down by the stage so they could merge that table with another and plant themselves front and center. Cameras immediately began snapping. The group photographed the walls, the band, and the regulars, who watched on with slightly horrified amusement, as if watching a middle-aged version of *Jersey Shore*. Carlene spotted Lorraine and Michael in the middle of the group.

"Hey, Lorraine," Michael yelled.

"The lungs on him," Ciaran said under his breath. Now that he mentioned it, it did seem as if all of them were yelling. Were Americans always this loud? Carlene had never noticed it before. Michael was pointing at an Irish man who had been doing a bit of a jig to the music, minding his own business. "Get a load of this," Michael screamed.

"I'm Twittering about it as we speak," Lorraine said. Carlene finally met Ronan's gaze. It would have been impossible not to; you could feel the heat coming off his grin. She'd never seen him look so happy. The regulars were all staring at Carlene too.

"Are those your folks?" Eoin said.

"God, no," Carlene said. "Definitely not."

"They're from Ohio too," Ronan said. "So they're practically family."

"They are not practically family," Carlene said. Eoin, Anchor, and Collin got off their stools and wandered over to say hello. Everyone offered to buy them drinks. They wanted virgin strawberry daiquiris, iced teas, and Cokes. Declan was the only one keeping her sane. He handled all their requests with a smile, and when she went to help, he waved her away.

"But we don't make strawberry daiquiris," she said.

"Don't worry, pet," Declan said. "I'll find something red. We'll tell 'em it's the Irish way."

The band played "Danny Boy." Anchor and Eoin soon returned to the bar, but Collin stayed and entertained the tourists. He even danced for them. Carlene raised an eyebrow at Anchor and Eoin.

"Riverdancing," Anchor said with a smirk. "Bet ye miss me heavy metal now." One of the larger men in the group stood on a chair and started videotaping.

"If he falls off that chair, you'll be liable," Ronan said.

"America is a litigious society," Anchor said. Carlene asked the man to get down. She looked around for Michael and Lorraine, and finally spotted the pair in the center of the hooplah, huddled around their video camera. Then, to Carlene's surprise, Ciaran's wife, Jane, walked in the bar. Carlene hadn't seen her since the hen night. Apparently, Carlene wasn't the only one surprised. Ciaran flushed, quickly slid his pint glass over to Anchor, leaned in and asked for a pint of water. Carlene complied, although Jane didn't appear to be there to check in on her husband. In fact, she didn't even acknowledge him. She was carrying a large dress, concealed in a garment bag. Sally tore out from behind the bar.

"Is it my dress?" she asked.

" 'Tis," Jane said. "I was passing by the shop when Annmarie asked if I'd drop it in to ye." While they talked, Carlene snuck a glance at Ronan. Then suddenly, she felt someone staring at her. Carlene looked up to find the woman from the museum staring at her. In that one glance, it was as if she knew exactly how Carlene felt about Ronan McBride. She looked at her with pity, and a touch of judgment, as if she thought it was Carlene's fault for getting involved with him in the first place. Sally was now holding the garment close to her body and swaying in the middle of the floor. Ronan stared at the back wall of the bar.

"You can't see it," Sally called to Ronan, even though he wasn't making the slightest attempt to do so. "It's bad luck."

"So is marrying the wrong person," Carlene said under her breath. She thought she said it soft enough that no one could hear, but Ronan's head snapped toward hers and their eyes clashed.

"You should know," Ronan said. Carlene looked away first.

"Do you mind if I hang it upstairs?" Sally asked.

"No bother," Carlene said. Sally hurried up the stairs with it, along with several of her girlfriends in tow. The band took their first break. Lorraine was setting up a mini–video projector on the table and aiming it at the back wall. When the projector was turned on, the wall behind the band flooded with light.

"Show time?" Anchor said. They hadn't even asked Carlene's permission. Did they really think they were going to take her entire bar hostage by showing pictures of their trip on her back wall? Carlene took her frustrations out on the limes in front of her. Slice, slice, slice.

"Oh no," Ronan said. He shot out of his stool. Carlene stared at the back wall as the video started to play. The Cliffs of

Moher loomed large on the wall. Sally and Jane were coming down the steps. They stopped halfway. Carlene watched as an image of her and Ronan kissing by the cliffs filled the space. Lorraine's voice could be heard on the video.

"Look at the lovebirds," she said.

"Don't spy on people, Lorraine," Michael said. Carlene watched as the scene she'd been playing over and over again in her mind played out in front of the entire pub. She watched Ronan's arms circle her back, drop to her lower waist, and hold her tight as they kissed. Heads snapped from Sally, to Carlene, to Ronan, and back again. Lorraine looked over at Carlene with a clueless grin on her face.

"I got you two," she said. The Americans clapped. Carlene lowered the knife in her hand and looked at Sally. Sally turned and sprinted up the steps. Jane stood stunned for a moment before running after her, but first treated Carlene to a parting word. *Whore.*

Ciaran slid his beer back from Anchor and pursed his lips, but didn't make eye contact with Carlene.

Ronan remained standing halfway between the bar and the video, which still played. On the wall, Carlene watched Ronan take her hand and lead her away from the cliffs.

CHAPTER 35

A Note of Clarification

For a few minutes nobody except the group of Americans moved. Then the band started up again, although quieter, and this time the tune was not as jaunty. In fact it sounded more like a country ballad in which the singer has lost his dog, job, Chevy, and woman, all in one go. Joe walked in the door and stood nervously by the entrance as if anticipating a sneak attack. Sally stomped down the steps with her wedding dress in hand. It was out of the garment bag now and displayed in all its glory. It was a gown fit for a twelve-year-old princess, covered, as Carlene had suspected, with hundreds of glittering crystals.

Once again Sally stopped halfway down the stairs. She screamed at the top of her lungs. The band stopped playing. Everyone turned to her.

"You asked me to marry you when we were fifteen!" Sally shouted.

"Sally, please," Ronan said. He lowered his head to the bar.

"You wrote 'Be Mine' in the abbey. Remember? You stuck the note in the tower wall for me to find."

"Sally," Siobhan said. "Not here."

"Yes, here," Sally said. "And then you proposed in the exact same place."

Siobhan stood. "How's that now?" Siobhan said.

"Siobhan," Ronan said.

"He left me another note in the tower," Sally said. "It said 'Marry me.'" Sally stuck her hand in her cleavage and pulled out a tiny note.

"Can I see that?" Siobhan said. She moved to the bottom of the stairs and held her hand up to Sally like a Good Samaritan helping a jumper off the ledge.

"Leave it be, Siobhan," Ronan said. Siobhan looked at the note, then looked at Ronan. She handed the note to Katie.

"I've been waiting for you for fifteen years, Ronan McBride," Sally said.

"Tell her," Katie said. "Or I will."

"Tell me what?" Sally shrieked.

"Can we go somewhere private?" Ronan said. Sally took the wedding dress in both hands and pulled. It started to tear.

"Tell me," she said. "Or I rip it to shreds."

"I'm sorry," Ronan said. "I'm sorry."

"Sorry for what? Kissing that whore? Cheating on me while we're engaged? Or dragging out the engagement for fifteen fucking years?"

"All of it," Ronan said.

"I was going to help you," Sally said. "With your problems."

"I know."

"What problems?" Siobhan said.

"You should really say 'which problems,'" Katie said. "If she lists them all, we'll be here all night."

"Sally, can we please not do this here?" Ronan said. Carlene wanted to save him from this humiliation, but she didn't know what she should do. She looked to Declan, but he was suddenly fascinated with a jar of paper clips on the back bar.

"Why are they looking at the note like that?" Sally said.

"It's not Ronan's handwriting," Katie said.

"What?" Sally said. "Yes, it is. I was there. Do ye think I don't know when I'm being proposed to? Tell them."

"I didn't write the note," Ronan said. "Either of them."

" 'Be Mine'?" Sally said.

"It wasn't a love note at all," Ronan said. "It was a tip on a horse."

"What?" Sally said. Carlene didn't think Sally could screech any louder or higher, but she was mistaken.

"A friend was leaving me a tip for a winning horse in the abbey. You found the note first."

"Why was he leaving you the note there?"

"Because fifteen-year-olds aren't supposed to be seen with bookies, and we didn't have text messaging back then."

"But you said—"

"I know, I know what I said. I was fifteen, Sally. You were all bubbly about it and I lied and told you it was a love note for ye, okay? The horse didn't even fecking win, if that makes you happy."

"And 'Marry Me'?" Sally said. Ronan pulled the folded newspaper out of his pocket. Carlene looked away. Obviously, he'd been carrying it around for the past week, unable to bring himself to show it to her. But now he handed it over, like an accused man handing over the murder weapon.

"Number eight," Ronan said.

"You're gambling again," Siobhan said. "I don't fucking believe you."

"I don't get it," Sally said. "We have fecking text messaging now, Ronan McBride. Why is someone still leaving you notes? What are you, a child?"

"It was just someone messing," Ronan said. "Racehorse Robbie bet me I couldn't quit gambling—"

"Another bet you're sure to lose," Siobhan said.

"He's had a couple of wankers following me around twenty-four/seven. Then outta the blue some fella rang and said he left a tip on a winning horse for me at the abbey. I told myself no matter what I wasn't going to bet—but I had to have a look and see what he was on about."

"But you texted me," Sally said. "You told me to meet you there."

"I was working at Mickey John's," Ronan said. "My phone was on the bar. I didn't text you, Sally. We were both set up."

"It's all been a lie," Sally said. She slumped on the stairs. Carlene felt a rush of concern for her. She suddenly seemed more like a child than a woman. She'd spent fifteen years concocting this fantasy around Ronan based on secret love notes and ruined abbeys. Carlene looked for the woman from the Ballybeog Museum, and once again she found her staring at her. It was extremely disconcerting. And things were way too tense at the moment to stop and ask someone who she was.

"How much did you lose this time, Ronan?" Siobhan said.

"My pride," Ronan said. He glanced at Carlene. "I'm really sorry, Sally," he said.

Sally pointed at Carlene. "You," she said. She threw the dress on the stairs, stomped down the rest of the way, faced Carlene, and squared off with her.

"Shit," Carlene said. Declan grabbed her arm and whispered in her ear.

"I don't think she's gonna hit ye," he said. "But ye might want to think about ducking just in case."

"Thanks, Declan," Carlene said.

"No bother, pet," Declan said.

"You never said a word," Sally said.

"This isn't her fault," Ronan said.

"Shut yer gob," Sally said.

"I'm sorry," Carlene said. It was a little too late, but she really was sorry. She didn't come here to steal the loves of other people's lives.

"I quit my job, I followed you here, I helped you get this place up and running, I helped paint yer fucking wall!" Sally said.

"I know. I know, I'm sorry," Carlene said.

"I blathered on and on about Ronan being the love of my life and you never said a fucking word."

"I should have," Carlene admitted. She wasn't going to apologize any more. Sally wasn't really listening anyway.

"How long have you been shagging him?" She turned to Ronan. "Did she win this pub fair and square?" Joe, who up until now had been standing in the doorway listening, stepped farther into the room.

"Of course she did," Katie said. "I drew the name m'self."

"Maybe this could use some lookin' into," Joe said. The three McBride girls turned and glared at him.

"There's nothing to look into," Siobhan said. "Sally's upset is all."

"But how do we know that Ronan and this girl weren't lovers before she came here? Everyone is hooking up on the Internet these days. This whole raffle could have been a right trick!" Joe said.

"You got your money, Uncle Joe," Clare said.

"I'll give it back to you," Joe said. "Plus interest. It's the pub I want."

"You can't have it," Carlene said. "It's legally mine."

"We can get a judge to review this," Joe said. "This could have been a scam."

"Ronan and I met at the Galway Races," Carlene said. "After I won the pub." She looked at Ronan, who now had his face buried in his hands. "Tell them," Carlene said. As if physically linked together, all three McBride women stood.

"You were at the horse races?" Siobhan said. "After losing the pub?"

"Jaysus," Clare said. "He's still at it. He goes and loses Father's pub and he's still gambling his life away."

"You promised," Katie said. She had tears in her eyes. "You promised over Da's grave!"

Ronan didn't lift his head from the bar.

"This needs to be looked into," Joe said. "Investigated."

"Why on earth do you still want this place?" Siobhan said. "You've more than enough money to set your tanning beds up somewhere else."

"It's just convenient here is all," Joe said. "I can keep an eye out from next door." Carlene was so engrossed in the conversation that she didn't see the woman from the Ballybeog Museum until she was standing only a few feet away from her. She held out a book.

"Here's the book ye wanted," she said. Carlene couldn't believe she chose this moment to hand it to her, as if nothing else were going on. "*The Souterrains of Ireland*," the woman said.

"Thanks," Carlene said. She took the book and quickly stuffed it beside the cash register. "What's your name?" Carlene said. But she was too late, the woman was already out the door. "Declan," Carlene said. "Did you see the woman who gave me the book?"

"Sorry, pet," Declan said. "I had me back to her."

"Is anyone still working?" Riley said. "I wouldn't mind a fresh pint."

"The party is moving to Finnegan's," Sally said. She swiped Riley's pint glass off the bar, then worked her way down, removing everyone's drink and dumping what was left in their glasses down the drain.

"Sally," Carlene said.

"They're my lads and they'll go where I say," Sally said. "Right now, the pub is closed," she announced. "Everybody out." One by one the lads slowly stood, removed crumpled bills from their pockets, and set them on the bar. Sally pushed the money back. "It's on her," she said. Even the McBride girls got up to leave. Carlene was surprised to look up and see the band, as well as the Americans, pack up as well. One by one, the pub started to empty. Ronan and Collin remained at the bar. Sally stood in the doorway watching Ronan until Jane took her by the arm and led her away. Collin came up and whispered in Carlene's ear.

"How was that for a bad boy?" Collin said.

"What?" Carlene said.

"Who do you think the fella was that called Ronan and texted Sally?" Stunned, Carlene stared at Collin. He grinned.

"Thanks for the advice," he said out loud. He strolled out the door.

"What was that all about?" Ronan said.

"I think you should go too," Carlene said. "I'm tired and I have a lot of cleaning up to do."

"I'll help," he said. She didn't protest. They worked in silence, washing glasses, wiping down tables, upending the chairs.

"I'll get the jacks," Ronan said. He headed off to clean the bathrooms. Together, they finished in two hours. The place was spotless. It made Carlene sad. She liked the noise and mess of a pub.

"Thank you," Carlene said. "But you should go." She wanted him to argue. She wanted him to stay. He nodded.

"Are you still browned off at me too, Miss America?" Ronan said.

"You and me," Carlene said. "We mean well. But we keep making a mess of everything."

"Aren't you being a little dramatic?" Ronan said.

"Am I?" Carlene said. "You didn't even tell her. I don't even know if you ever were going to tell her." Ronan nodded.

"Fair enough," he said. His voice was stiff, defensive. He walked to the door, turned, and spoke softly. "Bye awhile," he said. Carlene waited until he walked out and closed the door.

"Good-bye," she said.

CHAPTER 36

Pulling Out the Punches

The day following the Americans from Hell incident, Carlene wasn't sure what to expect. Would she have any customers? She'd been awake all night, throwing covers on and off, turning this way and that, looking out the window and realizing she'd never been somewhere so dark—at home there were always streetlights even at night, but here the sky was cloaked in a deep cushion of black. Had she been in a better mood it would have been comforting; as it stood, it made her feel isolated and so alone. She obsessively replayed the events of the evening. Sally's torn wedding dress hung in her closet like a ghostly reprimand.

Carlene tried not to think about Ronan, but her thoughts kept returning to him anyway, like a homing pigeon returning to his perch long after his coop had been torn down. Ronan was so beautiful, and aggravating, and immature, yet caring, and funny, and every time he messed up he was too easy to forgive because you could tell he meant well. There was a softness to him, a vulnerability that Carlene wanted to leap in and fix, yet there was also a wall, which he would run and hide behind the second he felt she was getting too close. How much was he still gambling? Did any of them believe that he had really quit?

Carlene woke early the next morning and picked up the book on souterrains, just to get her mind on something else. She had just fixed herself a cup of instant coffee and opened the book when Ciaran's wife, Jane, burst in the door, followed by Ciaran himself, eyes firmly planted on his feet, like an infant discovering them for the first time. Jane looked as pretty and perky as ever, except for the large white bandage on her neck. Ciaran glanced up, mouthed "Sorry," and returned his gaze to his fascinating feet. Jane barged up to the bar. Despite her petite frame, she looked perfectly capable of kicking Carlene's ass.

"Where the feck do you get off?" Jane said.

"Pardon?" Carlene said. Jane ripped the bandage off her neck. There, Carlene could clearly make out teeth marks.

"Ciaran," Carlene said. "I didn't tell you to bite her neck."

"You said follow her passions," Ciaran said. "Her passions are fucking vampires. I thought she'd fancy a nip." Jane put her bandage back on and shook her finger at Carlene.

"First Sally, and now this? I wish Joe McBride would have turned this place into a spa. At least then I'd be getting my nails done instead of slapping some sense into my husband. You won't be entertaining Ciaran anymore here. That's a promise."

"I'm sorry," Carlene said.

"Mind yer own business or I'll come back and mind it for ye," Jane said. Then she stormed out. Ciaran stood in her wake.

"Ciaran," Carlene said.

"I know, I know," Ciaran said. He remained standing.

"I think you'd better go with her," Carlene said.

"Right, right," Ciaran said. "Listen. Can I just get a wee drink to take away?"

Carlene couldn't sleep that night either, so a little after one in the morning, she called her father. Maybe, for once in his life, he would comfort her. Maybe he had some great advice that would save her from all of this.

"What time is it?" he asked straightaway.

"It's one twelve here," she said.

"You should be in bed." Carlene heard water running in the background. It continued throughout the call.

"How are you?" she asked.

"I'm not well," her father said. Carlene settled in and listened to his complaints. His joints were bothering him, his back ached, his hands were chapped, they were discontinuing one of his favorite cleaning products, and he was going to sell the gym. Carlene, who had been lying down, sat straight up in bed.

"Why?" she said.

"Because you were supposed to be here to run it," her father said. "You were going to take over for me."

"Since when?"

"I thought it was obvious. I was slowly giving you more and more responsibility. You had your own office."

"It was a janitor's closet, Dad."

"It was spotless, and that desk fit in there," her father said.

"I don't know what to say. Sell if you want to sell."

"Why don't you just come home?" Without waiting for her reply, he started in on the woes of running the gym. She was so deflated by the time he was done that she didn't even try to talk him into visiting. Just once, she would love to say, "How are you, Dad?" and hear, "Grand, grand. You?" in response.

And he didn't even know what a failure she was here. Maybe he was right. Maybe she should come home and run the gym. It didn't dawn on her until she hung up. He hadn't once asked her about her.

Carlene had underestimated Sally's influence. A week went by with only a few visits from Declan. He seemed so concerned for her, and she was grateful for his company and his assurances that things would get better. He did everything he could to cheer her up, including bombarding her with jokes. "Have you seen the Ballybeog cemetery?" he asked her.

"I have," Carlene said.

"Did you know that nobody who lives near the cemetery is allowed to be buried there?"

"No," Carlene said. "Why not?"

"Because they're not dead yet," Declan said. His visits kept her sane. One day he saw her book on souterrains and started leafing through it.

"Why the interest?" he asked.

"I'm just . . . curious about all things Ireland," Carlene said.

"Ah, right, right," Declan said. Carlene felt a rush of guilt. Here was maybe her only friend left in Ballybeog, and she was lying to him. She couldn't help it; the souterrain was her secret, the one thing keeping her sane. "Remember you asked me if I knew who gave you this book?" Declan said.

"Yes," Carlene said. "I'm sorry you didn't see her. She's the same woman I ran into at the Ballybeog Museum."

"I reckon I know who you're on about," Declan said.

"You do?"

"It sounds like Ellen," Declan said.

"Ellen," Carlene said. Why did that name sound familiar?

"She's Pat McGee's daughter. Stays in her room most of the time." That was it—she'd heard the women on the bus to the cliffs talking about Ellen.

"Why do you think it's her?"

"She's a skinny thing with short dark hair. Very pale."

"That's her. Well, that's great, right? It means she's coming out of her room."

"I heard Pat McGee say so the other day. Seems she's been coming out of her room since you came to town."

"Me?"

"You've got your own Irish stalker!"

"That's so great," Carlene said. "I wish she was a paying stalker."

"Don't you worry, pet. They'll come back."

"Thanks, Declan." He got up to leave, then stood by the door watching her.

"I love Sally like she was me own daughter," Declan said. "But I've always known Ronan wasn't the man for her. She won't see it for a long time all right, but you did her a favor. And let me tell you, chicken. That home movie? That was some kiss. Some kiss, all right. I'd say Ellen isn't the only one you've lured out of hiding. I think if you played your cards right, you might just talk that boy into settling down." Before Carlene could argue otherwise, Declan winked and was out the door.

Carlene scrubbed the floors. She polished the bar. She polished the brass rail at the foot of the bar that she always forgot about because she was always on the other side. She polished the tables and the chairs. She cleaned windows inside and out, mopped and swept the floors, and walls, and pictures, and shelves, and knickknacks. She played all of her favorite songs from the jukebox. She played a game of pool by herself. Then darts. She lost both. She cried. She danced. Every morning she crawled thirteen steps into the souterrain and back. She played with Columbus. She rearranged the furniture on the back deck and picked fresh wildflowers every morning. Ronan called several times, but Carlene didn't call him back.

On her sixth day of solitary confinement, Ronan showed up at her door carrying a computer. It was an older model, a dinosaur by most standards, but she was so thrilled to see it, she had to refrain herself from dropping to her knees and clinging to his legs. Ronan cleared a space in the back of the bar, and within a few minutes, she was hooked up and online.

"I didn't know I could get Internet," Carlene said.

"I installed a satellite," Ronan said.

"When did you do that?" Carlene said.

"A few days ago," Ronan said. "You were out." It must have been on one of her walks. She'd been taking long walks into town and around the abbey. Ronan looked around the empty bar.

"How ya keeping?" he said.

"Grand, grand," Carlene said. She turned away so he wouldn't see her tears. She hated crying. She'd been doing a lot of it lately.

"It will all settle down," Ronan said.

"That's what Declan said," Carlene said. Ronan started for the door, then stopped.

"I would have told her," he said. "I was planning on it that night. It's why I had the newspaper article in my pocket. I've no excuse for dragging it out—other than I'm not very good at facing up to things, I guess."

"I believe you," Carlene said. "But you and me. I don't know—"

"Right, right," Ronan said. "No bother."

"Wait," Carlene said. "There's something I want to show you. It's out back." Ronan's cell phone beeped. He flipped it open and read the message.

"Can we do this another time?" he said. "I have to run." Carlene nodded. "Bye awhile," he said.

Why did she let him do that to her? The minute he left, Carlene felt as if a huge hole had opened up inside her. It wasn't a blessing to find someone who made you feel so alive, it was a curse. She had been so looking forward to finally showing him the souterrain. Where was he going in such a hurry? Was he dating someone else? Was he gambling? And which, she chided herself, would bother her more? She was too restless now; she had to do something.

In the shed, Carlene found a bag of sand and a long piece of rope. Carlene tied the sandbag to the rope, borrowed a ladder from Joe, and hung it from the wood-beamed ceiling. Voilà, she had her own punching bag. She worked out for about an hour, going through all her old boxing drills. It felt great. On the third day of this routine, she felt someone at the window watching her. Two middle-aged women stood in her front yard, looking in. Carlene waved. At first, they just stared, then slowly, they lifted their arms and waved back. They started to walk away. Carlene ran to the door and threw it open.

"I'm open," she said, hoping her perspiration wouldn't drive them away. "Are you here for a drink?"

"Actually," one of the women said, pointing at her, "we'd like to do that to ourselves."

"What?" Carlene said. What had she done to herself?

"Boxercise," the other woman said. She looked down at her body. "We need to get in shape."

"The annual Ballybeog Talent Show is coming up, you see,"

the first woman said. "I'd like to be fitting into me dress by then."

"Boxercise?" Carlene said. "Both of you?" They nodded in unison. "Well then," Carlene said. "What time can you be here tomorrow?"

The next morning, six middle-aged women and one sixteen-year-old girl showed up for boxercise class. Carlene was impressed with their outfits—they were new and trendy. Carlene put on some upbeat music and took them through her routine. They loved taking turns on the punching bag. It seemed there were a lot of women in Ballybeog who just needed to hit something.

"You own a boxing gym back home in Ohio, is that right?" one lady asked her.

"My father owns the gym," Carlene said. "Although he might be selling it."

"You wouldn't want to go home and run it?" another asked. There was no malice in her voice, only curiosity.

"I'd rather make a go of it here," Carlene said. As soon as the words were out of her mouth, she knew it was true. This was her home now; at least, she wanted it to be.

"So you grew up boxing?" the girl asked.

"Yes," Carlene said. "I even married a boxer. Well, semiprofessional anyway. He was Irish too." She was feeling so good, endorphins flying through her body, her mouth just didn't know when to stop. She didn't even realize what she'd said until she'd noticed that her class had come to a dead stop.

"Keep going," Carlene said. "One two, one two." The authority in her voice surprised even herself. But suddenly, their questions came faster than their jabs.

"You're married?"

"To an Irishman?"

"A boxer?"

"Does Ronan McBride know this?"

"Does Sally Collins know this?"

"Where is he?"

"Does he know you're here?" Carlene wished she had a whistle to blow.

"I'm not married anymore," Carlene said. "I found out he was marrying me just for a green card. He disappeared soon after the ceremony. When I tried to get a divorce, I found out the minister who married us in Vegas wasn't even really ordained. So I was never really married, you see. Not that he knows it. I haven't heard from him since. I guess he'll find out when he goes to apply for his green card. Now. Move. Move, move, move." Slowly, they started moving again. Jabbing, jumping, kicking.

"Is she taking the piss?" Carlene heard one woman ask the other.

"No talking," Carlene said. For the next half hour, she killed them with aerobics.

They stayed for a spot of lunch. It was their idea. They offered not only to buy the sandwiches, but to prepare them as well. They popped into Joe's and came back with their arms full of food. Carlene supplied the drinks. At first, they gossiped amongst themselves while Carlene happily ate her sandwich. Then the conversation slowly turned back to Brendan. They were really interested in her now, and not just the fake polite interest. They told her how they don't believe in divorce in Ireland, it's not like America where everybody gets divorced. Carlene assured them once again that she was never really married, and she tried to get their minds off it by asking the married ones to share their secret to a lasting relationship. The woman who'd been married the longest said, "We don't see each other and we don't talk to each other. That's the secret."

The conversation moved on, and Carlene loved listening to their gossip.

"Did you hear about Maggie Mahoney?"

"Ah, right, dreadful."

"Who's Maggie?" Carlene asked. They filled her in. She lived in the next town. She was a young widow, who after five years of being alone had just started dating again. An older gentleman. One by one, the women added to the story.

"Old enough to be her grandfather, so."

"They were going at it day and night, bouncing off the head-boards." The story halted as a few titters and giggles escaped the crowd. Hands were put shyly over mouths, heads shook, laughter spilled forth.

"Ah, dreadful." They must have noticed the lost expression on Carlene's face. The woman sitting nearest Carlene leaned in.

"He had a heart attack, you see."

"Oh no," Carlene said.

"While they were bouncing off the headboards," another clarified. Carlene put her hand over her mouth, shook her head.

"When she was coming, he was going," the oldest in the crowd blurted out. The women rocked with laughter, then crossed themselves.

"May he rest in peace."

"She got her piece, now he's getting his." The laughter started all over again. They crossed themselves again.

"Ah, dreadful."

"That poor woman. We'll have to take her a stew."

"Ah, go on, tell us more about Brendan," one woman said. "Were you married in America?" They were all watching her, waiting. This was what it would take to fit in—a little soul baring. Trust was built on confiding in others, owning up to your mistakes. And, if nothing else, Carlene's wedding had been amusing.

"Okay," Carlene said. "I'll tell you about my wedding day."

CHAPTER 37

Las Vegas, Nevada
Are You Lonesome Tonight?

Carlene stood in front of the ordained minister who had the power invested in him by the Universal Church Online and tried to avert her gaze from his hill of a stomach. It strained against his creased forest-green dress shirt. He was milliseconds away from popping a button. Carlene wanted to stop the proceedings. Didn't their ceremony deserve the respect of a fresh, pressed shirt? Surely Brendan noticed. Why didn't he say something? Did the minister's wrinkly green hill of a stomach remind Brendan of the rolling hills of Ireland?

And was that really a white carnation attached to his baby blue blazer with a safety pin? It was a big pin too, as if made to fasten a giant diaper. Great, now she was thinking of diapers at her wedding. That couldn't be good. Besides which, everybody knew carnations were white trash flowers. She wanted to reach out and rip the carnation off his chest. Brendan was the fighter. Brendan should be livid. Brendan should be crouching ready to deliver the one-two punch!

Carlene dug the nail of her ring finger into her soft palm. If she pressed hard enough, could she make her love line bleed? She tried, but there wasn't any blood, only a short, sharp pain.

She glanced at Brendan, so tall beside her, so handsome in his tux. She ignored the part of her that wanted to punch him in the stomach as well. "You clean up nice," she leaned over and whispered. Whenever she had a bad thought, like wanting to punch someone in the gut, she would immediately follow it up with something positive. If she thought the bad thought silently, but said the good thought out loud, then that was the one that would count in the end. Wasn't it?

Brendan's lips stretched a tiny fraction, as if it was the best he could muster, as if it hurt to smile. He swallowed hard. His chin shook and his Adam's apple jerked. His nervousness startled her. Did he want to call the whole deal off? She hated this, standing next to each other all stiff and made up. She was used to seeing him with boxing gloves, a mouth guard, and green silk shorts. Maybe that's the way they should keep it. Half-naked and from afar.

One the other hand, it was nice to see Brendan's face free of sweat and blood. She liked the slant of his jaw, his heart-shaped chin. His was a strong, handsome face with full lips and prominent cheekbones. His blond hair was cut short and a patch of freckles paraded up his neck. Only his hands showed the toll his five years of professional boxing had taken on him; knuckles so swollen they couldn't find a ring big enough to fit. Being a lefty, he'd broken the bones in his left hand fifteen times, compared to only six on the right. His nose wasn't the prettiest sight either, but its slight bump gave him character. He was wearing way too much cologne, though, a mix of musk and peppermint. Carlene suddenly wished she had a mint, anything to rid herself of the taste of cheap tequila on the back of her tongue. If she wasn't careful, she was going to cry.

Carlene sniffed and held her head up like she'd seen Brendan do after countless fights. This was her wedding, she had better start enjoying it. Focus on the positive. She loved her shiny gold dress, long and low cut. It clung to her ample breasts. She had a nice rack. She looked down at her nipples. It was chilly in the chapel. Her long blond hair hung in ringlets past her shoulders, a thousand spiral staircases stepping away from her head. They felt a little too tight, and she still had a headache from the hairspray fumes. Brendan paid for the stylist. Her name was Sue and she told Carlene she was going to get the fuck out of Vegas the minute she hit the super slots. Carlene, who worked hard for every dime she ever made, could never understand those who were so willing to just throw it away.

On the other hand, she was taking quite a gamble marrying Brendan, wasn't she?

Carlene's lips were so glossed she had to keep them slightly open. She hated the gummy feel when they touched. Her eyelashes were curled to the ceiling and caked with so much mascara she was afraid to blink. The straps on her gold stiletto sandals dug into her polished toes. At least she would look good in her wedding photo. The photographer, all dressed in black, paced the back of the room. He doubled as a dealer, and warned them his shift was starting. He told them he only took pictures after the ceremony, when it was too late to turn back, like the kind captured at the apex of a roller coaster, preserving the terrifying moment before everything plunged straight downhill.

In her hands, Carlene held a single white rose. She wanted a hundred, an armful. When Brendan handed it to her, she should have insisted on more. She didn't like the cardboard Elvis cutout front and center either. He towered over them in a white suit sparkling with sequins. His right arm extended out, and his finger pointed at her like he was going to recruit her into the army right after the ceremony. Next to the minister was a four-foot pedestal topped with a vase of blue plastic flowers. They looked like they belonged at funeral for a giant Barbie doll. Carlene had just turned twenty-seven. This wasn't the wedding she dreamed of as a little girl.

Had she been in charge of the planning, she would have done things differently. They could have gotten married next to the Sphinx, or in the Eiffel Tower, or in front of the fountains at the Bellagio. Why couldn't he have put more than a good laugh, a couple of margaritas, and a run to the Elvis Chapel into it? And what was wrong with her? She hadn't even said "I do" and she could already feel herself morphing into a nagging, neglected wife.

"Do you take this woman to—" The minister started to cough. Brendan looked at Carlene and crossed his eyes. Good old Brendan. That's why she was doing this, because he was wonderful and made her laugh, because she loved him. That was something, wasn't it? Carlene turned her head slightly and covered her mouth, so the minister wouldn't see her laughing at him. He was still coughing, a smoker's cough, filled with phlegm, and his jowls bounced up and down from the force. Carlene opened her mouth in a pretend yawn, anything to stop the laughter roiling inside her, busting to get out. Just then, the minister's offending button popped free from his straining stomach and shot into the air. It landed smack on the center of Carlene's tongue.

"Jaysus," Brendan said. "That's some balls." His hands flew up to his head. Carlene opened her mouth as wide as she could, terrified she was going to swallow the button and choke to death. Would Brendan get to stay in the country if she died now? No, because they hadn't even said "I do." But if they had and she died—

The air conditioner rattled and then groaned to a stop. Heat descended like a swarm of locusts. The minister yanked a wrinkled blue tissue out of his blue suit and held it out to Carlene like a consolation prize. Who the fuck wears a dark green shirt with a baby blue blazer? Carlene spat the button at the Elvis cutout. It stuck just beneath his nose.

"Good shot," Brendan said. He grabbed her hands and pulled her toward him. His grip was strong, decisive.

"I do," he said. He took the platinum wedding band they had purchased ten minutes earlier from Discount Diamonds out of his pocket and slipped it on her finger. Carlene stared at it. It did not come with any diamonds. The minister looked at Carlene. Brendan squeezed her hand. "Your turn," Brendan said.

"Oh," Carlene said. "Me too." She tried to slip Brendan's ring on his finger, but she couldn't get it past his knuckle.

"Good enough," Brendan said. He pulled his hand away. The

minister pronounced them husband and wife, picked up a remote control from the podium, and pointed it at gigantic speakers suspended from the ceiling by frayed bungee cords. They
crackled to life and Elvis's booming voice filled the tiny chapel.
*Are you lonesome tonight? Do you miss me tonight? Are you
sorry we drifted apart?*

Brendan gave her a small kiss. His lips were chapped, and her
excessive gloss helped to coat them. That's good deed number
two I've done today, Carlene thought. *Honey, you lied when
you said you loved me,* Elvis crooned. Carlene turned to have
her wedding picture taken, but the wedding photographer slash
blackjack dealer was gone. Carlene painfully stepped to the pew
where she set down her purse. Her heels were killing her. How
could something so beautiful cause so much pain?

She dug her iPhone out of her purse and clicked on the camera application. Just married a guy you barely know so he can
stay in the country? There's an app for that. . . . She held the
phone at arm's length and snapped her own picture. *I'm Mrs.
Brendan Hayes,* she thought. *That's some balls.*

They hit a bar and drank. She knew Brendan could drink, but
the amount he consumed that night should have been lethal. He
was too drunk to make love, and he passed out in their heart-
shaped bed. Carlene stared at the ceiling and knew she had
made a mistake. It was almost a relief when she woke up and he
was gone. She never saw him again. A month later she received
a letter from the Elvis Chapel with their sincere apologies, but
anyone who had been married by Minister Harrison was not
legally married. Turned out his online license had expired. The
chapel offered to cover all expenses to Vegas for a replacement
wedding. A replacement groom they couldn't come up with. It
was strange; Brendan was out there somewhere, thinking he had
a wife. He'd find out, she guessed, if he ever tried to put the
paperwork through for citizenship.

Ballybeog, Ireland

When Carlene was finished with her story, the women all rallied around her, asking her a million questions. Had she Googled

him? Did he come back to Ireland? What county was he from? Was she still heartbroken? No, she told them, she was totally over Brendan Hayes. It was the truth, and it felt good to say it. If only she wasn't in love with Ronan—only then could she say she'd truly learned her lesson. She'd been so harsh on him the other day, but he was right, she was just as messed up as he was—different mistakes, same flawed human being. She didn't mention Ronan or any more of her flaws to the women. One secret at a time, she thought—otherwise there would be nothing left for tomorrow's class.

Chapter 38

Down Under

When Carlene was a kid, you couldn't buy mini-bottles of hand sanitzer with clips to attach to your key chain like you can now. So her father sent her to school with industrial-strength bottles, enough to sanitize a small village. The bottles weighed down her backpack, and Carlene developed shoulder pains and back-aches, but nothing was worse than the fear of someone discovering the bottle in her bag. She took to wrapping them in brown paper bags like a bum with a bottle of vodka.

She would hunch over the bag nervously, strategically placing her head so her hair would hang over the bag and shield the large bottle from view. Sometimes, if she forgot to screw the cap on tight enough, the sharp smell would permeate the classroom. It wouldn't take long for people to start sniffing, looking around, and asking, "What's that smell?" She sniffed the loudest and was always the first to ask the question.

In addition, every two days her father supplied her with a box consisting of a dozen pairs of blue rubber gloves, one for each hour, which he actually thought she would wear. There were six hours in a school day, so the box was supposed to last her for two days. His first act of business when she came home from school was to check the box to make sure there were six left for the next day, before an air kiss to either cheek and a "How was your day?"

Carlene wondered how in the world her father could actually believe that she would wear them. It would have been social suicide, and of course she never did, not once, and at the end of the day she'd march to the nearest garbage can and throw away six pairs of brand-new gloves. She didn't feel too guilty; it was his ritual, not hers, and he was out of his mind to think she would don blue rubber gloves in front of her classmates. She convinced herself he did know she was throwing them away, but he wanted to be soothed by the fantasy anyway, so she went along with the game. She made it through middle school unscathed. All that changed the first day of high school when she was partnered in chemistry class with Shawn Cole. She'd had a crush on him forever. *Chemistry*. Could the universe have been more clear? Carlene was so excited, she forgot to hide her backpack.

When she stooped over and retrieved her notebook, all she could think was—*Don't let him see the back!* That was where she'd scribbled *I Love Shawn Cole* about a hundred million times. So when he glanced over, saw her bag, and exclaimed, "What is this?" her first thought was that he could see through her notebook to the back of the book, that not only was he the cutest boy in school, but he had x-ray vision as well—truly, a score. But instead, he reached over her and pulled out the industrial-sized bottle of antiseptic and the box of rubber gloves. The smell of latex and sanitizer permeated the classroom. Even the stench of plugged-in Bunsen burners couldn't disguise it. To Carlene's horror, Shawn pulled gloves out of the box, one by one, like a magician pulling on an endless string of scarves. When he got to the last pair, he put them on and launched into a comedy routine. The class erupted in hysterics.

By the end of the day, Shawn Cole picked a new lab partner. Julissa Lions. Carlene had always secretly admired her; she was so pretty with long black hair and shiny pink lip gloss. Julissa's backpack was filled with neon-colored pencils, gum, and a pack of Kool menthol cigarettes. Julissa's mom, Cathy, always picked

Julissa up after school, and Carlene had taken to hanging around, just so she could see Cathy Lions pull up in her blue station wagon. Julissa would always get into the passenger seat and lean over and kiss her mother on the cheek.

Carlene imagined she and Julissa were sisters, pictured herself getting into the passenger seat leaning over and kissing Cathy Lions's cheek. She had been determined to become best friends with Julissa Lions. But that day, after Julissa snuggled up to Shawn, she turned to Carlene, laughed, and called her Germ Girl. It didn't make sense—if she'd called her Clean Freak she would have understood, but no, Germ Girl. The nickname would stick with her for the rest of high school.

Carlene vowed from that day on, she would not be her father's prisoner of clean one more second, hour, or precious day of her life.

She gathered all the gloves Shawn had strewn around the room and put them back in the box as neatly as she could so it looked as if she hadn't touched a single pair. She bypassed the trash can at the end of the day. When she came home, if her father noticed she'd been crying, he didn't acknowledge it. Instead, he counted the gloves like he did every day. There were twelve pairs in the box. He counted again, like she knew he would. He counted again, and again, and again. She wished she had another pair of gloves to slip into the box, just to watch him short-circuit.

"Tell me you took two boxes of gloves to school today," her father said.

"No," Carlene said.

"No, you won't tell me, or no, you did not take two boxes of gloves to school today?"

"No, I did not take two boxes of gloves to school today." She mimicked her father's clipped speech back to him. With each second, her defiance grew, which both fascinated and appalled her, yet she couldn't bring herself to stop.

"It looks as if you didn't use a single pair of gloves today," her father said.

"That is correct, sir," Carlene said. Her father looked at her as if he'd never seen her before. And then it hit her. All these years. He really, truly thought she'd been wearing the gloves. It wasn't a self-soothing game. She pitied him, then hated him, then hated herself.

"There are still twelve in the box," he said.

"Count them again," she said. The image of Shawn and Julissa hovered in her mind, cuddled together in chemistry class, laughing at her. Her father counted the gloves again.

"Twelve," he said. He held out the box. "Count them."

"I don't need to count them. I just counted you counting them. You counted them twenty-seven times." Michael Rivers rubbed his hands on his pants, kneading his fingers into the folds that he ironed no less than three hundred times that morning. Carlene wanted to scream that it didn't make sense for a person to iron their pants three hundred times and then rub creases into them with their fingers. She didn't know how this showdown was going to end, and she was both thrilled and terrified that she'd finally stood up to him. She was prepared to be grounded, or shunned even, but nothing could have prepared her for what came out of his mouth next.

"Your mother would have been very disappointed in you," he said. He cradled the box of gloves to his chest and walked out of the room. He never made her wear them again. But it didn't matter. He'd won. She'd never been able to get the sting out of his parting comment. *Your mother would have been very disappointed in you.*

Carlene would wear gloves today, but this time it was of her own free will. She was going to go down into the souterrain, and this time she was going to crawl all the way through. She would go early in the morning—there was no way she was going to crawl around down there in the dark. She would leave a note on the bar, telling anyone who cared where she was, in case she never returned. Surely, if enough time went by, someone would come into the pub and see her note.

Would it be Ronan? Should she make it a love note? Tell him that despite his fatal flaws she thought he was beautiful and amazing? Or should her note say: *Be Mine?* She didn't write any of that, instead she drew a map to the souterrain. Then underneath she jotted down:

> *I, Carlene Rivers, being of sober mind and body,*
> *announce that upon my death in a narrow*
> *underground passage, I leave this pub to:*

She wrote, *Ronan.* Scratched it out. *Nancy.* Too busy; suppose she got distracted running both the café and the pub, and there went the best cappuccinos in Ballybeog? Carlene didn't want that on her conscience. Carlene scratched Nancy out as well and wrote: The half dozen. *There, that's the way it should have been in the first place.* There were six of them, they could rotate their shifts.

Carlene wore a small backpack too, the first time since high school. She would bring enough water and food to last her a few days. After a bit of deliberation she also brought a small kitchen knife and a bottle of hair spray that she could use like Mace. She would also carry a flashlight. She thought of going to the hardware shop to see if she could buy a miner's hat with a light on it, but in a town that oozed gossip, she decided it wouldn't be the best move.

She went at six A.M., when the sun was just beginning its ascent. A yellow ball hiding behind gauze-curtain clouds. It smelled like fresh grass, dirt, and heather. She fed Columbus, then kissed her little head for luck. She wished she could take the kitten with her; after all, she was the one who discovered the passage in the first place. As she padded across the moist ground to the trapdoor, she felt happier than she'd been in a long time. Maybe all women had a little Nancy Drew in them; Carlene was certainly relishing the adventure. How often in life, as an adult, did you get to explore hidden passages?

She hadn't gleaned much information from what she'd read in the book so far. She'd tried to stay up late last night reading it, but it was very technical. She didn't know how someone could make a book on secret passages a snoozer, but the author had managed it quite well. All she knew was that Ireland was full of such spaces, from Dingle to Donegal. Some were made of limestone and timber, others were just plowed earth. A good number of the souterrains were located near ringforts, which bolstered the argument that they were originally built as places of defense.

Others said that they weren't defense at all, they were simply used as cold storage to preserve food. Later, it was said that cattle thieves or IRA members used the underground spaces to hide weapons or themselves, but it was pretty much agreed that the spaces had been built long before. The exact age was unknown, and again subject to disagreement. Some thought they dated all the way back to the Bronze Age, others dated them as late as the eighteenth century. Some had spaces where you could actually stand up in them, some had multiple passages ending in beehive-shaped rooms. Carlene couldn't wait to see what hers was like.

Dropping down onto the chair was easy. She'd done it many times. The familiar smell of wet limestone and dirt was surprisingly comforting. She wore jeans, tennis shoes, a sweatshirt, a rain jacket, and heavy work gloves. She didn't want to cut her hands on anything as she crawled. She dropped to her hands and knees and breathed. *I can do this.*

She shone the light down the passage. The beam of light only illuminated ten feet ahead. She would need both hands to crawl. That meant tucking the flashlight into her shirt. When she felt as if she'd made enough headway, she would stop and shine the light again. It wasn't a perfect plan, but it was better than nothing. It was now or never. Carlene started to crawl.

It was damp, and within a few feet her knees were wet and aching. She should have worn knee pads. The space was barely big enough for her and the backpack. It scraped along the timber roof, shaking loose dirt and pebbles as she crawled. The backpack snagged a few times, and Carlene had to force her way through, after which the light sprinkling of dirt turned into a downpour. *Please don't cave in, please don't cave in.*

She stopped after about ten paces and breathed. It was so dark. The space wasn't large enough to turn around. If she wanted to go back now, it would mean crawling backward. If she wanted to quit, now would be a good time. She reached into her shirt and pulled out the flashlight. Her hands shook as she turned it on and shone it down the passage. Still, more of the same, for at least another ten feet. She started up again.

Right hand, right knee, left hand, left knee. The farther in she went, the more the temperature dropped, until soon it felt as if she were crawling through a freezer. The food-storage theory was starting to gain credibility. Imagine having to crawl through here every day for milk. Carlene started to sing to herself. She'd never been one to sing much before, but everyone over here did it, no matter how terrible their voices were, and it seemed to make them deliriously happy, so she was going to try singing too.

She didn't know enough words to the Irish songs she liked to keep herself entertained, so she started in on a military cadence of right, left, right, left. She stopped after what felt like ages, and this time, when she turned on the flashlight, she could make out a large opening just six feet away. Her heart began to pound. It was a dark, dark hole. Anything could be there. Anyone could be in there. What if someone was living down here? Surely, they'd heard her coming. But could someone really just be sitting there in the dark, waiting to pounce? Unlikely. Unless they were asleep. Imagine waking a sleeping terrorist. It was just after seven in the morning. Most criminals were probably night owls. Carlene held her breath, kept as still as possible, and listened.

Besides an occasional drip, it was deadly silent. *There is no one in there, there is no one in there.* What kind of animal might burrow its way in here? Obviously, this was built by man. She didn't know any animal who knew how to lay a limestone floor and a timber roof. But had an animal taken advantage of the space to hang out? Was she going into a fox den?

Shit, she hated herself for getting herself into this, and knowing that there was no way she could turn back now. If she didn't go all the way up to the entrance, she would torture herself about it for the rest of her life.

The thought made her keep crawling. Finally, she was at the mouth of the opening; she could feel the dampness spreading even before she turned on the light. She took a moment and tried to look into it without the flashlight, but it was pitch black. She breathed. She listened. She heard water dripping. It was definitely wetter in here. She took a deep breath, said a little prayer, and turned on the light.

It was a small, round, dirt room, a tiny cave. Against the back wall a bench had been carved out of stone. It looked as if she would be able to stand up in the middle of the room, but have to scrunch over on the sides. Carlene had to admit that after all the fear, worry, and fuss, it was a tad disappointing as far as hidden underground spaces were concerned. She shone the light along the left wall, half expecting to see old milk bottles or something to prove that it had been a caveman's refrigerator. Instead, it was eerily empty. She read that some of the spaces had a duct in the ceiling and a fire pit. Excitement, strike two—this one did not. Confident and calm, she swung the light to the right. There, lying on the floor, was a human skeleton.

Hanging off its bones was a tattered gray dress. The skull was tilted back, the jaw gaped open as if she died mid-scream, empty eye sockets stared at the ceiling. Carlene screamed, and screamed, and screamed, but she couldn't move. Then adrenaline kicked in. Ignoring the pain in her knees, Carlene began what could only be described as sprint-crawling. As she scrambled out as if her life depended on it, the lone light continued to shine upon the abandoned bones.

CHAPTER 39

Bringing in the Guards

There was no question of what to do—the police had to be called. Carlene had no idea who was lying down there or for how long, and although it was some comfort that it was a skeleton and not a fresh body, it was still something she could not mull over, not for a second. She rushed into the pub and picked up the phone. There was no dial tone. Carlene put it down and picked it up again. It was definitely dead. She examined the lines going into the phone. It seemed perfectly fine. She ran upstairs and grabbed her cell phone out of her purse. Shit. What did you dial for 911 in Ireland? How could she still not know?

She ran over to Joe's shop. He was seated at the counter, hunched over, reading his newspaper.

"Call the police," she said. "Quick." She didn't know why she said quick—the skeleton had been down there for quite some time—but she still felt panicked.

"What the devil is going on?" Joe asked. He looked her up and down. She forgot what a mess she was, dirty and wet, and shaking.

"I found a skeleton on my property," she said.

"A what?"

"A woman, Joe. I found a woman's skeleton."

"How do ye know it's a woman?"

"It's wearing a dress."

"Right, right," Joe said. "Where did ye find it?"

"Underground," Carlene said.

"You dug up a grave?" Joe asked.

"No," Carlene said. "Please. Just call the guards." Carlene had rushed in so fast, she hadn't even bothered to look around. Now she sensed people staring at her. This time it wasn't a christening, but there were several women doing their shopping, and all had stopped to listen to her. If she had hoped to keep this a secret, there wasn't a chance of it now.

It didn't take long for Mike Murphy and a second guard to arrive, followed by Father Duggan. Joe tagged along, as well as all five customers who had been in the shop. Carlene wished she had time to change and take a shower, but they were all anxious to get to the skeleton. Carlene wanted to ask Father Duggan why he was there—it was obviously too late for last rites, and besides, how would they know if the skeleton was even Catholic? She realized, as they all gathered in the backyard, that she should call the McBrides. She asked Mike Murphy if he would wait for them before going after the skeleton. The guards spent the time circling the entrance to the passage, then they cordoned off a square around it with crime scene tape.

Carlene used the phone in Joe's shop to call Mary McBride. Katie answered and Carlene quickly filled her in. Katie agreed to call the rest of them, including Ronan. When Carlene returned to the passage, the guards were taking pictures of the entrance.

"How did you find this?" Father Duggan asked Carlene.

"My cat found it," Carlene said. The folks who gathered in her backyard were all chattering at once, wondering whose body it was. Joe pulled her aside.

"Listen," he said. "If this property is a crime scene, it may change things."

"What things?"

"What if Ronan raffled off the property to cover up a murder?" Joe said.

"You're accusing Ronan of murder now?" Carlene said. "What kind of miserable old man are you?"

"I—I—"

"Whoever it is down there, she's been dead a long time, Joe. Way before Ronan's time. Maybe it was you. Where were you about a hundred years ago, Joe?"

"Look at you. Getting a bit cheeky, aren't ye?" Joe said. He was right. She even felt a bit cheeky. It felt great. Maybe facing your fears and getting the shit scared out of you was good for your soul. Joe seemed less impressed with her spiritual development.

"You should sell this place before it becomes a circus," he said.

"It already is. And you know what? I like the circus. The circus is exciting." Carlene moved away from Joe and stood as close to the guards as she could. Finally, Katie arrived with Siobhan, Clare, Liz, and Mary McBride. Just when Carlene was debating whether or not to ask for Ronan, she saw him, pushing through the crowd, coming toward her. Carlene didn't know what came over her, but she ran to him. She knew very well he could push her away, reject her, and yet she kept running. He stood still, but when she threw herself into his arms, he didn't push her away. Instead, he hugged her, rubbed her hair.

"Shh," he said.

"I wanted to tell you about it," she said. "I was going to the other night—"

"It's okay—"

"About what you said—"

"We've both made mistakes, let's just focus on this for now, all right?" Ronan said. Carlene nodded, even though she wanted to grill him. What mistakes had he made? Was he talking about her, calling her a mistake? Or did they involve Sally? Had he gone back to her? They didn't have time to talk any further; the first guard was dropping down into the hole, trying to drag a stretcher with him. Carlene wanted to say that the skeleton probably didn't need a stretcher, but what did she know?

While everyone stood and watched, Father Duggan gave a short prayer. Declan arrived and said he'd put on cheese toasties in case any of the crowd wanted to come in for a wee drink afterward. She was comforted with pats on the hand and several murmuring, " 'Tis awful, now tell us again what it looked like?" It seemed like forever before Mike Murphy poked his head back up and the crowd backed away, waiting for the stretcher with the skeleton to come back up. Instead, he came up, quickly followed by the other, no stretcher to be seen.

"She won't fit, will she?" someone asked.

"Is she a large skeleton?"

"Did someone say it 'twas a giant?" The guard ignored them; instead, he walked right up to Carlene and pointed his finger at her.

"Did ye know it was against the law around here to lie to the guards?"

"What?" she said.

"There's no skeleton," the other yelled. "The tomb is empty." The crowd tittered.

"Are you sure?" Ronan asked.

"She's empty," Murphy confirmed. "No sign of nothing." He held up Carlene's flashlight. "Except this," he said.

"That's mine," Carlene said. "I dropped it when I saw the skeleton."

"The skeleton that doesn't exist," the second guard said. He turned to the priest. "Father, if you're going to say a prayer for anyone, it should be this American girl who thinks it's funny to be wasting our time with tall tales."

"She has to be down there," Carlene said. "I just saw her."

"How about we all go inside for a wee drink," Declan said.

"I'm telling you, less than an hour ago there was a skeleton in there. If it's gone, then somebody took her."

"And who do ye think would be doing this?" the guard asked.

"Somebody's been doing a lot of things around here," Carlene said. "Stealing the Guinness kegs, putting up plywood walls, and crashing trees through the front door of the pub, stealing cheese." She shot Joe an accusatory glance.

"I was sittin' in me shop all mornin'," Joe said. "You saw me." Joe looked at Ronan. "You're the one who wants this pub back," he said. "You're the one who was foolheaded enough to lose it in the first place."

Mary McBride stepped forward.

"Joesph Paul McBride," she said. "I will not have you talking to my son that way."

"Listen up," the guard said. "Show's over."

"Come on in and have a wee drink," Declan said.

"There's only two possible answers here," the guard said. "One, the skeleton felt better and walked out on its own accord; or two, someone is playing a prank."

"Or she's lying," Joe said.

"That would be three," Murphy said.

"My phone was dead," Carlene said. "I think the lines were cut."

"That sounds serious to me," Ronan said.

"All right." The guard sighed. "We'll check it out."

The phone in the pub was working again. Carlene was furious. Who was doing this to her, and why? After answering all the questions she could to the guards, she went up and showered while Declan minded the bar. *Everyone either thinks I'm crazy, or a liar, or both,* she thought as she watched the dirty water swirl down the drain. But she knew the truth. There *was* a skeleton, her phones *were* dead. Someone was trying to set her up, drive her out. The excitement of the souterrain itself got lost in all the talk of the missing skeleton. What was she going to do? She'd have to write down a list of suspects. And she knew, no matter how much she wanted to exclude him, Ronan would be on that list.

When she came back down, showered and dressed, she was surprised to see a full bar, including all of her regulars. She was so happy to see Riley on his stool, she almost hugged him. Even Ciaran was sitting at the bar with Jane. Everyone was talking about the skeleton and the souterrain. Apparently, everyone knew about the underground space, especially the children of Ballybeog, who invented numerous games around it. But until today, nothing mysterious had ever turned up in it.

Katie patted the bar stool next to her, and Carlene happily joined them in a drink. If there was ever a time for a stiff one, this was it. Carlene was pleasantly tipsy when Mike Murphy burst in the front door holding the skeleton.

"Is this the skeleton you saw?" he said.

"That's her," Carlene said. Lucky for the dress, or Carlene wouldn't have been sure.

"I found her in the bushes," Murphy said.

"Are you sure you didn't find her in the closet?" Laughter ripped through the bar.

"Who do ye think killed her?" Declan said.

"She's not a murder victim," Mike Murphy said. "She's from Gerald O'Sullivan's fifth class."

"How do you know?" Carlene asked. Murphy turned the skeleton around. On the back of the skull, in thick black marker, someone had written: *Gerald O'Sullivan, Fifth class.*

"Someone's playing a prank on you, chicken," Declan said.

"What's the difference between a chicken and its egg?" Riley said. Nobody asked, "What?" "The chicken is involved, but the egg is committed," Riley said.

A few of the men in the pub had instruments with them, and soon they were playing, and people were singing at the top of her lungs. As Carlene sat back and listened to the music, the laughter, and the craic, as people came up and touched her on the shoulder as they winked and assured her she wasn't in any real danger, that they would all look out for her, Carlene hoped that whoever was doing this to her was there to see what an utter failure their latest shenanigans had been. Still, the next time might not turn out to be a party. Carlene was going to have to find out who was out to get her, and she was going to have to do it soon.

CHAPTER 40

Everything's Better with a Tan

Ellen, the depressed, carb-deprived, farmer's daughter / stalker, was Carlene's top suspect. She decided to spend her mornings investigating and her evenings working. The morning of her first investigation, she started out at Nancy's. It would be torture to do a stakeout on a empty stomach.

"How ya," Nancy called when Carlene walked in. The place was bustling. Nancy's younger brother and mother were working behind the counter—the mother was cooking, the brother handling the cash register, and Nancy was waiting on the tables. Carlene ordered a cappuccino and an Irish breakfast, and, in a secretive voice that most would associate with a drug deal in an alley, asked if Nancy would leave out the black and white pudding. Nancy's laughter rang through the little café.

"No bother a't'all," she said. When Carlene was stuffed and heavily caffcinated, she asked Nancy if she knew Ellen, who sometimes worked at the Ballybeog Musuem. "The museum?" Nancy said. "Why it's been closed for ages, lad," she said. So Declan had been right about that. Carlene must have wandered in on a day where the door had been left unlocked, and Ellen had followed her in and stood in the corner. Creepy, and sad,

Carlene thought. Although she was starting to see how all this rain could turn a person a little creepy and sad.

After the big feed, Carlene thanked Nancy, tipped generously even though you weren't supposed to tip in Ireland, and wandered down the street to the museum. On the way, she waved at folks as she passed, but this time not all of them waved back. Carlene was totally dejected—they all waved BS, Before Sally. It didn't take long to reach the museum. The morning's light mist had turned into a downpour. Carlene had to pee. She pulled her hood up over her head and stared at the little house / museum. All the blinds were drawn. For the heck of it she crossed over and tried the door.

It was locked. She had no tricks up her sleeve, no slick moves with credit cards or bobby pins. Carlene's first stakeout was a bust, called on account of rain and a full bladder.

Carlene's boxercising class had gained notoriety, and soon she had twelve women all dying to hit something. The punching bag was by far the group's favorite. She wondered if some of them imagined their husbands sitting at the bar without them as they pummeled away at it. Gossip spread about Carlene's brief marriage to a semiprofessional Irish boxer from the North. It soon became apparent that in addition to hitting something, the women wanted details of Carlene's secret shame. To think, all the years she'd suffered over Brendan Hayes, and now he was paying off. She dropped hints about their relationship, leaving crumbs of promises that if they kept coming to class, those who hadn't heard it already would eventually get the whole story.

Carlene led the ladies through a particularly rough workout, twice their pace, with additional squats, kicks, and plenty of punches. By the end, she was the only one still jumping and kicking. The rest of the women were laid out across the bar, fanning themselves. Before they could start up their usual luncheon, however, Carlene shooed them all out. She had to shower and shave and dress to kill. She had a date.

*   *   *

They lay on their backs in the little cave, as Carlene was now calling the souterrain. Carlene studied the stone ceiling, illuminated by the lantern Ronan had brought down (along with two pints of Guinness) and wondered how many other people had looked up at it in their lifetimes.

"When do you think this was built?" Carlene asked. "And why?"

"During the famine is my guess," Ronan said. "To preserve or maybe even hide food."

"That's so sad."

"Yep."

"Not much of a hiding place if everyone knows about it." Ronan rolled over, put his hand on her waist, and rotated her so they were face-to-face. Carlene loved being this close to him, underground.

"Who are you trying to hide from?" he whispered.

"Myself."

"If that were possible I would have ditched meself a long time ago."

"Touché." Ronan suddenly smiled.

"What?"

"I'm just glad there wasn't a real dead body down here. It might detract from what I'm about to do." His eyes traveled over her body.

"Drink a Guinness?" Carlene guessed.

"Among other things." His hand circled her neck, his lips crushed down on hers, and this time his kiss was different. It wasn't an impetuous thank-you-for-picking-a-winning-horse like their first kiss at the Galway Races, or shy, slow, and guarded like the kiss they shared when he tried to tear down the plywood wall, or jealous like at Finnegan's where she confronted him about his engagement, or comforting like the kiss on the cliffs when she was confessing what happened with her mother. This kiss was purposeful, and strong. This kiss was a statement.

This was the kiss of a man who was no longer holding back.

If she was willing, he was going to take her, right there, in the little cave of the soutterrain. So she let go. She let go of her fear of small spaces, she let go of guilt, and she let go of propriety. She was going to enjoy each and every second of this, their first time, even if it was their last. She wanted to touch, she wanted to taste, she wanted to make up for a lifetime of blue rubber gloves. Ronan pulled back to take off his sweater. He lifted her and placed it underneath her.

"Does that help at all?"

"It feels like I'm lying on a cloud."

"Liar."

Carlene smiled and traced the outline of Ronan's lips with her finger. Then she kissed the scar above his eyebrow. Finally, she smiled at him, a smile that told him exactly how much she wanted him, right here, right now, and this time, he wasn't going to run away. "Liars should be taught a lesson."

Ronan planted soft kisses all over her face, then he pressed his body against hers. She loved the strength of him, the smell of him, the intoxicating sounds coming out of him. His moans made her feel desired, and they hadn't even gotten to the good stuff yet. She was one to talk, shamelessly rubbing against him with soft little moans of her own. They probably didn't need the glowing lantern he'd brought down, splashing their dirty shadows against the wall; his grin alone would have lit up the darkness. His eyes seemed to feast on her whenever he looked at her, she couldn't wait until they took her in ungloved and unclothed. He touched her nose with the tip of his index finger.

"Are ye saying you want me to teach you that lesson, Ms. America?" Carlene slowly slid her hand down his chest and over his stomach, stopping only when she reached the bulge in his jeans. Ronan buried his face in her hair and groaned.

"Fair play," he whispered, and his hands came down softly on her breasts, cupping them as his thumbs skillfully circled her nipples. Carlene arched into his touch.

"Oh God," she said. "Oh God, oh God, oh God."

Ronan shook his head and grinned. "I'm doing all the work, and he's getting all the credit?"

Carlene laughed, and Ronan laughed, and then he shut her up with another kiss, and soon his hands started roaming. She cleared her mind of everything but the sensations spiraling through her body, until even the cold, hard ground fell away.

It seemed he was going to take his time, his hands were going to touch every inch of her, slowly, then he was going to retrace the spots he touched with his tongue, and it was driving her to the brink of madness. She loved the feel of his rough hands, his smooth tongue, even his stubble grazing against her exposed skin. He really and truly wanted to completely unravel her. This was what he'd wanted to do to her from the moment she'd looked up and caught him staring at her in the fountain. And now, it was finally happening. The whole place could cave in on them when they were done for all she cared, as long as she got to have all of him first. She wanted him so much that when his hand finally dropped to the zipper on her jeans, and his fingers slid first lightly over, then into her panties, she was so turned on she was starting to think by the end of this there might be a real dead body lying in this little cave after all.

If you only watched their shadows on the wall, you would have eventually seen dark shapes coming together, blending into one, stretching and retracting, faster and faster, the shadows climbing higher and higher, then peaking and dropping, then shifting so that the smaller shadow was now on top, then starting all over again, stretching and retracting, and retracing, and splashing, and climbing, writing *we were here* with the outlines of their bodies, pulsing across the damp stonewall like a lifeline.

CHAPTER 41

Sunny Days

At the following week's boxing class, Carlene was so engrossed in the routine that she didn't see the man staring in the window. Mrs. Mahoney, who was standing closest to the window, constantly checking her reflection, noticed him first. Carlene was contemplating buying window shades so Mrs. Mahoney would stop staring at herself. She yelled at her to concentrate. Mrs. Mahoney said she couldn't help it; she was delighted with her weight loss since starting the class, not a whole stone lost yet, but certainly a pebble. The second Mrs. Mahoney spotted the Peeping Tom, she alerted the rest of the ladies with a scream that emanated from the depths of her bowels. Carlene hoped she would remember to tell her to save that kind of screams for her kicks.

"Jesus," Mrs. Mahoney said. Additional screams echoed through the room. The man's face disappeared from the window. Carlene ran for the front door, quickly followed by the entire class. Even though they could only see the back of him, it was easy to recognize Joe McBride, hightailing it back to his shop. The women, who seemed too tired when Carlene asked them to speed shadow-box in between sets, suddenly surged forward after Joe. Maybe she should add "chasing perverts" to the routine. He didn't stand a chance of reaching the safety of his front door. Sensing he might be crushed underneath a dozen sweating women, he halted, frozen in space.

"Ye wee pervert!" one woman yelled.

"I'm thrilled to bits," the woman closest to Carlene leaned over and whispered. "I've never been noticed by perverts before."

"I wasn't looking at yous like that," Joe said, sounding genuinely horrified. "I was waitin' until you were done jumping about the place so I could tell you ladies, who are looking trim and slim by the way, all right, I was jest bidin' me time to tell ye all about the benefits you may wish to reap from a gorgeous, golden tan." He thrust up a flier that showed a picture of a very tan, bikini-clad model.

"Boxercise isn't just about looking good," Carlene said. "It's about owning your power. Right, ladies?" The women gathered closer to the flier.

"Jaysus," one woman said. "I'd love to look like her."

"And you can, ladies," Joe said. "You can all have a natural glow."

"Tanning beds cause cancer," Carlene said.

"So does drinking, and smoking, and eating tuna fish with mercury, and stress, and genetics, and darn near breathing," Joe said. "But at least with tanning you get a nice brown glow out of it." The woman began passing the flier around.

"Well, where is it?" a woman asked, looking around. "In the shop? You won't find me lying there in my skivvies while folks are picking out their potatoes in the next aisle, you can betcha," she said. Joe gave Carlene a look. See?

"But would you be willing to tan in the pub—if say there was a privacy curtain around ye, and it was offered after your jumping-around class when there 'twasn't a fella to be seen?" Joe said. Right so, the women said. They might be willing to do it then.

"Joe," Carlene said. He held up an index finger.

"One tanning bed," he said. "For now. All the profit goes my way."

"That sounds like a win, lose proposition," Carlene said.

"I'm not finished. If ye do this, I'll stop consulting my solicitor about the shady nature of ye winnin' that raffle."

"There was nothing shady about the raffle," Carlene said. "I got lucky. For once in my life, I got lucky."

"Just one tanning bed," Joe said. "For now. See how it goes."

"It's a pub," Carlene said.

"Looks like it's also a gym now," Joe said. "That probably violates the conditions of your business license, so."

"Unbelievable," Carlene said.

"A spa, ladies," Joe said. "Am I right? And what the feck is a spa without a tanning bed, I ask ye. And did ye know a good tan reduces the appearance of ungainly cellulite?" And with those words, Carlene knew she would soon be running a pub slash spa. *The Half Tree. A good place to drink and die, and meet yer Maker with a heavenly tan.*

Carlene didn't think she was going to have to babysit the tanning bed, but she realized her mistake the day Riley wandered over and fell asleep in it. His body was fine since he'd gone in with all his clothes on, but his face was redder than usual. He had the ruddy nose and cheeks of an alcoholic, but now he also had a blistered forehead and chin. From then on Carlene made sure to unplug the tanning bed and keep the curtain open so that nobody else could sneak in for a "nap." The lads thought it was great, and were not at all happy that they weren't privy to use the spa. Sally came back that day, and although Carlene prepared herself for a fight, Sally told her the hardware shop sucked and quietly asked for her job back. Carlene took her to the back porch to talk.

"I know what you're going to say," Sally said. "You're worried I'm mental. You think I'll go psycho on you."

"Given the circumstances," Carlene said, "I just don't see how it would work out."

"Because of Ronan?" Sally said.

"Mostly," Carlene said.

"I know you're still seeing him," Sally said. "I've accepted that."

"I just don't feel comfortable—"

"Just give me a chance, will ye? You were right. What was it you said I should do again?"

"Become the man you want to marry," Carlene said. It was actually a slogan she'd seen on a feminist postcard, but it was good advice nonetheless.

"Right, so," Sally said. "I need to become the man I want to marry. Ronan was never in love with me. I've been holding on to a fantasy."

"I'm glad you recognize that—and you're a lovely girl—"

"Are ye gonna give me my job back or aren't ye?" Sally said. Carlene wanted to say no. She wanted to warn her that Ronan had been coming around a lot lately. She didn't want Ronan to feel uncomfortable either. But Sally looked so depressed. And she'd been extremely helpful to Carlene when she first hired her. It seemed wrong to turn her away.

"We can try it out," Carlene said. "See how it goes."

"Brilliant," Sally said. "And you've nothing to worry about. I hate men—especially Irish men."

"They are the best of men, they are the worst of men," Carlene agreed. If Sally got the reference, she didn't comment on it.

"One more thing," Sally said. "Does the job include free boxercising classes and unlimited use of the tanning bed?"

It had been four days since their passionate lovemaking in the souterrain, and no sign of Ronan. Carlene wanted to blame Sally; maybe somehow he'd heard she was back and he was afraid to come in.

It wasn't true, and even if it was, who wanted to date such a coward? No, it was Ronan being Ronan, performing his well-honed disappearing act. Maybe he was off gambling, maybe he was with another girl, maybe he'd found a proper job and was so busy growing up that he just didn't have time to visit. Or call. Or text. Or send a homing pigeon. Maybe, after making love to her, he was done with her. Or maybe he'd dropped dead replaying it over and over again in his mind like she'd been doing. Or maybe it was so amazing that he was terrified. She was terrified too. How could they ever follow that one up? It had been real; it had taken lovemaking to a whole new level, one she never even knew she could reach. If they could do that in a damp little cave, think of what they could do with roses, champagne, and a proper mattress. But now he'd disappeared. What a talent she had. Like a slutty magician. Sleep with a man and make him disappear.

But what if something terrible had happened? What if Racehorse Robbie was after him to pay up, and he was out doing something stupid? Carlene wasn't going to call him any more; it might trigger the obsessive dialing she went through during her breakup with Brendan. Besides, she had another tool on her hands, seven of them, in fact. The McBride women loved her. Carlene decided she would go to mass, and if they didn't invite her back to breakfast again, she could at least casually ask about Ronan. Just because she wasn't going to obsess on him didn't mean she wasn't going to casually check out whether or not he was okay.

CHAPTER 42

Goats Will Eat Anything

Carlene wasn't religious, but she loved the inside of the Catholic church. She loved the old wood, the stained glass, and the people of Ballybeog who came to sing and pray. Mary McBride was indeed in attendance, but only Katie was seated next to her. Carlene took a seat toward the back; she didn't want to crowd them during the service. She would wait until it was over to say hello. Just the fact that they were here was a good sign; if anything was terribly wrong they probably wouldn't be here at all. And, Carlene suspected, had anything tragic happened, she would be the first to hear about it given that the pub bred gossip like stagnated water bred mosquitoes. It would have been heavenly if not for the fact that several people seemed to be intently studying her, only to look away as fast as they could when she returned their gaze. Was she still persona non grata in Ballybeog, or was it all in her head?

She waited for Mary and Katie outside the door. It was a rare, sunny morning. At first, the McBride women didn't seem to notice her, and were already several feet past her when Carlene called out to them. Mary's face immediately broke out in a smile, and she reached for Carlene with both hands.

"How lovely to see you again," Mary said.

"Me too," Carlene said. "Hi, Katie." Katie stepped forward and hugged Carlene. She wanted to cry, and was immediately ashamed that she was so starved for affection.

"Where's the rest of your gang?" Carlene said. She tried to sound cheerful, and not at all like she was checking up on Ronan.

"I tell ye," Mary McBride said. "It's a great shame that I can't get them all here every Sunday. But they all have their own lives now, I suppose."

"Unlike me, right, Mam?" Katie said. She winked at Carlene and linked arms with her mother.

"Speaking of busy lives," Mary McBride said, "we're on our way to Siobhan's house. But it was lovely to see you." Normally, Carlene would have received an invitation. She tried not to take it personally. They turned and walked away. Carlene couldn't help but notice it was at a pace so brisk that she would have had to run to keep up with them. No more advice, no more questions, no more answers. She wasn't going to worry about Ronan one more second either. It was her own fault—she knew Irish men were their own breed, the kind that could draw you in and then inflict significant pain once you realized they were never going to live up to their charm. Ronan McBride wasn't hers, and he never would be. It was time Carlene started focusing on what mattered; her pub. At least she still had that.

It didn't take long for Joe to pay another visit to Carlene's boxercising class. This time Mrs. Mahoney didn't scream, she just waved and wiggled everything she was working so hard to whittle down. Carlene spoke to Joe outside, insisting that the ladies didn't want him in their space. His profit on the tanning bed was dwindling; after several of them had burned, they weren't keen on using it anymore. Carlene was about to point this out when he interrupted her with his own agenda.

"I'm going to bring ye three more beds," he said. "So the ladies don't have to wait."

"No," Carlene said. "In fact, I wanted to tell you that it's not working out."

"That's because they don't want to wait in line," Joe said. "Three more beds, for now, and they'll be less of a line."

"There's something wrong with the tanning bed," Carlene said. "It gives everyone a sunburn. Nobody wants to use it."

"Nonsense," Joe said.

"I'm sorry," Carlene said. "I want it out."

"You want part of the profit, is that it?"

"No," Carlene said. "I don't want it at all. It's just not going to work out."

"I hope you're not going to force me to speak to a solicitor."

"Go right ahead," Carlene said. "Because you're not turning my pub into Tan Land, and I've been very nicely trying to tell you that your product is defective."

"The three new beds won't be—maybe the women have the dial turned up too high—"

"It doesn't matter. I don't want it in the pub anymore."

"I see. Well, you'll be forcing me—"

"Do what you have to do," Carlene said. "Because I won the pub fair and square. And you made off with a hundred thousand euros."

"Made off? Talk about fair and square, I won that hand fair and square."

"Maybe you did. But you won it from your nephew who has a gambling problem. Didn't that bother you at all?"

"Doesn't it bother you at all to be knockin' boots with that same gambling man?"

"Good day, Joe. If you don't get your tanning bed out of here by this time tomorrow, I'll have some of the lads deposit it in your front lawn."

"Gone," Carlene said.

"What do you mean gone?" Becca said.

"I don't know. He's just disappeared. From my life anyway." There was silence on the other end. Carlene half expected Becca to say "I told you so." To her credit, she didn't.

"Have you seen my dad?" Carlene asked.

"Levi, Shane, and I had dinner with him last week," Becca said.

"How is he?" There was another moment of silence. "You have to tell me, Becca. Is he okay?"

"He had little baby-sized gloves for Shane."

"Of course he did."

"He seemed . . . smaller," Becca said.

"What?"

"I know it sounds weird. He just looked . . . little."

"Like a shrunken old man?" Carlene said.

"Something like that," Becca admitted. "I think you should come home."

"What?" Carlene said.

"I hate to say this, but I don't think he can survive without you."

"Are you kidding me here?"

"Carlene, I'm dead serious. I know you don't want to hear this, but I really think you should come home."

"Becca, don't. This is my time, remember? My chance?" Carlene waited for Becca to agree, but she was met with silence. Carlene thought she was going to lose it. She didn't know whether to cry or scream. She'd been so homesick, so excited to talk to Becca; now she just wanted to get off the phone. Becca was saying the very things Carlene was deathly afraid of—that she was selfish, that her father would suffer without her. Why couldn't Becca just tell her what she wanted to hear? Just once? She was supposed to come running home because her father looked smaller? Maybe Becca was just jealous. She'd always been jealous of Carlene—she couldn't stand not being in the spotlight every single second.

"Jesus," Carlene said. "My whole life you've been telling me to get out from under my father's illness, and now that I have, now that I'm actually making a life for myself—one not many people get a chance to experience, by the way—you're telling me to give it all up and come home?"

"I always thought you were exaggerating about his . . . peculiarities, but after seeing him . . . I just really think you should come home for a visit," Becca said.

"He can visit me."

"You know he won't."

"It's his own fault."

"You're right, you're right," Becca said. "I just felt sorry for him, I guess."

"He has that effect on people. I'm sorry I got so angry."

"No sweat. But listen, I gotta go. Shane has a piano lesson." Riley yelled over to Carlene for another beer.

"He's still only four or five months old, right?" Carlene said.

"He's not playing yet, but I have him listening to Chopin. He loves it."

"I'm sure he does." They said their good-byes and pretended to totally make up, but they were both putting on an act. Carlene could hear it in their voices, feel it in her stomach. Anchor came out of the bathroom holding his nose. He jerked his thumb toward it.

"You're going to have to do something about the jacks," he said. "It's deadly in there."

Carlene lay in bed thinking about her father, and even though she couldn't stand how guilty it was making her feel, it was still better than thinking about Ronan. Columbus jumped up and began kneading her chest. It took her several tries and multiple turns before she settled her little body down to sleep. Carlene stroked her head and reminded herself as she fell asleep to the rain beating down on top of her that she was still a very lucky woman.

Carlene awoke to the sound of a bleating goat. She rubbed her eyes and looked out the window. It was still raining, a light mist, but she couldn't see whether or not there was a goat in her backyard. There had to be. He sounded way too close. She padded downstairs and headed for the kettle. It was funny how used to instant coffee she'd become. And it was no longer something she just tolerated, she actually looked forward to it. She was so groggy she almost didn't see the goat standing in the middle of the pub.

He bleated again. Startled, Carlene looked up, saw the goat, and screamed. It wasn't that she was afraid of goats, she just wasn't expecting to see one by the pool table. Life, she realized, was all about expectations. Apparently, the goat wasn't expecting her either. He took one look at her and ran. "I have that effect on men," Carlene called after him.

Unfortunately, he didn't have much room to run, and he smacked straight into the closed front door. Oh God, she didn't know they were that stupid. Panicked, the goat turned around and stared at her as if it were her fault. Somebody had gotten in again. Somebody had deposited a goat in the middle of her pub. Somebody was definitely trying to drive her mad. Did goats bite? Should she approach it? Call for help? Was this Joe? The tanning bed was still there—she was going to have to ask the lads to take it over and dump it on his property. She hated stooping to his level, but she'd already warned him.

"Do you mind if I fix myself a cup of coffee before I deal with you?" Carlene said to the goat. He didn't mind; he was too busy gnawing on the doorknob. She should probably just go over, open the door, and let the goat out. But where would he go? He obviously belonged to someone. She couldn't chance letting him go only to find out at some later point that he had been run over. Her reputation had taken enough of a hit, and she wasn't going to add goat killer to the list. Should she call Ronan? She'd resisted thus far, not wanting him to think she was clingy or desperate, but wasn't a goat in your pub reason enough to call? She could say, "Hey, when you worked and lived here did you ever wake up to find a goat in the middle of the room?" And, "Do you know if you startle a goat, it'll smack into a door?"

It was too early to call anyone. Maybe she would just keep him. That would show whoever had done this. She would make a little pen for him out back and pretend she was thrilled to have a goat. He would be a good lawn mower too. Usually a boy from town did her mowing, but the kid probably wouldn't mind a little help. The goat didn't like the sound of the kettle screeching either. *He must come from a very quiet farm,* she thought as she made her coffee.

She had barely taken a sip of her coffee when there was a pounding at the door. Both she and the goat jumped, although she was the only one who was scalded. The goat began to wander around the pub. Carlene pulled her robe around her and went to the door. There stood Mike Murphy and his sidekick, the same one who had gone down into the soutterrian in search of the skeleton.

"Good morning," Murphy said. Carlene remembered Ronan had called him Mike, but since she didn't think it was appropriate to call an officer by his first name, she didn't use it.

"Good morning," Carlene said.

"May we come in?" the shorter one said. She didn't know his name, and he didn't offer it. Carlene stood aside and allowed them to enter. They began walking briskly toward the bar when the goat bleated. The two of them halted, then looked at the goat. He was chewing on the cord to the tanning bed.

"Damn it," Carlene said. She ran over. The goat, startled once again, ran away from her, slipping on the recently mopped floor. Carlene picked up the chewed cord, which thank God had been unplugged, and rolled it up. Mike, she noticed, had removed a notepad from his pocket.

"There's one violation," he said.

"Excuse me?" Carlene said.

"I'm afraid having barnyard animals in a pub is a public health violation," he said. *No shit, Sherlock,* Carlene wanted to say. Oh, why couldn't they have at least let her finish her first cup of coffee?

"He's not mine," Carlene said. "He certainly wasn't invited."

"Come again?" the one who wasn't Mike said.

"I woke up, came downstairs to make myself a cup of coffee, and found him standing in the middle of the room. I don't know who is doing this to me—but you have to believe me. Someone is fucking with me big-time." She wondered if she shouldn't have said "fucking" in front of the guards, but this was Ireland, so she was probably okay.

"All barnyard animals need to be kept outside," Mike said.

"He's not mine," Carlene said. "I told you, someone broke in and left him here."

"Someone broke in?" non-Mike said. "How?" Carlene started to pace. For once she saw the point of it. She wanted to scream. She wanted to throw them out. They were bothering her more than the goat.

"I don't know," she said. "There's no obvious signs of a break-in, so obviously, whoever is doing this must have a key." She assumed there were a limited number of people who could have a key. Joe, Ronan, Sally, Declan? Maybe it had been a mistake to let Sally back in. Maybe this had been her plan all along. Drive Carlene insane, drive Carlene out of Ireland.

"We've been informed that you are trying to run a spa out of here," Mike said. "If that is the case, it violates the terms of your business license," he said.

"Who?" Carlene said. "Who informed you?"

"That's confidential," non-Mike said.

"But it could be the very person who is fucking with me," Carlene said. "It could be the person responsible for the plywood wall, and stealing the kegs, and putting a skeleton in the souterrain, and now dumping this fucking goat on me!" She was losing it, she knew she was losing it, but she was so, so tired, and if she admitted it to herself, she missed home. Even the thought of scrubbing the floor for the fifth time with Lysol sounded better than being here. She looked outside. The windows were smeared with rain. She couldn't see a thing. "Does it ever fucking stop?" she asked. She marched over to her cup of coffee, sat at the bar, and started to drink it.

"Are you running a spa out of here?" Mike asked.

"No," she said.

"What's that?" he asked. He pointed to the tanning bed.

"That," Carlene said, "is another man's dream."

"Beg your pardon?" non-Mike said.

"That is Joe's foolhardy get-rich-quick dream. That is a tanning bed. Personally, I think he should have gone with sunlamps. That I could see a use for. I could use a fucking sunlamp right about now myself."

"She's certainly got the hang of the word 'feck,' hasn't she?" non-Mike said. "That looks like a fire hazard," he added.

"It's not plugged in," Carlene said. "And I told Joe to get it out of here. If it's not out of here by this afternoon, I'm having the lads take it over and dump it on his front yard."

"Illegal dumping," Mike wrote down. "Another violation."

"Now you're violating me for things I haven't even done yet?" Carlene said. Mike took off his hat and gestured to one of the stools.

"Be my guest," Carlene said. "Would you like a cup of tea?"

"No thanks."

"Coffee?"

"We're on duty."

"A drink?"

"Just a small one." After she'd fixed their small drinks, Mike rubbed his face and sighed.

"Look," he said. "I've nothing against Americans. I was really excited when they elected Obama. He's got Irish roots. Did you know that? But he's not very popular anymore, is he?"

"That's the American way," Carlene said. "We like to build 'em up and tear 'em down." She stared at the guards. "I'm starting to think it may be the Irish way as well."

"Ballybeog is a very small town. We were quiet before the raffle. This situation has upset a lot of people," Mike said. "Personally, I think you're grand. I have no problem with ye being here. But you can't go around breaking all the rules and think we're going to sit back and let you turn this place into a spa," he said.

"Or a petting zoo," non-Mike said.

"Or some kind of haunted house what with all your skeletons," Mike said. "We've got better things to do with our time."

"I understand," Carlene said. "The tanning bed and the goat will be out of here today. I am going to get security cameras and I'm going to catch whoever is doing this to me."

Mike wrote out a ticket.

"In the meantime," he said. "You're shut for the next thirty days."

"What?"

"After thirty days we'll come back and inspect. If everything is up to code, you can reopen."

"But I told you, it's not my fault."

"We can't look like we're giving you special treatment," Mike said. "It wouldn't look proper."

"Thirty days is nothing," non-Mike said. He pointed to the tanning bed. "You can catch up on your tan."

CHAPTER 43

The Visitor

Ronan didn't come into the pub. He still didn't call, didn't text, didn't e-mail. Even though Carlene had finally caved and left him a message that the pub had been shut down for a month, he didn't respond. That was beyond cruel. Unless he was the one who had been doing this to her all along. Don't trust an Irishman, isn't that what she'd always heard? She felt like one of those pathetic, hapless women who didn't know her husband was a serial killer. When Carlene ran into any of the McBrides in town, they were polite, but the conversation was always brief, and they never mentioned Ronan. It was obvious he didn't want anything to do with her anymore. It was maddening how surgically he had disappeared from her life. She reminded herself that she was now a lucky girl, and therefore, there must be a reason for it, she would be better off without him. It was easier to convince herself of this while she was busy working, or taking her walks about town, but it was almost impossible when she was alone with her thoughts, lying upstairs in the bedroom at night, where Ronan himself used to sleep. And there was nothing keeping her from ruminating, no boxercise, no regulars to keep her company, no tanning bed, no goat. Even crawling into the soutterain had lost its magic.

It was at the beginning of the second week of such torture that she decided now would be a good time to see the rest of Ireland. After all, there was nothing she could do here, and once she got the pub up and running again, who knew when she'd have the chance? She'd go to Dublin, and Cork, and Dingle, and Kerry. She could be a visitor, not an intruder. She would also buy and set up security cameras; surely whoever had been tormenting her would definitely take the opportunity while she was away to do something. Then she would have them on camera and it would be dealt with once and for all.

She spent two glorious weeks as a tourist. In Dublin, Cork, and Limerick she took the Hop-On Hop-Off buses, and immersed herself in the sights. Dublin was a big city with a lot to see. Besides sightseeing, she went shopping on Grafton Street and at night was thrilled to go to OPP, Other People's Pubs. They were huge pubs, designed to attract tourists, with traditional music nightly. She was fascinated by the Kilmainham Gaol, and she loved wandering through St. Stephen's Green. At the Guinness Brewery she skipped all floors but the top floor where you could get your free pint of Guinness and look out over the city.

Cork and Limerick were smaller, but just as fascinating. She was finally getting used to the fact that everywhere you went in Ireland, no matter how small, there was probably at least one local castle. She loved County Kerry—the scenery was gorgeous with the Ring of Kerry—and she loved Dingle, a quaint, small town with boutiques, and pubs, and Fungi the dolphin, whom she never did get to see. She finished her trip off in Kinsale, a gorgeous beach town with gourmet restaurants and cliffs dropping off into the ocean—only unlike her trip to the Cliffs of Moher, she was doused in sunshine.

She traveled by trains, buses, and taxis, something she was told wasn't the thing to do. She would eventually start driving here, but constantly feeling like she was on the wrong side of the road wasn't her idea of a relaxing vacation. By the time her two weeks were up, she was ready to go back to her pub. She would only have one more week left of her forced closure, and she was planning on starting over. She was the girl with all the luck after all, and surely things would calm down.

As her taxi pulled up to her pub, déjà vu washed over her. No one was hanging out of her tree with a chain saw, thank God, but there was a large crowd of people gathered in her yard. They were drinking and having a grand old time. Anger coursed through her. Why were they always partying without her? She flew out of the cab, grabbed her suitcase, and paid the driver as fast as she could. She was going to throttle whoever had done this. No matter how much of a party pooper it made her, they could not do this in her pub while she was away. As she made her way through the crowd, folks patted her on the back, or grabbed her in hugs, all smiles, which made it difficult to glare at them. Carlene burst through the door and spotted him immediately. It was hard not to—he was holding court in the center of the pub. Carlene felt as if she'd been shot with a tranquilizer gun. She was stunned, sluggish, and fighting gravity. There, being treated like royalty, stood Brendan Hayes.

He had yet to spot her. Declan and Sally were behind the bar. Carlene ran up to Declan. Maybe she could get Brendan and everybody else out of here without Brendan ever laying eyes on her. Or maybe she should go away, sneak out until the party was over. She scanned the crowd and didn't know whether she should be relieved that Ronan wasn't there, or heartbroken that Ronan wasn't there.

It dawned on her, as she watched Brendan, the guy who used to consume her every thought—his tall presence, his shaved head, his bulging biceps, huge smile, bright blue eyes, and deep echoing laugh—that as she looked at him now, she felt absolutely nothing. It was Ronan she was thinking about. And she wasn't going to run away from her own pub.

"Declan," Carlene said. "I'm not allowed to be open for business for another week. We have to get everybody out of here."

"It's a party, luv," Declan said. "It doesn't count."

"Why didn't you tell us you were married to Brendan Hayes?" Sally said.

"Because what happens in Vegas stays in Vegas," Carlene said. "And because it was never legit."

"You might want to tell him that, chicken," Declan said. "He's telling everyone he owns half of the pub." Carlene marched over to the bell that Declan always rang near closing time. She rang it, and rang it, and rang it, again, and again, and again, until people finally looked up.

"Party's over," she said. "Everybody out." Brendan actually lit up when he saw her, which wasn't surprising since he was so lit up. He bounded over to her.

"Carlene," he said. "Look at you. You look gorgeous." So did he. On the outside.

"You too," Carlene said. "Now get out of my pub." Brendan leaned on the bar and grinned.

"Did you forget?" he said. "We're married. Half of this pub is mine." Carlene leaned in toward him and tried to imitate his grin.

"Number one," she said. "The marriage was never consummated because you were always to drunk to get it up, remember? Number two, the minister forgot to renew his license. I got a letter from the state of Nevada saying they would pay our airfare and hotel for us to come back and get legally married. How did you not know that? Oh, right, you disappeared. If you let me know your legal address, I'd be happy to send documentation. And while I'm at it"—Carlene lowered her voice, although he probably didn't deserve it—"I can send the picture I received of you in the mail from your friend Trent in Tampa." Brendan's grin evaporated.

"I don't know what you're on about," he said.

"Well, maybe a picture of you in my red thong with little

white hearts will refresh your memory. I've been needing a theme for my Christmas card this year. Or I could hang it in the pub. You can keep the thong, by the way. Think of it as an almost-married gift." Brendan looked stricken. He glanced around the bar. Then he slammed down his pint. One by one, Carlene's regulars stood. They crossed their arms, glared, and formed a semicircle around Brendan.

"What's all the shouting about?" Angus said.

"Is he bothering you, chicken?" Eoin said.

"If he's bothering you, then he's bothering us," Collin said. Carlene wanted to kiss them and kick them at the same time. If Brendan chose to fight, he could probably stand his own against them all. They probably knew it too, yet there her lads stood.

"I think he was just leaving," Carlene said. "Am I right?" Brendan looked stunned; it was the first time Carlene had ever stood up for herself with him. He glanced at the men surrounding him.

"I just came to tell ye, we were never married in the first place," Brendan said. "So stop calling me, and texting me, and Twittering me. I don't want anything to do with you, or this middle-of-fucking-nowhere pub." He pushed his way through the lads, who bumped him a little harder than necessary, but eventually let him through. *Thank God,* she thought as she watched him leave, *I didn't get his name tattooed on my ass.*

"He is so hot," Sally said. She looked as if she was going to run after him.

"He's a heartbreak waiting to happen," Carlene said. "You want to be happy? I already told you. Become the man you want to marry."

"What kind of shite is that?" Riley said.

"The kind of shite that prevents women from falling all over men because we think, mistakenly, they have something we don't. They look good, or they tell a good story, or they box, or they play guitar—"

Or when they make love to you they find your g-spot and every other letter of the alphabet—

"I play guitar," Collin said. His T-shirt had two pictures of King Tut on the chest. It read: STOP STARING AT MY TUTS. He winked at Sally.

"You don't need to chase after anyone, Sally," Carlene said. "Look at you. You're perky, smart, funny. Why don't you fall in love with yourself? That's what 'Become the man you want to marry' means. Do that, and I promise you, they'll be chasing you."

"Looks to me like you should be taking your own advice," Sally said.

"That's the great thing about life," Carlene said. "It's never too late to start."

Her emerald earrings were gone. When she wasn't wearing them, she always left them in a little bowl next to the cash register, and suddenly they'd vanished. It was her father who pointed out she wasn't wearing them. They'd recently started to Skype. On her computer screen, he looked withered, and broken. He begged her to come home before he lost the gym for good. He told her the men at the gym wanted her back. He told her Becca wanted her back. He said he didn't understand how she could turn her back on all of them. Then he asked her why she wasn't wearing the earrings. She pawed at her earlobes, stunned. She told her father she would think about it, and ended the call before she started bawling. Her father wasn't good with emotions, happy or sad. She turned to find Declan staring at the computer screen where the image of her father had just been. His mouth was slightly open. He was probably wondering why they were both wearing blue rubber gloves, but she didn't have time to explain.

"I lost my mother's earrings," she said.

"Don't worry, pet," Declan said. "We'll find them." He helped her look. They examined every inch of the pub. Declan looked downstairs while she looked upstairs. When they didn't find them, Carlene and Declan, bless his heart, even crawled through the souterrain. She'd never looked so hard or so long for anything, not an easy feat with her eyes swollen from crying.

At least the pub was thoroughly clean; positively every surface was gleaming. Declan finally made Carlene stop and sit while he fixed her a sandwich and a drink. She didn't realize she was still wearing the gloves until Declan gently pulled them off her and threw them away.

"I wasn't trying to listen in, pet," Declan said. "But it sounded like your father is trying to convince you to go home?"

"He can't run the gym by himself," Carlene said. "If I don't go home, he's going to lose it."

"What are you going to do, petal?"

"I love it here," Carlene said. "But I worry about my father. I've tried to get him to come visit, but even that's too much for him. I don't think I can take hurting him like this. Even my best friend, Becca, thinks I should come home. Besides, not everyone in Ballybeog loves me being here either." It was all she could do not to mention Ronan, and how he was gone, gone, gone. She played with her naked ears. "I think maybe losing my mother's earrings is a sign."

"I've got a sign for ye," Declan said. "Open."

"Open?"

"It's the best sign you could ever ask for. You hang it over your heart. Open. Don't you let a few begrudgers get you down. You do what's in your heart. As long as it's flipped to Open, you'll know what to do."

"Open," Carlene whispered.

"Open," Declan repeated with a wink.

Declan had given her a lot to think about. On the one hand, she absolutely loved her life in Ballybeog. Her time here had been a gift. For the first time in her life, she felt as if she belonged. As crazy as it sounded, whenever she heard the word "home" she thought of Ronan, and her kitten, and her little pub in the middle of nowhere.

But her father was in pain. Becca still thought she should go home. And if she didn't, what would happen to the gym? Her father only had two things in his life: the gym and Carlene. And it was looking as if he'd never be willing to visit her in Ireland.

Could she really be responsible for him losing the only two things he loved in life?

And then there was Ronan. Ronan was in her heart. She missed him with an intensity that at times threatened to bring her to her knees. But he was gone. And his heart had been this pub, and it had been taken from him. In essence, because the raffle had only been open to Americans, it had been taken from everyone in Ballybeog as well. Luck was one thing, but as the man at the festival told her, "You can't win if you don't play." Given the way they were shut out, it was a miracle folks around here were speaking to her at all. Carlene knew what she had to do. She had to make things right. An open heart didn't mean every man for himself. It meant doing what was best for the greater good. It meant doing in your heart what you knew to be the right thing to do, even if, maybe especially if, it also meant saying good-bye.

CHAPTER 44

The Do-Over

She called Ronan first. His phone went straight to voice mail, but she left a message anyway. Declan told her to follow her heart, but her heart was confused, and torn in several directions, and slightly bruised. Surprisingly, deciding to leave the ultimate decision to luck brought about a peaceful feeling in Carlene. For once she was taking control and letting go at the same time. She set the date for exactly two weeks from now. It would give her time to prepare, to say good-bye. She would probably be home before Christmas. At least she was giving something back, and she could think of no better present to the town, no better tribute to the folks of Ballybeog. They had given her so much in such a short time.

She broke the news to Mary McBride and the half dozen in person. They sat at Mary's table, drinking tea. Carlene knew they were stunned by the news, and several times they asked her if she was sure, but eventually they squeezed her hands and told her she should indeed follow her heart. It wasn't an easy thing to tell them, especially since part of her thought she should just give the pub back to them, but she stuck to her original idea. Her intention had already been voiced; it was floating out there in the great beyond, as alive as electricity, and no matter how difficult, she would see it through.

It didn't take long for the news to spread. Once the McBrides knew, she simply told a few of her regulars, and from there, gossip took flight. Her message to Joe was nonverbal. She grabbed the bulldozer and headed straight over to the shop. He was in the back, stacking shelves. She quietly left the clock on the counter and walked out. She erased COME SEE THE YANK, which was still written on the sandwich board, and replaced it with COME ENTER THE RAFFLE. OPEN ONLY TO THE RESIDENTS OF BALLYBEOG, IRELAND, followed by the date and time.

Carlene hung up the phone and stared. There, in the little bowl beside the cash register, were her emerald earrings. Stunned, she reached for them, half expecting them to disappear. Had Sally simply borrowed them? What did this mean? Did it mean she was doing the right thing, or that she'd made the worst mistake of her life? It didn't matter, she thought, as she put on the earrings. It was too late to turn back now. *Iacta alea est.* The die is cast.

It was the biggest crowd she'd ever seen in the Half Tree, bar none. Bigger than the tree-trimming ceremony, bigger than the skeleton crew, bigger than Brendan's grand entrance. Had it not been for the fact that the local guards were drinking it up with the rest of them, Carlene would have been afraid of being shut down for being over capacity. Even the other publicans were there, no doubt hoping to win a second addition to their livelihood. Joe was dressed in a tuxedo and guarding the raffle box like it was the last keg of Guinness on earth. The rules were clear. Everyone could enter only once. She didn't want to charge them a dime, but the McBrides insisted she charge the same twenty euros apiece. She relented; although it would never amount to the same money they'd won raffling it off in America, it would still be enough money to see her home and then some.

There was no sign of Ronan, nor had he ever acknowledged her message. That was it, then; it was so obviously over. Johnny

Spoons and his band began to play. Carlene left Declan and
Sally tending bar and threaded her way over to Mary McBride.
She grabbed her by the hands.

"Does Ronan know about this?" Carlene said. "I have to ask
before we draw the name." Mary McBride squeezed her hands.

"He knows, luv," she said. "And believe me. He's made his
wishes very clear."

"Oh," Carlene said. *He's made his wishes very clear.* Meaning his absence was proof that he didn't care. He wasn't even
going to enter the raffle. She could have restricted him from entering, everyone would have understood that. But she didn't.
And he couldn't even acknowledge that. "At least he knows,"
Carlene said. She hurried back to the bar. She didn't want Mary
McBride to see her pain. Maybe Ronan hated her for not just
giving the pub back to them where it probably belonged.

"You okay, pet?" Declan asked.

"Fine," Carlene said. "It's almost time."

She couldn't wait for Ronan any longer. It was way too
crowded, and people were starting to get drunk. If she didn't pick
the winner soon, they'd have a mob on their hands. Declan,
who made it clear he wasn't entering the drawing, was desig-
nated to pick the winner. He stood on top of a table near the
windows. The crowd closed in. Carlene stayed behind the bar,
taking everyone in. Joe, of course, was standing as close to
Declan as he could get, his hands clasped below his chin. The
half dozen and Mary McBride hung back. Katie was watching
Carlene. Ellen, her stalker, was there, dressed all in black. The
band was on stage. The ladies from her boxercise class stood together. The man from RTÉ was there, ready with camera and
microphone. Sally and Declan were behind the bar with her, and
all of her regulars were sitting in front of her. Collin started a
drumroll on the bar. Declan reached his hand into the box. Carlene's heart was suspended in midair. Declan pulled a folded
piece of paper out of the box and cleared his throat. The little
pub went from all out noise to deathly quiet in seconds flat.

"Carlene," Declan said.

"I'm ready," Carlene said. "Just read the name."

"I just did," Declan said. "Carlene Rivers." Her regulars whooped.

"What?" Joe yelled. He grabbed the paper from Declan's hands.

"That's not possible," Carlene said. "I didn't enter."

"Draw another name, why don't ye," Eoin said. Carlene was slightly surprised, but quickly hid her hurt.

"Yes," Carlene said. "There's been a mistake. Please choose another name." Declan reached into the box again.

"Carlene Rivers," he said. This time the entire pub cheered.

"This is outrageous," Joe yelled. Declan kept drawing names from the box.

"Carlene, the Yank, Blondie from Cleveland, Yankee Doodle Dandy, the Pain in the Ass from America, Carlene, Carlene, Carlena," he said.

"Carlena?" Carlene asked. "Someone wrote Carlena?"

"It's a vote by proxy," Declan said. "But it's a vote nevertheless." Carlena. Carlena, Carlena, Carlena. Ronan was the only one who'd ever called her Carlena. *He made his wishes very clear.*

"I don't understand," Carlene said.

"Congratulations," Anchor said. "You just won a pub in Ballybeog." He stuck his hand out. They shook. "I'm the ambassador of craic," he said with a wink. Collin was wearing his SUPPORT YOUR LOCAL BARTENDER shirt. He winked at her.

"You all entered my name?" Carlene said. She could barely speak.

"We did, yeah," Ciaran said. "Now give us a pint or we'll have to bite yer neck."

"I wish I'd come up with the idea meself," Danny said. "But we all knew it was a good one when we heard it."

"Don't get a big head over it," Sally said. "We just figured whoever won the pub was gonna be hated by everyone else in Ballybeog, and why put ourselves through that when we've already got you to hate." She said it with such a big smile that Carlene had to smile back.

"Ladies and gentlemen," Johnny Spoons slurred into the microphone, "the people of Ballybeog have spoken. Long live the American girl. Now, let's put this fucking raffle behind us and get our dancing shoes on." Joe, who looked as if he were still trying to protest, was swept up in a sea of bodies and voices raised in cheer. Carlene was still stunned.

"Are ye just gonna stand there with your mouth open, or are ye going to pour us a pint?" Riley said.

"Give her a chance to catch her breath, dear." Startled, Carlene saw a small woman sitting daintily next to Riley. They held hands on the counter. Riley caught Carlene staring.

"This woman's looked after me for forty-six years," he said. "Would you look after a man for forty-six years?"

"I wouldn't look after you for forty-six minutes," Anchor said. Carlene didn't answer. Between the lump in her throat, and pouring free pints, there was nothing left to say. As it stood, she wouldn't get a chance to speak anyway. A loud cracking noise thundered through the pub. All heads snapped to the corner of the room. The tanning bed was plugged in, and the cord was sparking. It flopped on the floor like a recently caught fish. She didn't even have time to panic. The lads were up and on it within seconds.

"Where's your extinguisher?" someone yelled. Carlene had no idea; she didn't even know if she had one. She was terrified someone was going to throw their pint on it, and rushed to get a pitcher of water. Was water okay for an electrical fire? She couldn't remember a single bit of sound advice.

"Everybody out," she shouted. She could live if her pub burned down, but she would die if anything happened to any of her lads.

Everybody agreed; she was incredibly lucky. Joey, the singing fireman, was standing closest to the flames when they sparked up. Within seconds, he had put out the fire with an extinguisher Carlene didn't even know she had. By the time everyone was out, so was the fire. Declan turned to Carlene.

"You're one lucky gal," he said.

"What's so lucky about winning a pub, only to have it burn down?" Joe said.

"Ah, it'll be grand," Anchor said. "It's just a bit crispy on one side."

"Is it okay to go in?" Carlene said. Before she could move, she spotted a familiar figure pushing through the crowd. It was Ronan. Carlene's heart stopped.

She saw him take in the charred wall of the pub. The heavy smell of smoke hung in the air, causing many in the crowd to cough. Ronan didn't see Carlene—he was looking at the fire damage, the expression on his face downright panicked.

"Carlene?" he yelled. Anchor stepped up next to him.

"What happened?" Ronan said. "Is Carlena okay?" Anchor's face morphed into that of a grieving man.

"They're going to do all they can," Anchor said. "But it doesn't look good." Ronan tore past him into the pub.

"What are you doing?" Carlene said.

Anchor grinned, flashed her the horns. "Only messin'," he said. Carlene ran into the pub after him, and soon the crowd followed. Ronan was standing in the middle of the room like he didn't know where to turn.

"Jaysus," he said. "Please, no. It's my fault. I should have stayed and protected her." He dropped to his knees. "God," he said. "I swear. I'll go to mass, and I won't skip out. I've already been to gambling rehab. I'll settle. Just let Miss America be okay." He pulled something out of his pocket and held it up. "This is the penny she dropped into the fountain the day I met her. She was fucking gorgeous. Okay, I probably shouldn't say fucking, right, Lord? I'll stop that, I promise. Maybe I caused her bad luck. Maybe I shouldn't have gone back after her penny. But I took one look at her and realized I wanted to be the man that made her wishes come true." Carlene put her hand over her mouth. She looked at Anchor. He flashed her a grin and the horns.

"Ronan," Carlene said. "I'm okay." Startled, Ronan whipped his head back. Anchor started laughing.

"Only messing," Anchor said. Ronan ran up and grabbed

Carlene. He buried his face in her neck and gripped her so tight she couldn't breathe. She pushed him away enough so that she could feel her rib cage again, and stroked his hair.

"That scared the shit out of me," he said.

"I'm okay," she said. He slid down to the floor, bringing her with him. They sat, embracing and entangled.

"Were you really in gambling rehab?" she said.

"Thanks to Racehorse Robbie," Ronan said.

"What?"

"Our little bet," Ronan said. "I had a fallback. If I lost, I either owed him a hundred thousand, or I would agree to go to gambling rehab," Ronan said. "It was in Dublin. There were no phone privileges or I would have called you."

"I had no idea," Carlene said. "I thought you hated me." Ronan opened his hand and held out the penny.

"I do," he said. "I fucking hated you the moment I laid eyes on you."

"I fucking hated you too." She kissed him, then took the penny. "I can't believe you went in after this," she said.

"I can't be sure it's yours." He dug in his pocket and brought out a handful of pennies. "So I reckon one of these has to be Miss America." She laughed as he took her hands and poured the pennies into them. There were so many, they overflowed her palms and began trickling to the ground. "Lucky girl," he said.

"I don't need luck," she said. "I have you." Singing Joey entered and walked over to the tanning bed, which looked like a cremated coffin.

"Here's your culprit," he said, holding up the frayed cord. "These things are a huge fire hazard." Carlene whipped around to glare at Joe, but he had mysteriously disappeared. "You're going to need a new wall, and a new stage," he said. "Probably looking at ten thousand or so euro—not too bad in the scheme of things, right?"

"You can use the money from the raffle," Katie said.

"Can I get a wee pint?" Riley called from his stool. "All this fire business has me mind in a jam." Carlene heard a meow. Columbus jumped on the counter, tail twitching. Carlene swooped up the kitten and held her close. Riley banged his empty pint glass on the counter. Carlene picked up the glass, then leaned over and kissed Riley on the cheek.

"Mind yerself," Riley's wife said. "You won't be so lucky if you don't keep your paws to yourself."

CHAPTER 45

Crying Wolf

Carlene walked into the pub and was so astonished at what she saw, she simply stood and stared. Her regulars were all there, gathered around her computer. They were all wearing blue rubber gloves. On the computer screen was her father. They were all laughing and talking, including her dad. Carlene snuck up behind them.

"What's going on?" she said.

"Hello," her father said softly. "I see you're wearing your mother's earrings. That's a good sign."

"Hi, Dad," she said.

"I've met your friends," he said. "I like them." One by one, Carlene glanced at her lads. Anchor, Eoin, Collin, Billy, Ciaran, Riley, Declan, and Ronan. When Ronan caught her eye, he winked at her.

"They say you're doing a fabulous job," her father said. "And they insist that I come see for myself."

"That would be great, Dad," Carlene said.

"I won't make it for Christmas, but maybe the spring."

"I'll buy your ticket," Carlene said.

"Too late," her father said. "They already did." He waved a ticket in front of him. It was wrapped in plastic. Carlene nodded, restraining herself from ambushing the lads with a hug. Her father hated public displays of affection. A few minutes later, they were saying good-bye, and her lads were all waving good-bye with their blue rubber gloves.

"Thank you," Carlene said when the screen went dark. "Now please take those fucking things off." The men laughed and removed their gloves. Declan held up a jar behind the bar.

"That'll be one euro for cussing, young lady." Carlene bought them all drinks on the house, including Declan. It was nice to see him sitting on the other side of the bar for a change.

"How in the world did you get him to agree to visit?" Carlene asked them.

"It's the accent, petal," Declan said with a wink. "Charms them every time." She waited until they were gone. Then she picked up the phone and called her father again. She guessed she was still a bit of a coward herself, because she wasn't going to video phone him; she knew she couldn't look at him when she said what she had to say. She was just grateful when he picked up.

"Dad," she said. "I need to tell you something. It's about Mom. It was all my fault."

Carlene walked and walked. The Irish countryside and miles and miles of limestone walls comforted her as she replayed her conversation with her father over and over again. It was almost too much to absorb, and she knew, had the revelation come any earlier, she might not have been able to handle it. But out here she was different. She'd changed. She was stronger.

Her mother didn't have a weak heart. Her mother had chronic depression and a razor. She'd first tried to kill herself when she was sixteen. She spent the next few years in and out of hospitals. And then, at nineteen, she fell in love with Mike Rivers, and he fell madly in love with her. The first few years she was married, love seemed to work miracles, and Renee's depression seemed to all but vanish. Then gradually, it came back with a startling vengeance. That day on the bus they were going to a pharmacy for her mother to pick up medication. She'd promised Carlene's father she would take it. That afternoon, she came home and they fought. Over nothing. He didn't even remember, except that she was in a mood. She opened her medication and poured the pills down the drain. Her father called Grandma Jane to pick Carlene up. Then he told her mother he would leave if she didn't get help, didn't take this seriously. They fought some more. Her father got in the car to drive, to clear his head. He was gone less than an hour.

He found her in the bathtub. Carlene couldn't imagine what that must have been like. It explained a lot. Why they moved so soon after her mother's death. He spared her the details of the scene, but she could imagine, she could hear the pain in his voice.

"I cleaned and cleaned," he said softly. "But it wasn't enough. It was never going to be enough."

It was a total shock, and she had a lot to work through now. So did her father. But it was there, in the open, where they could finally deal with it. And at least in one sense, the gloves were finally off.

The lads all pitched in to fix the wall. Anchor, Eoin, Ciaran, Collin, and Billy had torn down the old wall before she could say shamrock. All they asked was for free drinks and free rein of the jukebox. Carlene didn't mind the heavy metal so much this time; they worked faster. With the help of the lads, Joe sheepishly removed his charred tanning bed, gave her back the bulldozer clock and ten thousand euros for the damage. He also handed her a large bag, but when she started to open it, he held up his hand.

"You can check that out later," he said.

"Thank you," Carlene said.

"You know what this place could use, though?" Joe said. "A deprivation tank. They're supposed to be good for the soul—"

"Go home, Joe," Carlene said. Then, before he could run away, she leaned forward and kissed him on the cheek.

The Half Tree—Present Day

The cake was four feet tall. The David had never seen anything like it. He carried it like a child, afraid of tipping it on its head. Once it was safely in the back of the van, he began talking.

"This is so good," he said. "I am glad he came home. I am glad Carlene didn't lose the pub, and they are still in love. But I am confused. Who is Sally marrying?"

"Herself," Katie said.

"What is this?" The David said. "A joke?"

"Nope," Siobhan said. "She wanted to wear the dress, and drink champagne, and dance, and eat cake. So she took Carlene's advice and she's throwing herself a wedding reception."

"Without a groom," The David mused.

"You should ask her to dance," Katie said with a wink. "Now let's get this cake there before she murders us."

By the time they got back with the cake, there were so many people they were spilling outside onto the little yard. The David spotted Carlene and Ronan immediately. They were both working behind the bar. Every once in a while he noticed they would stare at each other and smile before turning away. This made him feel very good; in fact, the knot in his stomach was loosening. He walked up to Sally and asked her to dance. When it was over, Sally stood by the cake. Carlene rang a little bell behind the bar, and the place quieted down. Sally held a knife in one hand and a glass of champagne in the other. She held her glass high.

"I'm becoming the man I want to marry," she said.

"For fuck's sake," Anchor said.

"If you're a man, then I'm gay," Collin said.

"Me too," Billy said. There were several wolf whistles.

"Can we get on with this?" Riley said. "I'm dying of thirst here."

"I am liking this very much," The David said. "I would like to marry me too."

"I want to thank everyone for coming to my party," Sally

said. "Now, I'd like to invite up all the men who want to feed me a piece of fucking cake."

"I'm so happy that at least one piece of my advice worked out," Carlene said. She was talking to Sue, who was wearing a sleeveless lavender dress. She looked gorgeous. Her hair had just been colored, even darker red and spikier than before. Despite Carlene begging her to, she wasn't drinking stiffies; instead she was sipping on a cup of tea. Carlene was happier than she'd ever been. It had been several days since the fire and you couldn't even tell. In fact, it was much better now—they even bought her a new dartboard that hung straight. She'd been back in business, and it was better than ever. She seemed to have crossed over some invisible line, from blow-in to local. She was one of them now.

"It's a beautiful fake wedding reception," Sue agreed. "Are ye gonna be next?" She glanced at Ronan, then grinned at Carlene.

"We're going to see if we can get the hang of co-running the pub first," Carlene said. "Besides, he's a terminal bachelor, or so everyone says."

"We're all terminal," Siobhan said. "Not here for a long time—"

"Just here for a good time," Carlene finished. She grinned. Then before she knew what was happening, she saw a blur of red whizzing toward her. Just as she registered what it was, it smacked her in the face. Carlene didn't think roses could hurt so much.

"Carlene caught the fecking bouquet," Sally said. "Just my fecking luck."

Carlene snuck out of bed early the next morning, praying she wouldn't wake Ronan. Lucky for her, everyone had pitched in and cleaned the night before, so she wouldn't be going downstairs to a mess. In all the excitement since the fire, she had forgotten two things. One, she wanted to see what was in the bag Joe had given her, and two, she'd never checked the security cameras. When she opened the bag, she momentarily forgot about the cameras. There sat an actual coffeemaker, a grinder, and a bag of beans imported from Italy.

The cameras were designed to play any images they recorded on a miniature screen built into the device. Carlene held the camera in her hand and stared at it for a moment before turning it on. This one had been aimed at the front door. She had another one aimed at the back door. If neither of them showed anything, it either meant that the culprit hadn't struck in a while, or they were using another way in. She stared at the camera. Did she really want to know? After all, she hadn't been vandalized or pranked since she'd won the pub the second time. *Know thy enemy,* she thought as she pushed Play on the camera. As the images came into view, she stared, dumbfounded.

"What are you doing?" Ronan stood on the stairs, looking half-asleep. Carlene almost dropped the camera. She had to think quick. She didn't want him to see it, but if he caught a whiff of her shock, he'd insist. Carlene held up the camera.

"I tried to catch the prankster with this," Carlene said.

"And did you?" Ronan asked.

"Let's go to breakfast. I'll tell you all about it after a good feed."

"Nancy's?"

"Where else?"

Carlene politely declined tea, ordered French toast and three cappuccinos. Ronan ordered the full Irish breakfast. Carlene waited until they were full. She didn't want to begin the next part of their adventure keeping any more secrets.

"You know what Declan told me when we first met?" she asked. Ronan eyed her.

"Nod and smile?" he said.

"No."

"Sometimes when you're a publican, you've gotta be a bags?"

"No."

"What's for you won't pass you?"

"No."

"Say nothing till you hear more?"

"Okay, yes, he's said all those things, but—"

"Don't get your knickers in a twist?"

"Ronan."

"Sorry. It's just—he's got a lot to say."

"He just said that no matter how friendly they were to your face, or how begrudging behind your back, that you could always count on Irish people to rally around you when things were at their worst—when you really needed them."

"And they did—didn't they?"

"Yes. That's what I'm saying. They were there for me when the wall went up, they were there when the kegs went missing, they were there when the skeleton was found."

"So it all turned out for the best."

"That's the point," Carlene said. Just then, a short, elderly man walked up to the table.

"You're the pub winner, aren't ye?"

"I am," Carlene said. She introduced herself.

"Hello, Ronan," the man said.

"Hello, Gerald," Ronan said.

"Listen," Gerald O'Sullivan said. "If you see Declan around, will ye tell him I'll be needing my skeleton back?"

"What?" Ronan said. He was almost out of his chair. Carlene pulled him back down.

"I'll tell him," Carlene said.

"Thanks. I didn't think I'd be missing her, but I do," Gerald said. "She's my one and only."

"We'll get her back to you as soon as possible," Carlene said.

"I hope she worked out for you," Gerald said. "What was it, a Halloween party?"

"Something like that."

"Ah, right so. Glad you enjoyed her." He winked and walked away.

"Declan?" Ronan said. "And you knew?"

"I saw the tape this morning," Carlene said. "He came back for the goat."

"I don't understand," Ronan said. "Why would Declan do this to you?"

"Let's get out of here, and I'll tell you all about it," Carlene said.

They walked hand in hand down the street. It was a grand fresh day, and the sun was out. Everyone they saw waved, and they waved back. Christmas lights were already up on several of the shops. Carlene couldn't wait to decorate the pub. There was nowhere on earth she'd rather be for the holidays. Without even discussing it, they headed for the abbey. They stood on the little bridge overlooking the stream. In the distance, the sun rose behind the tower. Ever so gently, snow began to fall. Carlene jumped up and down.

"It's snowing!"

"Have ye never seen snow before, Miss Lake Erie?" Ronan said. Carlene punched him on the shoulder.

"It's much more magical here." Ronan put his arm around her and pulled her close.

"So tell me why I shouldn't slug Declan," Ronan said.

"The Boy Who Cried Wolf," Carlene said.

Ronan's eyes narrowed. "That's the little fucker who keeps pretending there's a wolf at his door, screaming and hollering until the whole town comes running, then when they work out he's a nasty little liar, they ignore him, but the next time there really *is* a fucking wolf, only it's too late for the little bugger?"

"That's the one," Carlene said.

"What about it?"

"Nobody likes a winner, Ronan. So Declan decided to do something to get them to like me. The kegs, the wall, the skeleton—all pretty harmless, but it brought people running."

"Jaysus," Ronan said.

"Yes," Carlene said. "That's some balls."

"As soon as enough of this white stuff falls, I'll have a ball for you," Ronan said. He shook his head. "Declan, Declan, Declan," he said.

"I'd say he's going to stop now," Carlene said. "From now on, I'm on my own." Ronan took her hand and kissed it.

"I wouldn't say that," he said. "I wouldn't say that at'all." He leaned forward, and kissed her. It was gentle, and strong, and full of promise. He pulled away, took her hand, and headed for the abbey.

"Where are we going?" she said.

"To the tower," he said. "There's a note waiting."

Carlene stopped. "Ronan?" she said. He kissed her again, quick and hard, and laughed.

"It's a surprise," he said.

"A good surprise or a bad surprise?"

"That depends how you look at it."

"I can't take any more surprises Ronan, really I can't. Please, just tell me."

"I'll tell you this much," he said. "There's a fecking note waiting. You see, I've got a tip on a girl."

EPILOGUE

Declan—One Year Later
Say Nothing Until You Hear More

Would ye mind putting these on? I'm not much of a fan of blue rubber gloves meself, but we've got a visitor coming. If you think you look funny in them, you should see all the lads wearing them. It's gas. It might seem a little strange to you, but we're used to strange around here. Matter of fact, I've just come from Joe's deprivation tank, and I'll tell ye, I'd take these rubber gloves over it any day. I don't know what I was supposed to feel in that thing, but deprived about sums it up. It's been a year since the Yankee Doodle came to town, can you believe that?

It's Saint Stephen's Day and that's a big day in the pubs. Everyone is cracked from spending so much time at home with their relatives on Christmas Day, and we'll have a big crowd all right. Johnny Spoons is coming. Our visitor, Michael Rivers from America, will arrive before the crowds, and then go back with Mary McBride when things get too crazy for him. Thank you for all the friend requests, but I've been off that fecking farming game since my virtual dog ran away.

As far as our little love story goes—I'm not going to say I told you so, but did you see the bling on her finger? I will say that I'm a little sick of the two of them smiling all the fecking time.

Ah, but I'm just an old begrudger. I wouldn't mind getting my smile on meself, so come on, ladies, if you're in the area, stop in for a wee pint on me. It goes without saying, you've got to be a good-looking bird. And when it comes to our lovebirds, I guess what I've always said is true after all. What's for you, won't pass you. That's all the Irish wisdom I have for ye today. I know you're wanting more, but I have to cut you off. Sometimes when you're a publican, you've gotta be a bags. But come back to-morrow, and I'll freshen your pint, and I may just have another wisdom nugget for ye, all right. After all, you can only fill a pot of gold with one coin at a time. Ah, sure. Say nothing until you hear more.

Please turn the page
for a very special Q&A
with Mary Carter.

Was it challenging to write a book that takes place in another country? What kind of research did you do for the novel?

It was extremely challenging. In fact, when I first suggested the idea of this novel to my editor, I didn't think he would be interested in it. When I found out he loved the idea, I freaked out a little. I felt completely over my head and was slightly terrified of what I had gotten myself into.

As far as research, I hung out at a lot of Irish pubs in New York. Truth be told, I was hanging out at them long before I wrote the book. It's part of what inspired me in the first place. Like Carlene in the book (and many women), I'd always had a weakness for Irish men—the charm, the accent—the world of trouble. I think I'm more immune to them now, and I finally have a balance of Irish friends who are women. I still love the culture, however, and the music, and the craic.

Tell us about your trip. Did you love it? Was this your first time in Ireland? Are the Irish really as friendly as everyone says?

It was truly the trip of a lifetime. I spent a month in the Republic of Ireland. I was in Dingle, Adare, Killarney, Limerick, Kilmallock (my favorite), Charleville, Cork City, Conna, Youghall, Castlemartyr, Kinsale, Dublin, and Galway. I made it out to the Aran Islands for a day as well. I went to several horse races, and thanks to a friend who is also a bookmaker, even won a few bob on the ponies, played poker until five in the morning (and came in second!!!), hung out in numerous pubs, saw the sights, marveled at the street performers in Dublin and Galway, took every Hop-On Hop-Off bus there was, went to a stand-up comedy show in Galway, ate so much I gained ten pounds, watched Tiger Woods play in Adare, and saw incredible live music from traditional to rock. Most of all I met incredible people. They were even friendlier than everyone says, and more than willing to help me out with an idea, a joke, a line, a book, a tip, a lesson, or a fact for the novel. Even though I had a complete outline and had written a draft of the novel before my trip, the experience definitely helped shape and enrich the final manuscript.

Do you have Irish in your family?

On my mother's side, it's mostly Irish Catholic. My great-great-grandmother (there may be one more great in there, I'm not sure) was from Ballymena, County Antrim, in the North (where Liam Neeson is from, by the way!). She immigrated to Philadelphia. We don't have terrific records—or even the correct spelling of my great-great-grandmother's surname—and I have yet to visit Northern Ireland, but I would certainly love to one day. Besides being a big tea drinker and having red hair, and quoting saints, my mother (and grandmother and maternal aunts) embodied the Irish spirit, always making me feel as if Ireland was my distant home. I do realize the Irish encounter this a lot—wannabes, so to speak; regardless, sometimes culture is so passionate and pervasive, the place may be far removed but the identity remains strong for generations to come. Besides, my name is Mary Patricia, and you can't grow up with that name without thinking you must be just a little bit Irish.

Why do you think so many people want to be Irish?

I definitely think it's the fun we seem to think of them having nonstop. They do know how to throw down and have a good time. They appreciate good conversation. They are witty, and intelligent, and friendly, and very quick to come up with a snappy line or words of wisdom. They are prolific and musical. Their country is stunningly beautiful, and the Guinness is smooth, the women are admirably spirited, and there is a bit of risk-taking type of danger in some of the lads. They carry the strength of a people who have experienced atrocities, yet survived and thrived. And the accent. Have I mentioned the accent? Who wouldn't want to be Irish?

Isn't there a dark side to drinking? Why didn't you address the dire consequences of alcoholism in the novel?

You make a million decisions when you sit down to write a novel, and one of them concerns its tone. Yes, of course, alcoholism, everywhere in the world, is a serious problem. Riley is one character in the book you could say is an alcoholic. So was Carlene's ex-boyfriend, Brendan. But had I delved into this topic much more, it would have been a very different book. Without being too idealistic, I wanted more of a fun, romantic story that focused on the positive aspects of pub life in Ireland—a sense of community, a place to share stories, a place to laugh, a place to get away from your troubles. That was the type of experience my heroine, Carlene, needed to have in order to grow and make up for the lack of affection and sense of community that was lacking in her life. Every pub probably has your token drunk slumped at the bar by the end of the evening, but that's not the majority. Stereotypes of the Irish and drinking abound, and I didn't want to play into them. I've met plenty of Irish people who don't drink at all. I wanted that sense of the pub as a home away from home to be the primary focus of the novel.

Are your characters based on people you know in real life?

Yes, many of the characters in this particular novel were *inspired* by real people. And I get this question a lot. But what people need to understand is that a character often embodies several people a writer has met in their life, all shaped and morphed and rolled into one character—with a little bit of the writer existing in each character, and this funny thing characters tend to do, which is take on a life of their own during the writing process. So by the time it's all said and done, even though the idea for a character may have been sparked by so-and-so, by the time they are fleshed out, they are truly their own people. That said, I met so many great folks in Ireland, I did do a little "character stealing" for some of the smaller roles. And even though the story is based in Galway, which is on the West Coast of Ireland, I primarily based the town of Ballybeog on my favorite town in Ireland—Kilmallock, County Limerick. I took creative liberties, of course, and it must be reiterated that it is a work of fiction.

What are you working on next?

I am working on a new novel for Kensington—the juicy details of which I am going to keep to myself for now, but soon you will be able to read more about it at marycarterbooks.com.

THE PUB ACROSS THE POND

Mary Carter

ABOUT THIS GUIDE

The suggested questions are included to enhance
your group's reading of Mary Carter's
The Pub Across the Pond.

DISCUSSION QUESTIONS

1. In the beginning of the novel, a crowd is gathered at Uncle Jimmy's pub. They are waiting on a bride. What is the general mood of the crowd, and how do the various characters feel about love? How does the atmosphere change with the arrival of the German student? How do they react to the proclamation that he is thinking about killing himself?

2. Ronan McBride is a gambler. Carlene Rivers, according to her best friend, Becca, is "the unluckiest girl in the world." Who is actually luckier—Ronan or Carlene? What chances do each of them take in the novel, and which one of them makes the biggest gamble?

3. "Luck is like the weather. It can change like that," an Irishman tells Carlene in the beginning of the novel. How does Carlene's luck change throughout the novel? Is she lucky or unlucky? How does she behave when she considers herself lucky as opposed to when she considers herself unlucky?

4. How does Ronan feel about Carlene when he first spies her standing in the middle of the fountain in Eyre Square? Is it different from how he expected to feel about her? Why does his reaction to her bother him? Would Ronan have fallen in love with "Unlucky Carlene," who never would have ventured into the fountain in the first place?

5. Does anything in Carlene's past prepare her to run a pub? What does she get from the Irish culture that she'd been lacking her whole life? What role does touch play in Carlene's past, and how is it different when she comes to Ireland?

6. What does Carlene see as some of the cultural differences between the Irish and Americans? If the Irish festival in Dublin, Ohio, were to take place in Ireland, what would be the difference?

7. How did growing up around mostly women affect Ronan? How did growing up among mostly men affect Carlene?

8. The Irish are known as the friendliest people in the world. Is every Irish person Carlene meets friendly? If not, who isn't? How do the people of Ballybeog react to Carlene? Who likes her? Who doesn't? Can she trust all of them?

9. How does Carlene react to the mysterious pranks being played on her, and Joe's never-ending quest to take over the property?

10. Why does Carlene continue to wear the blue rubber gloves even though her father isn't around? And when she was with her father, was she enabling him by agreeing to all of his rituals or was she just being a good daughter? Would she have been able to get him to stop? Would he have let her stop?

11. Why doesn't Carlene name the cat or the pub right away? What does this say about her?

12. How does Ronan treat Carlene? Is it different from how he treats the other women in his life? Is he consistent or erratic with her? How does Carlene's past relationship with an Irish man affect the way she interacts with Ronan?

13. What kind of relationship does Carlene have with her regulars? Would her experience have been different if

there were no regulars, just new customers coming in every day?

14. Sally tells Carlene that Irish women don't like her. How does Carlene react, and what does she think of Irish women? Is Sally telling the truth? Does Carlene's relationship to Irish women change by the end of the book?

15. Carlene tells Sally, "Become the man you want to marry." How does Sally decide to implement this? Is Sally a changed woman by the end of the book?

16. What role does music play in Irish culture? Is it any different from American culture?

17. What role does the pub play in Irish culture? Is it any different from bars in America?

18. How is the second lottery of the pub different from the first? What does the outcome say about Carlene's presence in Ballybeog? In which circumstance do you think Carlene was luckier?

19. Carlene was deeply affected by her mother's death and carried residual guilt. Her father was deeply affected as well. If Ronan hadn't pushed her, would Carlene have ever shared her "confession" with her father? Would their lives have been different if the two had broached the subject early on? Does Carlene change when her father finally reveals the truth about her mother's passing? Does her father?

20. Do you think Carlene and Ronan will live happily ever after? Will they actually get married? Will they continue to run the pub? Why or why not?

GREAT BOOKS, GREAT SAVINGS!

When You Visit Our Website:
www.kensingtonbooks.com
You Can Save Money Off The Retail Price Of Any Book You Purchase!

- All Your Favorite Kensington Authors
- New Releases & Timeless Classics
- Overnight Shipping Available
- eBooks Available For Many Titles
- All Major Credit Cards Accepted

Visit Us Today To Start Saving!
www.kensingtonbooks.com

All Orders Are Subject To Availability.
Shipping and Handling Charges Apply.
Offers and Prices Subject To Change Without Notice.